"An impressive novel."

—Piers Anthony on *Sacred Ground*

"Absorbing—one of those books one reads eagerly from page to page, caught up not only by the action but by the interplay of character."

—Andre Norton on *Sacred Ground*

"Lackey has two great strengths as a writer: her ability to tell an exciting story and to create sympathetic characters who inspire effortless identification. Lackey is one of the best storytellers in the field."

—*Locus*

"Shows a sure touch with the wonder and adventure that characterize the best fantasy writers."

—*Romantic Times*

"An undoubted mistress of the well-told tale."

—*Booklist*

TOR BOOKS BY MERCEDES LACKEY

THE HALFBLOOD CHRONICLE
(with Andre Norton)
The Elvenbane
Elvenblood

DIANA TREGARD INVESTIGATIONS
Burning Water
Children of the Night
Jinx High

Firebird
Sacred Ground

FIREBIRD

Mercedes Lackey

A TOM DOHERTY ASSOCIATES BOOK
NEW YORK

This is a work of fiction. All the characters and events portrayed in this book are either products of the author's imagination or are used fictitiously.

FIREBIRD

Cover art by Vladimir Nenov

A Tor Book
Published by Tom Doherty Associates, Inc.
175 Fifth Avenue
New York, NY 10010

Tor Books on the World Wide Web:
http://www.tor.com

Tor® is a registered trademark of Tom Doherty Associates, Inc.

ISBN: 0-812-55074-9
Library of Congress Card Catalog Number: 96-23841

First edition: December 1996
First mass market edition: September 1997

Printed in the United States of America

0 9 8 7 6 5 4 3 2 1

To Natalia Marakova
Always, for me, *the* Firebird

CHAPTER ONE

ANOTHER SLIVER of silvery-pale wood joined the tiny pile at Ilya Ivanovitch's feet, and the rough shape in his hand became a little more foxlike. The wood rasped against the sword calluses on his palm as Ilya narrowed his focus to the lumpy head, turning the carving this way and that, frowning at it, oblivious to everything else. Sun-rays baked through the linen tunic on his back with the fever-heat of high summer; the sharp, resinous scent of the block of wood in his hands tickled his nostrils. Under that scent lay others: the green musk of herbs crushed under his feet, the sweet and heady fragrance of wild roses somewhere nearby, the tannin-rich breath of the forest all around him, the all-too-earthy scent of horse-dung. Birds vied with insects to fill his ears, but could not overwhelm the gentle rustling of the leaves as a fitful breeze floated by. Last year's leaves crunched and rattled under the hooves of one of his father's horses as it nosed through the grass between the trees, looking for something more succulent than the tough strands of a full summer's growth.

The horses had just been moved into the forest for fall grazing. They were fat and spoiled from a spring and summer of good clover and tasty grasses, but they might need that fat come the winter.

He set the sharp edge of his smallest knife against the wood; this would be a tricky cut, for the ear was one of the hardest bits to carve. He wanted it thin, so that the light would glow through it if he held it up to the sun.

Slowly, carefully, he shaved and shaped the nubbin of wood; with every sliver, it took on more delicacy, more life.

His brows furrowed as he squinted, and he lost track of scent, sound, even the heat on his back. His world became the bit of wood and the blade that was sculpting it. From white wood, imperceptibly the blunted triangle transmuted to a thin sliver of white flesh and fur. In a moment, he would finish with it and move on to the other ear—

"Hoy!"

Out of nowhere, a hand descended to thump him on the back, hard enough to knock the wind out of him. His arms jerked, and the blow sent him flying off his seat toward the ground. Helplessly, he watched as the knife soared off in one direction, the carving in another. Steel honed to astonishing sharpness glinted in the sun as it turned, end over end, moving with dreamlike slowness. Then time caught up with him again, and he landed on his knees in the grass, his chest tight as his lungs realized there was no air in them.

He struggled for a moment to catch his breath, his ribs aching, throat straining. Finally, after an eternity, a breath came, filling his lungs with welcome harshness. He took another; another—got himself under control. No point in getting angry, for that would only give his brother another excuse for boorish behavior.

"Hello, Pietor," Ilya said with resignation as soon as he could speak. He remained where he was and turned his head, but not with any haste, to look up at his older brother.

Pietor grinned whitely down at him, very pleased with himself, and shook his blond hair out of his eyes. "So, little brother, I find you at secrets. And what witchcraft were you up to, out here all alone in the forest? Consorting with the *leshii?*"

Ilya sighed. Every time he went off somewhere by himself, one or more of his brothers was convinced that Ilya was up to no good. Probably because every time one of Ilya's brothers went off alone, he *was* up to no good.

"No witchcraft," Ilya replied. "You don't believe in the forest spirits any more than Father does, I'm hardly alone with the horses all around, and it's not what I would call *forest.*" Ilya rose slowly, dusted the grass off his knees, and looked for his knife and the carving where he thought he'd seen them land. The former he found quickly enough, and he thanked his stars that it was undamaged. It had taken a lot of work to get the blade that sharp, and he had not been looking forward to the hours he might have to spend smoothing a nick out of it. His luck couldn't hold, however, and he already anticipated that the carving would be ruined. He had a visceral memory of the blade biting savagely into the wood before both knife and carving flew off.

When Ilya picked the bit of wood up out of the grass, he saw with a sinking of spirit that his gloomy expectation was correct. The ear that had taken him so long to shape had sheared off under his blade, leaving a ragged stump behind.

"Are you contradicting me, little brother?" Pietor's grin turned malicious, and the ominous tone of his voice warned of a drubbing to come. But at this moment and place, Ilya wasn't terribly worried about the implied threat.

For one thing, Pietor was alone, and none of his brothers had been able to succeed in beating him alone, not for the last year or more. Two or more *together,* now, that was a different tale altogether, and Ilya would have to find a way to distract Pietor long enough so that he would forget the so-called "insult" so that he didn't manage to gather allies.

Pietor wasn't very bright, and he didn't have a terribly long attention span; however, it wouldn't take much to distract him. It always took Pietor a while to organize himself enough to collect a group to beat Ilya up, and during that time he was vulnerable to interference. With any luck, by the time Pietor got back to the palace to rouse one or more of the others, he would have forgotten why he had gone looking for them in the first place.

"What you wish, brother." Ilya shrugged and tossed the ruined carving out into the forest, sheathing his knife so casually that not even Pietor could take it as an insult. A dun mare grazing nearby looked up at the motion as the bit of ruined wood sailed past her nose, snorted, and went back to single-minded munching. "You'll make up your own mind about what I said no matter what I tell you. So it doesn't matter what I say now, does it?"

Pietor's white-blond brows furrowed together and his vacant blue eyes grew even vaguer as he tried to puzzle through that. Finally he gave up. "You think you're clever, smarter than all of us, don't you?'' he challenged. "Too clever by half!"

Enough of this nonsense. I'm not in the mood. "I don't have to think anything, I only have to listen to you and I know what the answer is," Ilya replied, narrowing his own eyes and staring right at his brother with a challenge of his own. "What do you want, anyway? Why did you come sneaking out here, following me around like a thief or a gypsy? Do you covet my knife, or were you hoping I had somehow found a treasure you could steal?"

The abrupt change of subject and the unexpected challenge left Pietor floundering for a moment. "I—ah—" The young man backed up a step as he attempted to handle two thoughts at the same time and failed utterly. He stared into Ilya's face, and Ilya had to choke down the urge to say anything more. Pietor was thoroughly confused *and* briefly intimidated. Best leave well enough alone.

"Never mind." Ilya stalked off, startling two more horses into a brief canter before they settled again. He left Pietor standing dumbfounded in his wake, mouth hanging open stupidly.

Not that it's an unusual expression for dear Pietor, he thought savagely. *A whole afternoon's work ruined in a heartbeat by that oaf!* Ilya'd hoped to have the carving finished by supper as a surprise for Mother Galina; he was glad now that he hadn't promised her anything, as he often did when he planned to carve her something. *The worst of it is, I think he knew exactly what he was doing. He might not be bright, but he's cunning. He probably saw me out in the forest-pasture and realized how caught up I was in what I was doing; saw his chance to sneak up and play me another rotten trick.* That was altogether like Pietor. He was never happier than when he got a chance to spoil something of Ilya's as well as add another to Ilya's ongoing collection of bruises.

The day was still sunny and beautiful, but a dark cloud hung about Ilya's soul. He hated going back to Mother Galina empty-handed, even if he *hadn't* promised her anything; in his own heart, the promise had been made.

But a splash of pink in a patch of sun caught his eye, promising help with his predicament, and he made a brief detour toward the tangle of thorny branches. *Roses! Of course! A bouquet won't last as long as a carving, but with any luck, it'll last long enough for me to carve her another little beast.*

With great care for the thorns and one ear cocked for Pietor's approach, Ilya cut several branches bearing three or more of the flat-petaled pink blooms with their centers of molten gold. The soft petals trembled as he stripped blood-hued thorns from the fibrous green stems with the aid of his knife. It had always seemed appropriate to him, given the number of times the sturdy barbs had bitten into his flesh, that the thorns of the wild rose looked as if they had already tasted blood. When he had what he considered to be a sufficiently large bouquet in light of his failure to produce a carving, he resumed his journey back to the palace, home of his father the tsar and all of his brawling brothers.

Tsar! He's only a boyar, but he has to call himself a tsar to prove he's stronger and more important than his neighbors. Then what do his neighbors do? They call themselves tsars! Tsar Ivan actually ruled a little more land than most of the other neighboring "tsars." Part of it he had acquired by marriage, part by warring with his neighbors, both of which had been successful pursuits. All three of his wives had gotten substantial marriage-portions of land and beasts settled upon them by way of a dowry. Ilya's mother, the middle wife, had been the least successful in regard to land, having brought with her more horses than hectares, and Tsar Ivan still coupled Ekaterina's name with a certain degree of failure. She had failed him in two ways: She had borne him only one son before dying, and had brought him only a fraction of her own father's holdings.

Not that Father needed any more sons! Ilya thought sourly. *He's quite surfeited with such blessings as it is!*

As Ilya neared the palace, the sounds of a normal afternoon among Tsar Ivan's offspring met him long before the palace itself was in sight. Shouts of pain and triumph shook the leaves—the birds had long since scattered—and the clangor of metal on wood, wood on wood, and metal on metal punctuated the din. Arms practice or outright quarreling—it didn't much matter which was going on, they would sound the same, and none of Ilya's brothers ever held back in either.

When the tsar's numerous offspring and probable by-blows

weren't battling one another, they were either preparing to battle a neighbor or, more rarely, drinking and carousing. Ivan encouraged them in all three pursuits; battle with a neighbor would probably add more land to his kingdom, while brawling and drinking were both activities that were hazardous in and of themselves. Tsar Ivan was in the peculiar position of having had *all* of his sons survive infancy and childhood, including the ones whose mothers had not survived the births. Ilya and Sasha had both survived the travail of their arrival and the scramble for a suitable wet-nurse afterward, even though both their mothers had been cooling in their coffins before a nurse could be located among the serfs and servants. While this strange circumstance of a plurality of male offspring was gratifying to Tsar Ivan's pride and implied certain things about his virility, it also created a difficult situation. Obviously only one son could inherit, but which should it be?

In most families there would be no question but that it would be the oldest; however, Ivan was a law unto himself. His steadfast unbelief in the spirits of forest, hearth, and field was no more than a reflection of his contrary nature. He had thus far declined to make a pronouncement that would render his choice official, leaving all the sons in a perpetual state of servile uncertainty.

Ilya suspected that he knew why. *Father doesn't trust us. Not any of us.* That fact was clear to anyone who had a reasonably acute mind. Tsar Ivan never went anywhere without his bodyguards, not even to bed, and the way he eyed his numerous offspring left no doubt in Ilya's heart that Ivan anticipated attempts by his loving sons to murder him as a matter of course. He was not about to shorten his own lifespan by giving one of them a real and tangible reason to want him out of the way.

I don't know why. He didn't have to murder Grandfather to inherit. But maybe he sees us as a wolf pack. One wolf is not necessarily dangerous, or even two—but a pack can kill your horse in its traces and have you before you've run more than a few steps.

So Tsar Ivan encouraged fighting among his sons for more reasons than one. He obviously wanted the kingdom to go to the heir that was the strongest; battling one another kept his offspring in outstanding physical shape for real warfare. And in addition, well, if one of them managed to kill one of his siblings, there would be one son less to make attempts to take the crown by force. Ivan had no intention of actually doing away with any of his dangerous offspring, for that would be murder—

Ah, but if one of us happens to eliminate another, it's hardly his problem, is it?

Ilya took a circuitous route through the trees around in back of the palace, by way of the kitchen-garden and the nearby pigsties. There wasn't much left in the garden by this time of year and the ground lay fallow, waiting for the seeds for next year's planting; what remained green was mostly the tops of carrots, turnips, onions, and beets in neat rows, ready for harvest before the earth froze. The rest had already been harvested and eaten, put into storage, or preserved; the earth had been turned under after a liberal application of pig-manure.

The pigs themselves were happily wallowing in mud in their sturdy sties, blissfully unaware that the date of their demise could not be far off. Once the nuts fell, they would be herded into the forest to gorge themselves and put on more weight, and that would be the end of their carefree existence. The first hard freeze would signal butchering-time, and both porkers and cattle would become future meals, safely preserved to provision the long winters. Ilya both anticipated and dreaded that freeze. Butchering the animals and feasting after would keep his brothers too busy to think of trouble, but the boredom of the long winters only gave them more time and opportunity to make his life miserable.

Ah well, worry about that when the snows lock us in. Maybe the wolves will eat Pietor this year when he goes out in his sled, and that will leave me one less idiot to contend with. Of course, they'd probably eat the horses first, unless Pietor was out with Alexi or Yuri, and one of them got thrown to the wolves so that the other could escape.

He entertained this pleasant thought while he walked down the dusty path to the kitchen. The heavy wooden door leading into the kitchen stood wide open, and no wonder: Heat from the bread-ovens came blasting out to meet Ilya, and the servants working inside were half-naked, bodies, arms, and faces streaming sweat. Ilya stood in the doorway for a moment, taken aback by the sight; the only light came from the ovens themselves, a red glow that brought to mind the fires of the Infernal Pit. It bathed the glistening faces and limbs of the laboring servants, bent over their tasks at the three huge wooden tables like so many dwarfish spirits in bondage, or tormented souls paying the price of their sins. For a moment, the kitchen appeared as haunted and unchancy as the bathhouse, which had its own resident spirit, the *bannik,* a creature known to kill those who offended it.

Quickly Ilya crossed himself to avert any inadvertent curses brought on by that thought, and backed hastily out of the doorway. Mother Galina wouldn't be in there; the place was hot enough to make an ox faint. So if she wasn't in the kitchen, she was probably in the dairy, overseeing the results of the afternoon milking.

The dairy adjoined the kitchen and was as pleasant as the kitchen was hellish. It was the best-built construction on the property, for one of Ilya's ancestors had a great fondness for butter and cheese and had given his dairy-herd, both cows and goats, pride of place. It was the only building that was constructed entirely of stone, with a stone floor, and the water from the spring that served the entire palace was tamed to a trough running right through the center of it. In winter, the great brick stove at the end made it just warm enough to be bearable, but in the summer the cool was delightful. Ilya had spent many long summer days here as a child, watching the cheesemakers with fascination, helping to churn the butter, getting teased by the dairymaids. Later the teasing had turned to flirting, and the flirting to skirt-chasing, which had resulted in Mother Galina banishing him from the dairy unless he had reason to be there.

So I moved my hunting-grounds to the pastures, and no one the wiser. A big belly or two had probably resulted from his games in the grass, but he never found out about it officially. Ivan had an unwritten but ironclad rule about his sons' (or his own) bastards: Any serf-girl finding herself in the family way by any of the men was to present herself quietly to the chief steward. Provided that she didn't make a fuss, she'd find herself rewarded with a dowry, a husband of her station or above, and a new position on the palace staff. Ilya suspected that his father chose his own girls from among the ones so promoted, for certainly there were one or two of Ilya's own former milk-maids whom he had seen sporting silver-and-amber trinkets *he* had never given them and that none of the other sons could have afforded either. The best he or his brothers could manage for a girl was a string of glass beads or a length of cloth filched from the stores.

As he pushed the wooden door of the dairy ajar, the first person who caught his eye was not Mother Galina, but a new-comer, an unfamiliar, fresh-faced milkmaid, all pink cheeks and blonde braids. She stood at one of the smooth slate tables, kneading the last of the whey out of a cloth full of curds. The shapeless, coarse linen smock of the serfs was pulled in tightly around a tiny waist by a spotless apron embroidered with flow-ers and deer in tiny, careful stitches of black wool. Her smock was short enough that she displayed not only a pair of pretty little feet, but slender ankles and a hint of graceful calves. The string tying her smock at the neck had come undone, allowing one shoulder as smooth as cream and the very beginning of the swell of a shapely breast to show. The maid looked up and caught him staring; she gave him an impish smile and a slow, languorous wink of one limpid blue eye. He straight-ened, feeling suddenly much more cheerful.

"Stop flirting with my girls, you shameless hulk!" He jumped and gave the expected yelp as the end of a cheesecloth hit his rear with a sharp snap. The girl giggled and turned her attention back to her work without the slightest sign of shame; he whirled around to catch Mother Galina in a bear-hug that left her breathless. The spry little woman was not quite as slender as one of his maidens, but she was hardly much heavi-er. Beneath her matronly blouse and skirt, she was surprisingly limber for an old babushka.

"Why would I flirt with a silly girl when the most beautiful woman here is you?" he cried, loud enough for everyone in the dairy to hear. More giggles followed that pronouncement, and Mother Galina extricated herself from his arms with a blush and a slap, which missed his cheek, as it was supposed to.

"What mischief have you gotten yourself into that you

come barging into my dairy like a clumsy ox?'' she demanded, her bright black eyes twinkling under her bushy eyebrows. ''What is it that I must rescue you from this time? Or is it one of my maidens that must be rescued *from* you?''

Her brows and the little that could be seen of her hair under the scarf that all respectable women wore was black, as black as it had been the day she arrived at the palace. No one knew where she came from; she had simply appeared at the kitchen door, claiming to be an expert dairy-woman. That day had been particularly disastrous in the dairy: The butter wouldn't form in the churns, the cream had soured, and some of the cheeses had been discovered to be rancid rather than ripening. The chief cook, who never had liked dairy-work, had told her that if she could redeem the situation, she could have the dairy and the position of first undercook.

He really hadn't expected her to be able to do anything, but he had been at his wits' end. He had never regretted his hasty promise. By nightfall, sweet pats of butter were stored in wooden butter-buckets in the spring, the cheeses had been saved, and the soured cream had provided an excellent sauce for dinner.

Now, Galina's arrival and, more particularly, her success had not gone unremarked, far from it. There had been some muttering about Galina being a spirit—perhaps the *domovoi*'s wife—but Ivan had put a stop to such mutterings quickly. ''There *is* no house-spirit, so how can there be a wife?'' he had shouted out one night at dinner. ''The next person who blathers about the *domovoi* will get a pot thrown at his head, and it won't be by a spirit!'' He then proved that he wasn't bluffing by knocking one poor serf senseless for hours, and topped himself by growling that he'd do worse than that the next time.

So ended the talk, especially as Galina produced nothing more supernatural than good butter. Eventually, most folk forgot she hadn't been born on Ivan's land, particularly since a great deal of Ivan's land was ''newly'' acquired. Mother Galina had made herself the undisputed ruler of the dairy, as much a part of the household as those who had served Ivan's family for generations.

Nor was that all she had done. Ilya had been about three

then, and as wild as a little gypsy. His wet-nurse had long since gone on to other things, Ivan's current wife cared nothing for him, and he wasn't yet old enough to begin the proper training of a warrior. He could no longer recall what had brought him to the dairy shortly after Galina was placed in charge, but thereafter, she became his unofficial nurse and substitute mother.

"I brought you these," he said, holding out the bouquet of roses, "just to prove the loyalty of my heart to you." Fortunately, he had not stood in the doorway of the kitchen long enough for the heat to wilt the delicate petals. As Mother Galina closed her hand about the stems, a wonderful perfume arose from the blossoms, filling the dairy and causing more than one of the dairymaids to sigh over her churn. Galina buried her rosy face in the flowers, her own expression that of deepest pleasure.

"You're a good boy, Ilya," she said at length and appropriated a milk-jug from among those that stood in rows on a shelf along one wall. Filling it with water from the trough running the length of the room, she dropped the bouquet in and set it up on the shelf again, out of harm's way. She had to stand on tiptoe to do so, but Ilya did not offer to help, having learned the futility of any such offer long ago.

"There. Now we can all enjoy them," she said with satisfaction, and, if possible, the heady aroma of roses grew even more intense. She turned once again to face Ilya, her plump hands resting on either hip. "Now—what *really* brings you here? Which of my girls are you bent on chasing this time?"

"I had no intention of chasing *any* of them when I walked in here," he protested with absolute honesty. *Of course not; it was only after I came in that I saw one I intend to pursue!* "I just came to bring you a gift, that's all! Must everything I do have some ulterior motive?"

"Not everything," she replied. "Just *most* things."

He winced, for Galina had an uncanny ability to see right through even the most clever falsehoods. He had stopped trying to lie to her when he was five, and now very strictly tailored only the truth when she asked him an uncomfortable question. Even so, he often had the feeling that she could see into his very heart.

"You sound like my father," he growled, "seeing plots in casual conversations and an assassin behind every bush. He sent Pietor out into the pasture to *spy* on me this afternoon! Pietor accused me of sorcery! Only The Most High God knows what my father thinks I'm up to now!"

But Galina only chuckled and patted him on the arm. "Pietor sent himself into the pasture this time," she assured him. "And as for the sorcery—there was a band of gypsies here selling trinkets earlier this afternoon, and he probably got the idea to look for witchcraft in ridiculous places from one of them. I doubt that he would be able to come up with anything so creative himself."

He relaxed a little, only now becoming aware how tense he had been in the first place. "And maybe by the time he gets home, he'll have forgotten the idea," he said hopefully. "Don't you think?"

"At least by the time supper is over," she told him. "Your brothers have fewer wits than one of my cheeses. So, that brings us to supper; would you rather that you found a basket of bread and cheese by the back door tonight, or will you be a man, face them down, and have your supper with the rest of your family?"

That was no question and they both knew it, although there had been plenty of times when he had managed to construct an excuse justifying that basket by the door, and there probably would be again. His absence would be noted if he didn't go to dinner; he might as well face them all, or someone would create a rumor. He would hope that Pietor had forgotten his suspicions of sorcery, and be done with it.

Too bad Father believes in sorcerers. You'd think he'd be as scornful of magic as he is of spirits and demons, but that *he believes in.*

Or maybe he just believed in the will of his sons to use any means in their power to get rid of him.

"With luck, they'll all get too drunk to find their beds," he said by way of reply. "Na, I'm a man grown, Little Mother, I can face my own family over bread and soup. So long as I don't have to do so more than once a day."

Neither of them paid any attention to the girls and the three young boys eavesdropping shamelessly on their conversation.

The dairy-workers were only serfs, they weren't even freeborn servants; Ilya was alone in the family in treating them better than the dogs, but it didn't matter to him if they listened to what he said or not. Gossip in the huts didn't concern him, not even if the gossip *did* make him out as a sorcerer. He'd have to be a singularly incompetent sorcerer, anyway, to let his brothers beat him to a froth on a regular basis.

"If Pietor casts black looks on you, you might suggest to one of the others that he was hoping to involve you in a conspiracy," she suggested. "Yuri—he could suspect a plot just by seeing two serfs visiting the privy at the same time. You're clever enough to hint without actually saying anything. The rumor will get back to Ivan before the end of the meal, and it won't do Pietor any good; he'll believe a conspiracy before he'd ever believe in sorcery."

"I'll think on it," he temporized, and kissed her brow as she flushed with pleasure. "That might do me more harm than good, though. You know that Father thinks I'm already engaged in plots against him; I don't need to add to that. It's easy enough to see where Yuri gets his suspicious nature."

She nodded solemnly. "Do what you think is best; you hardly need *me* to give you advice anymore."

"Now that is surely the biggest lie you ever told me, Babushka," he chided with a smile. "I shall always need you to give me advice!"

"Ah, when the eagle is flying, he doesn't need his mother to count his wing-beats," she replied, once again cheerful. "Now off with you! I have butter to press before dinner."

She turned back to her work and was soon engrossed; he paused at the doorway long enough to whisper to the attractive blonde. "Moonrise. The north meadow?"

She nodded, ever so slightly, and he left the dairy with a bounce in his walk. The north meadow, bordered by the spring that supplied the palace and dairy with water, was a favorite meeting-place of his. There was a weeping willow on the banks of the stream whose branches formed a curtain even in the fall; the ground beneath it was soft with moss. Perhaps in any other household but Ivan's the serfs would fear to walk there after dark, afraid of the water-dwelling *rusalka* or the meadow-haunting *polevoi,* but not here. Ivan would have thrown pots at anyone telling tales of spectral herdsmen all in white, or ethereal maidens waiting to pull the unsuspecting under to drown. The shelter of the willow's bough was a good place to sit and play the balalaika, and if a milkmaid happened to hear the music and was curious about who was playing there, well, that was no one's business but hers.

And even if her courage failed her and she didn't appear, it was still a good place to sit and play the balalaika.

He marched toward the palace with trepidation, but the sounds of combat no longer troubled the air, and he breathed a sigh of relief. After a good workout or a good quarrel, the rest of his brothers were usually too tired to want anything but their suppers. *He* always took his practices in the morning; the others liked to lie abed as long as possible. If he showed up early, he had the courtyard and whichever warrior who wanted to practice with him all to himself. That was one reason why his brothers were no longer able to beat him singly; concentrated practice was much better than an uncoordinated brawl.

However, those solitary practices were not doing much to alleviate his father's suspicions either.

Father thinks I'm trying to train myself in treachery, in back-stabbing and ambush. Huh. If I killed him, I'd only have a hundred times the trouble I do now! All my brothers would be trying to murder me in turn, rather than just beat me up now and again.

He crossed the yard and entered the wooden palace, easily the largest building for leagues and leagues around. He actually couldn't imagine anything bigger; his head swam if he tried, although old tales spoke of palaces with hundreds of rooms, with towers and domes that touched the sky. Such places were as nonsensical as stories of *banniks* in the bathhouse—who would live in such a palace? How could they find their way about? How could food come from the kitchen to the hall in any kind of edible state?

This place was enough of a barn as it was. Dozens of peasant huts could fit inside; in the great hall, there were tables able to seat a total of fifty people at a time, and there was even a second story, where the tsar and his wife and guards lived with the tsar's own set of servants. This was the only dwelling Ilya had ever seen with wooden or stone floors instead of a dirt one—very grateful to the feet in winter.

Outside, the shutters and parts of the wall were painted with brilliant decorations: swirls of leaf and bursts of blossoms, with joyful birds like nothing ever seen in the forest. The exposed beams were carved into fanciful shapes; animals and birds and fish piled atop one another in a blatant disregard for the fact that fish did not ride atop bears, nor foxes fly. Inside the building there were more carvings on every beam, painted this time, and on the floors lay the hides of sheep and bear, and even a carpet or two taken from Turks. Heated by tiled stoves, cooled in summer by the breezes coming in the open windows, it was a marvel to Ilya every time he looked at it. There were dozens of rooms, entire rooms devoted to spinning and weaving, to drying and preparing herbs, rooms just for storing things. Each of his brothers had his own small room, there was a chapel for the priest, rooms where the servants slept, even a room made to catch all the thin winter sunlight so the tsarina and her ladies could sew in comfort in the coldest and bleakest of winters. He could hardly imagine how ordinary men had built the palace; it just seemed too big for human hands to have made. Small wonder that serf-girls longed for the sort of promotion that permitted them to work or even live inside it.

The hall was the largest room in the palace, and served for every kind of gathering. It held carved wooden benches and tables enough for all the family, all of Ivan's warriors, and a few of the most important servants. Ilya paused just inside the door to see how the land lay before entering. The kitchen-staff was already spreading out the plates and bowls of food, although Ivan and most of his sons had not yet arrived. A little relieved, Ilya took a place on the bench beside Sasha, the brother nearest his own age, and reached for a bowl of mashed turnips. Sasha ignored him, since he was only reaching for vegetables; Sasha became annoyed only when someone got at the meat before he had a chance to pick it over.

Dropping a bit of butter on top of the turnips, Ilya intercepted the boy carrying the borscht and got a bowlful. Meals with the family were always like this: intercept or grab what you wanted, or do without. There had never been any polite passing of plates among Ivan's offspring; it was every man (and woman) for himself.

More and more of the family and household drifted in; by this time, Ilya had bread and soup, turnips and onions, and the meat was coming around in the form of stewed rabbit. There would probably be venison or boar in a bit; Ilya didn't care to wait for a heartier meat. He liked rabbit well enough, and Sasha didn't, so when the platter passed by he stabbed a hind-quarter with his knife and carried it in triumph to his own plate. They all ate on plates now, though when Ilya had been very young, there had been plates only for Ivan and his tsarina. But the third wife, Ekaterina's successor, had brought with her artisans as well as livestock, and one of them had been a pot-ter. There was a fine bank of clay on the property, hardly touched except to make tiles for stoves until the skilled potter arrived, and now they all had plates to eat from and pottery goblets to drink from, with more to trade outside the kingdom. Ilya understood that there had been some grumbling in the kitchen about the extra work involved in cleaning the plates, but once Ivan threatened to take off the hand of the chief troublemaker, there had been no more complaints. The tsar did not like to be considered backward and savage, and his new mother-in-law's audible sniffs at the sight of the few wooden implements he'd had until then had been enough for him to order the plates to be made and used at all meals.

The hall was lit by torches and oil-lamps, and the flickering light made it difficult to judge expressions. Ilya ate warily, trying to ascertain if anyone was giving him a more suspicious glance than usual, but he couldn't tell if there was anything going on in anyone's mind except thoughts of what to inter-cept next as the servants went around. Ivan, who was hacking his way through a thick slab of venison, seemed preoccupied with his dinner. His third wife, still pretty in spite of the odd beating and her husband's neglect, leaned over to make sure Ivan got the greater share of a special dish of eels in broth, something he particularly enjoyed, that had been served only to the important members of the family.

By this time, Sasha was cramming venison into his enor-mous cavern of a mouth, and Ilya was just about full. He appropriated another piece of bread and spooned honey over it, leaning back to enjoy his treat and his goblet of wine.

"How'd practice go?" he asked his brother. Sasha shrugged.

"Mischa broke that new guard's arm; there'll be hell to pay when Father finds out. Alexi cracked a rib and Boris sprained his ankle. Pietor showed up late, so Mischa addled his wits for him. About the same as usual."

"Ah." He took a bite of the honeyed bread, followed it with a gulp of sour wine. "Pretty new laundress," he offered, knowing that Sasha preferred to find *his* girls among the washerwomen.

Each of the brothers had his own "territory" for skirt-chasing. As the eldest, Mischa tended to tread the dangerous path of chasing the house-servants; dangerous, because that was where their father also found his frolics. Gregori and Boris kept to the kitchen-girls; Pietor, Yuri, and Alexi favored the goat-and sheep-herders, or went out among the farms and fields to see what human crop had matured.

Sasha grinned ferally at the mention of the laundress. "Mine," he stated, with an edge to his voice. "And don't forget it."

"I wouldn't think of it!" Ilya replied fervently, for Sasha had a heavier hand than any of the brothers but Mischa. Ilya never had figured out why he had the dairy as a hunting-ground all to himself. Maybe it was Mother Galina's presence; the others all seemed unaccountably afraid of her.

Too bad for them; the milkmaids were some of the prettiest girls in the palace, and they were always clean and sweet-smelling, for Galina would not permit dirt in her dairy. Of course, the laundresses were always clean and sweet-smelling too, but they had coarse, rough hands that were not to Ilya's taste. The milkmaids' hands were soft from working with the butter and cheese.

Content, Sasha turned his attention back to his food; Ilya contemplated the rest of his loving family.

There was not the slightest shadow of a doubt who their father was; they were all variations on the theme of Ivan. Tsar Ivan, at the center of the head table, though going slightly to fat, still boasted enough muscle to daunt even Mischa, his eldest son. All of the men of the family were tall, blond, blue-eyed, square-jawed. Ivan's hair was going to silver, and his harsh features softening a bit with the fat of good living. Mischa was actually shorter than his father, a bit stockier, a bit broader. The next, Gregori, was probably the closest copy of the way Ivan had looked as a youth; he had everything but the hard muscles of a serious warrior that Ivan had boasted, and that was because he was lazy. Pietor, taller than either, with hair so light it was nearly white rather than blond, and rough, blunt features, looked as stupid as he was. Sasha was darker than Ivan; his hair was more golden-brown than straw-colored, and his features more arrogantly aquiline, but another streak of laziness kept him from living up to that implication of arrogance.

Then comes me. There were no mirrors in the palace except for three tiny hand-mirrors of polished metal that were the proudest possessions of the tsarina and her two chief ladies, but Ilya had seen himself in the reflections of a quiet pond often enough to know that the tsar could have no fault to find with his parentage. His hair was more gold-colored than straw, his features a little leaner than his brothers', but he had all of the family stamps: broad shoulders, square jaw, bright blue eyes, strong muscles. The traits that set him apart were subtle, probably too subtle for Ivan to notice—intelligence in the eyes, a hint of good humor about the mouth, and a stubborn set to his jaw.

Then came the younger brothers, Alexi, Boris, and Yuri. They looked alike enough to be triplets, and only if you paid close attention could you see that there was a year separating each of them from his sibling. They looked like slightly brighter, slightly less muscular copies of Pietor.

Strong like bull, dumb like ox, hitch to plow when horse dies. That's my family.

You could easily see Ivan's by-blows among the servants, too—his sons' bastards weren't old enough yet to take any serious tasks, but Ivan's own wood's-colts served their legitimate brothers with no sign of envy. Square-built, coarse-featured blonds abounded among the servants currently waiting on the tables, though most of them seemed, if possible, to be even duller of wit than the legitimate offspring. It was as if the mothers of all these children contributed nothing to their looks, a fact that Ivan took great pride in.

They didn't contribute anything in the way of wits either, as far as I can tell. Then again, Father's taste runs to girls as stupid as sheep.

The only woman at the head table was Feodora, Ivan's third wife; all the rest of the women, including Feodora's two cousins who acted as her ladies, sat at the lower tables. All of them were in positions lower than men of the same rank. Ivan had fixed ideas about the appropriate status of women in his household. He considered them slightly more important than his cattle and goats, but less so than his best breeding stallions.

Mother Galina had spoken some choice words to Ilya on *that* subject over the years, although she had been very careful to keep her opinions just between the two of them.

The hall was a noisy place at supper, with men shouting at one another in order to be heard up and down the lengths of the tables, and it didn't get any quieter as the evening progressed. As soon as most of the food was cleared away and there was nothing left but fruit, strong drink, and pastry, dice cups and counters came out and the gaming began. Someone set two of the dogs to fighting, and a betting-contest broke out over the outcome. Yuri, Gregori, and Pietor leapt over the table to join the fun; Sasha slouched forward onto the table with a belch.

Ilya tried not to squirm with impatience as he watched for a chance to leave. How long until moonrise? It couldn't be too long, but he had to wait until all his brothers *and* his father were sufficiently distracted before he tried to make an escape.

Out in the dark, smoky hall, more men gathered around the struggling dogs, shouting and waving their fists in the air to encourage their chosen hound. The growling and yelping dogs had everyone's attention now, despite Feodora's expression of distaste. She would probably be leaving the table soon, permitting her ladies to follow her, but it would be noted if any of the men left this early.

A moment later, the tsarina rose and all but fled the room, her two women and her servants scuttling after her. That was the signal for every other wife and daughter to leave as well. Now, except for serf-girls with pitchers of drink, there were only men in the hall. The dogfight was an even one, and had gone on longer than Ilya had expected; it might prove to be just the distraction he'd been hoping for. Now Mischa and Alexi had left their seats, and even Ivan leaned over the table, intent on the outcome. Only Sasha yawned lazily and ignored the affray.

I won't get a better opportunity than this one. Ilya decided to take his chances and slipped out of his chair. At just the moment that he stood up, Sasha stabbed him with a swift glance.

Ilya took another chance, and leaned over to whisper in his brother's ear. If it had been anyone other than Sasha, he wouldn't have dared, but he and Sasha shared a weakness for women that occasionally made them allies.

"I've got a girl waiting," he said hoarsely.

Sasha seized his wrist in a crushing grip. "*Not* the laundress," he replied challengingly.

Ilya shook his head—minimally, so as to avoid catching Ivan's notice. "Dairymaid," he mouthed. "New one."

"Must be the season for new girls." Sasha let him go with a sly wink.

"I've got to piss or I'll burst!" his brother said loudly, and lurched to his feet, waving to Ilya to follow.

Ilya did so, grateful that Sasha's weakness for girls was so powerful, he was willing to forget any quarrel. Once they were out in the hallway and the noise of the dogfight faded, Sasha let out a burst of laughter and slapped him on the back hard enough to make him stagger if he hadn't been ready for it. "I was waiting for *you* to start watching the damn fight so *I* could sneak away!" he chortled, very pleased with himself. "You know if the old man saw us trying to sneak out, he'd want a piece for himself!"

"Laundress at moonrise?" Ilya asked. "In the laundry?" The laundry made a very convenient place for Sasha to meet his girls, and the convenience was matched by the comfort of tumbling on the piles of soiled linens and clothing.

Sasha shook his head. "One of Feodora's maids, in the wool-shed."

Ilya whistled. "That's coming pretty near to Mischa's ground, isn't it?" he asked, amazed that Sasha dared even think about "poaching."

"Well, Mischa can get used to it," the other replied with bravado—and Ilya had the feeling that it wasn't all bluff. *So Sasha is going to challenge the heir-apparent. Well, better him than me.*

"As for me, I'm taking advantage of the fact that it is still pleasant at night," he said, soothingly. "It won't be long before I have to get into the cow-barn with them and bundle in the hayloft under whatever blankets and old furs I can find."

"The more fool you for not keeping your girls on the string when they come into the palace," said Sasha smugly, and slapped Ilya on the shoulder so that he staggered a little. "Well, good hunting among the cows! I'm off to my little bundle of fleece."

They parted ways. Ilya did not go directly to the door leading to the kitchen-court and thence to the meadow. Instead, he slipped into the servants' area, to the tiny, windowless, chill little closet beside the dilapidated chapel, the cramped cell of a room allotted to Father Mikail. As he expected, the priest was taking his dinner with the servants now that the family and the important folk of the palace had eaten their fill. With him would be Ruslan the Shaman, giving mutual protection and bolstering the frayed dignity of each other. Of all the free-born and (theoretically) highborn folk in the palace, *they* were the lowest in rank, and no more than nominally above the servants, and in reality treated with less respect than anyone other than a drudge.

There wasn't room for anything in this room but a small chest and a bed, so Ilya didn't need to be able to see to get what he wanted. He knelt down in the darkness, reached under the bed, and felt among the wool slippers, winter boots, and odds and ends that needed mending until he felt the neck of his balalaika. He kept it in Mikail's room to prevent his brothers from cutting the strings—they wouldn't actually break it, because they *might* want him to play at some point. But they knew that he usually played it when he was trying to attract a girl, and if he found it with the strings cut he'd either have to spend precious time restringing and tuning it, or do without and risk losing the girl.

It was easier just to hide it with Mikail. With his instrument

in hand, he made his way out to his meeting with the pretty
dairymaid.

Once he got into the kitchen garden, he relaxed. It was just
dusk, easy enough to see where he was going, and at this point
only one of his brothers would be likely to stop him. He came
to the fence, crossed the stile into the meadow, and made his
way slowly through the waist-high grass. The dairy cattle
wouldn't be put here until first frost, so he didn't need to
worry about being interrupted by a curious cowherd or stepping in a heap of dung. The soft, cool evening air, scented
with the flowers that grew thickly underfoot, brushed his skin
gently. Crickets sang among the grass-stems, and somewhere
nearby a nightingale poured out her heart to the stars that were
slowly appearing in the east.

Ilya planned his campaign as he walked, instrument slung
over his back, hands swinging at his sides. *She seemed agree-
able, but I doubt she'll let me get too far tonight.* He never
forced his women, taking his cue from Sasha, who felt the
same way. As far as Ilya could tell, given that the serfs would
not protest anything to a member of the family, the brothers
were about evenly divided on their initial techniques when it
came to tumbling girl-flesh. Pietor, Alexi, Yuri, and Gregori
had a certain reputation for ordering a girl to come to them
and taking what they wished from her. He, Sasha, Mischa, and
Boris preferred girls who came willingly. Ivan—who knew?
None of Ivan's wenches ever talked.

*Well, no one would ever deny Father anything, so even the
unwilling girls probably pretend to be willing.*

So, tonight would be the start of a new campaign. There
would be lots of kissing and caressing, and maybe the girl
would let him go farther than that—but unless she already had
a position inside the palace in mind, it would take another two
nights at least before he stormed the ramparts and the gates
opened for him. Still, the conquest itself had its rewards, because once the girl yielded to him, it was only a matter of
time before she looked elsewhere than him for a lover—not
because he was a *bad* lover, but because there wasn't much
to be gained, in the way of presents or position, by being his
lover. He'd know his time was over when she wheedled him
for a position on the palace staff, or when she just showed up

there by herself. The latter, of course, could be accomplished by going to the steward and claiming to be with Ilya's child, whether she was or not. The steward would ask Ilya if he had taken the girl, Ilya would naturally admit the fact, and she would have a better job than she had before, one with all sorts of advantages attached. For a girl used to spending the winter in a peasant hut, huddled at night in a box of straw under a single blanket, the prospect of a winter in the palace was often incentive enough to make her eager for Ilya's embraces.

It really didn't matter to the steward if a girl lied about being with child. If no baby appeared in eight months, well, things happened. According to the steward, the serfs were only slightly more intelligent than the cattle, and just about as reliable. The steward's answer to the lack of a baby was simple: Girls miscarried all the time, or sometimes girls just didn't count properly and thought they were pregnant when they weren't. His contempt for the intelligence of the serfs was rivaled only by his contempt for the intelligence of the female serfs, although he *should* have known better, considering the sly tricks that were often played on him. To him, the girls were not only untutored serfs, they were female, and couldn't be expected to calculate anything as complicated as the number of days from one moon-phase to the next.

Ah, with this little rosebud, Father will probably set a claim on her himself as soon as he sees her. He sighed, for it was a vexing thing constantly to lose lovers to his father. Still, it couldn't be helped. He would enjoy this one as long as he had her, and hopefully when she was ready to move up in the world she'd be honest about it to him.

IT was past midnight by the moon when he left his little Ludmilla drowsily content beneath the willow and picked his way back across the meadow to the palace. To his surprise and gratitude, the city had capitulated with only token resistance, and the gates had been thrown wide open to the conqueror. As it turned out, she was already conquered, for Yuri had broken the gates and pillaged the city ahead of him, which accounted for her pliancy—

Not that it matters to me. The difference between us has

made her so very sweet, yielding, and grateful I hardly needed to be more than usually charming!

And unlike real cities, girls could be pillaged many times over with the same level of satisfaction. He did wonder, though, why she hadn't gone to the steward rather than showing up at the dairy. Perhaps the position in the dairy *was* her reward, and she had singled him out with an eye to rising higher. Well, good for her; she was a toothsome little thing, and she had given him as much satisfaction as he had given her.

Actually, with far more satisfaction on her part, given that it's me instead of Yuri. Not only is his siege-engine rather pathetic, but he has no idea of how to use it. He smiled smugly to himself, for he had played her like his balalaika and wrung the sweetest music out of her before he took his own full pleasure. She'd seemed pleased enough with the string of red glass beads he'd gifted her with afterward. No, she had nothing to complain about from him . . . and *he* wasn't going to suffer the twinges of guilt he often suffered if a girl turned out to be a virgin.

All that crying and carrying on—even if more than half of it is an act, it still makes me feel as if I've stolen something. He *knew* why they did it: The guiltier they made him feel, the better the presents they could coax out of him. That still didn't keep him from feeling guilty.

So a girl like Ludmilla, already "spoiled" and now perfectly happy to give up any pretense of reluctance, was nothing short of perfect.

He was so wrapped up in satisfaction that he wasn't paying much attention to his surroundings as he sauntered past the chapel to replace his balalaika in Mikail's room. The servants were all in their beds by now, except for the girl his brother was with, and it was in her interest not to attract his attention. And as for his brothers—well, Sasha was likely as full of contentment as Ilya was and unlikely to pick a quarrel, and the rest were full of drink and snoring. The night was his—

Or it was until a hand shot out of the darkness and seized his wrist.

For one moment, Ruslan's wild tales of the vengeful and dangerous *domovoi* raced through his mind, and he bit back a yell as he grabbed for the hand holding him. In the next moment, he recognized the feel of the shabby vestments and the skinny arm, and he plucked the clutching hand off his wrist with a feeling of annoyance.

"What are *you* doing here?" he asked Father Mikail crossly. "It's late. If you're going to be up, shouldn't you be praying or something?"

"I have been praying, knowing what *you* were probably doing," the old priest said reproachfully. "Ilya, Ilya, you aren't even *pretending* repentance for despoiling another poor girl!"

"She was already nicely despoiled before I got to her," he retorted, stung. What was wrong with the old man? Jealousy?

That might be the case, since it sounded as if Mikail was not going to give in tonight.

"And that makes it better?" Mikail's voice took on a querulous tone, which only irritated Ilya more. "It is no less a sin, and worse because you are unrepentant!"

He throttled his irritation; he was not going to let the old crow ruin a perfectly fine evening. "Look, I'm not going to quarrel with you," he replied abruptly in a low whisper. "It's too late, and I'm not going to attract a horde of servants by having an argument out here in the open where we can wake them up. You can call me to task in the morning if you're still of the same mind."

With that, he thrust the instrument into the priest's hands and stalked away, and his irritation melted. For all intents and purposes, the argument was over before it began. Father Mikail was too timid to pursue him tonight, and too diffident to confront him by daylight, especially as he must know that Ruslan would not agree with him on this subject. *He must have seen me going out, and he's been praying for my soul ever since,* he thought, amusement returning to him. *Poor old man. He must never have been young; all he can think about is sin and damnation, and he's so desperate to keep his soul clean that he never enjoys anything for fear it's sinful. That's not the life for me! Plenty of time to repent before I die—right now I want to make sure I have lots of things to repent of when I'm old!*

There was not even a whisper in the darkness behind him;

Father Mikail had faded into the shadows, obediently carrying the balalaika with him.

Ilya sighed. Poor Mikail. Only the priest and the shaman were held in greater contempt by Ivan and his sons than the despised Ilya. It was hard to believe that anyone could be lower in the palace hierarchy than Ilya, but the very things that the two men represented were the things that Ivan despised the most.

But if Mikail was despised, the shaman was actually in worse case. *He* didn't even have quarters in the palace; he was relegated to a hut next to the bathhouse.

Poor old Ruslan. Bad enough that he is a shaman; it is worse that he is an inheritance from Grandfather.

Ivan's father, Vasily, who had not styled himself a tsar but a boyar, had been a thorough-going pagan. He had believed, fervently and wholeheartedly, in every sort of spirit ever imagined, from *bannik* to *rusalka,* from *leshii* to *vodianoi.*

On his orders, every means of propitiating those spirits had been utilized. He ordered the cooks to leave pots of unsalted porridge in the attic for the *domovoi* and pannikins of sweet cream in the meadow for the *polevoi.*

Ilya sighed as he thought of his grandfather, who he knew of only from the stories of others, and it occurred to him, as he stealthily opened the door to the tiny room he called his own, that Ivan's steadfast refusal to believe in *anything* supernatural, Christian or pagan, might have been because of Vasily's unshakable belief. Ivan often pointed out that no matter how much porridge was left in the attic, the usual household mishaps continued to occur—and that the cattle strayed from the meadow when the fence came down, not when someone forgot to put out the cream. Vasily had spent a great deal of the family treasure on propitiating the spirits, and Ivan loudly pointed out that no great good had ever come of that— nor had any great harm ever come from his insistence on ignoring the spirits.

It was Ivan the unbeliever who had improved the family fortune, who had raised himself to the rank of tsar, who had increased the familial landholdings by manyfold. Granted, he was just one minor tsar among hundreds beneath the Great

Tsar of Rus, but still—that was better than a boyar. It was more than Vasily had done.

If you think that life is all about getting more land, more cattle, more power—I don't know; what's all that without happiness? Or, at least, enjoyment?

Ilya closed the door and opened the shutters and moonlight poured into his room; it wasn't a very big room, but it was larger than a servant's, and it was furnished befitting a son of the tsar, if a despised one. He had a chest—carved by his own hands, but of good wood—in which his clothing was carefully folded. His bedstead held a goose-feather bed, one of Ivan's cast-offs, covered with coarse linen sheets, mended blankets, and the furs of two bears and a wolf he had killed himself. On a table beside his bed was a lamp, unlit, and a pitcher of water. By the brilliant moonlight he made certain that none of his brothers had sabotaged his bed. He had not once omitted to check, not since he was six—not even when he was drunk, injured, or otherwise operating at a disadvantage. His brothers seldom resorted to such childish torments anymore, but he had learned the value of taking precautions.

While he was at it, and while the moonlight was still pouring in the open window, he checked the rest of the room. He found nothing, but it never hurt to be certain. There'd been vipers left in his room before, and less dangerous but equally unpleasant "surprises."

The moon crept down below the treetops, sending his room into darkness as he finished his checks. Only when the room was completely dark and he was certain that his sleep would be undisturbed did he throw the bolt on the door, close and lock the shutters, and strip himself down to the skin for bed. He was already clean, and he yawned hugely, quite ready for sleep. He'd bathed in the river with Ludmilla, both before and after his amorous exertions—not only was he fastidious, but he'd often found a little water-play to be very erotic, provided the girl wasn't afraid of the water.

It would be too cold for that before very much longer. There had been a bite to the water that had been pleasant, given the heated condition of their bodies, but it was a chill which presaged the ice of winter.

And soon comes the end to all dalliance under the willow. Ah, well.

He envied Sasha the "possession" of the wool-room; the rolled fleeces would be far more pleasant for tumbling a maiden than the prickly straw of the cow-barn.

It could be worse. I could be freezing my privates off in a woodshed or something, which makes it difficult to remain in the proper mood. I could be picking up fleas in a serf's hut. I could be taking my chances in the bathhouse. I could be doing without altogether!

There was one small stumbling-block to overcome in gaining the safe use of the barn now and again. He wondered what the chief herdsman would want for a bribe this year; last year it had cost Ilya an old cloak and a beautifully carved bone whistle for "special favors."

Without those favors, though . . . well, the amount of discomfort and hazard involved in a winter seduction would probably guarantee his chastity until spring.

I can't blame the man for wanting his little reward. In his place I'd want a little extra for all that extra work.

The man made certain that Ilya got warning and a way out of the barn if any of his brothers showed up looking for him. He'd also built a cozy little hay-cave up in the loft, a place where Ilya could leave a couple of old blankets, and he'd seen to it that the cave wasn't disturbed until spring, no matter how much hay was thrown down for the stock. *Of course, he probably used it himself, for trysts with girls other than his wife. I know I would have.* All he had to bring was a brick or a stone, hot from sitting in the stove and wrapped in an old piece of fur. With the addition of that heated stone, such a cave made a fine trysting-place.

Ruslan approved of Ilya's trysts almost as much as Father Mikail disapproved, though that approval was voiced only to Ilya himself. When Father Mikail flung himself into one of his lectures about sin and the consequences for Ilya's soul, Ruslan only pulled his beard and nodded wisely. The shaman would never have disagreed with the priest on a topic so fundamental to Mikail's beliefs in front of Ilya. The two took very good care never to contradict each other in public so as to present a united front.

But in private—well, Ruslan took great proprietary glee in Ilya's conquests, as if he felt Ilya's success was a reflection of his own virility. Ilya was both amused and embarrassed by his interest.

Ilya folded his clothing neatly, then climbed into bed and pulled the covers over his head with a sigh of relative contentment. He was clean, sated, and more or less unbruised. For the moment, life was good.

I could wish for Father Mikail to agree with Ruslan about my girls, but other than that, I haven't anything to complain about tonight. For a moment he felt the sadness of isolation, of a loneliness he tried not to think about too often. The priest and the shaman were his only two real friends besides Mother Galina, and they were hardly the kind of friends a young man craved.

On the other hand, they're better than nothing.

Perhaps Mother Galina had known he needed men to guide him, for she had sent him to both Mikail and Ruslan the winter she arrived.

The memories intruded on sleep, as vivid as a memory of a few days ago. He had been with her in the dairy as the first snow of the season fell; when the last of the dairymaids left, she had looked out at the fat flakes as if she was trying to make up her mind about something. She stood in the doorway, and he stood beside her, watching the ground whiten as the light faded into blue dusk. He didn't remember being cold, for some reason, but he vividly recalled licking his finger clean of cream filched behind Galina's back. Finally she spoke; that is where his memory failed. He didn't remember now what she had told him; he only remembered crossing the snow-frosted yard and entering the palace, remembered walking toward the chapel, looking for two old men. He had found them both in the chapel itself, sitting on a pair of stools with a small table between them, with the faded, painted eyes of the icon of Jesus watching them from above the altar, and he did remember quite clearly what they had been engaged in.

A game of chess. And if Father Mikail had ever considered that it might be a trifle irreverent to play a game of chess in the house of God, he had obviously put that thought aside. It was, after all, the only place where he and Ruslan could be

guaranteed not to be harassed with scorn for such an effemi-
nate pursuit.

The two of them had set up a board between them, and the
state of the set showed how little anyone else cared about this
particular pursuit; they didn't have all of the pieces and had
substituted stones for the missing pawns and a pinecone for a
missing rook. The rest of the set was as battered as might have
been expected; two of the knights were headless, and the remaining pawns were hardly more than man-shaped lumps rid-
dled with toothmarks and clearly rescued from dogs and
teething babies. He also remembered what he told them when
they looked up in startlement.

"Mother Galina says you are to teach me."

Teach him what? they had asked him.

"Everything," he had told them soberly, then stuck his finger in his mouth. The two men had immediately forgotten their
game and concentrated on him.

From that time on he'd had two refuges instead of one: the
dairy and the chapel.

For some reason, even to this day, Ilya's brothers were unlikely to even venture into the chapel, much less bother him
there, and he was quick to take advantage of that. Perhaps it
was a lingering vestige of the piety their mothers attempted to
instill in them, a respect for the place if not for the priest.
Perhaps it was just the haunting eyes of the icon above the
altar, eyes that remained remarkably penetrating despite the
faded condition of the icon itself. Whatever the reason, as
often as it was possible to escape from the incessant practices
designed to make him a fighting machine, or from the torments
devised by his brothers, he would head for the chapel. At any
time of the day, he would find one or both of the old men
there, ready to continue with his lessons. Ruslan taught him
all of the lore of spirits and magic—never mind that the old
shaman couldn't actually work any magic himself, which certainly contributed to the reasons he was held in contempt—
and dozens of songs and heroic tales. He'd also given Ilya his
first knife, and showed him the bare rudiments of carving.

*And the only reason Father allows him to stay is because
of a deathbed promise to Grandfather that he would never
turn Ruslan out. Poor old man; it must be very hard to remain*

where you are so despised because you have nowhere else to go.

Father Mikail was a newer arrival, brought in the household of Ivan's first wife. Ivan permitted him to stay only so long as he didn't interfere in anything important—which essentially meant that he was permitted to teach Christian doctrine to the family, serfs, and servants only so long as those lessons didn't interfere in their duties. And he was permitted to hold holy services whenever he liked—so long as family, serfs, and servants didn't escape tasks in order to attend services. Perhaps when he had first arrived, he had been appalled by the presence of a pagan shaman in Ivan's household, but it couldn't have been long before Mikail realized that he and Ruslan were better off as allies than antagonists. And eventually these two oddest of bedfellows had become friends.

Mikail taught Ilya how to read and write, as much of chess as he could absorb without squirming with boredom, and despaired of making a good Christian soul out of him—not because of Ruslan's interference, but because of Ilya's own nature.

He never will make a good Christian out of me; I'm too fond of my pleasures. But he is a good teacher; he'd have to be, to teach a brat like me how to read without resorting to violence!

In return for all these favors, the first major carving project Ilya ever embarked on was a new chess set for the two of them.

You can follow my progress as a carver in the set itself, he thought with drowsy amusement. *From the first pawn to the last tsar. That first pawn is almost as clumsy as the ones the dogs chewed on, but they won't let me replace it. On the other hand, the White Tsar is not bad, even compared to what I'm carving now. . . .*

But even as he thought about his chess set, his carving, he began to relax, and as he relaxed, he started to fall asleep. He tried to keep a grasp on his thoughts, but they began to slip away from him in a confused jumble of clumsily carved pawns that gave way to a carved fox that laughed at him with sparkling eyes and turned into Ludmilla.

*　　*　　*

IN the morning, he woke with the first crowing of the roosters, feeling (as always after a night of dalliance) quite self-satisfied and pleased with the world. The first rays of the morning sun sent fingers of light through the cracks in his shutters, and the rooster crowed again. Dust-motes danced in the golden light, and there had been a time when he was a child that he could have gazed dreamily at that dance for hours.

He made a mental note of the cracks; as always, the weathering of the wood opened places for winter wind to come through, and no servant would bother to repair the shutters in his room. Cracks in the shutters were tolerable in the summer when all that might come in was a bit of rain, but when winter descended in earnest, there would be snow sifting in through those cracks, and that would *not* make for pleasant waking of a morning. *Get some moss and a little tar; stuff the cracks, then tar them over. That should hold until spring; then it won't matter anymore.*

Anything done to his room, other than sabotage, he did for himself, more often than not. While the outside-servants seemed to think well enough of him to accept his bribes and remain bought, the house-servants knew they could get by with neglecting him. They never quite dared descend to outright insolence, but they were quite well aware that they could get away with simply not performing their assigned tasks where he was concerned. By now he was so used to this state of affairs that it was easier just to take care of things himself.

First thing to do after I eat. I think I might be able to safely skip sword-practice this morning. Considering what Sasha had said last night about the damage done to the tsar's fighters by his sons, sparring partners might be thin on the ground this morning.

He stretched and yawned hugely, clambered out of bed, and dressed himself in shirt, breeches, boots, and sash, carefully tidying his room before leaving it. There was very little chance that he would avoid his father this morning, but given the way that his brothers had been swilling down honey-wine last night, he might be able to elude most of them before they appeared at breakfast with aching heads.

But as he approached the great hall, he heard his father roaring at someone, clearly in a temper. Although the words did not carry to where he stood, hesitating, the tone certainly did.

Tsar Ivan is very unhappy this morning, and it doesn't sound to me as if his unhappiness is due to a bad head from drinking last night. The last thing in the world he wanted to do was to encounter Ivan in a temper, so he made a hasty detour to the nearest exit. *I'd better find out why he's roaring before I take my chances around him.*

It wasn't the first time he'd retraced his steps of a morning and took himself out into the yard. At least the weather was good; a bit cool, but sunny and clear. He wouldn't have to plow his way through a snowstorm to get to a place of refuge or to get a bite to eat.

He stopped long enough in the kitchen to filch a basket and fill it with hot bread. The head cook glared at him but didn't dare actually rebuke him—he was, after all, a son of the tsar, if the most despised son of the tsar. If he wanted to filch bread, then that was his right.

There was one place to go where he would get sure news of what had his father in a froth, and that was the dairy. If he went to the dairy for shelter as well as news, he really ought to arrive bearing gifts. And if he *really* wanted to hear gossip, the gift had better be food. When the girls were distracted, they tended to chatter, and chatter was precisely what he wanted.

Mother Galina and her workers seldom ever got hot, fresh bread since their work kept them away from the kitchen and the servants' table until after everyone else was finished eating. The maidens greeted him and his basket with cries of pleasure, and even Galina smiled and condescended to allow a brief rest while they all ate chunks of hot bread dripping with sweet, melting butter and drank pannikins of milk still warm from the cows.

Ilya kept quiet; if there was anything of note about the tsar's anger, he'd hear about it sooner if he didn't say anything directly. Once they "forgot" he was there, they'd start to gossip freely, giving him no more regard than one of the cowherds.

There's some advantage to being the despised one, he thought to himself, sitting on a stool in the corner beside

Mother Galina and licking butter from his fingers. *People forget to guard their tongues around you.*

His charming Ludmilla, his companion of the previous night, was nowhere to be seen, but he hadn't really expected her to be here this morning. The dairymaids took turns at milking; those who milked the cattle in the morning worked in the dairy in the afternoon, and vice versa. Just at the moment, he really didn't want to see her; if it so happened that *he* was the one who had incurred Ivan's wrath, he didn't want the complication of Ludmilla to deal with. She'd either try to dissociate herself completely from him—the likeliest outcome—or feel she had to defend him. In either case, he had long ago determined that he personally would come out a loser. Either Ludmilla would quickly find another lover among his brothers, or she'd incur even more wrath on *his* head by being outspoken in his defense.

As the bread disappeared, the chatter began. At first it was entirely inconsequential nonsense, but finally one of the youngest girls said, into a conversational lull, "Did you hear the tsar this morning? He was bellowing like a bull with a cow in view!"

"I heard him," one of the older women said, "but I didn't get a chance to find out why he was so angry. Does anyone know? Is it going to give us any trouble?"

Just what I'd like to know!

"Not *us*," another older woman said smugly. "But there may be more than pots flung before the day is over. My husband's brother's second son heard that it's the orchard-workers who are in trouble."

"Tell, tell!" exclaimed two or three of the girls at once, for there was ongoing rivalry among the "outside" serfs and servants for relative importance to the household. At this time of year the orchard-workers were in ascendancy, and serfs working elsewhere were always eager to hear of any trouble coming to them.

"Oh, it is quite serious!" the woman said with unconcealed glee. "*Someone* was robbing the tsar's cherry trees last night!"

There were gasps all around the dairy, and Ilya's own eyes widened. *No wonder Father's in a temper! I wouldn't be one of the orchard-guards right now for a brand-new sable coat and fur-lined boots to match!*

One of Tsar Ivan's most treasured possessions was a tiny orchard of a dozen special late-bearing cherry trees. Of all the things in the world, Ivan's two favorite dishes were eels in broth and cherries in cream. He had specially planted these trees so that he could have cherries long after the native trees had been picked bare.

And he guarded the fruits of those trees like a jealous sultan guarded his harem. He had bird-nets strung over them, and set small children to frighten away pests by day, older gardeners to do the same by night. He often went out personally as the cherries ripened to see just how much of a harvest he could expect, and the servants claimed he counted the cherries on the tree and demanded an accounting for each one.

So, after all those precautions, to have his trees robbed of their fruit in the night—

Ilya shook his head slightly, not only over the news but over his incredible good luck to have been with a girl during the night hours. If Ivan took it into his head that one of his sons might have robbed him of his precious cherries—*Oh, I am glad I was with Ludmilla last night! If Father's suspicions fall on me, I'll have an alibi, and so will Sasha!*

But a moment later, Ilya jumped to his feet. Now that he knew *he* was in no danger, he had to hear about all of this firsthand! And to do that, he had only to stroll into breakfast as he had begun to.

He dropped a kiss on Mother Galina's head. She smiled at him, making no move to leave her own stool. "Don't say anything to anger him further, dear," she cautioned. "But bring me back the rest of the gossip when you can."

"I shall, Babushka," he promised fondly, for somehow he had the feeling that this was no simple case of a thieving serf or a hungry animal. No, this was something special, and promised enough excitement to take the attention of everyone off him for a while!

And who knows? Perhaps this might lead to a way that I can leave this place, he thought as he hurried toward the palace again. *For that, I would almost sell my soul itself.*

CHAPTER TWO

IVAN WAS still bellowing when Ilya strolled casually into the great hall. The tsar paid no attention to him whatsoever, which was a good sign, a sign that he, at least, was not under suspicion. He gathered up cold meat, warm bread, and something to drink and took a seat at one of the lower tables where he had a good view of the proceedings.

On his knees in front of the tsar was the chief gardener, and from the man's posture, he was just about to go down on his face and grovel before his master. Ivan's face, flushed scarlet, held a curiously fixed expression, one that his family and those who served him knew meant that his anger had mounted to the point that anything could happen. It was entirely possible that if the gardener did not satisfy him with enough servility, Ivan would kill him on the spot. The tsars, little and great, held the power of life and death over their people, and Ivan had never hesitated to exercise that power in the past.

The gardener, though personally unfamiliar with the danger signs of Ivan's rages, must have sensed that, for he abruptly fell on his face, just before Ivan drew his sword. Ilya still could not make out his words, muffled as they were by the fact that the man had his face pressed into the floor, but his tone betrayed panic.

That, at last, placated the tsar. Ivan took a deep breath, slammed his blade back into the sheath, and his high color faded a little. "In the future," he said in a tight voice, "you will never, *never* say to me, 'It is not my fault.' The gardens are *your* responsibility, and what happens in them *is* your fault. You would do well to remember that."

Ilya feigned that he was ignoring the entire scene, but his father's words clarified the situation. *Ah. I thought that there was more to this than just the theft of cherries—there's no reason to become that angry over a simple theft. But Father can't stand not having someone to blame when things go wrong. And once his temper's up, don't stand in his path, don't contradict him, and don't try to push the blame off on someone else. Even I know better than that.*

The gardener glanced up, then whimpered, evidently just now realizing how close he had come to death. His abject fear had satisfied Ivan's blood-lust; the tsar's face returned to normal, and he spat to one side of the man's head. "Get out of here," Ivan snarled, turning on his heel and flinging himself down into his chair. "Send me someone who can tell me exactly what happened. I'll deal with you later."

That "someone" turned out to be the chief of Ivan's guards, a stiff-necked, haughty man that Ivan had recently raised to the rank of boyar by investing him with land and a substantial house of his own. Sidor was under no illusions; Ivan had made him, Ivan could break him, and would do just that if he wasn't pleased. He went to one knee with his head bowed as soon as he came into Ivan's presence, and he waited to speak until Ivan gave him leave.

"Well?" Ivan growled, sitting back in his chair and toying with his sword-hilt. "What have *you* to say for yourself?"

"It is my failure, oh, Tsar," Sidor replied promptly. "If I had been properly strict, my men would have been properly vigilant, and—"

The tsar waved his hand in a dismissive motion. "Yes, yes, that's obvious, isn't it?" Ivan interrupted impatiently. "Whip the sluggards who fell asleep until they can't stand." He leaned forward over his knees, his blue eyes blazing. "Now tell me what happened and why."

Sidor nodded his head stiffly and did not lose one whit of his subservience. "There is not much to tell, oh, Tsar. The first watch had retired just before moonset, and the second watch had come on. The trees were untouched as they made their first inspection. They took their places, and that is all that they can recall, until they woke up with the men of the third watch shaking them." A sneer crept into his hitherto cold, unemotional voice. "They claim they must have been overcome by sorcery, that a witch or spirit must have attacked them."

Ivan, who had observed the men of the garden-watch drinking their fill of potent honey-wine the night before, snorted, but made no comment of his own. Ilya hid his face behind his cup in case his father should look up and see the satisfaction in his eyes. The time of the theft was right so far as Ilya was concerned; he had a perfect alibi if he needed to produce one. But the hapless soldiers could not have concocted a tale more calculated to incur Ivan's scorn and anger if they had tried.

Sidor continued the story, reflecting his tsar's contempt for anyone who would be so foolish as to try to deceive the tsar with a tale of spirits. "When the men of the third watch inspected the trees, all of the ripe fruit had been stolen, and some fruit that was not quite ripe had been discarded on the ground. The bird-nets had been pulled back from the branches. There was no sign that any of the gardeners' ladders had been used to climb the trees, but that doesn't mean it didn't happen that way." Sidor shrugged. "It was very strange that those men fell asleep for that long; even if they had been very drunk, I will say that much in their favor. There must have been noise, a great deal of it, when the thief climbed the trees, but they slept through it somehow. None of us could find any sign of how the thief got into the garden or left it."

Ivan grunted, his brows furrowing. "A clever thief could have given them a bottle of mead laced with something to make them sleep, and if they shared it around—well, right there would be your explanation for why they didn't wake up. You can be sure none of them would admit to such a thing, either." He brooded, slumped in his chair for a moment, his face sullen with knitted brows and his lips twisted in an angry frown. "Well, after the men see what happened to the sluggards, there won't be any more of that. Do as I said; beat them. And while you're at it, beat the head gardener." He looked up again, and there was an avidity in his eyes that made Ilya shudder. "Beat them bloody; make an example of them. Bring them before me when you are ready to punish them."

"Shall I set extra guards tonight, oh, Tsar?" Sidor asked carefully.

"What, on *fruit trees?*" Ivan exclaimed with a snort. Ilya smothered a grin of amusement at his father's expense. "There's enough snickering about my cherry trees as it is. No, the regular guard will do; whoever the prankster is, he'll get a rude surprise if he makes another attempt." His expression turned crafty and cruel. "Then he'll be caught, and a theft of cherries is a theft all the same. A man who'll steal cherries will steal anything else, and there is only one punishment for thieves in my land."

Ilya's amusement turned to a shiver of revulsion. Ivan's punishment for thieves was considered extreme even by his allies. Ilya's father had taken a leaf from the book of the Turk and the Tartar who were cruelty incarnate, but had gone one step further than even those demonic barbarians. Instead of cutting off only one hand, Ivan cut both hands off a thief. Then, with the stumps seared with a hot iron, the poor wretch would be carried out to the edge of the forest and left there.

There was little doubt that the bears and wolves would make short work of a weak, helpless man with no hands. Ivan would, once again, hammer home a lesson to his family, servants, and serfs.

It was a lesson that Ilya had learned long since—but his brothers might not have realized that Ivan could and would apply his laws and his will to them. *Could this have been a prank by one of my brothers?* he wondered. *If it was, I hope he realizes how angry Father is, and has the sense to keep his mouth shut about what he did. I'm not sure Father would spare even one of his own children in the mood he's in now. It isn't a matter of a few cherries anymore, it's a matter of control, pride, and power.*

Ilya knew better than any of Ivan's sons that it was the rankest folly to challenge Ivan's hold on any of the three.

"Did you make any inquiries around and about? Did you ask who wasn't in his bed last night?" Ivan continued.

Sidor nodded, and his posture wasn't nearly as servile as before. He must have guessed that Ivan wasn't going to punish *him* by now; his confidence had returned, and with it, all of his arrogance. "The servants aren't talking, of course. Peasants; they'll all stick together against their masters." He spoke with the contempt of one only recently elevated to the position of master. "Still," he continued, "if it is one of the servants, you'll catch him at his tricks and then he'll serve as a good example to the rest."

Ilya had had enough, both of breakfast and of his father. Quietly, so as not to draw attention to himself, he stood up and left the room. Perhaps it might not be a bad idea to go find someone to spar with after all. This was not the time to draw attention to himself by acting differently from his brothers.

He took himself outside as quickly as his feet could carry him without running. The best thing he could do right now would be to look busy, but as if he were completely unaware of the theft in the garden. No one had noticed him at breakfast; the farther removed from the situation he was the better.

The warriors practiced in a yard formed by two wings of the house and the stable, with a shed where the arms were kept making a partial fourth side. The buildings kept most of the wind off and gave partial shelter from snow and rain, but the yard still turned into a muddy mess any time there was any significant amount of rainfall. It was better than practicing in the open, and that was all Ilya could say for it. The yard itself was not much different than the stableyard. There were a couple of crude benches along one side, seats that had been made by propping half a log on legs pounded into the earth, and there was a fighting-dummy at each end of the yard, but other than that it was bare.

There wasn't anyone in the yard or the shed when Ilya got there, which was a little odd but not unheard of. Perhaps word had already spread of the punishments to be meted out to the hapless garden-guards, and the curious or callous were gathering to watch. That didn't matter. Someone would come along to spar with sooner or later. In the meantime, Ilya picked up a blunt old practice-sword and a scarred wooden shield and began methodically working against the practice-dummy.

It was hard work, since both the sword and the shield were heavier than the ones he'd be using in actual fighting. He flailed away at his targets, ducking the return blows as the dummy swung around and the weighted mace it "carried" hissed through the air above his head. It was hardly worth bouting against the dummy except for exercise these days; he had the timing of the dummy worked into his nerves, instinct, and muscles after so many years of practice against it. If all opponents were as predictable as the dummy, he wouldn't ever worry about going to war.

He got himself into the rhythm of—*strike, strike, duck, block*—and it lulled him into a trance. He didn't even notice that he wasn't alone in the yard anymore until a hand lashed out from behind and grabbed his wrist in a grip like a wolf-trap and spun him around.

He found himself looking, startled, into the cold, blue eyes of his oldest brother. Beside him were Pietor and Gregori.

"What have you been up to, sorcerer?" Mischa snarled. "Stealing, and leaving others to take *your* punishment?"

They gave him no chance to reply before Mischa's other fist drove into Ilya's stomach.

THE candle-flames illuminating the chapel were doubled and tripled in Ilya's vision, and he clutched the side of the door while the walls spun around him. Someone moaned, and after a moment, he recognized the voice as his own.

The two men, bent over their chess-game beneath the painted icon of Christ, started and looked up straight at him. "Holy Mother!" Father Mikail exclaimed, knocking over his stool in his haste to stand. "Ruslan—"

"I see, damn them, they've been at him again!" the shaman snapped, shoving the chessboard and table aside roughly, so that the pieces scattered across the floor. "You think I'm blind as well as stupid? Let's get him down before he falls down!"

Ilya clung to the doorframe with the last of his strength, just inside the chapel, barely able to see his mentors through eyes swollen until they were mere slits in his face. In fact, there seemed to be several of them. He blinked, trying to make the many condense back into two. When he looked again, Ruslan and the priest were already at his side, though he hadn't seen them move toward him. When he realized they had reached him, he let go of the doorframe and fell into their arms. They each draped one of his arms across their shoulders and half-carried him into the chapel.

Pain overwhelmed every other sensation, confusing every-thing, and yet he felt as if he was separated from it, rising above it, floating somewhere just over his body. He wasn't certain just what was broken this time: a couple of ribs, by the stab every time he took a breath. The rest of his injuries were all to softer things than bones—Ludmilla wasn't going to admire his face for a while, which might be just as well. Considering what Mischa had done to Ilya's privates, he wasn't going to be using *them* for some time, so it wouldn't matter what Ludmilla thought.

They're getting better at this, my dear brothers. More pain in less time. He'd have giggled if it hadn't hurt so much. *How efficient . . .*

Ruslan and Mikail helped him over to a pallet in one of the two side-chambers at the rear of the chapel, a pallet that was kept there permanently, just for him. This refuge had been in place since Ilya's brothers had begun beating him on a fairly regular basis. They lowered him down onto the pallet, but his head was still spinning so much that being prone didn't make much difference—he still seemed to be floating above his body.

Then, abruptly, he snapped back into himself, though he still felt detached from the pain, almost as if he was too numb now, his mind too battered to feel anything. He heard whimpering and knew it was his own voice, but felt separated from that as well. Still, he knew that in a while he would lose that detachment and begin to feel his hurts again, and then he would be very grateful that he was lying down.

Mikail knelt down beside him as he lay on the pad, while Ruslan went off after his herbs, returning in moments with all of the usual things he needed to tend to Ilya's injuries. The priest bathed the cuts and bruises with a soft cloth dipped in cool water, while Ruslan dealt with the herbs. Unfortunately, this was all very routine for them and for Ilya as well.

"What was it this time, boy?" Ruslan asked as he measured ground herbs into a wooden cup and accepted the stoup of wine the priest handed him. "What excuse did they have this time?"

It was difficult to talk around his split and swollen lip, and with a spinning head, but Ilya had plenty of practice in speaking under such handicaps. " 'ietor," he said thickly. "Tol' 'i'ha an' Gregori I wa' a 'orceror. Tha' I'd 'agicked 'way 'ather's cherries. 'u' guards tried tha' one wi' 'ather, an' he ha' 'em whi'ed, so 'i'ha didn' dare take it t' 'ather.''

"Pietor was the instigator. He managed to persuade Mischa and Gregori that Ilya is a magician, that he was the one who stole the tsar's cherries by magic. But the tsar was already in a rage because the orchard-guards tried to use sorcery as an excuse for their failure," Mikail translated at Ruslan's blank look. "So the brothers knew if they went to the tsar with another tale of sorcery, it would look as if they were trying to shift the blame from their friends among the guards to Ilya. Everyone knows that guarding the cherry orchard is such soft duty it only goes to Mischa's and Gregori's friends. This is one time when trying to blame Ilya would only have gotten the others in trouble. And what probably made them angry enough to come after Ilya in a group was that Pietor convinced them that Ilya really *is* a sorcerer and is using his magic to cause trouble for them and their friends. They knew the tsar wouldn't listen, so they decided to mete out their own justice."

"Idiots," Ruslan muttered. "Doesn't it occur to them that if Ilya was a powerful enough sorcerer to steal cherries, he'd be stealing gold instead? That he'd be wealthier than anyone we've ever heard of, that *he'd* be the tsar? Or that he would be in the palace of the Great Tsar, and not here at all? Pah!" He spat.

Ilya's head swam as Ruslan raised him up enough to drink down the bitter potion. The two men exchanged angry asides concerning Ilya's brothers while Ilya closed his eyes and waited for the pain to subside.

The voices buzzed above his head in a meaningless drone, and dizziness caused by Ruslan's drugs joined the disorientation caused by Mischa's hamlike fists. The voices came and went, and the only change was one he was already prepared for, since this was hardly a new experience. His pain eventually disappeared under the wave of nausea and intoxication that surged outward from someplace inside him. The nausea he could fight; he didn't bother fighting the intoxication.

He drifted; it wasn't sleep, exactly, but it certainly wasn't waking. He couldn't hold to a thought for very long, but he really didn't care.

Once, in a moment of silence, he cracked his eyes open to find himself alone. The icon of the Virgin gazed down on him, the flickering candle-flames giving her a spurious illusion of life, her eyes large and blank as those of a deer surprised by a hunter, too stunned and frightened to move.

What was she afraid of? Not him, surely. Maybe Mischa. If Mischa was angry enough, he'd tear down the icon of the Virgin without even thinking twice. Afterward, maybe, he might be afraid of curses or God's anger, but not at the time.

Ilya closed his eyes again; his imagination was running loose again. The icon was only paint and wood, but her servant, at least, had the power to help him. Father Mikail would once again see to it that no one molested him while he recovered. As long as he was out of sight in the chapel, this was the safest place for him until this current situation passed. What he endured now was the worst he'd suffer—by tomorrow he would be better. In a few days, if nothing was broken, his bruises would be fading into yellow and green. Ruslan would poultice the worst of them with wormwood and wine, which would ease the pain as well as make them heal faster.

It wasn't so bad. There were plenty of people who endured more; most fighters, for instance, who risked death every time their employer went to war. *If only I could get away. Far, far away.* Ah, but he might as well wish for a fortune in gold, one of the Mare of the Night Wind's flying foals, and the hand of a beautiful tsarina with her own lands, while he was at it. There was no real escape from here, not without more danger than he faced from his brothers. Once again, he reminded himself of the hazards of leaving. If he left on foot, he'd be limited in what he could take with him. He'd have to pass through leagues and leagues of wild forest, full of wolves and bears, if not *rusalka, vodianoi,* and *leshii.* If he made it through the forest without being eaten, he'd then have to stop for supplies, and to get supplies he'd have to sell his services since he didn't have much in the way of valuables to sell. That brought up more problems, since all of the neighboring tsars and boyars were either related to Tsar Ivan by marriage or bloodlines or were enemies. He couldn't sell his services to relations, obviously; they wouldn't dare shelter him, they'd definitely recognize him, tell Ivan. They might even imprison him, then send him under guard back to his father. The only services that Ivan's enemies would be interested in would be Ilya's fighting skills.

Which would mean that sooner or later I would be fighting my own family. Not a good idea; the moment one of them recognized me, I'd be dead. I'd be worse than dead, if they captured me.

If he took a horse, Ivan would have him tracked to the ends of the earth as a thief, and once Ivan caught him, Ilya would suffer the same fate as any thief. Ivan had made that perfectly clear over the matter of the cherries, and he wouldn't hesitate a heartbeat if Ilya took a horse.

Oh, I don't care for that idea. Die eaten by beasts, die by torture, starve to death, or die by torture. Not a very wide choice of fates.

The best thing he could hope to do, quite honestly, was to outlive Ivan. Then, in the confusion following the tsar's death, he might be able to get a horse and a mule, load them up, and slip away while his brothers were fighting over the throne. In the chaos and conflict following, they might not miss what he took, and they certainly wouldn't miss him until he was long gone.

So strange. They all seem to think of me as their enemy, when I'm the brother who's the least likely to cause any trouble. I don't want to be tsar. I don't even want to be a boyar. I would be very contented to sit at any of my brothers' right hand, agree with everything he said, and chase the girls. That would make a perfectly fine, full life as far as I'm concerned.

It didn't make any more sense than Ivan's continued suspicions. *Only someone like Father would be so certain that the son who makes no overt grasps for his power and position is the one that's the most dangerous.*

And it never seemed to occur to any of them that, as Ruslan had pointed out, if he were half as skillful as they thought he was, he wouldn't *be* here.

If I was an expert poisoner, they'd all be dead—one dose of poison in the mead one night after the women have retired, and it would all be over. If I was a real sorcerer, I'd be in the court of the Great Tsar, dripping gold and jewels with every step, with a hundred Turkish slave girls at my beck and call.

That particular image caught his fancy, and his drug-fogged mind played with it for some time in a most entertaining fashion.

What a fine life that would be! Nothing to do but please the Great Tsar now and again and amuse myself! It wasn't hard to conjure up the proper picture from all the books and tales he'd absorbed over the years. He pictured himself arrayed in a splendid gold-embroidered floor-length vest of scarlet silk-velvet, black silk breeches, and a gold-embroidered silk shirt of deeper scarlet. Around his neck was a huge necklace made of gold plaques set with rubies, and his shirt was belted with a sash made of cloth-of-gold. His boots were of the finest black bullhide, polished to a high gloss by one of the throng of dusky-skinned, dark-haired beauties who swarmed about him, half-fainting in the anticipation that he would notice one of them. He would live in a palace made of white marble, a place that rose from among its gardens like a fantasy of cut snow. He'd furnish it with thick Turkish rugs to soften every footstep, and huge porcelain stoves in every room keeping the winter chill so far at bay that roses would bloom in the rooms at Christmas. He would have hundreds of servants—most of them pretty girls, of course—and every day he would choose from all the delicacies of the world to eat. Smoked sturgeon, roast pork, great slabs of beef; things he'd never tasted but only read of, like pomegranates, peacock, sugar-frosted cakes as tall as a man—all these things would grace his table, and his girls would feed him with their soft little hands. He'd conjure wondrous feats of magic for the Great Tsar, but only when *he* chose to, making it very clear that he was doing the Tsar a favor by doing so. And at night, his girls would press closely about him, begging him with their eyes, each of them—*Take me, oh, mighty lord, oh, great master, take me—*

Acute pain woke him out of his daydream as the imagined vistas of luscious woman-flesh caused his wounded privates to stir—or attempt to. The attempt didn't last long, but the ensuing agony was more than enough to make him lose all interest in pursuing that particular dream for now.

He opened his eyes again. Father Mikail sat beside him,

reading, but the moment he tried to sit up, the priest put his book down and restrained him with a firm hand planted in the middle of his chest. That was easily enough done, since Ilya didn't really want to move anyway.

"It's after dinner," the priest said, anticipating what he'd want to know after many repetitions of this same scene. "Long past. Mother Galina brought some food for you; are you in any mood to eat it?"

He wasn't, not really, but he knew from past experience that Ruslan's vile brews required the leavening of food or they wouldn't stay down. And if there was a state worse than the aftermath of one of his brothers' beatings, it was the aftermath of one of his brothers' beatings combined with retching his guts up.

He nodded, and Mikail helped him sit up enough so that he could, with a little help, spoon the warm concoction of cream, porridge, and a little honey into his mouth. He sighed, thinking of his daydream of mounds of pastries, roast ducklings, vats of blood-sausage—cream-porridge was a sad contrast, and Father Mikail was no substitute for a dusky-sweet Turkish slave-maiden.

As he had expected, the moment he finished the porridge, the priest had another potion for him to drink. The bitter taste made him shudder down to his toenails, but Mikail was not a cruel man, and gave him a good cup of honey-mead to wash the taste out of his mouth.

"I have a new *Natural History* here," Mikail said, after he'd helped Ilya back to his prone position. "Father Vlas sent it over a few days ago. Would you like me to read to you?"

I don't remember him mentioning that book, Ilya thought dizzily. *I'll bet he was waiting until after he'd finished it to say anything. He'll probably combine it with copying lessons so we can make our own copy.*

Very few of the neighboring tsars and boyars held Ivan's views on religion; Mikail's plight was viewed with sincere pity by most of the other household priests round about, and most of them were quite prepared to loan Father Mikail precious books since there was little else they could do to soften his lot in life. No one else would have been willing to replace him, and the Patriarch was *not* going to permit this household to go without a priest after fighting so long to get one admitted.

"Please," Ilya managed, although he didn't think that Ruslan's potion would permit him to enjoy much of the new book. Still, it would give him something to think about besides himself.

"'In the country of Africa are many strange Beasts,'" Mikail began, going to the front of the book and starting over again. "'From Great to Small, there are none like unto them in these northern Climes. . . .'"

Ilya drifted off again under the influence of Ruslan's potion, ears filled with Father Mikail's pleasant voice, mind filling with strange images—the Phoenix, the Lyon, the Monocerous, the Parrot.

The beasts came to life in his dreams, alternately playful and threatening, at one moment as sweet-tempered as a lapdog, and in the next tormenting him without mercy. Then, finally, they all turned on him.

A pack of Lyons, yellow as cured hay, with huge tufted tails and heads as big as bushel-baskets, followed by a hunting-party of the strange humans called Monopods, who had only one foot and moved about by hopping, chased him up a tree. The tree itself was quite bizarre, covered with huge purple fruits, like grapes, but smelling of roses. He poked his head above the top branches, into the sunlight, and as he searched the ground for a way to evade the Lyons circling the base of the tree, a huge shadow passed over him, blotting out the sun.

He looked up, too late to duck. All he saw was a pair of enormous feet, each as large as a man, and he screamed as a Roc plucked him up the way a falcon would seize a mouse, carrying him off. The pain of its talons piercing his shoulders was terrible, and as he struggled in the creature's grasp, afraid that at any moment it would lean down and bite his head off, a flash of fire darting up from below made the Roc bellow.

It was a Phoenix, which flew at the Roc, battering its head with her fiery wings, and the Roc dropped him. He hung in the air for a single moment, long enough for him to realize what had happened and endure an instant of terror before plummeting out of the sky to his death. He screamed as the ground rushed up to meet him, flailing helplessly in a vain attempt to stop his fall.

He woke with a start before that final impact, sweating, and with every bruise aching fiercely. This time it was Ruslan waiting beside the pallet, with another potion, to be followed by a cup of milk-and-honey rather than mead. Ilya would have preferred the mead, but he knew better than to ask for it. Ruslan would only tell him he drank too much already.

"There's something strange out there tonight," the old shaman said, as soon as Ilya had drunk both cups down. "Ivan can scoff all he wants to, but there's something magical, some spirit loose in the air tonight, and if I had anything to bet with, I would bet that he loses more cherries before dawn."

Ilya reached up with one hand and felt his jaw before he tried to answer. Ruslan, never one to pretend to powers he didn't have, very rarely made such bald statements about spirits. Oh, he would warn Ilya against the *rusalka*, tell him what the signs were that he was in the presence of a forest spirit, but he seldom claimed that there *was* a spirit about unless he truly, sincerely believed that there was.

"What—what makes you think that?" Ilya asked carefully. His lips weren't quite so swollen; he could actually form real words again.

"There's a feeling out under the moon; the stars are nearer and brighter than usual, and the beasts of the fields are quiet, too quiet," Ruslan said irritably, rubbing his beard with one hand. "I saw a light in the forest near the orchard, and I heard singing, but it wasn't a bird or a woman's voice, but was something between the two. I saw the *bannik* in the woodpile near the bathhouse; tonight there is something about that makes spirits bold." He shook his head at Ilya's look of incomprehension. "I can't explain it to you, you don't half believe it yourself. Something's out there, that's all I can tell you. Go to sleep; sleep will heal you faster."

Ilya was not about to press for further explanation, not in his current situation. Even if Ruslan gave it, he might not understand it. And even if he understood it—well, Ruslan was right, he might not believe it. Obediently, he closed his eyes, and this time, if he dreamed, he didn't remember the dreams.

* * *

RUSLAN remained in a state of irritation for the next several days as Ilya recovered. Ilya knew why, but unfortunately there wasn't much he could do about it: Ruslan was angry because Ilya was hurt—again—and Ruslan was left to patch up the result. It wasn't that he begrudged the use of his skills and herbs on Ilya, it was just that he had to do so with such regularity. *That* was what made him angry and irritable.

Ilya's reaction was the opposite: The more he recovered, the lighter his spirits became. He really *wasn't* that badly off; things could be much worse. All he had to do was stay out of sight of his brothers; really, it was his own fault that he'd gotten beaten. If he'd just keep his mouth shut and not get in their way, they'd leave him alone.

Ruslan, however, was obviously not of that opinion.

"It's getting worse instead of better," he grumbled one day to Father Mikail, when they both thought Ilya was asleep. "And the boy doesn't do anything to provoke them; I've *watched* him. He generally goes out of his way to avoid them. Oh, once in a while he talks back to them, but they're so dim they usually don't realize what he's saying. At this rate, they're going to kill him before long, and we can't do a damned thing about it!"

"I could write the Patriarch again," Father Mikail said tentatively. "This could be considered to be a provenance of the Church, which holds kin-slaying to be a double sin, even as when Cain slew Abel—"

"And the Patriarch will just do what he did the last time: tell you to pray for Christ's peace to enter their hearts and send a letter to Ivan that the tsar will use for starting a fire!" Ruslan snorted. "Christ's peace, my—"

"Don't blaspheme!" Mikail interrupted sharply.

That was a silly thing to say. Ruslan's a pagan—

"It isn't blasphemy if I don't believe in your Christ, now, is it?" Ruslan countered, bristling. But at Mikail's stricken and hurt look, he grimaced and apologized for his rudeness.

"No matter—you were forgiven before you asked it," the priest said, as Ilya knew he would.

"Well, I haven't had any better luck than you," Ruslan said gruffly. "And maybe that is why I keep losing my temper. I've left offerings for the *polevoi*, for the *khoziain*, but the spirits of the fields are silent, and Ivan chased away the house-spirit a long time ago. I've prayed to Perun, to Rod, to Simargl, and they are as silent as your Christ." He sighed. "We're old men; all we can do is pray. I can't think of any means to get the boy out of harm's way."

"When I last wrote the Patriarch, I explained how much the boy loves learning, and he suggested the priesthood," Mikail said, shaking his head. "Ilya! A priest! We'd see Ivan turn beggar first."

Ruslan snorted. "If I thought for a moment that he'd agree, I'd even join you in trying to persuade our young blockhead to join one of your holy orders—at least if he wanted to become a monk, the Patriarch would stir his fat bum to protect the boy." He laughed cruelly. "After all, there would always be the chance that when Ivan dies, Ilya's brothers will kill each other, leaving Ilya the heir, and the land would go to the Church."

Mikail bowed his head and said nothing. He really couldn't deny what Ruslan had said; the Patriarch's greed for land was a byword even among Mikail's fellow priests.

But Ilya's thoughts were captured for a moment by the idea. To become a monk! That was a possibility that he hadn't thought of. He'd be able to study in a monastery library, read and write as much as he wanted to. More than that, it would get him out from under Ivan's thumb—he could even leave openly, and no one would stop him. After all, he wouldn't be running away, and he wouldn't be going to one of Ivan's enemies; there would be no reason to stop him.

Well—maybe. Ivan was peculiar that way. Even if he didn't want a thing, be it a spavined horse, a mildewed turnip, or an unwanted son, the moment anyone else expressed an interest in that thing, it suddenly became his most important possession. If Ilya told the tsar that he wanted to become a monk and that the Church had accepted him, it might be harder than ever to escape.

The more he thought about it, the more certain he became. *He'd never let me go, especially not to the Church. The bare thought of one of his sons becoming a priest or a monk would drive him wild. The idea of the Church getting anything that belonged to him, especially his own flesh—it would be worse than the rage over the stolen cherries.*

Besides, he didn't think he could live like Father Mikail. No fine food, no fine clothing, no pretty milkmaids waiting in cozy bowers—oh, that last would be the thing he missed the worst.

Could priests marry? He couldn't remember. But even if they could, they weren't supposed to chase girl after girl. If they were allowed to marry, it would have to be some dull, virtuous, housewifely creature; once wedded, there would be no straying from her bed, either, and where was the fun in that?

Was he really in that much danger? *My dear brothers never have done worse than crack a bone or two.* They didn't want to kill him, they just wanted to hurt him. Hurting him made them feel important. They needed him—if they killed him, they wouldn't have anyone else they could feel superior to.

Ruslan and Mikail are just overreacting, he told himself. *I can't blame them; I must have looked awful. Nobody's going to kill me—unless it's Father, and I'll just be careful never to make him angry or give him a reason to think I've done something against him. I know one thing: I won't insult Pietor anymore! He holds a grudge a lot longer than I thought he could. I'll just be very meek and quiet when I get around him. Father is the only real problem.*

He regained confidence as he regained strength, and the news that Mikail and Ruslan brought gave him more reasons not to worry too much, at least about the tsar. Just as Ruslan had predicted, the ripe cherries vanished from the trees every night, leaving only the unripe ones. And since no one could accuse Ilya of practicing sorcery while he was too battered even to stand, Pietor was going to be in big trouble with Mischa, if he wasn't already. Mischa didn't like being tricked into doing anything—even if it was something he didn't mind doing under normal circumstances. He would consider what Pietor had said to be an attempt at trickery.

So in spite of his mentors' conviction that his brothers were going to kill him, Ilya was quite certain he would be able to avoid anything worse than a beating for however long it took for Ivan to die. He'd made up his mind, though, after this last beating, that he was going to do his best to stay out of sight until that day arrived. *Then* he would be free, and he could make his escape. It couldn't be that much longer; Ivan couldn't survive too many more exhibitions of choler like the one Ilya had witnessed. He'd have a fit of apoplexy and choke to death.

But Ilya did wonder who was stealing the fruit. By now, Ivan must be so enraged that every little thing would set off a display of temper.

"Ivan is worse than angry," Ruslan told him when he asked about the state of things and whether it was safe for him to reappear. Interesting that everyone knew he went *somewhere* after a beating to heal, but no one seemed to know where he went, or to care. Maybe they all thought Mother Galina was looking after him.

By now, his head no longer threatened to split whenever he sat up, and Ruslan thought he might reappear for meals in the next day or so. Ludmilla still would not be enjoying his own particular skills for a few more days, but he could put her off.

If she was still interested. She might not be, after all the gossip about this latest beating. It would be only too clear that he was not the favored son in Tsar Ivan's brood. By now, she might have taken up with one of the others, even, and he'd have to find a new girl. It wouldn't be the first time, sad to say, and it wasn't going to be the last.

"No, Ivan is much worse than angry," Ruslan repeated, breaking into his reverie. "I haven't seen him like this in years; he's gone quite cold, calculating. The tsar has pledged himself to catch whoever or whatever is stealing from him. He's positive now that it must be one of his enemies, determined to torment him. I don't know, but if I was one of his enemies, I might do just that, on the chance that he'll fall dead in a fit of rage."

"What do you think?" Ilya asked curiously.

"Well, it isn't a serf, a peasant, or a servant," Ruslan told him, "because Ivan locked the palace up the night you were beaten, so that means no servants got out that night, and he put a heavy guard outside the orchard walls the next night, and no serf or peasant could have gotten past that many guards. Believe it or not, this *has* convinced Ivan that someone is working some kind of witchery or sorcery against him, because no matter how dire the punishments are, men left inside the orchard to guard the trees are found asleep by their replacements.''

Ilya blinked. ''I suppose that a really clever thief might be able to slip them something to make them sleep and get in anyway. You're right, though, it couldn't be a servant or a serf; those cherries aren't worth that much to one of them.''

Ruslan nodded. ''Ivan thinks it's magic some enemy of his is working. I'm not so certain. I've been all around those fields, and I haven't found anything there. No buried spells, no spells tied to the trees, no signs of man's magic at all, and if there were signs to find, I would be able to find them.''

''So what do *you* think?'' Ilya asked, although he was fairly certain what Ruslan's answer would be.

Ruslan coughed. ''I think it's a spirit. Maybe a *polevoi;* that would be the most logical. I think they've finally gotten tired of him and his boasting, and a spirit is teaching him a lesson.''

Ilya shook his head. ''Why would a spirit steal the ripe cherries and leave the rest for another night? Why wouldn't a spirit take everything all at once?''

''Why does a spirit do anything?'' Ruslan countered. ''If we could understand them, we wouldn't need to be so very careful around them, now would we? We'd know what pleased them and what angered them, and we'd always be able to stay on their good sides.'' And that, for him, was the end of the argument.

It might have been the end of it for Ilya too, except that now his curiosity had been aroused. *He* could think of any number of ways that a very clever thief could get in and out of the orchard without being seen. Through the treetops themselves, for one—the wall around the cherry trees wasn't more than eight feet tall, and the trees easily overhung it to mingle their boughs with their more ordinary sister-trees whose fruits were already harvested. A very clever thief would climb into the trees at a distance and work his way into the orchard without ever setting foot on the ground.

Ivan had made plenty of enemies. This might be part of some larger scheme. Perhaps, once the fruit was all gone, the thief would find a way to let Ivan know who he was and why he had stolen the tsar's treats—providing a bushel or so of fruit, or a vat of preserved cherries by way of proof. The next step might be a threat—"See how easily I stole your fruit, think how easily I could take whatever else I want. Think how easily I could do things beside steal." He might offer to return the fruit for a high price. Perhaps he would pass himself off as a real sorcerer and let it be known that Ivan could hire his services. Ivan might even be persuaded, given that his hot anger had given way to cold. If such a thief was that clever, he could arrange it all without putting himself in any danger until he knew Ivan's mind.

But if this was all by the hand of a clever thief, the man had only had to deal with Ivan and his men so far, and they didn't have any more imagination than a herd of cows. Ilya wondered if he should get involved.

He spent the rest of that last afternoon debating the notion. If he *did* catch the thief, or even got a good enough look at him to identify him, Ilya might earn some real and tangible evidence of Ivan's gratitude. And if he was suddenly the favored son, the others wouldn't be able to beat him up without getting Ivan angry. Or at least, they wouldn't be able to come at him in a gang; Ivan would insist that any fighting be one-on-one. That in itself would be an improvement. He might not be able to *beat* Mischa alone, but he could keep Mischa from hurting him; he knew he could hold his own against any one of his brothers, so long as the fight was fair.

On the other hand, what if the thief was one of the brothers? Ilya would be in a worse situation than he was now, for none of the brothers would risk the chance that Ilya would tell the tsar the identity of the thief.

Even if it was a stranger, it still might be too risky to try to catch him. There would be nothing to stop a stranger from trying to kill the one who caught him.

And it would be a great deal of work; probably far more work than it was worth. On the whole, maybe it would be better to just watch and wait and see what happened.

So, very near supper-time, Ilya decided it was time to go back, face his family, and see what more had happened during his recovery.

The clothing he'd last worn was a dreadful mess: torn at the seams and at the knees and elbows, and stained with his own blood and Ruslan's poultices. Neither Ruslan nor the priest ever seemed to think of bringing him new clothing whenever he wound up in their hands—or maybe they didn't want to risk giving away the fact that they were sheltering him by rummaging through his things for fresh clothing. He'd have to give his current outfit to Mother Galina and beg her to clean and mend it for him. He certainly could not appear at supper like this.

There was other suitable clothing in the chest in his room, thank goodness—although it was mended and still bore the faint stains of a previous beating. The few servants he encountered pretended that there was nothing wrong with his appearance—or pretended not to see him at all. He discovered when he entered the room that Mischa hadn't taken his need for revenge into destroying Ilya's room and its contents, as he'd done once when they were all much younger. His room was pretty much as he had left it, except for the dust that lay over everything. He flung open the chest, seized the clean clothing on the top, and changed into it quickly, intending to be in his place before any of his brothers were.

He managed that, moving into the great hall before anyone had begun serving, walking straight to his usual seat at the end of the high table, and simply sitting down nonchalantly.

It isn't as if I haven't done this before.

Although the smug looks and snickers his brothers aimed at him as they entered the great hall (probably in response to his bruised and battered condition) were uncomfortable, at least he was sitting down and eating as his brothers took their own seats. He could pretend to be so interested in his food that he didn't notice. He would not have been able to make such a pretense if he'd been edging his way past them to his bench—and they'd have had plenty of opportunity to trip him, punch him in his bandaged ribs, or grab a wrist to twist it, knowing he wouldn't be able to move out of their way quickly enough to escape.

Every bite of this meal was wonderful after so many days of whatever Ruslan or Mikail could filch, all of it cold by the time it reached him. Galina had always sent over breakfast, but her idea of a convalescent meal was porridge, porridge, and more porridge.

Someone had killed a young wild boar, and the odor of roast pork made his mouth water and his stomach growl. He had no hesitation in reaching for the platter bearing chunks of smoking meat and helping himself hugely. There was plenty of pork to go around, for once; the men down at the lower tables didn't seem to have much appetite tonight. Perhaps that was due to Ivan's glowering expression of smoldering rage; he glared down at his fighters and guards as if he would much rather have had them on rations of bread and water in the stableyard than feasting at his table. Ilya knew from experience that having Ivan watch every bite you took wearing *that* expression was enough to put the most hardened warrior off his food.

There were no such looks levied in Ilya's direction, and he heaped his plate and ate with a good appetite, if with a somewhat sore jaw. In fact, aside from one glance at his least favorite son, Ivan had ignored Ilya completely. It occurred again to Ilya that Mischa had inadvertently done him a good turn by beating him up and laying him out for all this time. There could be *no* thought that Ilya was responsible in any way for the thefts. Which was just as well, for Ivan was obviously taking this personally; *very* personally.

Finally, when the meal ended, the women left the hall, the pitchers of mead came around and cups were filled sparingly and well-watered under Ivan's glare, the tsar stood up. Silence fell immediately across the hall; not even the dogs under the table whimpered or barked.

There had been a half-bowl of cherries in cream on the high table, which Ivan had devoured with a look that should have curdled the cream. Evidently someone had been gathering what could be gleaned when the thief was done, and the scant harvest ate at Ivan's heart like a canker. There couldn't be much left on the trees by now.

Ivan glared once around the hall. "You have failed to prevent the thief from his work," he said abruptly. "I will try rewards; perhaps that will give enough reason to succeed. Whoever catches the thief will be my heir." There were startled looks all around the tables at that, for Ivan had never made any attempt to designate an heir before. "Tonight it will be Mischa's chance to try, and his brothers will follow in order of age. And after them, as long as there are cherries left, anyone can try.''

He sat down heavily, looking at no one. Mischa shoved his cup of mead aside, stood up, and bowed to the tsar.

"So long as I do not encounter sorcery, I will not fail you, Father,'' he said stiffly. "But I am only a man; I cannot prevail against a sorcerer.''

"Then you will not be my heir, will you?'' Ivan countered testily. "Succeed, and you will have the prize—fail, and your brothers will have the chance to succeed where you failed.''

Mischa said nothing more; he only bowed again and left, presumably to go straight to the orchard. Ilya stared after him, and found himself seized in the grip of a strange and unaccountable impulse to follow him. Strange—because he really had no reason to follow his brother. *He* certainly didn't want to catch the thief; the last thing he wanted was to be named Ivan's heir. Success would not make him more beloved, either to his father or his brothers. His father would be certain that the only reason he had caught the thief would be because of collusion between them. And as for his brothers—jealousy would give them a reason they hadn't had before to consider cold-blooded fratricide. He could only get himself into more difficulty if he succeeded.

No, there was no reason for him even to try to catch the thief. Nevertheless, his unquenchable curiosity made following after Mischa irresistible, and it was all he could do to remain seated at the table. He never could resist a mystery to be unraveled. Ruslan and Mikail alternately praised and chided him for his avid curiosity, swearing it was going to lead him into trouble one day, but also telling him it drove him to learn as quickly as a born scholar. He waited a decent interval and then rose to his feet, trying to look exhausted, limping as if his injuries pained him. No one paid him any attention at all; those who were to be on duty tonight were gambling or playing games of chance, but quietly and without drinking their usual amount of wine. Those who were not on duty were drinking as if to make up for their fellows' abstinence.

Ilya slipped out the nearest door and followed silently in Mischa's wake. Tonight, there was no moon, and it was only his own familiarity with the area around the palace, learned by treading the paths of the estate by night in his endless assignations, which enabled him to move without betraying his presence to his brother. Mischa had no such practice. Up ahead, he stumbled and swore grimly; twice he fell, which was certainly not going to do his temper any good.

Interesting. I do believe that this plan was as much a surprise to brother Mischa as it was to me.

At the entrance to the orchard, two guards stood under a pair of torches; Ilya shied away from the area of light and took to cover until he got into the deeper darkness under the orchard wall.

In the back of his mind, he was a bit bemused by how quickly he managed to blend in with the night. As insects and a bird or two mingled their songs with the rustling of the trees in the breeze, he drifted along in the shadows beside the wall like a windblown leaf. This could have been a dream, or one of Ruslan's stories, for surely nothing short of magic could make a man so at one with the world around him. He moved so quietly, so easily—he had never moved so well in his life. It was so strange, yet so easy; so entirely wonderful.

He experienced an intoxication that he couldn't define, and yet he had never been so entirely sober. He didn't make a single misstep; it was as if he had eyes in his feet. He knew where every stone, every branch waiting to trip him up lay, and he knew it without knowing how he knew. He had never felt quite so alive, and every breath filled him with more energy. He avoided the two guards he spotted patrolling the walls outside the orchard as if he were invisible.

As he paced carefully beside the wall, he came to the first tree overhanging it: a plum tree, long past harvest time. Ivan *should* have ordered the trees to be trimmed back, especially given the thefts, but the tsar's greed had obviously overcome his good sense.

Ilya climbed the tree easily, in spite of his aching ribs. In fact, he didn't even notice more than a little discomfort. All he was really conscious of was the wind in his hair, the rough bark under his hands, the sway of the branches under him. He'd been climbing trees since he could toddle, and these orchard trees, with low-hanging branches, were intended to be easy to climb so that they were easy to harvest.

Not surprising that our thief has been so successful. He has probably taken this very road into the cherry-orchard. I wonder if I'm likely to run right into him?

He edged along the branch, belly pressed to the surface of the limb, until he sensed another branch reaching toward the one he was on from the cherry tree on the other side of the wall. It was hardly more than a darker shadow and a whisper of leaves, but he recognized it for what it was immediately.

He put out his right hand and touched it, smoother bark than the tree-trunk beneath him; he grasped it, pulled himself across to it. It sagged under his weight but held, supported as it was by the top of the wall itself. It was but the work of a moment, then he was across and down, and his feet touched the soil of Tsar Ivan's private preserve.

The first thing that struck him was that the bird-nets had been removed from the trees, probably because they were totally ineffective at stopping the thief. He peered through the columns of tree-trunks and saw by the flickering lights in the middle distance that Mischa had not inconvenienced himself too much in this duty; he'd set himself up very near the orchard gate and probably wasn't going to stir himself farther. Ilya slipped from shadow to shadow among the trees, working himself nearer and nearer to where Mischa had made his outpost, and finally took to the branches again, swarming up the trunk of the tree like a cat.

From here he found he had an excellent view of the area beside the gate where Mischa had set up a kind of camp. The tsar's orders had specified only that Mischa was to watch, not what he was to do while he did so, and Mischa took full advantage of that neglect to specify himself what he should and should not do. Even as Ilya watched, servants brought a stool, torches, a basket of food, and set them all up with an obvious eye to creating a comfortable situation for his passing the hours of the night.

It wasn't long before Mischa and the two guards, who were obviously friends of his, were arranged in a circle, tossing knuckle-bones and betting various personal objects on their outcome. They were paying no attention whatsoever to the trees, but then, so far as Ilya could make out, the cherry-thief had never appeared this early in the evening, so perhaps Mischa wasn't being as cavalier about his duty as he seemed.

Ilya assumed a comfortable position in the cleft of the trunk, propped up yet out of sight, where he could see Mischa and at the same time have a good view of the rest of the orchard. He kept his left eye closed when he watched his brother and the rest, so that when he looked away from the circle of torches, he did not have to wait for his eyes to adjust to the darkness. This was an old trick he had learned a long time ago when he began meeting girls in the fields by night. He wondered if Mischa knew it. Certainly after being under all those torches, he wouldn't be able to see anything at all even if he heard the thief, but it didn't appear that Mischa was very worried about that particular problem.

As for Ilya, he was actually getting comfortable, even feeling a measure of smugness at his own cleverness. This was a good idea; whatever was going on here, if the thief did not know that Ilya was up in the tree, Ilya might be able to catch him at work even if Mischa didn't. And once Ilya knew who the thief was, he might be able to use that information. If he could actually, physically catch the thief—well, there were all kinds of possibilities. It was just possible that, in order to keep from being taken before Ivan, Ilya could persuade the thief to help him get away from Ivan.

I could help him steal horses, maybe even some of Father's valuables, then we could create the signs of a struggle and my own death! Father would hardly go looking for me if he thought I was dead. . . . His imagination ran wild with schemes for getting away. Of course, they all depended on the thief being both clever and cooperative. Granted, that was an unlikely outcome, but it was worth considering.

He was doing just that when—

``**HOY!** *Wake up, you lot! Gawd, the tsar is going to have your ballocks in a vise!*''

Ilya woke up with a start at the shouting just beneath his perch; he lost his balance and grabbed for the tree-trunk beneath him as he tried to remember exactly where he was and why he was here at all.

Underneath his perch, three guards were shaking Mischa and his two friends awake, cursing and berating them. The torches they had set about their post were about two-thirds burned down—and Ilya could tell just by looking at the branches around his perch that the ripe cherries were gone, leaving behind only the green.

So, the thief *had* found a way to make them all sleep—and without knowing that Ilya was up in the branches of the tree! In fact, the thief had to have been within touching-distance of Ilya while he slept and *still* he had not awakened!

Thanking the saints who watched over fools that it was still black night, he slipped down to the ground under the cover of all the noise and sprinted to the orchard wall. He dared not be found here, lest Mischa decide to declare that he was the thief. It was the work of a moment to get up a tree and over the wall, but his earlier feeling of extraordinary well-being was gone. His ribs ached as he pulled himself up into the tree and across to the matching tree on the other side of the wall; his back hurt, and he was conscious of a dozen places where he had scraped himself on the rough bark. He was excruciatingly careful about getting back to the palace, freezing in the shadows and listening and looking in all directions before moving to another bit of cover. This was *not* the time to get caught outside his own chamber!

In fact, perhaps I'd better take an alternative route inside, just in case Father has guards watching the halls.

He didn't often need to get into his room via the window, since it was a tight squeeze for anyone with shoulders as broad as his, but tonight it was probably worth a little skin to take that route. There was plenty of cover between himself and the palace, and he used every bit of it to get into the shadows shrouding the building itself. He crept up along the palace wall on his hands and knees until he was just below his own window, and felt for a sliver of wood he kept stuck in a crack under the window-frame; he pulled it loose and used it to slip the catch on the inside of the shutters. Putting the sliver back, and straining eyes and ears against the night to be certain that he was alone and unobserved, he then heaved himself up onto the sill. With a grunt of pain as he wriggled in sideways and the window-frame compressed his broken ribs, he levered himself inside and dropped down to the floor.

Safe. He refastened the shutters, stripped off his shirt and breeches, and quickly slipped into his bed where he was supposed to be.

But of course, at this point it was impossible to sleep. He stared into the darkness for what seemed like a very long time, listening for the return of Mischa and the two guards. He had a notion that Ivan might be doing the same, and that their reception by the tsar was going to be anything but silent.

Just as he was about ready to give up and drift off into sleep, he heard a distant commotion. Heavy footsteps thudded up the staircase to the tsar's special chambers; they sounded, at least to him, as if those who climbed the stairs were reluctant to make that journey. He heard a far-off murmur of voices, then his father roaring something. With this much distance and so many walls between his room and the tsar's chambers, it was impossible to understand the shouted words, but the tone was clear enough.

Well. I don't think Mischa is going to have much opportunity to worry about me for a while. It was hard to keep a certain amount of self-satisfaction out of his thoughts, for this certainly was one of the brighter moments of his life. Mischa, of all people, was in trouble with their father! And he was not going to live down the tsar's disappointment in him for quite some time. *Still. How was it that I fell asleep? I wasn't tired, I hadn't been drinking—in fact, the last thing I remember is settling in for a long watch. Is the thief somehow putting something into the food? But why would it affect only the guards in the orchard?*

As Ivan's voice, muffled by layers of wood and stone, continued to roar incoherently on, Ilya worried at that problem until he lost it entirely in the labyrinth of sleep.

THE next day, as they sat together on a bench in the sun, he interrogated Ruslan and Father Mikail carefully, for he had decided to keep his own presence in the orchard a secret even from them. He told his two mentors everything that he knew without betraying that *he* had been the one who witnessed it all. Then he asked their opinions.

Father Mikail was very certain who—or what—was stealing the cherries. As the sunlight poured down over them like warm honey and the birds singing nearby seemed to mock all the shadowed thoughts of the night, the priest's generous mouth took on a grim cast.

"It's a demon," he said darkly. "Sent to punish the tsar for his blasphemy and unbelief. This is only the beginning. It begins by taking cherries, and it will end by taking his soul."

For a moment the words cast an eerie chill to the warm air. Could it be? Was that the answer? It was the one possibility that had not occurred to him.

But Ruslan snorted with contempt. "Don't be absurd!" he countered bluntly, as his fingers played among the small bones, carvings, and talismans woven into the fringes of his belt. "If it was a demon sent to punish Ivan, why hasn't it announced itself? I thought your demons always made a point of telling their victims just what was in store for them—or what would the point be of sending them? If Ivan doesn't know what's about to happen, he doesn't get a chance to repent now, does he? And if he doesn't get a chance to repent, isn't that mighty unfair of your God?"

Mikail opened and closed his mouth several times, looking remarkably like a startled fish, then shook his head. "I have no refutation for that. God would not give a sinner no chance to repent," he admitted, crestfallen. He bent his head, and Ilya suddenly noticed just how much gray there was among all the blond hair. Ruslan had always been grizzled, but when had Mikail begun to show his age? The priest sighed, unaware of Ilya's scrutiny. "I suppose it cannot be a demon after all."

He looked terribly disappointed, and Ilya couldn't blame him. It would have been such a triumph for him to have something like a demon to combat, and it would have been even better if in the course of his work he could have made a penitent convert of Tsar Ivan as well. Was Ruslan right? Ilya couldn't *think* of any tales of demons coming to torment victims without announcing themselves. Normally, it was the heathen, pagan spirits of the house, forest, and fields who carried off victims with little or no warning beforehand.

"It might be a saint," Mikail ventured, his brow creasing with doubt. "I'm sure I've heard tales of Saint Elijah the Prophet being *terribly* vengeful when he thought he was slighted—"

"Nonsense," Ruslan interrupted. "Every one of those tales

is just a story of the god Perun that you Christians stole for Elijah. And even *you* have to admit that such stories are hardly the kind of behavior you'd expect out of a saint!''

Glumly, Mikail nodded.

"So what do you think it is?" Ilya asked Ruslan. The old man chewed on his lower lip thoughtfully, as his fingers continued to move among his talismans.

"What I thought it was before," Ruslan told them both, eventually. "A spirit, either of the fields or the forest. And I'll grant you," he continued, turning to Father Mikail, "that there isn't a great deal of difference between a spirit and a demon, particularly where you priests are concerned. It may not be able to take Ivan's soul, but I think he's been lucky that so far all it's taken is his fruit. *Leshii* and *polevoi* aren't forgiving of those who forget to honor them, and I'll not be surprised if this spirit gets weary of cherries and looks for blood.''

The priest crossed himself hastily. "Holy Christ and His Blessed Mother forbid," he said. "Perhaps I had better go out and bless the orchard?" He looked frightened at the idea of confronting a spirit, but Ilya thought that he would probably go ahead and bless the ground if Ruslan thought it would help.

"That might only anger it," Ruslan cautioned. "These things have taken Christian priests before, old friend." His expression soured. "Consider this, before you think that this is something you really must do. Ivan hasn't *asked* you to do anything, and I don't see where it's your duty or mine to voluntarily help him in this.''

When Father Mikail looked at them both doubtfully, Ilya added his own voice to Ruslan's. "Think of this, Father. This spirit may be serving both itself and God. It is giving my father a lesson in humility that he sorely needs—indeed, it isn't only the tsar who is being humbled! Last night it was Mischa, tonight it will be Gregori, the next night, Pietor. I don't think that either Gregori or Pietor are going to have any more luck than Mischa, and this may be the first time in their lives that any of them has been defeated or humbled in any way. I believe that it will do them all good, though I think we ought to take pains to stay out of their way for a while.''

"And thanks be to God that they cannot find any reason to say you are to blame for this, Ilya," the priest replied, then sighed heavily. "Well, Ruslan, you are right; Ivan has made no requests of me, and I am in no way obligated to aid someone who has repeatedly spurned both Church and God. And Ilya, you are also correct; this could be God's way of giving the tsar a much-needed lesson in humility. It only shows that Almighty God can use even a pagan spirit to do His will."

Ilya grinned at the shaman, who winked a reply. "Going back to what this spirit is . . . If I were to guess," Ruslan continued, "I would say that the spirit is probably a *polevoi;* the spirits of the forest are usually stronger and more dangerous, and the spirits of our fields have been neglected for so long that they have probably become relatively weak. Still, *I* have no intention of finding out for certain by trying to propitiate it, and I would probably think twice about it even if I *liked* the tsar."

Mikail started to say something, thought better of it, and shrugged. "In any case, it is out of our hands. Now, young Ilya, about that section of Plutarch's *Lives* I asked you to read—"

"I am out of *my* expertise!" Ruslan exclaimed, as Mikail produced the book he had mentioned. "I shall be off—there are several things I would like to do." He smiled grimly. "Just in case this spirit *does* move its attentions onward, I intend to see to it that the three of us are protected."

Mikail nodded; Ilya was perfectly pleased to apply himself to the Latin that Father Mikail had requested he study, for he had the best answer he was likely to get about the thief in the orchard. A spirit *would* be able to make people sleep against their will, and a spirit would not have to trouble itself about getting past walls and guards. Though what a spirit would want with cherries he had no notion.

Then again, why does Ruslan set out porridge for the bannik *in the bathhouse and the* domovoi? *They are spirits, too.*

But spirits could also be warded against, and Ilya had every intention of trying his own vigil at least once more. Not tonight, for Gregori was a famous hunter and was also unlikely to fall prey to the overconfidence that had led Mischa to game and gamble and ignore his surroundings. Gregori might well be able to detect Ilya in the orchard—and if *anyone* would hear or otherwise sense a spirit approaching, it would be Gregori.

But Pietor was the worst hunter of all of Ivan's sons, and he was unobservant to boot. It would be no problem for Ilya to slip back into place in the treetops without alerting him.

But this time, when he did, he would have a way to keep himself awake, no matter what befell.

But it was a strange thing, to find himself actually willing to accept that there was a *spirit* working mischief out there, after all these years of hearing and half-believing in Ivan's assertions that such things did not exist.

TWO nights later, he was back in his tree-shelter, his coat covered with ward-charms and other protections he had learned to make after all of Ruslan's instructions. And to keep himself awake in case the charms failed, he had filched a half-dozen pins from the ladies' work-baskets. He had them strategically placed in his clothing, and he held one. If he fell asleep, one or more pins would jab him as his muscles relaxed, and in the meantime, he planned to stick himself at intervals with the one he held.

If this doesn't work to keep me awake, I can always see if Father Mikail won't allow me to call it a form of self-flagellation, so it would count as penance, he thought wryly. *If I'm going to hurt myself on purpose, I might as well get* something *out of it.*

Every time he got the least bit comfortable, he jabbed himself with his pin, all the while watching Pietor to see if his brother showed any signs of nodding off. Pietor had surrounded himself with a ring of torches, but he wasn't sitting, he was pacing back and forth like a sentry on duty. But Ilya knew his brothers, and he knew that with Pietor, good intentions didn't last very long. Sure enough, at about the same time that Ilya got tired of jabbing his right thigh and changed his target to the left, Pietor sat down under a tree with his back up against it.

As Pietor began to relax against the tree-trunk, Ilya jabbed himself with the pin—at precisely the same instant that a bird began to sing, very softly, somewhere in the far distance.

Wait—a moment— He felt his eyes start to close and, with alarm, jabbed himself in the thigh again. He jerked awake with the pain, not only of that self-inflicted injury, but with the added insult of three of the other pins sticking into him as he relaxed a bit too much.

Down below, Pietor's head nodded forward, his chin resting against his chest.

The fluting music neared, and whatever it was that was singing, it was *not* a bird. The tones were bird*like,* but the music itself, soothing, lulling, sending one into a trance, was nothing that ever came out of a bird's throat. Ilya stabbed himself again, fiercely, as he felt the music steal over his mind and start to send him into slumber again.

So *this* was how the thief was getting past the guards! It *was* magic, the first magic that Ilya had ever experienced, and there was no denying that it was powerful as well as subtle and clever.

Movement out among the trees caught his attention before he realized that it *should* have been quite dark out there, and he shouldn't have been able to see movement. But it wasn't just movement that had alerted him, it was a moving light, and it was up among the branches, not down on the ground.

The song neared, and insofar as he was able to figure, the moving light was the source of the song. He had to jab himself again and again to keep from being captured by those entrancing notes, but by now, he didn't care that his thigh was beginning to resemble a pincushion. Whatever this thief was, it was not a *leshii,* nor a *polevoi.* Neither of those spirits had ever been known to lull people to sleep with magical lullabies.

He hardly dared breathe, and yet at the same time he had the same, curious feeling of lightness, of *aliveness,* that he had felt the first night he had followed Mischa out here.

Maybe I'd better pretend that I'm asleep—Whatever was carrying that flickering light might not come too close if it thought that he was awake and could see it. On the other hand, he had the feeling that if he closed his eyes, pretending to be asleep, that pretense might turn into the real thing.

But the very appearance of the light now argued for a perfectly human thief rather than a spirit. What would a spirit need with a torch or a lantern? The light-source could only be a flame, not the spectral, blue-green globes supposedly borne by the *rusalka* and other spirits. He had no notion of how the thief was staying up among the branches of the trees—

Could he be climbing from tree to tree? Or perhaps he's on stilts, like a clown at a festival? That could be the reason why no one has found any sign of a ladder!

So he waited, every sense so acutely active that he could swear that he heard Pietor's breathing, felt the least little movement of air on his skin, smelled the cherries ripening just out of reach, and saw the sawtoothed edge of every leaf. Slowly, the flickering light worked its way nearer, one tree at a time. He held his breath, not daring to move. It was just barely concealed by the branches of the tree nearest his now. In a moment, it would come into view, and he would see the face of the thief at last.

In an agony of anticipation and impatience, he waited as the light danced tantalizingly just out of sight—now seeming as if it was about to come around to his side of the tree, now dancing back. He wanted to shout at the thief, demanding that he show himself, even though he knew that would be the worst possible thing he could do at the moment. But his nerves were strained to the breaking-point, and he didn't know how much more he could bear without losing control.

Then the flame hesitated, faltered, as if the unseen hand holding it responded to a cautious thought, a warning that all was not as it seemed.

He wanted to scream.

Suddenly, just when he thought for certain that the thief was about to turn and bolt back the way he had come, the flame darted around the concealing branches, and he saw the thief clearly.

It was a bird. A *huge* bird, bigger than any eagle he had ever heard of, a bird with a wingspan that was easily twice as wide as the span of both his arms.

A bird with feathers made of flame.

The bird sang softly as it plucked the ripe cherries and ate them one by one; as it hovered in place beside each branch, its feathers coruscated in ever-changing hues of scarlet, gold, white, and a touch of blue. He could not see the front of the head clearly, but it had a long, graceful tail that trailed halfway down to the ground, and its head was crowned with a crest of stiff feathers whose edges sparkled with the glint of faceted gems.

He gasped.

The bird broke off its song and whirled somehow, although he had never seen a bird able to fly the way that this one could, and stared straight at him.

That was when he finally saw the bird's face clearly, and gasped again as the strangeness of it struck him like a blow to the stomach.

The face was a beautiful yet disturbing mingling of human woman and exotic bird.

The eyes—they were not round, like a bird's, and they had whites as well as irises. The completely human, intensely blue luminescent eyes stared into his for one heart-stopping moment. Then, inexplicably, the face of the creature shifted and became wholly that of a bird.

Before he could even draw a breath, the bird made a most unmusical squawk of sheer terror. He had not even begun to move when it shot straight up into the night sky in a thunder of flame and feathers, arcing upward, a fiery comet in reverse.

Then it was gone, leaving only the dazzling afterimage burned into his mind.

CHAPTER THREE

HIS HANDS lost their grip, his mind went blank, and Ilya fell out of the tree.

He landed on his back with a dull thud, driving all the breath from his lungs. He saw stars, and his mouth opened in a silent gasp of agony. Somehow, perhaps because he was so limp with astonishment, he didn't do himself any serious injury, although he lay on the ground under the tree for several moments, thrashing and trying to make his lungs work. His injuries of the last beating reminded him with force that they were not quite healed. In all that time, neither his brother nor the pair of guards with him woke or even stirred.

Finally, with a sobbing intake of breath that broke the bizarre stillness in the cherry-orchard, he managed to get a gulp of air. After a second and third, he rolled over onto his side, wheezing and coughing. His lungs labored and his eyes watered with pain as he groaned. Still, despite all the noise he was making, the other three lay as if dead, with only their faint snores showing that they were asleep and not corpses.

His throat was raw, his chest afire, and his body felt bruised from toe to head by the time he managed to get up onto his knees, and from his knees to his feet. With every movement, he thought he was not going to be able to make the next, and yet he managed. As the moments passed and his mind cleared a little, he could think only of two things: the memory of the magical bird burned into his heart, and the urgent need to get out of there before someone came and found him.

Clutching his ribs in a futile attempt to make them stop aching, he realized that he was in no way going to be able to climb a tree, get over the wall, and climb another tree back down to the ground. He was going to have to take his chances with getting out the gate.

He found that he couldn't straighten up, and that his left knee hurt, so he bent over in a kind of stoop as he limped toward the gate as fast as he could go. Surely there wouldn't be too many guards here, would there? How many would the tsar have guarding his cherries when his son was supposed to be watching for the thief?

HE ducked from shadow to shadow in spite of the extra pain, but as soon as he got near enough actually to see the gate, he realized that he needn't have gone to all that trouble. There had been two guards left on the gate, and both of them were asleep, slumped down against the gateposts and looking like nothing so much as a pair of drunks caught on their feet when the liquor hit them.

He scuttled between them, noting that they were slumbering as soundly as the three still in the orchard.

At that point, with the dark path ahead of him and all danger of discovery behind him, his mind blanked, perhaps with shock. The next thing he knew, he was in his room; he was crouched on the floor beneath the open shutters with no memory of how he'd gotten there. With great difficulty, since his bruised muscles were all starting to stiffen, he pulled the shutters closed and fastened them, then fell into bed still fully clothed. For once, he didn't care if he slept in his clothing; he hurt too much to try and strip down.

Once he was actually lying down and able to relax, the pain started to ebb as cramped and knotted muscles unlocked. *On the whole,* he thought, as his mind began to work again, albeit slowly, *I've been hurt worse by beatings. I'll probably be a bit stiff and sore in the morning, but I can cover that easily enough. Maybe all those beatings have toughened me up enough that I can fall out of trees and not get hurt!*

That might be the case, but he wasn't about to thank his brothers for it.

What was it I saw? He couldn't close his eyes without seeing the bird, as if the creature had branded her image on the inside of his eyelids. Larger than any eagle he had ever seen or even heard of, with feathers that resembled flickering flames and a face that he would never be able to forget as long as he lived—what *was* she? He knew the bird was female; everything about her, from her face to her voice, had been completely feminine. Why had she chosen to raid his father's cherry trees, and how was it that her song, if song it was, could send people into a sleep so deep that it took tremendous effort to wake them?

Her eyes . . . they had been the most beautiful, the most expressive eyes he had ever seen in *any* face, beast, bird, or woman. Of a more intense blue than the clearest sky in high summer, there had been no doubt of the intellect and vivid personality behind those eyes. Nor was there any doubt that she had been as startled to see him as he was to see her. It had never occurred to her that anyone could escape being entrapped in her spell of sleep.

What was she? Where had she come from? And where would she go when the last of the cherries had been devoured? Why had she never appeared here before?

Would she come back? *I don't think so. I don't think that she'll take the chance, now that she knows there is someone who has seen her and knows how to defeat her magic. I wouldn't, if I were in her place.*

There it was, the word. *Magic.* He had to acknowledge it— he had seen magic, real magic, alive and at work. The bird herself must be magic, and what she had done to put the orchard-guards to sleep had to be magic. Tsar Ivan was wrong, and Ruslan and Mikail were right. Magic existed, it was real, and it worked even on those who did not believe in it. But even more important, creatures existed—supernatural creatures—that used that magic as naturally as breathing. If the bird was not a spirit like the *rusalka* or the *bannik,* then she was something like the Mare of the Night Wind or the Snow Dragon. She was certainly not the sort of thing one would find on a walk through the woods. She was something that was out of a book or a tale, and ordinary means of dealing with her simply would not work. Could she be shot with arrows or trapped with nets? Perhaps, but he would not count on it. She might be able to burn her way free of nets, outfly arrows—or both might pass through her as if she were made of fog.

There were things in the world that common sense dictated could not exist, logic failed to explain. And he would never, ever convince his father of that.

At least there will be more cherries left than there have been for a while. . . .

He giggled at that thought, his ribs and back aching. He had just seen the impossible, the inconceivable; he wanted to shout out his discovery to the whole palace, and he knew he was going to have to remain silent. He couldn't even confide his discovery to Ruslan; if he did, word would eventually leak out that he had been in the orchard at night, and Ivan would assume *he* was the thief, or that he knew the thief and was making up preposterous stories to hide the thief's identity.

Even if I could tell them, would I? If Ivan believed the tale of the bird with flaming feathers and the eyes of a beautiful maiden, he would want to kill her for her skin, or catch her to keep her in a cage as a trophy. How could he possibly permit that?

She cannot live in a cage. I know she cannot, I feel it. She is a bird, shy, but wild and free, and she could not bear to be in a cage where idiots could gawk at her. She will die first. And how could I be a part of anything that killed her? Now that I have seen her, I cannot imagine a world without her in it.

He dozed only fitfully for the rest of the night, his dreams haunted by wings of fire and startled blue eyes.

BREAKFAST was an entertaining meal, as Pietor got the tongue-lashing Ilya had expected for falling asleep just as his older brothers had. But then came a turn of events that neither Ilya nor anyone else had expected.

After the first failure, Ivan chose to make his sons' humiliation public, perhaps to add incentive for the next to try. He stood up and addressed Pietor at the high table once the great hall had a sufficient number of people there to form an audience. Pietor had clearly been expecting this; he left his breakfast half-eaten and set his jaw angrily. Ivan started his lecture in a tone loud enough to carry well across the great hall, as Pietor sat with his head hanging, and it got worse from there. Used to Ivan's ranting, most of the servants and family members went on with their meals, although some who had reason to rejoice in Pietor's failure hid their smirks behind their cups. Pietor endured the tsar's tirade, scowling, for as long as it took Ilya to eat a piece of buttered bread, but then, just as Ilya reached for his knife to cut a second slice, Pietor exploded with temper of his own.

"Demons haul you to hell, old man!" Pietor roared, shooting up to his feet and shaking his fist in his startled father's face. "I have taken all I *shall* take from you!"

Ivan turned red as a poppy and spluttered incoherently for a moment. Ilya and everyone else present stared in startled fascination; no one, *no one,* had ever shouted back at the tsar, least of all one of his children. "Who the hell do you think you are, you puppy?" he howled, spittle flying as he shook with rage. "You're my son, and you'll damned well take what I tell you—"

"That I will *not!*" Pietor shot back. "And as for the rest, you can call me your son no longer!" He swept dishes from the table in a dramatic gesture, and Ilya winced as they crashed to the floor and shattered. "I've had all I can stomach of your playing with us, making us dance like puppets, bowing and genuflecting to you as if you were Holy God, and all for what? So that you can dangle the hope of becoming tsar in front of each of us in turn? Well, I've had my fill of it!"

Ivan by now was so apoplectic that he could not even get out a single, strangled syllable; he stood rooted to his place, scarlet-faced and shaking, his eyes bulging and a fleck of spittle on his lips. It was the tsar's wife who asked, clutching her hands at her throat, "Pietor! What do you mean?"

"I mean I'm off!" Pietor snarled, flinging his arms wide. "I'm taking my inheritance, and I'm leaving! Don't think you can have me followed either, *Tsar Ivan.* You may think I am no hunter, but I know the forest better than any man here except my brothers, and I doubt you'll get one of them to chase after me!" His bark of laughter rang out in the tense stillness like the crack of a whip. "They'll be too pleased that there's one less competitor to follow me with much enthusiasm!"

And with that, while his father stood rigid with shock and anger, he turned on his heel and left, his boot-heels ringing on the hard wooden floor. Ivan continued to remain rooted where he was, face now nearly purple with rage, while the tsarina shook her head silently, her hands fluttering helplessly. Ivan seemed trapped within his own rage, and Ilya stared in morbid fascination, wondering if he might actually die of anger. How ironic if Pietor precipitated the tsar's death without knowing it!

How provident for me if he did! There will be such scrambling over the inheritance that I will be able to get away without anyone noticing until I'm long gone! Ilya was torn—to hope that the tsar would drop dead was unfilial, and Mikail would certainly say it was a sin, but—

Ivan still had neither moved nor spoken a moment later when a servant ran in, babbling that Pietor had taken two horses, one loaded down with a pack, and had ridden out of the stableyard at a gallop, heading into the forest.

He must have planned all this. He must have had the horses saddled, loaded, and ready. Holy Virgin, he's smarter than I thought! Much *smarter than I thought! Maybe he's not a fast thinker, but it's pretty clear he's a thorough planner!*

That was when the tsar finally came to life again. With a wordless shout of fury, he ran out of the room, heading for the stables, the tsarina in hysterical pursuit, crying and fluttering her hands. "Ivan! Ivan!" She wept as she ran. "Don't! I pray you! Don't!"

Ilya had sat through the entire scene in a state of amazement, as had most of the others here in the great hall. Some still sat or stood, frozen in various odd positions, as if they had been turned into statues. The rest only turned their heads to stare after the tsar, still not quite believing the scene that had just taken place before them.

The utter silence that had fallen over the great hall was so full of tension that Ilya wanted to jump to his feet, shouting, just to break it. Yet neither he nor anyone else seemed able to move, just as if they had been caught in a different kind of spell.

But as with all such spells, something did break it. A plate slipped from the benumbed fingers of a serving-girl, just out of Ilya's reach. He saw it drop, saw her eyes widen with horror, yet neither of them was able to move to catch it before it crashed to the floor, spilling its burden of sliced cold meat as it broke into several pieces, the sound shattering the unbearable silence.

The girl burst into hysterical tears, threw her apron over her head, and fled the room, weeping.

The spell broken, people began moving again. Another of the servants hurried to clean up the mess and salvage what he could of the meat before the dogs got to it. Five of the dogs converged at once on the fallen meat and began a snarling fight over it as the servant waded into their midst, kicking them ineffectually.

And everyone else, it seemed, began talking at once. Except for Ilya, who deemed it a good moment to make his escape, lest someone somehow managed to find a way to blame him for what had happened.

``**—SO** that was when Father got to the stable,'' Ilya reported to an avid audience of Ruslan, Mikail, and Mother Galina. They had gathered in the dairy; the dairymaids had been useless for work, so Galina had turned all the milk but a gallon or two into the souring vats and chased them all out. With the appropriation of a loaf of fresh bread from the kitchen, a few mugs, and some of yesterday's butter, the four were well fortified to discuss Pietor's defection. ''He found that all of the bridles had their reins knotted together, all of the saddles were gone, and all of the horses had been chased out into the field and thoroughly spooked. There was no getting near them for anything. It must have taken Pietor hours to do all that.''

''Unless he had help,'' Ruslan observed with a sly grin. ''What happened to the saddles? Those would be hard to get rid of.''

Ilya nodded. ''It turned out that the saddles had all been hidden up in the hayloft, but no one found that out until one of the stableboys stumbled over them. It took so long to catch horses and find the right saddles that Pietor had almost a half-a-day head start. They still haven't unsnarled more than a third of the bridles and reins.''

''It sounds as if he had this planned even before he went out into the orchard last night,'' Ruslan said, not making any attempt to conceal his grin. "Well! He has more intelligence than I gave him credit for!"

"I would say craft rather than intelligence," Mikail observed. "And I would also say that Pietor had help; I cannot imagine how he could have done this otherwise. At least one person must have stood guard so that he would not be caught at his work, and perhaps more than one person helped him."

Ilya nodded, pausing for a bite of bread-and-butter and a swallow of milk. "No one will admit it, though, and Father can hardly punish the entire stable staff, although I'm certain he would like to try right now."

"Even Ivan isn't that foolish," Mother Galina observed dryly. "Not if he expects to be able to ride or sell any of his horses for the next year. Ivan could punish a man or two on the suspicion that they had helped Pietor, and there would be nothing worse than grumbling and complaint—but punish everyone, and I don't have to tell you what would happen."

"He'd have every man and boy that had anything to do with the horses taking their revenge on him, but in ways he couldn't prove." Ruslan sat back and licked butter from his fingers, grinning with satisfaction. "Well, with a half-day's head start, no one is ever going to catch Pietor. Ivan might as well count the losses as gone forever. Two horses, Pietor's weapons and armor, and a pack of supplies—whatever else he took—oh, that's going to stick in the old man's craw for a long, long time."

"Where would he go, do you think?" Galina asked, echoing Ilya's own thought.

Ruslan shrugged. "Who knows? Through the forest, certainly, for he will be able to break his trail many times there. Pietor knows the forest, and he has more sense than to stop anywhere within Ivan's reach. He'll probably leave the trees in a few days and come back to one of the roads, and I don't doubt that there are plenty who would be willing to hire him as a fighter. He could find work for his sword almost anywhere, if it comes to that."

Ilya sighed. "There isn't a chance now that anyone else will ever be able to make the same escape," he said wistfully. "I wish I'd been as clever. Father isn't stupid, after all; he'll have the stable under watch from here on in, and it won't be guarded by anyone he thinks is suspect."

Oh, how I wish I had thought of delaying pursuit the way Pietor did before he got away, he thought with envy and regret. *I could have done what he did—and without ever confronting Father. I just wasn't audacious or clever enough to think of it. That could have been me making my escape if I'd been as cunning and bold as Pietor. He solved all the problems that I couldn't resolve. With a half-day head start, Father didn't send more than a token pursuit, and with two horses instead of one, Pietor can go anywhere, even to the court of the Great Tsar.*

Ilya would be berating himself for days over this one. If he had just had the sense to realize that pursuit *could* be delayed, and then deal with it!

But how could I have done what Pietor did without help? And who would dare help me? It's one thing for the stable-master to give me a safe trysting-spot; it's quite something else to help me knot reins and hide saddles. I know one thing; he wouldn't *have done it for me, not for any bribe I could manage. I wonder who Pietor got?*

"I would imagine that Pietor bought the help of the guards that were with him in the orchard, convincing them that they would be safer after he was gone," Galina said idly. "He was right, too! After all, now that he's run off, Ivan's mind isn't going to be on punishing them! Was there supposed to be anyone watching the stable last night?"

Ilya shook his head. "Not the stable or the paddock directly; there's no need right now. There aren't any mares in foal, the gypsies are long gone, and it's too early to worry about wolves. Father couldn't imagine any one of *us* daring to take his horses."

Father Mikail spread his hands. "There, you see? With perhaps the help of two friends, Pietor could have done everything last night and had his horses ready to mount and ride. My only question is why he didn't just *go?* Why stay and confront the tsar?"

Ilya snorted; the answer seemed obvious, given his brother. "Because it's Pietor, that's why! He knew what Father would do and say to him when he failed to catch the thief; he'd heard it twice before. His temper is just as hot as Father's. He couldn't resist the chance to tell Father what he thinks of him!''

"Ah, now that is a more logical explanation than the one I had thought of,'' Mikail said thoughtfully. "I had thought that he did so because he wanted to create more upheaval and confusion than would have occurred if he had simply vanished, because the more upset that there was, the longer it would take Ivan to organize pursuit.''

Ilya passed him more bread and butter and poured his own mug full of milk.

"I doubt he put that much thought into it,'' Ilya replied. "But being able to see Father going purple and spitting with rage—now *that* he would not be able to resist. Especially not since it gave him the chance to interrupt Father in the middle of one of his tirades.''

"And we still do not know what spirit is stealing the tsar's fruit,'' Galina said, shaking her head. "There is not much fruit left on the trees, and now I doubt we ever shall. And it *must* be a spirit, wouldn't you say, Ruslan?''

"I have no doubt,'' the shaman said firmly. "I favor the Old Man of the Fields, personally. By now that one must have a lively grudge against Ivan, and this would be a choice bit of revenge.''

As he and Galina entered a lively discussion of the characteristics of the different sorts of spirits that might be thieving the fruit, Ilya saw his chance, and led them into a discourse on spirits and supernatural creatures in general. He began planting hints and asking leading questions, all directed toward the goal of identifying his mysterious bird, and eventually he had an answer.

"A creature that flies but looks like a burning brand high in the sky—that would be the classical Phoenix,'' Mikail put in, after Ilya guardedly described the bird's burning feathers and how it looked in the distance. "You must be recalling that *Natural History* I read to you while you were hurt; the Phoenix is exactly like that, and is the bird that builds its own funeral pyre every hundred years, dies upon it, and is reborn from the ashes.''

The shaman burst out laughing, startling all of them. "Nonsense! I don't know what your Phoenix is, but Rus has no need to import foolish, suicidal foreign birds!" Ruslan countered. "Not when we have the Firebird, who is lovelier by far than your Phoenix and has no need to go killing herself!" He rubbed his hands together, warming to his subject. "Ah, the Firebird is a precious jewel indeed! She dwells beyond the North Wind, and she is a tsarina in her own right; when she chooses, she can put off her bird-form and become a beautiful maiden. She knows where the Tree of Immortality grows, and she eats of its fruit whenever she chooses. Her feathers seem to burn, but are not consumed, and it is said that she shines in the night like a thousand bonfires."

"I remember the tales! She sounded as if she was very beautiful," Galina said wistfully.

"Oh, she is! But it is the worst of all possible luck to see her unless she chooses to show herself to you, and worse still to take one of her feathers unless she gives it to you."

Ilya kept his thoughts to himself. *I don't know how my luck could be any worse than it is now,* he told himself. *And she didn't drop any feathers, so that is hardly an issue. But at least now I know what she is.* Somehow, being able to put a name to her made him feel a little better, although he didn't know why it should.

"The Firebird—I do remember that creature now, and I remember thinking how it seemed both like and unlike the Phoenix," Mikail put in. "I recall other things, Ruslan—you may say that seeing her only brings bad luck, but my recollection is that she is far more perilous than that."

"How so, Father Mikail?" Galina asked curiously. "I never heard that the Firebird was inclined to hurt anyone herself. In the tales, it was only those who tried to trap her who brought ill fortune on themselves."

"She is a temptation, that is what makes her so dangerous!" Mikail said gravely. "Like the succubus, that evil demon who imperils the souls of men by luring them into bodily congress, I was told that the Firebird seduces the mind and spirit. Once seen, she cannot be forgotten, and thoughts of her intrude on holier thoughts and even prevent prayer. It is a terrible thing to see her, for the mere sight of her threatens spiritual damnation."

"You Christian priests think *everything* threatens spiritual damnation, especially if it is a pleasure to look upon," Ruslan said crossly. "Believe me, it is enough that seeing her curses you with bad luck. Who needs to worry about damnation when every moment of your life something else is going wrong?"

That led the two into a spirited argument over whether it was worse to have one's soul or one's well-being in peril, and Ilya eventually left them when he became bored. He decided to make himself useful in the stable, helping to undo the mess that Pietor had left there. The stable-master gladly turned the great knot of tangled reins and bridles over to him, and he sat down with the snarled leather in front of him, glad enough for something to occupy his hands while he thought.

Maybe Father Mikail is right. I certainly can't get my mind off her. The Firebird continued to glide through his thoughts, and there was a growing need in him to see her again. *Was* there a chance that she would return to the orchard tonight? If there was even the slightest hope, he knew he had to be there. Perhaps she would think she had frightened him away; perhaps she would simply be more careful with her spell of sleep. Perhaps she would be tempted enough by the cherries to take that chance.

Ruslan said she could become a beautiful tsarina when she chose. After seeing her eyes, he had no doubt that this part of the tale was true. *If only I could see her as a maiden! I think— I think I might be content merely to* look *at her, if her eyes are a match for the rest of her. . . .*

With his mind involved in dreaming of what she must look like, his fingers flew unheeded, and he finally looked up in surprise when the last of the bridles fell from his hands.

With nothing more to do, he gathered up the bridles and took them over to the tack room, where he hung them on their pegs on the wall. The saddles, retrieved from the hayloft, had been neatly replaced on their stands. Everything appeared to be as it had been, except that the horses in their stalls either hung their heads with exhaustion or jumped at every sound, trembling.

Once again, he found himself at loose ends, unable to think of anything constructive to do with himself. He wasn't a servant or a serf, who had tasks assigned to him. His usual activities were severely curtailed by Pietor's escapade this morning. He couldn't ride, for all the horses were still exhausted, and most were so nervous that they shied and rolled their eyes at anyone who approached them. Several actually kicked the sides of their stalls in anger or fear if they heard someone walking in the stable. Whatever Pietor had done to spook them into flight had left them badly shaken; it might be days before the most sensitive were fit to ride. Ivan would be livid when he realized how much damage had been done.

As if he isn't already livid.

Knowing Pietor, Ilya could only think that he must have chased and beaten the horses until they were in a frenzy of fear and impossible to approach. Pietor treated horses as he did dogs: They either obeyed or were beaten. He would have had no compunction about mistreating them to serve his own purposes.

Ilya didn't dare go anywhere near the weapons-practice field, given that his brothers were probably all in a nasty temper and looking for someone to abuse. The oldest—well, their pride must be smarting, since Pietor had done what they had not dared, had defied Ivan and gone off with two horses and an unknown amount of booty. And the younger were afire with envy, and with anger, knowing that Pietor had spoken only the truth, and that Ivan was toying with them, and would continue to toy with them until the day he died. All of them must know that the tsar would punish them since he could not punish Pietor, and that life would be restrictive and uncomfortable for all of them for the next month or more. All that must be building up inside them, and they would be looking for an outlet for it. But they had no imagination at all; they would do what they always had and work out their frustrations in fighting. If Ilya came anywhere near them, they would have a real target for their anger. Somehow they would find a way to blame him for their troubles, and he would pay.

Let them abuse each other for a change. I'm tired of being their target.

He was too restless to borrow a book from Father Mikail to read and not feeling social enough to rejoin Ruslan and Mikail in their discussions. Going off into the woods or fields to carve would make Ivan suspicious and give his brothers an excellent opportunity to ambush him. So what did that leave?

He stretched with a groan as he turned toward the door to the tack room. His muscles still ached after his fall of last night, and it had been all he could do to keep from appearing stiff and sore. That would have raised questions, and with Pietor running off as he had, questions could lead to suspicion that he had helped his brother prepare for his flight. After all, who would believe his protests that Pietor hated him and would never have wanted his help? His other brothers certainly would have made no effort to substantiate his story.

Which meant it wasn't wise to sit in the sun for very long to bake his muscles—and again, that would put him where his brothers could see him; a very bad idea. It was too bad that the window of his room looked in the wrong direction, or he could go and lie on his own floor to get some sun and heat on his back.

But there *was* the bathhouse. . . .

Now that *was* a good idea! He knew that no one was likely to want to use it at this hour; if he fired up the stove himself, it would occupy his time and serve a useful purpose. Those who had been out searching for Pietor would be glad of the heated bathhouse, and those who had been trying to capture the loose horses would need it. If the horses were now kicking the sides of their stalls in agitation, they had probably been kicking their captors as well.

"I'm going to go use the bathhouse," he called as he left the stable. "I'll leave it heated and ready for anyone who wants to go after me."

"I will," the stable-master called. "And thanks to you. I got kicked more times than I care to think about, chasing down those damned spooked nags. By the time you're out, my bruises will be ready for a steam." Then he laughed. "And since you'll be first and I'll be second, I'll surely remember to leave the third steaming for the *bannik.*"

Ilya laughed, although he did not really know if the stable-master was serious or not. According to Ruslan, it was necessary that when the bathhouse was fired up, one must allot the third steaming to the *bannik,* the spirit of the bathhouse—but he had never heard of anyone here doing so. Did the stable-master or others actually make sure that the tradition was followed?

A few days ago he would have thought such a thing impossible, but if Pietor could manage to persuade people to help him, almost anything could be going on here, and Ivan wouldn't know anything about it if all the servants conspired to keep it from him.

He shrugged and headed down the path. It hardly mattered to him; he just wanted to ease his aches.

The bathhouse was quite removed from the rest of the palace buildings, a little two-room log hut set near to the stream to ensure that bringing water would not be a chore even in the dead of winter. Windowless and dark, surrounded by the shadows of the fir trees growing all around, it was a rather spooky place when all was said and done, and Ilya didn't wonder that bathhouses allegedly had their own spirits, the *banniks*. He'd never seen a single sign of a *bannik* about, and he probably used the bathhouse more frequently than anyone else—but after last night, he was no longer inclined to dismiss the tales of the *bannik* out of hand. He might not be alone.

Still, this was hardly the time or place when one could expect to see a spirit, with the sun high in the sky and birds singing in the thick boughs of the fir trees. Night; now *that* was when spirits appeared, not in broadest daylight. *All those stories, they take place at night, too. Only sorcerers and witches appear by daylight. And saints, too, but they don't count.*

As usual, the last person to use the bathhouse had left it bare of everything but soap and had failed to leave the doors open long enough for the steam-room to air out. *Probably one of my brothers; they think they never have to clean up after themselves.* With a sigh, Ilya opened the doors and hauled wood from the nearest woodpile until the breeze had taken most of the musty smell away. Only then did he feel his way into the steam-room, and in the dim gloom clean the ashes out of the stove, leaving only enough for a bed for the fire. Fortunately, the discourtesy of the last occupants had not extended to carrying away the tinderbox; he set a good fire with dry pine-needles and twigs as the base, then got it going after a few false starts with steel and flint.

While the fire heated up the stove and the inner room, it was time to haul water, and haul he did. The bathhouse needed a lot of water, water for throwing on the stove to make steam, water to heat on the stove for bathing, and the purest, cleanest water for drinking so that the bather didn't pass out.

When he finished filling all the buckets, he stood in the inner room until his eyes adjusted to the dark, and looked around. He surveyed the floor with disfavor; what was the point of getting clean when there was so much dirt on the floor that it was bound to make mud once the steam began? *What were they doing? Steaming with their boots on?*

There were blown-in leaves and other trash on the floor of the changing room, too, as well as dirt. *It looks as if I was the last person to clean up in here.* He made himself a broom of fir-branches and swept the place out, muttering under his breath that it was a shame that his brothers were such pigs. It occurred to him as he swept out the last of the trash that it had sounded as if he was apologizing to someone unseen for his brothers' conduct!

Oh well, there's no one listening. And even if there is, half the people here think I'm a little mad at the best of times. I don't suppose they'd find my talking to myself at all surprising.

Fresh bunches of fir-branches would complete the restocking of the bathhouse, and he went out to get them. It took him some little time to select the right size of branches, cut them properly, and bind them together into bundles. When he returned, there was someone already in the bathhouse.

It startled him when he realized that the steam-room was already occupied, for he hadn't noticed anyone approaching while he'd been gathering fir. When he opened the door to the inner room and saw a dark shape on one of the shelves, it took him aback. "Oh—" he said, peering into the steamy darkness, trying to make out who it was. "I beg your pardon, I hope you don't mind if I join you. Ah, here are the fir-branches. . . ."

He handed them in and felt the other take them, then grunt something that might have been "thank you." The bather sounded and looked vaguely like the stable-master, and Ilya retired to the other room to strip off his clothing before joining him.

He must have finished sooner than he thought. Well, that's fine, I didn't particularly need to be alone, and if one of my brothers shows up, he'll be less inclined to start something with another person present.

As his eyes adjusted to the gloom, it seemed that his identification was correct; it *was* the stable-master, lying back on a shelf with his eyes closed. Out of sympathy, Ilya kept quiet, making as little noise as possible as he bathed, then took a shelf himself and let the steam ease his own aches.

As his mind drifted in the heat, and his body relaxed, he found the image of the Firebird floating in the darkness behind his closed eyelids. She was as vivid and real to him now as she had been last night, and that alone was astonishing. Even the most exciting experience usually lost a little of its immediacy after a night's sleep, but not this one. He'd been certain, somewhere in the back of his mind, that when he woke up this morning his glimpse of the Firebird would seem like a dream, but if anything, it was the opposite. Pietor's dramatic scene, the discussions afterward, *those* were far more dreamlike than his memory of the Firebird.

If only I could see her again—

"Oh, you will," chuckled the stable-master.

"What?" he said, startled by the comment. *Did I say that out loud? I must have. Oh, fine, now he'll think I'm losing my wits. Well, perhaps he'll think that I'm simply lovesick.*

"You'll see her again. You've got that way with women, youngster. I hear a lot about you, all the time." The man chuckled again. "You would be amazed what women will say when they think there's no man about to overhear them, and they seem to favor the hay-barn and the bathhouse for their gossip-sessions in rainy weather. I hear plenty."

Oh, good. He must think I meant one of the dairymaids, perhaps even Ludmilla. He does think I'm lovesick. Ilya bit his tongue, blushing so heavily that he felt warmer than the steam wreathing around him. He wanted to ask what the stable-master had heard, but—

I'm not asking. Not for anything!

"Oh, they think you're a fine lad, and no mistake about it," the stable-master continued. "Even the ones that have gone on to the tsar wish they were still with you, and they'll tell the others as much when girls with fewer trinkets get to envying them. But you know how it is: You do what you have to in this world, and that's for women as well as men. If a girl gets a chance at the tsar, well, who's to blame her for taking it? Not when she's bound to get a good husband, a place in the palace, and a fine lot of trinkets out of it.''

Oh, I know only too well. How could anyone blame them?

"But you ought to know they think well of you," the man concluded. "I think so, anyway. You're a good lad, and they appreciate that."

"Ah," Ilya said faintly, "thank you."

He didn't know what else to say, so he said nothing, as the heat in the bathhouse built up to the point where he felt faint. How the stable-master was bearing it, he had no idea; occasionally the man would take up one of the bunches of fir-branches and lash himself with it, only to lie back down again. Finally Ilya rose, murmured something in the way of an embarrassed farewell, and went back out into the changing room. The cooler air put an end to his blushes, and the bucket of cold water he poured over his head helped revive him.

He scraped the water off his body with one of the sanded, curved, shaped sticks kept there for the purpose, then rubbed himself down with a bundle of birch-leaves. Once he was dry and dressed, he headed back toward the palace. His mind was on dinner, which was not far off, and he didn't really notice that there was someone approaching him on the path to the bathhouse until that individual spoke.

"Ah, I'm ready for that steam, and that's a fact," the stable-master groaned. "Thanks for setting the bathhouse up, lad."

Ilya stopped in the middle of the path as the stable-master went on, oblivious to anything other than his goal. He turned and stared after the man, dumbfounded.

But—but—the stable-master was just—but—I just saw—I talked to—

If the man in the bathhouse hadn't been the stable-master, then who—or what—*had* he been?

As he stared after the stable-master's retreating back, one of Ruslan's tales came back to him:

"When you see someone in the bathhouse, and later you find that others swear that person was elsewhere at the time,

then you have seen the bannik. *It is best to treat anyone you share the bathhouse with properly, with respect, for if by chance you do encounter the* bannik, *he is quick to take offense, and deadly when he does. He can kill a man by peeling the skin from him, and in other ways; he has killed a dozen or more strong men at once, and no one even heard them cry out. But if you are a good guest, he can be an equally good host.''*

That was what Ruslan had said.

It was *the* bannik. *Ruslan has seen him, he said so. Ruslan probably saw someone else that he knew was elsewhere, and that was how* he *knew what it was he'd seen.*

He licked lips gone suddenly dry and wondered if he should shout after the stable-master to warn him.

No—by the time he reaches the bathhouse, the bannik *will be gone. When he shows himself, it is only to one person at a time.*

He was so benumbed by his realization that he was already walking toward the palace before he was quite aware of what he was doing.

First the Firebird, then the *bannik*—what did it mean? Why was he suddenly seeing spirits and supernatural creatures? What was happening to him?

Could that last beating have driven him mad?

But Ruslan sees these things, or says that he does. And other people have seen them. Given how adamant Tsar Ivan was about the fact that such creatures did not exist, if anyone else had seen the *bannik* or the *domovoi* or any other spirit, would they have even mentioned such a thing?

Hardly.

Engrossed in his thoughts, he stumbled over a root in the path and looked down. When he looked back up again, the path was blocked by his brother Gregori, who held in his hands a short length of stout branch.

Ilya blinked at him, and quickly decided to take the route of conciliation. His brother's face was set in a grim mask, his eyes narrowed. ''Gregori! I just cleaned out the bathhouse and it's heated and ready if—''

He got no further, as a blow to his back knocked him to the ground and made him gasp for a breath that wasn't there.

He landed on his hands and knees, and a foot to his side sent him tumbling, choking on bile and pain.

Gregori and whoever had hit him from behind were not alone. He never got a chance to escape; he never even got a chance to recover from the first blows before they were on him. As blows and kicks rained on him from all directions, he could only curl up into a ball and try to protect what parts of himself he could.

HE woke to pain and darkness, more of either than he had ever experienced in his life. The pain was so intense it nauseated him. He was so cold that he couldn't even shiver; he was lying on some hard surface that radiated an aching cold into him that hurt more than it numbed. His left arm was twisted up over his head; it throbbed abominably, but the moment he tried to move it, he regretted it. Agony shot from his wrist to his shoulder, overwhelming everything, until it was all lost in merciful oblivion.

He swam gradually up into awareness again, and nothing had changed: not the pain, not the cold, not the darkness. His arm, his ribs and back, his legs, they all hurt worse than he had ever imagined anything could, even with his wide experience with pain. Nausea mingled with the pain, and he tasted bile in the back of his throat. Tears poured helplessly down his face, he moaned and sobbed, but there was no one to hear him, no one to help him this time.

He didn't know where he was, could not even move a single finger without awakening more pain; two more attempts to do so sent him screaming down into unconsciousness again. There wasn't any room for anything in his mind *but* the pain; it defined a suddenly narrowed existence, with the only certainty being that when it stopped, he would be dead.

He couldn't even think coherently enough to guess where he had been dumped, and it didn't matter; obviously his brothers had dragged him off somewhere so that no one would find him and rescue him. His only clues were a musty smell of decay and the terrible cold, and he was too disoriented to think what those clues could mean.

Neither Ruslan nor Mikail would find him in time to help him; his brothers must have made sure of that. He was utterly and profoundly alone, and not all of his tears or cries would change that.

"Oh, I wouldn't say that, Grandson." The voice was everywhere, echoing inside his head.

"Wha—what?" he gasped, blinking, wondering if the pain had driven him to hearing things.

"You're not entirely alone."

His eyes blurred, then refocused, as a pale smudge of light hanging in the air above him, a strange glow he'd thought was just another of the manifestations of pain, became brighter. A moment later, it was a well-defined sphere, floating above his head, fully bright enough to illuminate his surroundings.

The four walls around him were lit, dimly but clearly, by the cool, white glow. He turned his head a little to look, and when he saw where he was, he thought his heart was going to fail. Involuntarily he gave a yell of sheer terror, and his whole body jerked in a futile and illogical attempt to push it all away—and the ensuing agony of every shattered bone and torn muscle sent him crashing into unconsciousness again.

He floundered back up to consciousness with a moan; his head and body throbbed, and he thought for a moment that he was going to vomit. The bright sphere still hovered above him, but this time it was as tall as a man, and it appeared to contain something. . . .

Some*one*. Someone who leaned over and looked down at him with a face he knew by its resemblance to his father's.

"Gently, Grandson. I'll grant you, a crypt is not a pleasant place, but you'll only hurt—"

Ilya's scream drowned out the rest, and once again he plunged into darkness as his body spasmed with terror. The single glance had been all he needed to know where his brothers had left him, for he *was* in the family crypt beneath the church. He could not mistake the four rough-cut stone walls with their crude stone niches that held the mouldering remains of Tsar Ivan's father, grandfather, great-grandfather . . .

He's come to claim me. He's come to claim my soul! The charnel smell of death told him what his own fate would be—and the spirit of his grandfather, hovering above him, was surely there to welcome him into death, or perhaps *bring* him there if his hold on life proved too tenacious—

When he blundered into awareness again, the sphere of light and its occupant were still there above him. If this was a hallucination, he was still trapped inside it. He shut his eyes, desperately hoping they would go away.

It's the pain—it must be the pain. The pain is making me see things. He isn't there; not any more than the Virgin from the icon was looking at me the last time my brothers beat me senseless.

But the last time, he'd been safe with Ruslan, and not about to die—

A groan shook him, and his eyes opened involuntarily. His grandfather looked down on him with concern and care. *"This is bad, Ilya Ivanovitch. This is very bad. I had no idea that you were being mistreated so terribly. You must find a way to protect yourself from your brothers before it is too late."*

As if he was ever going to get a chance to. As if it was not already too late! Tears coursed down the sides of his head, burningly hot against his chilled skin and soaking into his hair above his ears. He closed his eyes and lost himself in pain and despair.

Some time later, he opened his eyes to darkness, tried to move, and the agony his attempt caused brought strange, animalistic sounds out of his mouth. But this time, he did not lose consciousness. He *had* to bring that arm down and get himself into a sitting position; that was his immediate goal. He would think no further than that. Weeping and howling with the pain it caused, he seized his left wrist with his right hand and pulled. Bone grated on bone, and pain made shafts of white light and stars dance across the darkness behind his closed eyes, but he managed to get his left arm down and lying across his chest.

Now for the next part.

Before he could change his mind, he rolled onto his right side and inched his way along the floor until he came to a wall. He didn't dare stop, no matter how much it hurt, or he knew he would never find the courage to start again. His breath came in short pants, and his left arm felt as if he had dipped it in molten metal; every time the bones grated together, it sent spasms all over his body. His ribs stabbed him with a dozen points of red-hot agony with every movement, and a hundred other injuries declared themselves to him with a hundred different pains, but he did not stop moving. Finally he achieved his goal; he sat with his back against the wall and his limp left arm cradled in his lap. When death took him, he was not going to meet it lying down. When his brothers returned, which they would, his corpse would greet them defiantly.

Once he stopped moving, some of his pain subsided, and he closed his eyes, wondering if that meant he was dying already. Had he jarred something loose in his crawl, was he bleeding to death inside? Now that he was still again, the sweat of his efforts chilled on his skin, and he shivered anew.

The shivering woke fresh pain in his body and arm; he opened his eyes in an automatic reaction—and shrieked aloud at what he saw before him. The globe of light was back, hovering now a little above the floor and before him, but in it was a stranger, a rough-looking, heavily bearded man in the furs of a hunter. What terrible spirit was this? The *domovoi* come to take him?

The man scowled and took several steps toward Ilya as he tried to shrink back into the wall that supported him. It was all the more horrible to see this man walking, for his heavy, thick-soled boots made no sound at all on the stone floor when they should have been falling with dull thuds.

The man leaned down and peered into Ilya's terrified eyes, practically nose-to-nose with him. And there was no hot brush of the other's breath on his face, only a clammy chill that surrounded the man the way the light did. Ilya stared into his eyes, too petrified to move or speak. The man frowned ferociously at him, and finally straightened up. *"You've got a mind, boy, why don't you use it to save yourself all of this?"* he snapped, as if he was angry with Ilya. *"Even your idiot brother Pietor found a way to escape! Gods! That my line has produced such a half-wit!"*

"Don't be too hard on him, Gregori."

Ilya yelped again, for his grandfather was back, clapping the stranger on the shoulder in a most familiar manner. The man turned toward him with a scowl.

"The boy hasn't helped himself at all!" the bearded man shouted, stamping one booted foot with frustration. *"Surely*

there must be a hundred ways to beat those fools!''

''The boy has done the best he could under the circumstances,'' Ilya's grandfather said soothingly, but the stranger was not to be soothed. He shook his head like an angry bear plagued with bees, in negation of what Grandfather had tried to tell him.

He rounded on Ilya and jabbed an accusatory finger at him. *''You!''* he shouted, as Ilya's heart tried to leap out of his chest with panic, and his chest tightened until he could not breathe. *''What have you done to—''*

This time it was terror as well as pain that overcame him, and he fainted.

He woke to find that he had fallen over sideways; his head didn't hurt in any new places, so presumably he had slid down the wall slowly instead of dropping straight to the floor. Fortunately, it had been his right side he had fallen onto; he leveraged himself up, panting for breath, and groaning with pain at every movement.

This time the darkness when he opened his eyes was very welcome to him; the darkness meant that there were no more spirits, or hallucinations of spirits. He leaned his head back against the stone of the wall and waited for the pain to subside again with his eyes tightly closed.

''You! Boy!''

His eyes snapped open at the new voice; there was another stranger standing before him, this time with a nimbus of strange, blue light about him instead of a glowing halo of white. This stranger was dressed in a bearskin robe covered with the ribbons, talismans, bones, and other artifacts of the traditional shaman. Ilya recognized it, for Ruslan owned such an outfit, though it was a costume that he seldom wore.

The newcomer, too, was bearded, but his hair was long, flowing down his back, and on his head he wore a headdress of deer-antlers. He carried a drum in one hand, the beater in the other.

He smiled grimly as he saw Ilya's eyes fixed upon him. *''Pay attention to what's around you, boy! Really hear what is said, don't just listen. You might learn something. Pay attention! Take note of everything that goes on! That's the way you'll learn what you need to know to get out of here!''*

He vanished with an audible *pop* before Ilya had time to react with more than stupefaction.

His mind began to work, sluggishly, a few thoughts making their way past the fog of pain. *Great-great-grandfather Gregori was a hunter, that's why my brother Gregori tries to be a greater hunter. Great-great-great-great-grandfather Potanka was a shaman, Ruslan told me so. Were they—*

Again, the light rose, this time with another stranger in the midst of it, a fierce boyar with a bristling moustache who took one look at Ilya and clapped his hand to his sword-hilt as if he was about to draw it and run Ilya (or something) through. Then, as if he thought better of the idea, he let his sword go and leaned over Ilya with a fierce but worried frown. With a little moan, Ilya lost consciousness again.

Time and time again he woke, to be confronted by either a stranger, or by his grandfather, or both together. His mind reeled under the images that presented themselves to him, and every time a new one appeared, his heart pounded so with fright that the blood roared in his ears until he passed out again. Some tried to advise him, some berated him, but he was so terrified he really didn't listen to any of them. He thought he must be going mad with the pain, finally, and began to scream at the top of his lungs. Perhaps if he screamed, the visions would stop.

It hurt to scream, and his fit of panic couldn't last for long, so he had descended to whimpering incoherently when a new light appeared. But unlike the others, this was a yellow light that flickered unsteadily, and it accompanied the distant sound of real footsteps on stone.

"Ilya?" called a distant, echoing, but joyfully familiar voice. "Ilya? Are you down here?"

"Here!" he cried out hoarsely, then doubled over, coughing, as the effort made his ribs stab into him like fifty knife-blades.

"Ilya?" Both the light and the voice were stronger now, and there was no doubt in his mind that this was no spirit or hallucination, it was really Father Mikail. "Ilya?"

"I'm here! In the crypt!" he managed, before another fit of coughing overtook him. He fought it down, and shouted with the last of his strength. "Here! In the crypt! Help me!"

The footsteps broke into a run, and as he fought against pain and darkness closing in again, Father Mikail appeared in the door at the farthest end of the crypt, a lantern held over his head.

And that was the last thing that Ilya saw for a very long time.

THIS time, he woke out of a drugged and dreamless sleep to find himself back on his pallet in the chapel, his arm already splinted and bound, his ribs likewise tightly bound. He assumed that the rest of his injuries had also been treated.

His head spun when he tried to move it, with the peculiar disorientation and bitter taste in his throat that told him Ruslan had dosed him thoroughly. Ruslan had treated him before when he'd been unconscious, trickling the medicines down his throat with care, a little at a time, to keep from choking him. That was why he wasn't feeling any pain now, and he mentally blessed Ruslan for his consideration.

"Don't stir much if you can help it," Mikail said, as he moved into Ilya's view and sat beside him. "And if you have to, tell me, and I'll help you shift yourself. They didn't kill you—but this time they actually tried to."

Mikail's expression was far more somber than Ilya had ever seen it before, and he wasn't certain what to make of it. Mikail had a basin and cloth, a pitcher and cup, and a prayer-book beside him. In the candlelight, it was impossible for Ilya to guess what time of day it was, but it did not feel as if he had been unconscious for more than a day or so.

He licked his lips, aware of a burning thirst engendered at least in part by the drugs. "Could I—have a drink?"

"Surely." Mikail poured a cup of something from the pitcher and supported Ilya's head as he held the cup to his lips. It was watered wine, cool and clean-tasting, and Ilya drank it down with gratitude.

Mikail helped him to lie down again, and placed the cup beside the pitcher. "I'll tell you what I know," the priest said, before he could ask any questions. "You've been drugged since last night when I found you after supper. I went looking for you when your brothers told your father at dinner that they'd discovered that *you* were the one who'd helped Pietor escape and that you had followed in his wake before they could catch you." He sniffed, frowning. "I didn't believe them. The tsar, oddly enough, didn't believe them on either count. I suppose that might have been because he had men guarding the stable and knew that the horse that you supposedly took was actually led out by Gregori and found roaming out in the orchard. The tsar didn't seem particularly interested in trying to find you, however, so Ruslan and I went looking."

Mikail patted his shoulder as he began to shudder, remembering the dark and the endless hours of fear in the crypt. Not the fear of death—he'd been angry that he'd been left to die, and afraid, but not *that* kind of fear. No, the real terror had begun when the spirits appeared. *There* are *things worse than death.* . . .

"We didn't find you in the usual places, so we split up. I thought I heard someone crying out as I searched about the palace, and I followed the sound under the chapel, through the maze that keeps thieves out and spirits in, to the crypt itself, and there you were." He shrugged. "That is all there is to tell."

"Except for what happened afterward—and the why of it all." That was Ruslan, coming in at last, burdened with a tray of hot food that interested Ilya not at all. He kicked a stool over and sat down at Ilya's feet. "This time, we not only didn't try to hide the fact that you were hurt, we made a great deal of fuss about it. We shouted and roused the entire palace, we conscripted servants to carry you out on a litter, and we made certain that Ivan saw you before we brought you here."

"What did he say?" Ilya asked weakly. His father had never shown any interest in his injuries before this.

"Nothing then. Later, he called all of your brothers in and ranted at them." That was Mikail, but he didn't look pleased that Ivan had taken an interest in his injured son.

"The trouble is, when he went after your brothers, it was because they lied, not because they tried to kill you. I don't think that was lost on them." Ruslan took out a knife and a piece of wood and began carving. "Later, he told us to take care of you, as if we wouldn't have without *him* telling us. That's about all that happened."

"Your brothers might leave you alone for a while, but Ivan

has given them the message that if they can arrive at a *reason* for getting rid of you, they won't be punished,'' Mikail said unhappily. ''What a father! Conniving at murder is bad enough, but conniving at the murder of your own child is a sin so terrible that he would never be able to do penance enough to save his soul, even if he repented of it!'' Mikail seemed almost as distressed about the state of Ivan's soul as about the peril of Ilya's body.

''As for why your brothers actually tried to kill you—that all boiled up yesterday afternoon before they attacked you.'' Ruslan didn't look up from his carving, but he scowled at it as if he suspected it was responsible for the entire situation. ''Ivan is certain that one of them helped Pietor and he's determined to find out who it was. He is also sure now that it was Pietor who was behind the theft of his cherries, since the thefts ended when Pietor fled.'' Ruslan grimaced, and kept his attention on his carving. ''Mind you, there wasn't that much fruit left to steal, so I suspect the reason the thefts ended was because the thief didn't want to be bothered with the little that was left.''

Or the Firebird was afraid we'd trap her, since I had seen her. . . .

Mikail nodded his agreement to all of it. ''He's convinced that the reason Pietor ran away is that he was the thief. He hasn't yet managed to contrive a convincing explanation for how Pietor managed to put all those guards to sleep, but I suppose sooner or later he will decide that Pietor hired one of those gypsy sorcerers to do it for him. Meanwhile, he's blaming your brothers for helping Pietor, and probably will decide, sooner or later, that one or more of them were in a conspiracy with him over the thefts. I'm sure they have thought of this, too. And they must know that the only way they can escape such an accusation is to get rid of you, then blame you as the conspirator. We think that was what they tried to do when they dumped you in the crypt, and Ruslan thinks they probably will keep trying. I—wish I could think otherwise, but I cannot.''

''How . . . pleasant,'' Ilya whispered. He blinked, as Ruslan and Mikail nodded grimly.

''The three of us *must* think of a way to make them leave

you alone,'' Mikail told him, his brows knitted with anxiety. ''I don't know how, but if we don't . . .''

He didn't need to finish that sentence. Before, all Ilya had to worry about was the risk that one of his brothers would actually injure him permanently. Now, the stakes were considerably higher.

Ruslan coughed. ''We thought about helping you to run away the way Pietor did,'' he offered, ''but it's hopeless. Ivan is locking the horses up in the stable under guard at night, and he has more guards patrolling the palace after everyone has gone to bed. He's making sure that no one else escapes him before he has a chance to discover who was helping Pietor. I don't think he's likely to change those orders before spring.''

And by then, my dear brothers might well take care of the situation for him. His head felt light and empty, and his broken bones throbbed with pain, making it hard to concentrate. *I have to find an answer. I have to!*

But not now. Even as he tried to think, the little energy he had ran out all at once, and while Ruslan and Mikail argued over his head, he fell asleep, despite trying desperately to stay awake and think.

``**YOU!** *Fool!''* The spirit rushed at him, brandishing a spectral saber. *''You don't deserve to live!''*

Ilya woke with a start and a yelp, sweating with fear; Ruslan's hand was on his uninjured shoulder, where the shaman had been shaking him to wake him.

''You were crying out in your sleep,'' the shaman said with a worried frown on his face. ''I was afraid you'd start thrashing about and hurt yourself.''

Ilya blinked at him, shivering. His nightmare had been a re-creation of his ordeal in the crypt, complete with the terrifying spirits tormenting him.

Well . . . not precisely tormenting him. Shouting at him, scolding him, hectoring him, just as they had in the crypt. That was bad enough, without being tormented. *One* spirit would have been enough to haunt his dreams for the rest of his life; after being plagued by a dozen or more, he wondered now if he would ever be able to close his eyes without fear. Would nightmares mark every attempt to sleep from now on?

It's a miracle I'm not mad—

Mad? I've got every right and reason to have gone mad! How many men could spend the night in a haunted crypt without going mad? How many tales are there of those who did?

And what if I had gone mad? What would my father, my brothers think and do then?

The idea struck him with the force of the first blow that had felled him, and he gaped at Ruslan stupidly as the implications of that thought ran through his mind.

Ruslan frowned at him. "What is it?" he asked and, when Ilya did not immediately reply, repeated more sharply, *"What?* I've seen that look on your face before; you've thought of something! What is it?"

He grabbed Ruslan's sleeve with building excitement. "What if you said I was mad?" he asked intently. "They left me in the crypt—what if that had driven me mad? Holy Virgin, I'd have every right and reason to have gone mad under circumstances like that, and there are a dozen tales of people who did. I could rave, put on quite a show for them to prove that I'd lost my senses."

Ruslan chewed his lip, scowling as he thought it over. "That could be very bad for you," he said finally. "They could easily declare that you're dangerous, and lock you in a room for the rest of your life. But let me think about this some more; there's some merit to the notion if I can just get past that little problem."

Ruslan hunched down on his stool, his eyes far away and his mouth set in a fierce frown as he pondered the question. "No," he said at length. "Not madness—not precisely. Not the kind of madness you were thinking of, with raving and carrying on. But if you'd been damaged—made feeble-minded—now *that* could be exactly what we need! They wouldn't lock you up; you'd be perfectly harmless, so they wouldn't need to. If you were able to take care of yourself in a reasonable manner, you'd be fine."

"Feeble-minded?" Ilya said, puzzled. What exactly did Ruslan mean by that? "You mean staring off into space all day? Sitting in one place, drooling and rocking?"

Ruslan laughed at his confusion. "Not that. Foolish! Like the silly son in the tales, the one who sits on the top of the stove talking to the fire and sings to the chickens. The one who makes up ridiculous tales about flying pigs and walking trees."

"The one who kills the Snow Dragon and marries the tsarina." Ilya wasn't going to laugh at anything for a good, long while, but he did manage a smile at the idea of acting like that. "How is that going to help?"

"In several ways, I think," Ruslan told him. "If you've become—well—an idiot, you are no threat to your father. How could he possibly suspect you of plotting to be rid of him when you can't even count your toes and come up with the same number twice?"

He's right about that—Father is hardly going to be threatened by a fool. "If he is no longer concerned about me, he wouldn't care at all what happened to me—and my brothers could do anything they liked to me without him saying a word," Ilya protested.

"That's true enough," Ruslan replied. "But think of your brothers. Is there any reason why *they* would bother with you if you were no longer a threat to them in any way? Think about it a moment, Ilya."

He closed his eyes and did think about it. *If I'm nothing, useless, no threat at all, completely helpless, in fact . . .*

It was so hard to think; he didn't hurt unless he moved, and since he had managed to protect his head with his arms, he hadn't suffered the injuries to his head that he had the last time, but he was still dazed and disoriented. The potions Ruslan fed him made it easy for him to sleep, and rather disinclined to move, but they didn't exactly help his ability to think.

Think! What would it mean to his brothers if he became the local fool?

"Let me tell you what I think, and you can tell this old man if he's seeing things or not," Ruslan said at last, interrupting his attempts to make his mind work. "I think that as you have been turning into a better fighter, they have been more worried about you. Is that right?"

"You might be right." He frowned. "I know that when they couldn't beat me up just one at a time and they *did* start to coordinate their efforts, the beatings got worse."

Ruslan nodded, pursing his lips thoughtfully. "Here's the

next thing. I think that as you have gotten older, they have been really concerned that you actually are a sorcerer. And I think that as you have shown yourself to be much more clever than they, they have begun to fear you, even as the tsar has. They feel that anyone who is clever must be capable of being a sorcerer or at least is able to think of ways to get rid of them too clever for them to guard against. That is why they were so afraid of you, and no matter how much you tried to reassure them, they would only be certain that this was a clever ruse to get them off their guard.''

Ilya nodded; all this made perfect sense, if you allowed for the fact that both the tsar and his brothers had a very skewed idea of the truth.

"So, if you become an idiot, you can't work sorcery, can you? You can't come up with amazing traps in the woods to make it look as if a bear killed them, you can't murder them with subtle poisons. And you can't fight, so it isn't even worth trying to beat you. Not only are you no longer a threat to them, but there is no glory or even satisfaction in beating you up, either.'' He smiled slyly. "Here's another thing. The maidens aren't going to be nearly as interested in an idiot as they are in the handsome and clever Ilya. They will not even have that to make them jealous.''

He gulped; that was one aspect that was not going to be very pleasant to deal with. *Better chaste than dead, I suppose.* . . . It wasn't an appetizing prospect, though. Perhaps he could find a way to attract the maidens as a stranger, disguising himself as a gypsy or some such thing.

Or perhaps some of them will decide to see if the tales are true, that a man who is deficient in his wits is well endowed elsewhere to make up for it, he thought wistfully, although he knew very well that neither of those possibilities was likely.

Better chaste than dead. And if he was an idiot—well, no one would entrust him with any kind of responsibility, which meant that when there was hard work to be done during planting or harvest and *everyone* in Ivan's little kingdom was expected to toil in the fields from dawn to dusk, *he* would be left to scare the crows with the littlest children, or bring water to the workers. So there was a good side to all of this.

"I think I can manage to be a convincing fool,'' he said

dryly to Ruslan, then sighed with resignation. "Do you think you could convince Father to come have a look at me? The sooner we start the story spreading, the safer I will feel."

Ruslan nodded soberly. "I think that you are right. Let me tell Mikail what we've decided and see if he can poke any holes in our clever plot. If he can't, we'll go off together to the tsar and see if we can convince him that it's important he come have a look at you."

"And I'll just rest here for a while." Ilya closed his eyes and listened to the sound of Ruslan's retreating footsteps. On the whole, this did seem the best way to ensure his safety, although now that Ruslan was gone, he could see a few more difficulties with it. Ivan would probably leave him completely alone, but his brothers were hardly known for their compassionate natures. He'd seen them pulling cruel tricks on the dogs, and equally heartless "jokes" on their own friends who might be drunk or otherwise incapacitated. He would end up being the butt of endless pranks unless he managed to stay out of their sight. He could count on being tripped and sent sprawling any time he walked near one of them, expect to have trash tied to his sash for the dogs to chase, plan on being given a bottomless bucket to fetch water. He would no longer be pursued, but he would be tormented from time to time. Whenever his brothers needed amusement, they would drag him out and amuse themselves at his expense.

I can bear that, I think. I hope.

At least it was better than waiting for ambushes, knowing that he would end up hurt, wondering how badly, dreading that it would be worse than before. It was *much* better than waiting for a dagger in the dark, or a fatal blow to the head.

Even if he wasn't sleepy, Ruslan's drugs had the effect of making his mind drift like a leaf on water whenever he closed his eyes. He could not have told how long it was that he lay that way, for he couldn't hold to thoughts for long unless he really concentrated and focused on them. There didn't seem to be any pressing reason to make the effort—which itself may have been another effect of the drugs—and he wasn't able to raise much concern either. So long as he didn't move, he didn't hurt, and that made it hard to care about anything.

"Ilya? Someone is here to see you." Mikail's voice, gentled, as if he were talking to a child, warned Ilya that the pair had managed to convince the tsar to come have a look at his offspring. He waited for a moment before opening his eyes, schooling his expression, readying himself, deciding right then what he was going to do.

When he opened his eyes, he widened them guilelessly, and smiled as if he hadn't a care in the world.

"Hello, hello!" he said brightly, and giggled at Ivan's dumbfounded expression. "Did you know that the sun and the moon are to be married tonight? I'm to carry the rings." *Should I pretend I don't know him? Better not; no point in doing anything that makes him suspicious.* He blinked at his father. "Tsar I-van, Tsar I-van," he chanted in a singsong, "cousin to the Moon-man!" He stuck one finger in the corner of his mouth and smiled.

The tsar frowned and turned to Mikail. "What is this? What is all this about? Why is he babbling like this?"

Mikail sighed and spread his hands wide. "As you see, Tsar, the boy has lost his wits. He babbles because his thoughts are broken past mending. I fear that the beating has damaged his mind forever and he will be this way for the rest of his life. He can't even keep his mind on his own nonsense for more than a moment or two."

Good! That gives me another cue. He pretended to lose interest in his visitors and began to walk the fingers of his good hand among the hills and valleys of his blankets, whispering nonsense to himself in a singsong.

The tsar watched him for some time more; Ilya continued to "play," taking the opportunity to catch a glimpse of his father out of the corner of his eye now and again. The tsar had never been any good at covering his emotions; at first, he was dumbfounded, then his expression gradually hardened into anger, but that anger was not directed at Ilya.

With a curse, he tore himself away from Mikail's side and flung himself out of the chapel, heading toward the great hall, still cursing. He was soon out of Ilya's sight, but Mikail stood in the doorway and watched with apparent satisfaction.

Finally he turned back to his patient. "He believes us," the priest said quietly, but with a half-smile. "And I would not care to be any of your brothers now."

Ilya looked at him with puzzlement. "Why? Why is he angry at them *now?* Why now, and not when they nearly killed me?"

Mikail turned to look after the tsar, then sat down beside Ilya. He had lost his smile, and his face was troubled. Ilya sensed that he had learned something about the tsar that made him a little ill. "Because—I think—he would not have cared if they killed you, but they have made you into something more helpless than a child, and helpless you will remain, a burden and a stone about his neck, useless and worthless, for as long as he lives. He will never be rid of that unwanted burden, and for that burden, he will never forgive them."

"Oh," Ilya said, for that was all he could manage. Finally he closed his eyes again and let himself drift. He didn't have to think about all of this right now, and he didn't intend to. This might be his last respite, and he was going to take full advantage of it.

CHAPTER FOUR

IF I were a lazy man, this would be paradise. Unfortunately, I'm not, and this is getting very boring.

Ilya watched the comings and goings in the great hall through slitted eyes. He lay atop the stove that heated the place, a structure built of bricks and faced with brown and white pottery tiles. It was more than large enough to hold him, standing as high as his chest, and long and deep enough for him to sprawl at full length on the top, even with his arms fully extended over his head. The really comfortable rooms in the palace—all three of them—had such stoves to keep them warm in the winter. Needless to say, two of those rooms, the great hall and the tsar's private quarters, were places where Ivan spent a great deal of time. The third stove heated the weaving room, a concession by Ivan to the fact that the women couldn't work in the winter without heat.

At the moment, with only the smallest of fires burning, it was barely warm on the top where Ilya lay, but it would never become uncomfortable, not even in the dead of winter, when it was kept going all day and all night.

This was the place where Ilya now spent a good part of every day—sometimes sleeping or pretending to sleep, sometimes just sitting and kicking his heels against the tiles, sometimes strumming on his old balalaika.

This was all at the suggestion of both Ruslan and Mikail. The top of the stove would have been a coveted place for winter lounging, except that a long tradition reserved it for the useless, the incurably lazy, the worthless. Perhaps this tradition had been started to keep the place from being contested; in winter, tempers grew short as the light faded, and an argument could escalate into a fight, which could end in death. But thanks to tradition, only a fool would sit on the stove, earning the contempt of every adult male and most of the youngsters. No one contested Ilya's place on top of the stove, which permitted him to watch everything and everyone while being left alone.

The main reason he was here now was to establish his presence as the fool on the stove before the snow fell, so that when most of the folk of the palace were crowded in here during the winter, his position and condition would be firmly established in their minds.

It was working. He had already overheard some of the servants referring to him as "Ilya the Fool," or as just "the Fool," and this was a good sign. Before very long, his new character would be set in their minds, as changeless as the rocks. Long after he was dust, there would be stories about Ilya the Fool to enliven winter nights.

I might as well give them plenty to laugh about. He decided to sit up and give up his pretense of sleep. He opened his eyes, yawned hugely, and stretched; no one paid him the slightest bit of attention. Blinking sleepily (and stupidly), he sat up and leaned back against the wall of the chimney behind him. *Well, now what am I going to do? I can't sleep, and I'm getting awfully tired of playing nonsense-music.*

The tsarina hurried by, her expression harried, as she searched among the servants for one who was not already busy with some task. This was a difficult season, with every servant and serf busy every waking moment. Not only were there the normal tasks, but this was the height of harvesting, with several crops coming in at once. The household chores took last place to the harvest, which often left the tsarina and her ladies to do jobs normally only a servant would touch. This did not do a great deal for her temper, and she would be willing to take almost anyone with a pair of hands to help her.

Her eye fell upon Ilya; she frowned slightly, and turned toward him.

"Ilya, I need someone to help in the wool-room," she said peremptorily. "Come down off that stove now."

Should I help her? He vacillated; he wanted to, if only to relieve his boredom, but if he did he would establish some sort of competence. That would be a bad precedent to set, just when he was trying to prove how utterly worthless he was.

Of course, the other option was to go with her and then make a mess of things, which would leave her with twice the work she had before. Fouling things would establish his worthlessness, but he didn't dislike her, and it would be cruel to double her workload with feigned incompetence.

He stared at her, his hand creeping toward his mouth until his finger finally reached the corner. He left it there, nibbling on the nail, while continuing to stare at her with blank eyes.

She must have been truly desperate, for she tried again. "Ilya, come down off the stove and follow me. I need help in the wool-room, the fleeces are too heavy for the women to carry."

That's not true; they're heavy, but the women can carry them if they do so one at a time. She's just looking for a beast of burden she can load all the fleeces onto at once. That made him feel a little better about playing the idiot.

He let his eyes unfocus as she continued to talk to him, at first coaxing, then nagging, her voice becoming shriller with each sentence. He ignored her for a while, but then, when she paused for breath to stare at him, he spoke. But not to her.

He stared off to one side of her. "The cabbages are dancing," he said clearly. "Can't you hear the brook playing for them?" He narrowed his eyes and whispered in a conspiratorial tone, "You know that the *domovoi* and the *bannik* are having a feast tonight."

She said nothing, but her eyes widened with a little fear, and she backed up a step. Now he looked down at her and smiled as sweetly as he could. "Are the honey-cakes done?" he asked. "I like honey-cakes. Do you like honey-cakes? I like honey-cakes. Are they done?"

Fear turned to exasperation. The tsarina's delicate features twisted in an expression of utter disgust. "Oh, go see for yourself, Fool!" she snapped, and turned on her heel to find someone more useful.

He picked up his balalaika and began to pluck aimlessly at it. The brief interaction had attracted some attention from the servants preparing the great hall for the evening meal. One or two of the upper servants stared for a moment or two, and several of the tsar's warriors snickered, but after a while, when nothing else happened, they lost interest in him.

Technically, he was supposed to be under the supervision of either Mikail or Ruslan, but so long as he didn't get into trouble, people were leaving him alone. It was just too much trouble to coax him down from the stove and lead him by the hand back to his "keepers." He wasn't very cooperative about being led, always finding something to distract him on the way—and unlike a small, willful child, whose manners he was aping, he was large and strong, and it was very difficult to move him when he didn't want to be moved. He had managed to watch a stream of ants for the better part of an afternoon yesterday.

When people were ignoring him again, he set his instrument aside and tucked his knees up, wrapping his arms around his legs and resting his chin on his knees. Now that there were more people appearing in the hall, things were a bit more interesting.

Scrubbing the tables and laying out platters of bread were the servants in drab brown woolen skirts and breeches and smocks of unbleached linen. Ivan's warriors, dressed in black breeches and half-corselets of light armor over tunics of brighter materials, were drifting in by ones and twos.

He hadn't had much chance to simply watch people before this, and at the moment, at least, it had the potential to be rather fascinating. When he'd been "himself," he hadn't dared permit anyone except the servants to catch him staring at them, because it might have been taken as a challenge. But now that he was the Fool, it didn't matter, and he could watch everyone from the tsar on down with the avid interest of a boy watching a frog. He'd learned a lot in the last few days, things that he wished he had known before.

The life of the palace swirled around him like a dance, but it was a dance with very distinct patterns, and rings within rings. The heart of the dance was the tsar, and everything revolved around him, like the virgin bride in the center of the wedding-dance, or the last sheaf of grain at harvest. But unlike the bride or the sheaf, the tsar remained the center of the dance no matter how circumstances changed.

The first circle surrounding him was composed of his sons, the captain of his fighters, and his steward. All of these had their own little patterns that brought them into and out of contact with each other, but the dance always brought them circling back around the tsar. Because the tsar was so suspicious of his sons, his closer partners in this dance were his captain and his steward, but he was the one who called the steps and the music.

Next outward came the tsar's fighters, a solid formation within the larger dance that in turn circled about their captain. Farther out came the superior servants, who were all freedmen rather than serfs. Sharing that circle were the tsarina and her women. This was a simple circle without much in the way of eddies and other patterns, except that the superior servants were barely subordinate to the tsarina, and were the equals of her women.

Then came the inferior servants, still free, but only peasants, while the superior servants had some pretensions at rank. Each group of these made their own patterns around their immediate superior and literally could not be co-opted by another unless their supervisor permitted it, or if the person who was commanding them was the tsarina.

Lastly, the drudges, who were all serfs, as much the tsar's property as his cattle and reckoned of less worth. These could be commanded by any of the servants above them in rank, but for all practical purposes there was no point in taking them away from the jobs that they knew. Superstitious and purposefully kept ignorant, they formed the larger part of both Mikail's congregation and Ruslan's pagan celebrations and rites, and generally worshiped both Christ and the old gods with equal fervor.

He had not much noticed them before, except for the few pretty maids among them, and he wouldn't have now if he hadn't been outside the patterns of the dance himself. Their place in the dance was minimal: to repeat the same steps in the same place, over and over, unless someone from one of the inner circles noticed one of them and called him (or her) into a new pattern. It suited the tsar to believe that they were happy, contented, and at one with the land. They would never give him a sign that this was not true, for although they worshiped him, it was out of fear, the way a whipped dog worships the hand that beats it.

And I—I am the Fool, the one who runs through all the patterns and disrupts them for a little while. Then I stand outside it all until the next unexpected moment when I break in.

Well, that was the theory he had, anyway. He hadn't really done much in the way of disruption since he'd healed up enough to venture out of his bed and into the rest of the palace again. Most of the disturbances he caused were among the folk of the third rank, the superior servants, the tsarina, and her household. Frankly, he didn't really want to regain the attention of either his brothers or his father, and he felt too sorry for the drudges and the lower servants to want to make their lives any more complicated. Ivan was probably still seething over the loss of not one, but two sons, and as for his brothers—well, they were still smarting from the various punishments that Ivan had levied on them for turning Ilya into a useless burden. If it hadn't been for the fact that getting revenge on Ilya would have been hollow, they'd have sought just that before now.

He scratched the end of his nose, watching the warriors come in and take their places at the long tables, seizing pieces of bread, grabbing at mugs and filling them sloppily from pitchers set along the center of the tables. Soon the varied scents of dinner drifted into the hall as the next lot of servants carried in platters loaded with meat and other dishes.

By the time Ilya had been able to rejoin the household, harvest was half over, and both day and night were distinctly cooler. There had been at least one hard frost, for the leaves had all turned. This would be the first year since he could remember that he had not been part of the harvest workforce, but no one trusted him to do anything other than frighten the birds off the grain and there were plenty of children to do that. During the harvest, everyone worked, and meals were eaten in shifts.

He overheard his name, and listened carefully; the steward was cautioning some of the house-servants not to let him wander out into the fields or he would get in the way of the harvesters.

"I don't suppose we could count on him to go fall into the river and drown," grumbled one of them.

The steward looked at him sternly. "*First* of all, he's a fool, not an idiot. Secondly, to wish such a thing is a violation of God's law. And thirdly, such a thing would bring terrible bad luck on us for years to come, and he might even come back as an angry spirit to haunt us."

The rebuked servant looked uneasy at that last, and Ilya reflected that before the incident of the cherry-thief, the third possibility would not have been mentioned. But now the household seemed equally divided between those who thought that Pietor was the cherry-thief, who had run away to escape Ivan's wrath, and those who thought the cherry-thief was a spirit and Pietor had been gravely wronged. And in any case, something of the subject of Ilya's unconscious ravings had reached the servants; it was commonly supposed that if the beatings hadn't damaged his mind, the spirits in the maze *had*. Which meant, of course, that there *were* spirits, and now it behooved a man to keep that in mind.

"We'll keep an eye on him," one of the others said, looking uneasily over his shoulder at Ilya. "Be bad enough having a spirit come back . . ."

He did not continue, but it wasn't hard to fill in the rest: *It would be bad enough to have a spirit come back to haunt the palace, but one who had died as a result of neglect, one who had been driven mad because of the actions of those within this house—* Such a spirit would be vengeful, and fully capable of exacting that revenge. Furthermore, such angry spirits were quite likely to destroy whoever and whatever came within their grasp, whether or not they were guilty.

This would be a frightening prospect for anyone who believed that Ilya would return after death. *It was a frightening prospect for me, in the crypt. I know what I saw, and I would do anything not to see those spirits again!*

He reflected that although he hadn't actually seen anything since his incarceration in the crypt, he hadn't been any place where he was *likely* to see something. It was commonly assumed even by Ruslan that there was no house-spirit, and Ilya had yet to move beyond the kitchen without being gently herded back to the house, so he would not have seen the spirits of the yard, the fields, the barn. He might have managed to convince himself that all those ghosts in the crypt had been hallucinations born of his injuries, except that he had seen two spirits before the beating, one admittedly at night, but also one in broad daylight.

He might have been able to dismiss the Firebird as a dream, eventually, even though she was still as vivid in his memory as if he had seen her only a few moments ago. But the person in the bathhouse could only have been the *bannik,* for there was no way that the stable-master could have been in two places at the same time. There was his proof that Ruslan, Mikail, and the drudges were all correct in their belief in such things.

Well, my brothers are due here at any moment, and I would just as soon be elsewhere. He sighed, and jumped down off the stove. One of the servants kept a sharp eye on him as he wandered in the direction of the chapel and out of the great hall.

Just as he reached the door of the great hall, Gregori entered. Something about the way that Gregori stared at him for a moment made him suddenly wary. There was a glint in his eye and a smirk on his face, the kind of expression he wore just before he would drop a hot coal on a dog's tail. Evidently Gregori, at least, had recovered from the tsar's tongue-lashings.

He's going to do something. Knowing that a prank was coming, Ilya kept his eyes fixed on the ground, but watched his brother closely under the cover of his long eyelashes. In this way he caught the surreptitious, sideways movement of Gregori's foot before he tripped over it.

He considered stepping on the foot for an instant, and thought better of the idea immediately. Instead, he allowed Gregori to trip him, but fell under his own control. It *looked* as if he had gone sprawling, but actually he landed without even taking a minor bruise.

Gregori got the laugh he had expected from those who witnessed the fall, and the shadow of ill-temper that had been in his eyes faded. Ilya sat up slowly, rubbing his head comically, earning another roar of laughter. ·

"My, oh my!" he exclaimed. "Was there an earthquake

just now? Or did the house-spirit make the floor heave up?''

Gregori laughed. He reached down and grabbed Ilya by the back of his shirt, trying to haul him to his feet before giving up. ''You tripped over your own big feet, Fool,'' he said, loud enough for everyone in the hall to hear him. ''Next time, be more careful of where you put them.''

Ilya sat up, but rather than paying any attention at all to Gregori, he stared at his feet for a moment, then began addressing them with a wandering harangue about being careful where they went. Shortly, Gregori went off to his position at the tsar's table, his lip curled with ill-disguised disgust, and the servants snickered as they listened to Ilya. Once Gregori was gone, he stopped right in the middle of a sentence, stared at the wall as if he had only just noticed it, and got to his feet again. He began shuffling, a few dance steps in a little circle, and the rest of those watching him lost interest as well. Once their attention was off him, he slipped away from the increasingly crowded great hall. The only person watching Ilya now was the single servant dragooned by his fellows into keeping an eye on the lunatic.

Ilya's restlessness had increased a hundredfold. He would even have welcomed the most menial work in the fields right now. *I have to get some exercise. I'm going mad with inactivity. And I don't want to get soft; Gregori and the others might not be trying to kill me now, but I'll have to be fit to meet more of those jokes of theirs.* He needed to be agile, to dodge plausibly whatever was thrown at him. He needed to be strong and flexible to make it appear that he tripped over obstacles and outstretched feet without really coming to grief. He had to find a way to keep himself in the same condition as any of the warriors.

But how?

He was already walking quickly, and frustration made him speed his steps. Before he quite knew what he was doing, he was running, easily outdistancing the surprised servant who had followed him.

He ran down the length of the palace, heading for the door that led to the gravel-covered yard between the palace and the barns and stables. It felt wonderful finally to stretch his legs, and as his muscles loosened and warmed up, he continued to run, out the door. He made an abrupt right turn as he burst out into the sunlight, and continued to run sunwise around and around the palace itself. He would have rather run out to the orchard or down to the river, but he was afraid that the servant detailed to keep him from getting himself into trouble would raise an alarm.

Besides, it was perfectly mad to run circles around the palace. No sane person would waste his time running for no other reason than to get exercise.

The hapless servant ventured out past the yard and cautiously waited at the point nearest the path leading to the river, while he circled the palace, head up, legs churning. After the initial burst of speed, he kept his pace down to something he could sustain for a while. With the bright blue sky overhead and the cool wind of autumn keeping him from getting overheated, there was a certain pleasure in the exertion, aimless though it was.

No, it's only aimless to someone who doesn't need to resort to subterfuge to keep in fighting trim. He passed the servant again, and to enliven the image he wanted to project, leapt and snatched at imaginary butterflies as he ran by. A couple of children toddled out from the cow-barn and watched him for a while, but what he was doing was not of enough interest to attract a crowd of adults.

Well, this would keep his legs in good trim and his wind strong. But he would need more than that; he needed activity that would stretch his muscles as well as strengthen them. He also needed something that could be done in the winter; once the snow closed around, he wouldn't be able to run anymore. What was enough like the exercises the fighters used to give him for that same sort of conditioning? Surely he could think of something!

Hah. I have it. And it will add one more log to the fire, so far as the question of my sanity is concerned.

He ran a few more laps around the palace, just to be certain that his legs were warmed up, then he stopped right in front of the servant. Ignoring the fellow altogether, he began to dance to a music only he heard.

Not just a bit of prancing and stamping, either, but the serious steps meant to impress onlookers, the ones that the young men performed to show off for the maidens—squatting kicks and split-jumps, whirling spins and spinning kicks, cartwheels and aerial somersaults, all of the moves that required agility, balance, and immense strength. In between each impressive move, he concentrated on intricate footwork, until sweat poured down his face and back and soaked his linen shirt. Only then did he slow, to give his body time to cool down, before he finished with a pose and a foolish grin plastered to his face.

The servant stared at him with a gaping mouth, looking more surprised than bewildered, and far too impressed by Ilya's fancy footwork.

Hmm. This is a good idea, but I shouldn't have been quite so enthusiastic in front of an audience. Ilya realized that he was going to have to do something to keep the man from spreading tales that might give some hint to his true mental state.

Mopping his brow with his sleeve, he sauntered over to the man and stared fixedly at him with that silly smile still plastered on his face. Finally, after he stared long enough to make the man uneasy, he leaned over and said in a confidential voice, "The *rusalka* taught me to dance, you know. But I have to dance whenever I hear her musicians playing, or she'll be very, very angry with me."

The servant's mouth snapped shut, like a frog with a fly, and his face paled. "She did?" he whispered. "You do?"

He nodded solemnly. "Of course," he replied. "Her musicians are the frogs, you know, which means I have to dance a lot. But I don't mind, I like to dance." Then he suddenly frowned, and the servant backed up a pace involuntarily.

"If I were you, I wouldn't go down to the river," he said fiercely. "She might drown *you*. She doesn't like *you*, she likes *me*. She likes *my* dancing." His frown deepened. "Maybe you'd better tell the rest, too. Tell them to stay away from the *rusalka*. She's mine."

"Of course, master, of course!" the poor man stammered. "I wouldn't think of it! I'll tell the others, you can depend on me!"

Ilya struck a pose copied from one of Gregori's lordlier moments. "See that you do," he said haughtily, and with lofty pride strode off down the path to the weaponry field, certain that the servant would not follow. Once he claimed that a *rusalka* was interested in him, none of the lower servants would dare to follow him. The river-spirits were some of the most dangerous of the natural spirits, for according to the tales, their power was not necessarily confined to the area of the river itself, and any particular *rusalka* had allies among nearly all the other water-spirits wherever one went. Besides, sooner or later *everyone* had to go down to the riverbank for one reason or another—to fetch water for washing, to bathe, to cross, or to fish. And once someone marked by the *rusalka* put a foot in the water, he was in her power.

Ilya's grin was genuine now. *Even if he decides that the rusalka is nothing more than a phantom of my madness, nothing is going to entice him to follow me anymore.*

He'd had another idea while he was dancing, and he wanted to collect the equipment he was going to need before it occurred to anyone to lock it up away from him. There wouldn't be anyone where the practice-weapons were stored right now; all able-bodied males were either out in the fields swinging scythes or in the great hall eating their heads off. With the servant gone, no one would see him or think to stop him.

It was the work of a moment to purloin a heavy wooden shield and wooden practice-sword, both of them double the weight of the real thing. He carried them off, not to his room, where they might be found and taken away from him, but to one of his old hiding places, used for secreting toys away from his brothers when he was a child.

He had several options among those places, but the one he felt the most secure about was the area beneath the raised floor of the bathhouse. No one wanted to step on cold stone floors once the bathhouse was nicely warmed. And no one would have wanted dirt floors, which would have turned to mud. The bathhouse was actually built on a raised platform, several hands above the ground level, with a tightly caulked wooden floor, the chinks sealed with pitch and rope. Caulking cracked and worked loose, though, so to prevent the winter wind from whistling up through cracks in the floor, the area beneath the bathhouse was walled in with extensions of the tight bathhouse walls themselves. That didn't stop clever animals from burrowing under it to make dens in the warmth beneath, and an enterprising boy with a knife and a great deal of ingenuity could easily create a removable hatch, one that would not be visible to anything but a close inspection.

No one as lacking in imagination as Ilya's brothers would ever have dreamed that someone would hide anything he really wanted in a place as inconvenient, awkward, and spooky as the bathhouse. As children, it wouldn't have occurred to them to look there, and as adults, even if they had an inkling that something might be there, they were above such nonsense as poking around under the bathhouse. That, of course, was what made it a perfect hiding place. And, of course, if the servants ever found anything hidden there, they would assume it was the property of the *bannik,* and quickly put back whatever they found.

The bannik! *I forgot about him—* Ilya paused with one hand on the panel of his hatch, and wondered if this was a good idea after all. As a child, he hadn't thought of the *bannik* when he was hiding things here, and the few times as an adult that he had used this place, he hadn't really believed in the existence of the bathhouse spirit.

On the other hand—he seems to like me. And he hasn't bothered me or my things in all this time. But now that I know he exists, there is no excuse for not asking his permission. He bit his lip, thinking. *I'd better say something, however awkward it is.* He cleared his throat and coughed once or twice.

"I beg your pardon, *bannik,* and I really don't mean to disturb you, but I need to hide these things from my brothers. Ah, perhaps I ought to explain why."

Feeling both awkward and rather foolish for speaking to empty air, he explained his situation, starting with the most recent beating. Given the knowledge of the household that the *bannik* had demonstrated at their last meeting, Ilya assumed that the spirit must keep himself current with the news of the palace, and it was quite likely that the word of Ilya's supposed condition was common gossip in the bathhouse. But the *bannik* could not know that the idiocy was feigned, nor could he know why it had been. That was what Ilya took on himself to explain. He could only hope that the spirit was still sympathetic enough to him that he would not mind the intrusion into his domain.

He waited, holding his breath, for some sign of the *bannik*'s approval or disapproval, but nothing happened. Finally, he simply let his breath out and opened the hatch.

There were still some things hidden in there: Ilya's toy sword, a box of pretty pebbles that he had collected, a top, and a bunch of feathers stuck into a ball of clay. All those things were covered with a thick layer of dust, and moths had been at the feathers. He moved these childhood keepsakes to one side and laid the practice sword and shield inside, then closed the hatch.

Dancing, fighting my shadow, running. Those should all keep me in adequate shape. On the whole, he was fairly satisfied with the progress of the day. It only remained to return to the palace and the great hall and resume his position on the stove.

But now that he had gotten outside for a while, he felt a great reluctance to go back in. Inside meant more idleness and boredom, and while he had managed to escape from the attentions of the servant meant to follow him, he might as well enjoy himself for a while. Granted, it was cold, but he had on a coat and the sun was shining.

The orchard! There wouldn't be anyone there; every apple but the most worm-eaten had been harvested days ago. The only creatures in the orchard were the horses, turned out to eat the discards and trim the grass and weeds beneath the trees. The horses weren't being guarded through harvest, for every hand was needed in the fields. The tsar was taking advantage of his horses' notorious reluctance to be saddled and bridled, and of their own greed to bring them back in at night when their mangers were filled with fresh hay and corn, to keep anyone from making off with one.

He got to his feet, dusted off the knees of his breeches, and sauntered to the orchard with his hands clasped behind his back, whistling tunelessly. It hadn't occurred to anyone to take his small carving-knife away from him, and it was in its sheath in his coat pocket; if he could find a good branch, there might be enough sound wood on it to carve something. Just now, it didn't matter what he carved; it would just be something to do.

Out in the open fields and the yards around the palace there was enough wind that it was rather chilly; in the orchard the trees cut the wind, and the sun was extremely pleasant. His muscles ached a bit from the unexpected exercise, and it was good to stretch, listen to the sparrows chatter, and let the sun beat down on tense shoulders.

He looked for a fallen branch of reasonable size, neither too old and dry nor too green, but there wasn't anything to be had, not even old or green. Probably the tsarina had sent some of the servant-children to glean the orchard for fallen and broken branches once the harvest was over, for apple-wood made a fine scent in the stove. In the spring, once winter was over, there would be more broken branches to collect for the stove. The tsarina was a frugal woman, inclined to make a thread stretch to cover as much as humanly possible. Very little went to waste in the palace since she had wedded Ivan.

He wondered if the Firebird had come here, too—there were far more apple trees than there were the tsar's special cherry trees, and she could have eaten her fill without anyone really noticing that any of the fruit was missing. It wouldn't have taken as many apples to fill her up as cherries, either.

His foot kicked up a windfall; there were more apples here than he had expected and he was a bit surprised that the tsarina hadn't ordered they be collected for cider. *The Firebird probably wasn't here,* he decided, picking up another bruised windfall, this one only a little soft in one spot, and taking a bite out of the unbruised half. It was warm, both sweet and tart, and the half that was bruised just beginning to turn, giving off a winy scent. *There's nothing special about these apples. Surely she only takes things that are rare and special.*

If *he* was tsar, he'd leave the cherry-orchard there, but he'd never harvest the fruit. He'd leave it all on the trees in hopes that she would come there again to eat, and he might catch another glimpse of her. It would be worth the entire orchard to him, if he could see her again.

Of course, if I convinced Father that she was real, he'd have bird-catchers out with nets and traps, trying to take her. He can't see anything that's rare without wanting to own it.

He nibbled carefully around the soft, pulpy bruise on his apple, and when there wasn't anything left on it that he wanted to eat, looked for a horse to give the rest to. One of the geldings he liked to ride was nearby; he chirruped to him and the horse lifted his head from the grass and swiveled his ears in Ilya's direction. Ilya and the stable-master were just about the only people who could approach the horses when they were loose in the field without them running off. Of course, given the way his father and brothers rode, he didn't much blame the horses for not wanting to spend any time under saddle, as it was rarely a pleasant experience for them.

Ilya held out the remains of the apple; the sorrel gelding's nostrils went wide as it sniffed, catching the heady scent of bruised fruit. It looked around, but saw no other apples nearby; that seemed to make up its mind, for the gelding moved lazily toward him, drifting sideways as if it was of two minds whether or not to bolt.

As it got within a pace or two of Ilya, it eyed him suspiciously, looking for any trace of a halter or bit. None of the tsar's horses could be enticed to hand if there was a bit of bridle-leather about. They knew every place a bridle could be hidden and every possible disguise for one. Head-shy and skittish, it took the stable-master himself to get any of them into tack.

Ilya laughed and held the apple out on his palm; again the gelding sniffed, testing for the scent of leather as well as of the apple, and the scent of apple-flesh decided it. A moment later, soft lips brushed his hand as the sorrel gelding plucked the remains of the apple, making it vanish as if by magic.

The horse shied just a little as he reached out to scratch its neck, but when there was still no sign of a halter or anything like one, it relaxed and leaned into his scratching and munched the apple meditatively.

"You know, if I had a way to take you and get away with it, I'd ride off with you now and we'd both be better off," he told the gelding. "Because then neither of us would ever have to put up with my brothers again. I have the feeling that between the fact that I'm the butt of all possible jokes and the fact that I'm not getting *any* woman-flesh anymore, pretending to be a fool is going to become very wearisome before the winter is over.''

"Oh, probably," the gelding agreed. *"Though I do think you're overly concerned about the woman-flesh. It really isn't that great a sacrifice to do without it."*

He blinked, and froze in place. He hadn't *really* heard that—had he?

"Don't stop scratching," the gelding said with irritation, leaning a little harder into his hand. *"What's the matter with you? You're not supposed to just stop like that once you've started a good scratch."*

"I—uh—I've never heard a horse talk before," he stammered.

"You never saw a Firebird before, either," the gelding pointed out. *"I would think that seeing her had something to do with the fact that you can hear me. Probably since you were awake when you saw her, some of her magic rubbed off on you. I have certainly been talking to you for some time, but you haven't heard me. Or else you just didn't understand me."* It reached down and lipped a bit of grass. *"Or maybe you just didn't listen. I do have Night Wind blood in me. If you'd been paying attention and hearing what I said to you, you might have understood me before this."*

"How did you know I saw the Firebird?" he asked, astonished.

"These things get around," the horse said vaguely. *"You can't keep secrets in a place this small. I think the dogs might have said something. They generally hear about everything that goes on in the household; that's how they know when it's a good idea not to be somewhere. I think the dogs heard you when you came in, and smelled the Firebird on you."*

He thought about the ever-present hounds, how they always seemed to be underfoot except during one of Ivan's rages or the times when one of his brothers was brooding about something. Had any of them been around when he'd slipped into the house that night? He thought perhaps he did remember them, wagging their tails when they recognized him.

"The dogs knew all about the Firebird, of course, but do you think any of the humans would listen to them when they tried to report what was happening in the cherry orchard? Of

course not! Now, the milk-cows knew about the Firebird too, but they aren't the brightest things in the world, and you can't always trust what they say. They'll believe anything anyone tells them. The milk-cows said that the dairy-maids said that you'd become a fool, but we told them not to believe what they heard," the gelding said, with a slightly superior air. *"The dogs knew all about what you and your friends were planning, and they told us. It's a clever plan, but it could use a little work."*

"Well, I've done the best I can!" he retorted, stung. Criticism from a horse was not what he had ever expected! "It isn't as if I've been in a good position to actually *do* much of anything, you know! I think I've done very well so far, in fact!"

"Don't be so prickly." The gelding snorted. *"I said it was a clever plan, didn't I? It's just that you could use a little work with the details."*

"Like what, exactly?" he asked suspiciously. Just what sort of advice could a horse give him, anyway?

"Like—you must know that you're going to get pushed, tripped, knocked about quite a bit, right?" The horse waited, looking at him expectantly.

He nodded.

"Well, then you ought to do something to protect yourself from what you can't avoid."

Ilya frowned. "I could—go to the wool-room and take as many gaudy rags as I can find, make those into pads for my knees and elbows. I should choose the gaudy ones, because they'll look more like something a fool would make to dress himself up than something I meant to use to protect myself. Have you any other ideas?"

"Just one." The gelding pawed the sod meditatively. *"Your brothers are all very predictable. I mean, we can even tell when it's about time for feeding by when we see them and what they're doing. They always do everything the same way, in the same order, at the same time every day. If they were cooks, you'd be eating pease-porridge every day until you ran out of dried peas. If you take the time to plot out their days, you'll have a general idea of where each one is so that you*

can avoid them. Avoiding one of their jokes is better than wearing padding to protect against it.''

"You have a point.'' It seemed a bit odd, taking advice from a horse, but if he remembered his old tales correctly, he wouldn't be the first to do so. Generally the horse in question was one of the Night Wind's foals, but it was still a horse. Besides, it was obvious that the gelding knew Ivan's household very well, and could probably be expected to render better advice on such matters than a heavenly horse would.

"Thank you very much,'' he said with feeling. "You've been quite helpful.''

The gelding shivered its skin all over and stamped one forefoot. *"Think nothing of it,"* the beast replied. *"Just keep me in mind for apples or carrot-ends. I like cabbage too, but it gives me wind. And a piece of bread is nice, now and again, if there's a scraping of honey on it.''*

"I'll do that,'' he promised. The gelding wandered away in search of more windfall apples, and Ilya did a quick mental calculation to determine where everyone in the household was likely to be at that moment.

The great hall. By now everyone is in there for supper; it'll be dark soon.

This would be a good time to go purloin those rags the horse had suggested. The only people in the wool-room would be servants, lower servants at that, and not permitted to question anything a member of the family did.

Even if that member of the family is a fool.

As long as he didn't run off with entire bolts of cloth, the tsarina would probably sigh with exasperation and ask the saints for patience, but do nothing more. After all, what was the point of trying to punish a fool? She probably wouldn't even complain to the tsar.

Even if she did, it wouldn't do any good. The loss of a few rags is nothing he is going to care about. Her frugal nature may be insulted, but that's just too bad.

Well, standing there wasn't going to get anything done, and the more time he wasted thinking about the horse's advice, the less time he would have to follow through on it tonight.

He shook his head, wondering if, after all, he really *was* mad. Not even Ruslan claimed to be able to talk to horses!

Could the horse be some other spirit in disguise? Could this all have taken place only in his own mind? One seemed as likely as the other at this point.

But I know this horse, I've ridden him more times than I can count, and I'd be willing to swear not only that the beast spoke to me, but that it couldn't possibly be a spirit in horse-disguise. Though he did say he had some blood of the Mare of the Night Wind in him—

Suddenly it all became too much for him to cope with. His head swam, and he staggered over and put a hand to the tree-trunk to steady himself. Then he looked up nervously, half-expecting the tree to say something as well.

But nothing happened. He swallowed with some difficulty, and wiped the back of his hand across his mouth.

Talking horses. Banniks. What next, I wonder?

He forced himself to think about the advice for a moment, instead of concentrating on who (or what) had given it. It was *good* advice, very clever and direct. If it hadn't come from a horse, he'd have had no second thoughts about taking it.

So whether it's coming out of my own imagination or really coming from a horse, I can't lose anything by following it, he decided. *It can't hurt to keep track of my brothers, and it can't hurt to pad my knees and elbows. Or my head, come to think of it. There's no reason why I can't make a stupid hat and pad it as well.*

It could actually be that this was a vision of some kind, all indirectly caused by his injuries, and brought on by all that strenuous exercise. Maybe he shouldn't have been surprised that he heard a talking horse; maybe he should just be grateful that he didn't hear voices telling him to do something really foolish!

The more he thought about it, the more logical that explanation seemed to be. It was certainly more logical than the idea that the Firebird's magic had somehow affected him.

That idea seemed to prove itself out, as none of the other horses seemed at all inclined to speak to him, no matter how hard he coaxed them with apples. They simply took his offerings, crunched them up in their strong yellow teeth, and went about their business, ignoring his tentative attempts at conversation. Finally, as the sky reddened with sunset, he gave up. He didn't have much time to carry out his raid on the wool-room if he was going to do it tonight.

THERE was only a single maid in the wool-room, which was a large chamber where everything needed to clothe the household was kept, from unspun and uncombed fleeces and hanks of flax to thread and finished cloth, to the rags carefully and thriftily cut from clothing that was too worn even to be made over again. They were called "rags" by default, but no one in the household would ever dare use these rags for cleaning. Household rags were made from old sheets and servants' clothing and undersmocks, but decorative "rags" were cut from the outerwear the tsar and his family and retinue wore. It was the latter that he was after; since there were no longer any children in the tsar's immediate household, adult clothing that was too worn to be cut down for someone smaller and too fine to be given to the servants was cut into strips to be turned into ribbons or wider strips to become the bases for bands of embroidery that could be applied to other garments. He didn't dare steal finished ribbons or embroidered strips, for the tsarina *would* have a fit about that, but if he could get his hands on raw-edged stuff—

He peeked in the half-open door and spotted a basket full of exactly what he was after, and while he was at it, it occurred to him that one of the batts of combed wool would make fine padding as well. He hid just behind the doorframe and watched the maid for a moment. As soon as she turned her back to the door, he moved.

He sprinted into the room, snatched up the basket of rags waiting to be worked into ribbons with one hand, and grabbed a roll of wool with the other. She saw him, but too late. He dashed out of the room again just as she was turning around, one hand outstretched to stop him, her mouth forming an indignant little O.

Her cries followed him out the door, but by then he was away, and there was no one to catch him. She certainly couldn't run after him, burdened as she was with heavy skirts, petticoats, and an apron.

Alone in his room with his booty, he took the largest of the rags, sandwiched wool inside, and made padded bandages out of them. He had an old cap that he padded with wool stuffed into the lining. The rest of the rags he used to decorate the cap and the ends of his bandages; by the time he was done, he had some very gaudy and odd-looking articles indeed. For good measure, he found as many odd bits of things as he could in his room, and festooned his bandages with something like a parody of a shaman's charms. When he tied them on, he looked as if a gypsy had purloined the costumes of a clown and a shaman and had combined them with his own dress for a most peculiar effect.

He rattled when he walked, the bits of inferior carvings, buttons, antler-tips, and bones clashing together with every movement. It wouldn't be possible to sneak around wearing these things, but that wasn't the point; the point was to avoid injury if he could. It would only take landing wrong to shatter a knee or an elbow, and he was quite well aware that it had been only luck that had prevented such an injury when his brothers had beaten him. Break a joint and he would effectively lose the use of that limb, for not even Ruslan could set such a break with any certainty of it healing well. It would *never* heal correctly, and the best he could ever hope for in such a case was that there would be some movement left in the limb when the splints came off.

When he was finished, it was very late, and he had completed his work mostly by moonlight. No one had come looking for him, so things had fallen out pretty much as he had expected: The maid had probably reported the theft, the tsarina undoubtably had thrown up her hands in exasperation, and no one had bothered to do anything about such a trivial infraction. After all, he was a fool, and fools did things that made no sense. Their actions were dictated by convoluted reasons of their own that no sane man could expect to understand.

He went to bed feeling rather pleased with himself, although he tried not to think too hard about the talking horse.

When he woke the next morning, it was with reluctance, for he had dreamed of the Firebird again. This time she was more maidenlike than bird, and he had pursued her across an endless landscape as she stayed just barely out of reach. And yet, she had kept looking back at him every time he thought of giving up the chase, as if she was luring him onward.

He'd had a similar dream the night before, and another, where he sat under a tree while the Firebird sang to him, three nights ago. In between those dreams he'd had the kind he'd expected: dreams of encounters with willing and nubile girls, as insatiable as any man could wish; but as time went on, he dreamed of the Firebird more and more, and of real women less and less. He had cause to wonder lately just what *that* meant!

He sat up in bed and stretched lazily, feeling only minor aches after all his running and dancing; he had half-expected to find that he was exhausted after so prolonged a dream-chase, but in fact, he felt remarkably well. *I needed that exercise,* he decided as he dressed himself in his rags and decorated cap. *No wonder I've been dragging about; I haven't had anything to get my blood stirred up since Ruslan took the splints off.*

He had to smile as he surveyed as much of himself as he could see by craning his neck around. His elbow-and-knee-bands were quite festive with all the colored streamers and the bits of flotsam dangling from them. If they were going to call him Fool, he certainly looked the part!

So, if I'm going to look the part, let me act the part as well! In high spirits now, he literally danced his way down to the great hall, hopping up onto the stove and surveying the place with a lordly air as he drummed his heels against the stove-front. The servants stared, then averted their eyes; the warriors and members of his family did more than stare. His brothers snickered, the tsarina and her women looked outraged and dismayed, according to their natures, and his father frowned with all the foreboding aspect of a thunderstorm. Ivan was *not* pleased to be reminded of the condition of his middle son.

He ignored them all, snatching what he wanted to eat from the trays that the servants carried by. He shortly had quite a feast laid out next to him on the stove, of buttered bread, apples from the late harvest, and a chicken-leg. This he ate while he continued to watch the room as if he were the tsar and not his father. He even issued orders to phantom courtiers and servants, brandishing his chicken-leg at them the entire time.

After a while, when he did nothing else outrageous, the

others began to ignore him. This was exactly what he had hoped for; he did not recall their attention by playing his balalaika or dancing, because that was not what he was after. He finished his meal, tossed the remains to the dogs, and lay down on the top of the stove as if for a nap.

Eventually the great hall was deserted, even by the drudges left to clean up after the meal. That was when he jumped down off the stove, stripped off his padding, and went to spy on his brothers, choosing Gregori as the first to follow.

In a matter of two or three days he had worked out what each of their patterns was, and had calculated the best places to be to keep out of their way. On the occasions when he couldn't, or when they actually came looking for him in order to have some fun at his expense, he was generally ready for them.

No matter what he was doing, he could always turn it into a display of foolery at a moment's notice. Whether he was running or practicing with his purloined weaponry, he could make it look as if he hadn't a sane thought in his head if he was caught. It took a lot of planning, but before the snow fell, he had an entire repertoire of nonsense he could insert for any occasion and on any cue.

Mother Galina didn't entirely approve of what he was doing, but she had to admit that he didn't seem to have another viable alternative. Ruslan and Mikail supported him, both with their protection and with further tales to the tsar and the household servants of strange things he was supposed to have done and said when they were "caring" for him.

No more animals spoke to him, which was a decided relief. He decided that the incident with the talking horse had been nothing more than a waking dream—or even a true dream, and he had only *thought* he was awake.

He even managed to get away with practicing with the heavy sword and shield in public by pretending to fight his own shadow. When he first began his exercises, he deliberately made his movements slow and clumsy because the warriors were watching him. Once they tired of the novelty of watching the Fool fight his shadow, he moved into *real* practice, feinting and striking against an imaginary opponent. It wouldn't have been good enough to keep him in practice if he'd been plan-

ning on real fighting, but it was quite good enough to keep
him in sound physical condition. The heavy shield and sword
built up his arms and shoulders the way running and dancing
built up his legs and back. Soon he was in the best physical
condition he had ever enjoyed.

He managed at last to get to the dairy and spend time with
Galina, and soon the servants stopped trying to chase him
away from his other refuge. What Ruslan and Mikail could
not tell him about household gossip, she could.

The harvest was soon over, the first snow came and melted,
and by that time he had established his new character so thoroughly that hardly anyone ever referred to him by his real
name, except Galina, Ruslan, and Mikail.

AFTER a strenuous workout, he was dozing on top of the
warm stove for a moment one day, when three of his brothers
entered the otherwise deserted great hall. The clatter of metal
and heavy footfalls alerted him and he sat up and watched
them warily as they approached the stove, hoping that they
weren't looking for him.

Unfortunately, they were.

"Hey, Fool!" Gregori called, with that false joviality that
made Ilya wary these days. "We were all going riding;
wouldn't you like to go with us?"

Something about his manner warned Ilya that it would not
be a good idea to refuse outright, so he tilted his head to one
side, stuck his finger in the corner of his mouth, and looked
at his older brother with as vacant a gaze as he could conjure.
"Ah?" he replied. "Go with you? Why, brother?" Some of
the dogs congregated behind the three, looking up at him from
between and around the brothers' legs.

"I said," Gregori repeated, with an edge to his voice that
hadn't been there a moment ago, "do you want to go riding
with us?"

The dog behind Gregori's feet whined, looking up at Ilya
with worried eyes. The other dogs all looked nervous and uneasy, and Ilya didn't blame them. Gregori seemed as if he was
in a bad mood today.

Gregori's hand clenched, as if he was hoping that Ilya
would give him an excuse to cuff him. Except that it probably

wouldn't stop at a cuff, although it wasn't likely to escalate to a full beating. Still—why risk even that?

"Ah, ride!" Ilya said brightly. "Ride, sure! I like to ride! Hey!"

He jumped down off the stove before Gregori had a chance to drag him down, and followed along in Gregori's wake. He was hoping for a chance to escape, but Mischa and Alexi kept him hemmed in, preventing any such notions. They clapped him on the back, staggering him, and laughed at his stumbling. He was very careful, however, not to stumble into Gregori.

He felt like a prisoner among them, and wondered what on earth he could do to make them entertained enough to let him go.

They did allow him to stop long enough to cram a coat on over his motley finery, at the same time that they donned their own, but that was all. When the odd procession reached the yard between the house and the stable, there were four beasts saddled and waiting for riders, and one of them was an old donkey normally used for hauling wood. Riding this beast was going to be bad enough, since Ilya's feet were going to drag the ground, but he saw that Gregori had a nasty, metal-tipped riding crop at his saddle-bow, and he guessed that his brother intended to sting the poor donkey into bucking or bolting as soon as he got into the saddle.

He stopped where he was, staring at the donkey, wondering how he was going to avoid injury to both of them. He didn't want the donkey hurt, for the poor little thing hadn't done anything to deserve ill-treatment. And he particularly didn't want *himself* hurt, which was what would happen if the donkey was maddened or frightened by the whipping.

The donkey was already frightened; its eyes showed white all around as it strained at its bridle, clearly wanting to escape. It looked at the riding crop as Gregori slipped the loop over his wrist as if it knew exactly what he intended to do with the whip.

They're going to make him buck as soon as I'm on top of the poor beast, and he won't be able to help it; if they hit the little creature with that crop, he'll have to buck!

The donkey wheezed, rolling its eyes to look at Ilya.

I'll mount him backwards! If I slap his rump, he'll trot off before they can grab the reins, and then I can dump myself off into the bushes!

That was the best spur-of-the-moment plan he could contrive. He shuffled over to the little beast and quickly climbed into the saddle. There he perched with his head facing the donkey's tail before his brothers could do anything about it. Gregori grabbed for the reins, which had been left dangling, but it was already too late. Ilya slapped the donkey's rump, and the clever donkey flipped its head, adroitly jerking the reins just out of Gregori's reach. The little beast trotted off as fast as it could put hoof to ground, heading for the nearest clump of bushes.

This was possibly the least comfortable way to ride that Ilya had ever encountered. He held on tight to the tail, but the donkey's jerky trot combined with the odd riding position jarred his teeth with every step. He was going to have bruises in places it didn't bear to think about when this was over.

The donkey brayed, and that was all the warning Ilya had as it stopped abruptly with its head down between its legs. It stopped *completely,* too, which was more than he was going to do, and he went sliding off over its neck backward into the bushes. Fortunately, they were junipers, and not the holly bushes that grew farther along. They were, however, quite prickly enough.

The donkey brayed again as it bolted, heading for freedom as fast as its four tiny hooves would take it.

He flailed around in the embrace of the bushes for a great deal longer than was necessary, because all of his brothers, and Gregori in particular, were laughing so hard they could barely stand upright. Gregori had braced himself against the doorpost, while the other two were holding each other up. Finally Ilya worked himself free of the springy branches and stood up with a fatuous smirk. "That was a fine ride, brothers!" he said clearly. "Why, I can't recall a better ride nor a finer mount! You must join me again some time!"

That sent them off into another paroxysm, and while they were holding their sides and wiping tears out of their eyes, he was able to stroll jauntily off to the safety of the chapel and the company of Ruslan.

He described what had happened while he picked bits of juniper out of his clothing and hair.

"It could have been worse," the old shaman said when he'd finished. "If that donkey had gotten out to the river and bucked you in—"

Ruslan shook his head, and Ilya only sighed. "My one saving grace is that my brothers aren't very bright," he replied. "If they were, I would be in very deep trouble."

ILYA woke with a start, his bedding in a knot, and his hair damp with sweat. He stared off into the darkness for a long time, listening to his heart pound.

This had been a very disturbing night, full of dreams that left him aching and frustrated.

His first set of dreams had all been about women. In the first dream, something unspecified had happened to Ivan and all of his brothers, leaving him the only heir. He'd been made tsar and was presiding over a festival at which there were no men, nothing but women, and there wasn't a single one that was less than pretty. Most of them he didn't recognize; there were shy, dainty maidens just blooming out of childhood, saucy girls his own age with tiny waists and flashing blue eyes, and handsome older women with the kerchiefs of married matrons covering their golden braids. He had been the center of a dance, during which he had partnered each and every female in the dream. All of them had flirted with him, the young girls with self-conscious blushes, and the older women with lightly veiled promise. He had known, in the dream, that when the sun went down, he would be dancing with them in another fashion entirely.

The second set of dreams had been even more explicit. He had been kidnapped by the Turks because it seemed that he was not Ivan's son, but the son of their Great Sultan. He had been presented with four wives and a harem of one hundred other beauties—and then the Great Sultan had sat down with him, telling him that he had something serious to speak with Ilya about. "I am old and no longer able to father children," the old man had said sadly, the white beard on his chin wagging comically with every word. "You are my only surviving son, and there must be other heirs as soon as possible. Ilya, you must go in to your harem and strive among the women until every one of them carries your child—and you must not come out again until you have accomplished this mighty deed!'' Then the sultan had taken him to the door of the harem and locked it behind him, leaving him alone with a hundred and four luscious girls, of all shapes, colors, and types, all dressed in little more than beads and scraps of silk.

That, sadly, was when he woke up. He'd gone back to sleep immediately, but instead of returning to the harem, he'd dreamed of the Firebird again. This time, to his disappointment, she was more birdlike than maiden, and she had carried a ripe cherry in her beak. She had swooped down toward him and he had opened his mouth like a baby bird—and as if she was feeding him, she had dropped the cherry into his open mouth. He could still taste the sweet juice of it. . . .

Now that is entirely too strange a dream, he thought, throwing the blankets aside. Or rather, trying to throw the blankets aside. He and they were so inextricably tangled that he couldn't just throw them off, he had to wrestle with them until he could get free.

He ran his hands over the tangle and sighed. *I am never going to be able to get to sleep again like this.* There was only one possible remedy, and that was to open the shutters and let some moonlight in so that he could see to straighten his blankets. They didn't let him have a candle and striker anymore, for fear he'd set the house afire. If he opened the shutters, that would let cold air in, too, but it couldn't be helped.

Maybe I ought to take to sleeping on the stove at night, too. . . . When he opened the shutters, a blast of cold air hit him and almost made him yelp, which might have awakened someone. It was in biting back that reaction that he happened to look down on the windowsill.

There, on the sill, red-black in the moonlight and shining as if it had been polished, was a single ripe cherry. A bead of juice or dew clung to the top, where the stem would have been.

He couldn't stop himself; it was as if he was in a dream, where he was compelled to do something he knew he shouldn't, but his limbs no longer obeyed the commands of his head. He reached out, picked up the tiny piece of fruit, and lifted it to his mouth.

When he bit down on it, the juice filled his mouth with sweet-sour flavor, exactly as it had in the dream. And, as in the dream, there was no stone to this cherry, for some sharp instrument (like a beak?) had already extracted it.

For a brief moment, his entire being filled with euphoria, a heady intoxication that was very similar to the way he'd felt in the orchard just before he'd seen the Firebird.

First the dream, then the cherry, now the intoxication. What was behind all of this?

Then the moment passed, leaving him standing in the moonlight, shivering from the cold breeze entering the window, with a bed to make up. And there was no sign of the cherry he'd just eaten except a few lingering fragrances—they were too fleeting and fugitive to be flavors—caressing the back of his tongue.

He turned away from the window, put his bed to right, and closed the shutters. He felt his way back to the bed and fell into it, fully expecting to lie awake for the rest of the night, but in fact the opposite occurred. He slept so late that if he had been Ilya instead of "the Fool," he'd have gotten into trouble. He didn't remember any dreams, not even fragments. Not a single girl from either of his previous dreams appeared, even for a moment. And since the only girls he *was* getting these days were the ones in his dreams, even in sleep he felt a deep frustration.

He was still tired when he did wake, and he resolved to be lazy for the rest of the morning. He hadn't managed to fasten his shutter properly last night, and a cold wind had penetrated into his room, leaving a drift of snow on the floor. When he convinced himself to get out of bed, he couldn't even have a wash, for the water in his pitcher had frozen. Right now, the top of the warm stove sounded very good indeed.

He dressed carelessly and drooped into the great hall. No one paid any attention to him at all; he intercepted a servant with plates of pancakes and helped himself, seizing a plate and heaping it high with buttered cakes and honey, taking his booty up to his accustomed perch to eat without disturbance. He was beginning to appreciate that there were advantages to being the Fool as well as disadvantages: He could take whatever food he wanted, even before the tsar got to taste it, and no one rebuked him. He could set his plate down on top of the stove and his food stayed warm for the entire meal.

It looked as if everyone else had suffered a frustrating night; the warriors all had hangovers from their drinking, his brothers had dark circles under their eyes and barked at one another, and even the tsarina was listless, picking at her food without really tasting it.

That was a shame, since the cooks had made a splendid meal. Of course, he'd gotten the best of it; perhaps the cakes that reached the tsar's table were cold or burned.

Well, serve them all right.

He stuffed himself with pancakes, eating until he couldn't touch another morsel. Then, as had become his habit, he tossed the remains to the hounds who gathered below him expectantly, awaiting the distribution of what he didn't want. Sometimes he acted as if he were a priest distributing alms to them, which the warriors seemed to find screamingly funny.

The dogs leapt for the fragments as they fell, tails wagging, but with a minimum of growling. They were in good humor this morning, even if the humans were not.

"Not bad!" said one, nosing among the reeds for the pancake bit. *"The Boy-on-the-stove is a generous one, there's butter on these cakes! Oh, good, good, good!"*

"Oh, yes!" chorused another joyfully. *"There is butter, you can taste it, smell it! Rich butter, lovely butter! I'd eat a brick if they'd butter it!"*

"I'd eat a log if they'd butter it," a third said wistfully, having nosed under the table too late to set a tooth to the coveted pancake fragments.

"I'd eat a featherbed if they'd butter it," put in a fourth, at which point all the hounds laughed as if he had told a tremendous joke.

"But you already did eat a featherbed, Silk-ear," the first laughed, explaining the joke. *"And you did it without butter!"*

Ilya sat very quietly, almost as surprised by what the dog said as by the fact that it was talking and he could understand it. Ilya recalled very well the incident in question, and it was a good thing for Silk-ear that the tsarina had no clear evidence of the identity of the criminal, or Silk-ear would have ended up as part of a meat pie. Or at the very least, his skin would have become a hawking-glove.

Ilya felt his mouth falling open, and quickly shut it. He lay down on the top of the stove, but not for his intended nap. He could hardly believe his ears, but the evidence was incontrovertible.

He'd heard the dogs talking—not a single horse talking only to him this time, but *all* of the dogs, conversing among themselves. As he continued to listen, it occurred to him that he was actually hearing two things: the panting and whining of adult dogs, and over the top of that, the voices speaking in a way he understood. This could *not* be his mind playing tricks on him, for there was no way for him to know which dog had ruined the tsarina's featherbed—and there was no reason for his mind to have recalled that incident.

He rolled over on his back—still hearing the dogs talking to one another: quarreling briefly over a bit of meat, planning to trip one of the servers if they could to get more of the pancakes.

I must be going mad, he thought abstractly. *Hearing the horse—that was the first sign of it. And now I'm going mad. . . .*

Fear sent shivers over his body in spite of the warmth of the stove. It was one thing to pretend to madness, but quite another to actually *be* mad.

"*Ha,*" said one of the dogs, right below his head. "*You have the fear-smell, Boy-on-the-stove.*"

He looked cautiously over the edge; one of the borzoi, the white wolfhounds, was looking up at him, tail wagging slowly.

"*You have the fear-smell,*" the dog repeated, looking up into his eyes. "*But there is nothing to be afraid of.*"

"I can hear you," he whispered, knowing that the others would only take it for more of his lunacy if they heard him.

Only this time, is it real lunacy?

"*Of course you can hear me, foolish boy,*" the wolfhound replied impatiently. "*You ate the Firebird's gift; I can smell it on your breath. You can hear all of us now, if you want to listen. But the fear-smell is disturbing the others; if you are going to smell of fear, you should take yourself somewhere else.''*

With that, the great, graceful dog, marked with a red leather collar as the pack-leader, turned and stalked away. Ilya stared after him, too astounded to move.

CHAPTER FIVE

THE HARVEST was over, the frosts turned to snow, the butchering done, and winter was fully upon them. It was still possible to hunt, though, and Ilya's brothers were out every day, bringing back deer and bear, rabbits and duck and geese, boar and great white-winged swans, as if they intended to single-handedly denude the forest, fields, and lakes of game. Perhaps they were taking out their own frustrations and anger on nature, since they could no longer do so on Ilya.

Breakfast was over, the brothers were gone, and Ilya reclined on the top of the stove, vaguely aware that there was some excitement among the animals, but too sleepy after a night of Firebird-chasing dreams to pay too much attention. Slowly, gradually, he had come to accept that he could hear and understand what animals said—and that if he *was* a little crazy, at least it was a useful kind of madness.

The dogs tended to get excited about very minor things, so he wasn't too concerned about what they had to say this morning. They were jabbering to one another now about preparations for a feast, but to the dogs, almost any large meal looked like a feast. Any time hunting was good and it looked as though more than one kind of meat was going to be served— particularly if it was game with large bones that they would get to chew when the humans were done—they thought it was a feast.

He liked the dogs, on the whole, but he had discovered that he had to make allowances for them. They were quite kind and protective where he was concerned, and careful about keeping him informed of the state of his brothers' tempers, but they weren't too bright, and they had trouble remembering anything that took place more than a week ago. In a dog's world, only three states existed: "now," "in a while," and "forever." If someone left, he was gone "forever," and when he returned they rejoiced as much as if he were back from the dead precisely because he'd been gone "forever." This would have been sad if they hadn't existed in a state of continuous optimism, certain that something good was going to happen in the next few moments. It took a lot, Ilya had learned, to break a dog's spirit. Not even his brothers had managed; only continuous and unrelenting cruelty could do it, and bad as they were, his brothers just weren't able to sustain that level of cruelty.

But when the cats started to gossip, Ilya woke from his half-doze and took notice. The cats never paid attention to anything that the humans did unless it was new and different.

"So what do you think Kicks-at-everything told Cries-a-lot?" the cat on the bench in front of the stove told the tabby that had just leapt up to join Ilya. "Kicks-at-everything" was Ivan, of course, and "Cries-a-lot" was the tsarina, who used tears in a futile effort to get her own way. *"He said they'd found a mate for one of the Monsters!"*

"No!" gasped the cat cuddling up beside Ilya, her eyes going round with astonishment. The "Monsters" were Ilya's brothers, a category from which he was excluded. The cats had adopted the dogs' name for him of "Boy-on-the-stove."

"You don't say!" the tabby continued. *"Who would be stupid enough to send them a mate? The Monsters should have been drowned at birth, not allowed to grow up and then mated!"*

"I don't know, but it must have been someone very far away," said the first cat, a privileged female who was allowed to grace the tsarina's lap because she was pure white, graceful, and had exquisite manners. *"But they are both very excited. The mate is coming soon, they said. Already there is excitement in the kitchen, and soon there will be much food."*

Ilya slipped down off the stove and left it to the cats; the white one jumped up to join her friend in a cozy gossip-session, casting Ilya a look of gratitude for his consideration in making room for her. They didn't have anything more of interest for him, since their speculations, like those of the dogs, had gone on to possible feasts and what might be filched from the kitchen or table during the confusion.

The tsar had found a wife for one of his brothers! That was fairly amazing—and it couldn't possibly be for any of the three oldest, since a wife would bring lands as her dowry, which would make them technically independent of Ivan. The tsar would never give them that much incentive to rebel, not after Pietor's defection. So it must be for one of the younger boys. Alexi, perhaps? Or Boris? Surely not Yuri. . . .

Well, there was one way to find out; if the dogs and cats knew, the next place for word to come would be among the tsarina's women, who would gossip to their maids, who would take it to the rest of the women of the household. It was time to head for the kitchen. Orders would already have been given to start baking—a wedding would mean a series of feasts, and much of the baking would have to be done ahead of time or there would never be enough bread, buns, and cakes. By now, the kitchen-staff would not only know *why*, they would probably have most of the details.

Ilya dawdled, even though he wanted to go there directly, because a fool never did anything directly. He happened to pass by a door and peeked out because it was the sort of thing a fool would do, and saw without much surprise that a light snow was falling, adding a new dusting of white to the layer already on the ground. Well, the cats were right about one thing—this new bride would probably be arriving very soon, if she was going to travel at all before spring.

He was a regular fixture in the kitchen now; he wandered through the orderly chaos, being avoided by the servants and cursed absently when he could not be avoided, until he got to his special kitchen-corner by the baking ovens. On his way there he filched a honey-cake from a tray left to cool, also because it was expected of him. The head cook swung her wooden spoon at his snatching fingers and missed, then went on with her conversation as if she had swatted at a fly rather than a person.

"So when he went off to the horse-fair, old Ivan managed to find not only a boyar with nothing but one daughter to wed off, but one who was stupid enough to wed the girl to one of *his* sons?'' the chief cook laughed. ''If I hadn't heard it from you, Anastasia, I wouldn't have believed it!''

''Well, if the rest of what I've heard is true, it's not surprising the old man is trusting her to little Boris,'' the maidservant said, taking a bite from a currant-bun and speaking through a mouthful of bread. ''They say she looks like a sow, with the temper of a mouse, and has the brains of a goose. Even *with* her dowry, they say he couldn't get anyone but Ivan to take her. No one else is that desperate.''

''Or that cunning,'' the cook retorted. ''That's one boy that won't have to be provided for, *and* the lands are too far away for Ivan to have to worry about his son going to war against him or running home to escape his wife.''

Ilya finished his cake and drifted back out, but a strange sadness made him seek his room rather than going back to his spot on the stove. Just at the moment, he didn't want to be around people at all.

So Boris was going to find himself shackled to a fat, ugly, timid, and stupid bride! Ilya felt more sorry for the girl than for his brother. Wedding vows were not going to make much of a change in Boris's habits, and it was entirely possible that his dear brother would start looking for ways to eliminate the boyar himself as soon as he settled in with his new bride. He certainly wasn't going to stop chasing girls, and Ilya doubted that he'd visit his bride's bed for longer than it took to get a son on her.

Ilya opened the shutters just a crack, wrapped blankets around his shoulders, and sat watching the snow fall.

It was barely possible that the boyar wasn't just desperate, he was cunning too, more cunning than Ivan. After all, accidents could happen to anyone. Once Boris produced a son, he was—well—superfluous. It would be supremely ironic for Boris to be plotting to get rid of his father-in-law while the father-in-law was plotting to be rid of Boris. *Old age and treachery will overcome youth and treachery every time,* Ilya thought cynically. *The old ones have had more experience, and it wouldn't take much to be smarter than Boris.*

Oh, what a family he had, that he should be thinking these things! He wished, as he had often wished in the past, that he had been born into a common household. Ivan might have even been a good father, if he hadn't had land and wealth. If he'd been a simple warrior, for instance, he would have welcomed the birth of each son as an addition to his fighting-force, and he would have trained them all to work together instead of plotting against one another. *We'd have been quite a force to reckon with,* Ilya thought wistfully, as he imagined what they all would have looked like, armored-up and standing behind Ivan, shoulder-to-shoulder. *We'd have had our pick of loot and girls—we could have gone fighting the Turks instead of the neighbors. We could have had songs written about us, and maybe even gone into the service of the Great Tsar. Mischa would have been our champion, I would have been the one to negotiate our fee—it could have been good.*

Ivan could have done that in any case; he could have seen his sons as assets and protection instead of rivals as greedy as he was. Ivan and his eight sons could have become legends, the sort that fathers told their children about to show them how important loyalty was. But Ivan had been born greedy, and he'd grown up greedy and wanting more, seeing rivals even in his own sons for the wealth and land he'd accumulated. Ilya sighed. Granted, his life had been comfortable, but he would have traded any amount of comfort for a life with fewer enemies among his own kin.

He certainly felt sorry for the poor girl who was coming into this with no notion of what she was about to get involved with. Even if she'd been clever and pretty, it would have been hard on her; Boris had plenty of clever, pretty girls to tumble, and he didn't have to go out of his way to please any of them. To tame Boris to her hand, she'd have had to be stunningly beautiful, clever and intelligent, and far more cunning and crafty than anyone here. Ugly and stupid—well, he could only hope that she was too stupid to be made unhappy by this, that she was so stupid that the mere possession of a matron's status and a wedding band would please her, because Boris certainly wasn't going to.

THE new bride, Katya, arrived with her father and his escort some weeks later, just before noon, in a light snowstorm. Since her father was a mere boyar, Ivan was not going to unbend an inch to meet them outside; he set himself and his family up in the great hall with the uneasy bridegroom firmly at his side, between himself and the tsarina. Waiting with them were all the wedding guests Ivan had invited, and most of the household. It made for quite a crowd, and there were servants peeking in from every doorway. Ilya watched their reception in the great hall from his place on the stove.

First came the boyar's escort, with tokens of the dowry and gifts for the tsar and his family; older men with long beards and serious expressions, they brought in rolls of legal contracts that Ivan barely glanced at, which was hardly surprising since he couldn't read, and lists of the properties that would be settled on the bride, which he also ignored. Everything that needed to be read he quickly passed on to the steward, who *could* read, and who would see to it that everything that had been agreed upon was there. More to the point at this moment, so far as the tsar was concerned, were the fine gifts, which Ivan seized with greed. The gifts were quite generous—silver goblets for himself and the tsarina, a belt of silver for himself and a massive necklace of amber and silver for the tsarina, a fine sword for Boris, and fur coats for the other sons.

When Ilya saw that last, a little of his family's greed rubbed off on him. He knew very well that if Ivan had anything to say about it, Ilya would never see so much as a scrap of fur. *I need that coat! I haven't had a new coat in years, and no one is going to waste one on me now that I'm the Fool!* He clenched his jaw and was determined that he should have his share. He jumped down off the stove and made his way through the crowd, reaching the wedding-party just as the boyar arrived at the last coat with no more sons being in evidence. "But don't you have seven sons still?" the boyar began, puzzled.

"Yes, but—" Ivan reached for the coat. "I'll—"

Ilya gave a great whoop and leapt forward, snatching up the coat and whirling it into a dance before throwing it over his shoulders.

"This must be the bride!" he crowed, giving the astonished boyar a great, smacking kiss. "Whoo, Boris! She's a saucy one! She'll set you a pretty dance, for sure!"

He turned to the poor, bewildered girl and seized her hand, pumping it with great enthusiasm. Poor thing; she was just as ugly and fat as she'd been painted, and from the dull, dazed look in her eyes, just as stupid as well. "Welcome to the family, Papa!" he shouted. "We'll be glad to have that pretty girl among us, you bet!"

Then he capered off, back to the stove, where he took off his coat and pillowed his head on it while the entire company stared. There hadn't been such a profound silence in the great hall since the day that Pietor rebelled and ran off.

The tsarina cleared her throat in the silence. "That is the middle son, Ilya," she said, with a malicious glance at Ivan. "I fear he is rather—simple."

"An accident! A blow to the head, and he lost his wits!" the tsar proclaimed hastily, as the boyar began to look as if he was thinking twice about this particular bargain. "A terrible thing, but it could have happened to anyone, and as you can see, the rest of my boys are a fine set of strapping, handsome, healthy fellows—especially young Boris here. . . ."

Ilya lounged at his leisure, ignoring the stares of the strangers and Ivan's near-frantic cajolery. He had mastered the art of seeming to stare at the ceiling while watching the room out of the corner of his eye. Ivan was certainly dancing a merry jig, trying to salvage the situation! The tsarina wasn't helping, either; she kept inserting little comments about "poor Ilya" that were intended to alarm rather than to soothe. And if the boyar had really cared anything about his daughter, the wedding would probably have been canceled right then and there.

But Ilya had been watching the party carefully, and had the feeling that there was more than met the eye here. His suspicions were confirmed when the boyar launched into a speech that sounded suspiciously rehearsed, just as Ivan began outlining the festivities to come.

"My friend," the boyar said, his face a mask of mock-regret, "I fear that I must return to my lands and leave my dear daughter in your hands. It breaks my heart not to see her wed—but terrible disasters occurred just before we left, and I cannot even stay the night. Had this blessed event not been of such great import to both our families, I should have asked you to postpone it until spring, but I know I can trust you to do all that is proper. . . ."

As the tsar stood there with his mouth agape in shock, the

boyar continued on in the same vein, edging toward the door as he spoke. He had obviously had this planned from the beginning, although the poor daughter clearly had no idea that this was going to happen, and stood, trembling, clinging to the arm of her elderly maid with her face going blotchy as she suppressed tears.

So dear Boris is not to go live with his father-in-law after all! The boyar is much cleverer than my father—

"And of course, in the spring, when our children are ready to start their own household on their new lands, we will be prepared to help them build their new home, the home they will share together—"

Which means that there is no house on those lands, no servants, no serfs, no livestock. No farms, perhaps? It makes one wonder—wide acreage is a fine thing, provided it isn't all swampland, or likely to flood at the lightest rain, or so full of rocks it's impossible to plow.

"—and now, I must bid you all farewell. No, we cannot waste another moment, urgent that we return—" With that and other such protestations, the boyar and his men detached themselves from the wedding party and all but ran out the door, leaving the tear-streaked, confused bride, her party of servants—a couple of dim-looking fellows who might have been kitchen-boys conscripted to play guards, and a single, elderly lady-in-waiting—and a pile of wedding gifts. And Ivan, who had gathered all of his relatives and allies as witnesses, was left to try and make the best of it. Silence as thick as a midwinter snowfall descended on the great hall, broken only by the whiny sniffling of the bride.

Before Ivan could say or do anything, the sound of rapidly retreating hoofbeats told everyone there just how eager the boyar had been to make his escape.

Ivan turned red, then white, then red again—and strangely enough, it was the tsarina who salvaged the situation.

"Well!" she said brightly. "I am sure that it is unfortunate for Katya's poor, dear father to have to return so quickly to his own land, but that is no reason why all of us should not celebrate such a *wonderful* occasion as fully as if he was here with us in body, as I am certain he is in spirit!" She left Ivan's side and took the arm of the unfortunate maiden, who timidly allowed herself to be led forward. "Come, Katya!" she proclaimed in ringing tones. "You shall have the place of honor beside me!"

She led the girl to the head table and sat her in the place her own chief lady usually had, leaving Ivan and Boris to sullenly take their own seats. "Let the feast begin!" she called gaily, quite taking over the proceedings as the remainder of Katya's escort were left to find their own seats among Ivan's people.

The poor maiden's blotchy face and dim eyes brightened a bit at the sight of all the food. Ilya acted as he was expected to, snatching what he wanted from the platters being carried by. At this point, several of the servants had made it a habit to pause briefly beside the stove to give him a chance to snatch; Ilya had the feeling that it tickled their fancy that the Fool got his pick before the tsar did. Before long, Ilya had his plate full of goodies, and could sit back in the shadows, munching and watching at his leisure.

Ivan was furious, that much was obvious. He knew now that he'd been duped, that the boyar had dumped an unwanted and unmarriageable daughter on him. He couldn't read the dowry list or the deeds to the property, but he probably figured it was worth about as much as the daughter, no matter *what* it said on the paper. He wasn't going to get rid of Boris without a fight, if that was the case, for Boris was hardly going to relish going off to build his own house in the middle of a swamp or a field full of rocks. That meant, instead of getting rid of a son, Ivan was now stuck with a useless cow of a daughter-in-law.

But Ivan was never one to give up, especially not when he'd been gotten the better of. He had revenge as a motive now, and as the evening wore on, Ilya saw the signs that his brain was stirring. It might take him a while to work it out, but by spring, he'd have found a way to get back at the boyar.

Boris, meanwhile, was just as furious and disgusted as well. Ilya didn't know what the tsar had told him about his prospective bride, but he'd bet it was nothing like the reality sitting at his mother's left hand. At this point, he was trying to think of a way to get rid of the girl and get back at his father, but Boris's brains were duller than Ivan's, and he probably wouldn't have an answer before Ivan did.

The tsarina was in her element, full of malicious enjoyment. She was the happiest person in the hall at this point. She had a palace full of people here to impress, and Ivan wouldn't dare do anything to her until they were gone, or all the festivities would grind to a halt and make him look even more a fool than he did already. She and she alone had the power to turn this fiasco into something better than it was, and she knew it. The new bride was worse than anyone had dreamed, and that meant that *she* would not be eclipsed in her own home by the newcomer; not even a wedding-day was going to make this girl shine, and the real star of the wedding would be the tsarina. Assuming the girl could actually *do* anything besides eat, the tsarina could make another handmaiden out of her. This might well be the happiest moment in her marriage to Ivan, for she had some splendid new gifts, and if she managed to turn this disaster into any kind of celebration so that people forgot or overlooked the fact that Ivan had clearly been duped, Ivan would be in debt to her. For once, *she* had the upper hand, and she was going to use that power for all she was worth.

The other brothers were jabbing one another with their elbows and making pig-faces (and probably grunting noises), united in relief that *they* weren't the ones being married off to Katya.

And as for the bride herself, she was finding solace for her vague griefs in her plate, literally inhaling everything that landed on it. She refused nothing, and the tsarina smiled poisonously as she heaped the girl's plate from every platter that came to the head table.

Poor thing, Ilya thought more than once as he watched the scene being played out in front of him. *Poor, poor thing. She has no idea what she's gotten involved in. Boris* will *marry her; he'll have no choice in the matter, unless some family disaster here makes it impossible. And short of someone dying or the barns burning down, I can't see that happening. I hope she doesn't fall in love with him, but I'm afraid she's going to, and unless Father finds a way to convince him, I doubt that the marriage is ever going to be consummated. I'll bet he spends his bridal night with one of the shepherdesses.*

Someone—probably the elderly lady-in-waiting—had taken pains to make Katya presentable. Sadly, it was a lost cause. Her hair, lank and thin, was of no color at all, and twining her braids around her head and surmounting her hair with a round headdress only made her head look rounder. Her face, puffy and vacant, was the color of dough, and her tiny eyes resembled a pair of currants sunk deep into it. Her nose was red and turned up at the tip, her mouth large, her teeth bad, probably from eating too many sweets. The fine blue wool tunic she wore strained over her pillow-breasts and barely contained the rest of her. Her clothing could have been cut down to fit three of the tsarina's women, and Ilya had to wonder if that was exactly what the tsarina had in mind in being so superficially kind to her. Would Katya's wardrobe shrink, as the wardrobes of the tsarina and her ladies grew?

No matter what happened here, Katya was the one who would suffer the most, and she was the one who deserved it the least.

Ilya lost his appetite, and decided to take himself into the kitchen. He slid down off the stove, taking his platter and his new fur coat with him. He might want the former, and he knew that if he abandoned the latter, someone would happily purloin it. He slid deftly and silently in between the hurrying servants, not playing the Fool because they wouldn't notice in their hurry, and tucked himself into the corner beside the oven.

Here in the kitchen at least, people were acting more normally. There wasn't the high-pitched, nervous chatter that there was out in the great hall, as Ivan's people tried to guess which way Ivan would jump, and strangers tried to make the best of a miserable situation. As platters came back from the hall, the servants seized them and divided the contents among themselves according to some arcane system only they understood. Here where people were talking normally, even laughing and enjoying themselves, Ilya was able to relax, too, and reapply himself to his food.

"Holy Mother, did you see that *bride?*" someone said, causing a flurry of laughter to erupt.

"I'd say Ivan got a bargain," someone else called. "He's

got three wenches in one for Boris! Too bad he can't divide her up and marry off Alexi and Yuri too!''

"She's easy to please, at any rate," one of the younger serving-girls piped up. "No turning up her nose at anything we've served her, and no complaints that something's a bit burned or the like. In fact, I don't think I've heard her say two words all night.''

"Well, *I've* been serving her escort, and they say the boyar's got a pretty little widow with property back at his home that he wants to wed, but *she* wouldn't share the house with the girl," said another in a carrying voice. "That's why he's hurrying back, and not some disaster at home, unless it would be that the widow would marry elsewhere while he's gone— the sooner home, the sooner wedded and bedded, and he's looking to make himself a son as fast as he can get himself between the sheets.''

"Oooh! Won't *that* be one in the eye for Ivan!" The cook herself chuckled. "Mark my words, he's been planning on getting the boyar's lands for Boris; now all he'll have is a great lump of uncooked dough and whatever bits of howling wilderness her father fobbed off on him!''

The kitchen was taking as much malicious pleasure in Ivan's downfall as the tsarina, and with as much cause.

So, the poor girl was as unwanted at home as she was here. Ilya felt even more sorry for her. For once there was going to be someone who was more despised in the palace than he was, and from the sound of it, her father didn't care any more for her than her father-in-law did. Small wonder she took refuge in her food.

THREE days of festivities had been scheduled before the wedding; everyone knew it, and Ivan could hardly get by with less. Boris stamped around with a face as black as a thundercloud, the rest of the brothers made every kind of tasteless joke imaginable, and the bride was so shy in the company of nothing but strangers that she would have hidden behind her maidservant if it had been possible. In a pretty girl, such shyness would have been sweet; in Katya, it was ludicrous and exasperating. It was hard to tell if Katya really understood how matters stood, or if she was just incredibly timid.

The first day was supposed to be a day of games and contests among the young men—mock-fights, tests of strength and endurance, all designed to make Boris look valiant, young, strong, and show him off like a hot stallion. But Boris did not deign to participate, although the prizes were good. Instead, he stood by himself on the sidelines, with his arms crossed and his hat pulled low over his eyes, while he glowered at all and sundry. The rest of the young men ran and jumped, tossed javelins at targets and battled in the snow with a will, while the poor, fat bride watched them without comprehension and bestowed the prizes with a trembling, pudgy hand when her maidservant prompted her. Rolled up in a cape of white wolf and ermine, she looked like a snowbank herself. Ilya, bundled warmly in his new coat and festooned with gaudy rags and his ridiculous hat, hung about the sidelines and watched his brothers carefully, figuring that their minds were already tuned to mischief, and waiting to see if he or the new bride was going to be the target.

They were indeed plotting trouble; the first prank that they devised was one he could do nothing about, though it was extremely cruel. Singly and together, they got the bride alone for a few moments and assured her that Boris was madly in love with her, and that the reason he was so sullen and quiet was because he was so overcome by passion for her that he didn't know what to say or do in her presence.

Now, Ruslan had always told Ilya that every woman, no matter how ugly, *wants* to believe that a man somewhere could love her, and poor Katya was no exception. So when Boris's brothers, all but the Fool, came to her assuring her with every possible oath that Boris, golden, handsome Boris, was mad for her—well, given her extraordinary stupidity, how could she *not* believe them? It was a tale of magic come true for Katya, and unlike Ivan's family, she believed in magic.

The fruits of their labor manifested that very night, at the feast that followed the games. In an attempt to make herself beautiful in the eyes of her betrothed, Katya succeeded only in making a spectacle of herself. Festooned with enough necklaces and bracelets to open a small shop, pudgy hands covered with rings, with her lank, colorless hair braided with red silk ribbons and wearing a scarlet-embroidered skirt and tunic, top-ping it all with a gaudy shawl worthy of a gypsy, with fringes twice as long as any other woman's, she attracted stares and snickers the moment she entered the room. And small wonder: She resembled nothing so much as one of the egg-shaped nesting-dolls given to little girls to play with. And oh, how she flirted and coquetted with Boris, who kept taking horrified glances at her and seeking salvation in the bottom of his wine cup.

But Ivan was in better humor with Katya and her father tonight; he'd had the deeds of the land she'd been dowered with examined carefully by his steward and a few of his poorer relatives—all people so impoverished and dependent on his goodwill that he felt safe in taking them into his confidence. Although all of it was wilderness, most of it was *not* swamp. It was, in fact, very valuable hardwood forest, and the source of all the skins for the fabulous fur capes and coats that Katya owned and that had been given as gifts. So he encouraged the poor girl in her delusions, filling her cup over and over again with particularly potent honey-wine, joking crudely about the kind of husband that Boris would make. Ilya cringed, and left the room early; the girl was drunk before the meal was half over, making a clumsy fool of herself, and unaware that people were choking down their laughter with their food.

It was obvious to Ilya that his brothers had found an entirely new and novel target for their humor. He would have liked to speak with either Ruslan or Father Mikail about the situation, but Ruslan was temporarily banished to the woods, because the boyar and all his people were sturdy Christians, and Father Mikail was taken up with the preparations for the wedding. There was no one he could turn to for advice. Mother Galina was completely uninterested in Katya's fate.

It was a real pity for the girl's sake that Ivan hadn't arranged to wed her to Ilya instead of Boris. Not that even the boyar would have put up with having a fool for a son-in-law—his expression had made that much clear when Ilya had pulled his own little prank to get his coat. But Ilya would at least have been kind to the poor thing, and tried to see to it that his brothers didn't torment her too much.

I would have taken her away to her dower-land, even in the middle of winter, even if we had to live in a wooden hut, he thought glumly. *Perhaps if she was happy, she wouldn't need to eat so much. Certainly having to work as hard as any peasant in the winter would slim her down!* If she wasn't the girl of Ilya's dreams, he would at least have kept his frolics with the peasant-girls discreet—unlike Boris, who would probably send her out of the bed-chamber so he could use it with one of his leman!

He decided to stroll around the palace in the dark; it wasn't really *dark* outside tonight—there was a full moon, and the moonlight reflecting from the snow made it almost as bright as day.

A peal of laughter rang out from the great hall, and Ilya had no doubt who had caused it. Poor Katya!

The great wolfhound, chief of the pack, joined him in his stroll. *"The new fat one is kind,"* he remarked to Ilya. *"I'm glad she's here. She saves bones for us, and slips us bits of good things under the table."*

Ilya looked down on the borzoi's long, lean head, and the dog's great, liquid eyes looked up at him. "She's going to need friends like you and the rest," he told the wolfhound. "No one else likes her, and the one they mean to mate her with hates her."

The dog wasn't surprised, for nothing much surprised a dog—it requires imagination to be surprised, and as Ilya had learned, they hadn't any. *"Stupid,"* he remarked. *"If they're going to mate her, they should treat her properly. Fat ones make good mothers."*

"Well, if Boris has anything to say about it, she won't get the chance to prove that," Ilya replied sourly. "You dogs ought to keep her company if you can. She'll be good to you."

The borzoi snorted agreement, then caught the scent of something interesting off in the direction of the river and loped off to investigate. Ilya continued his walk, ignored by the guards.

If only she wasn't so *stupid*. He would have been happy to let her in on his secret and at least keep her company if she hadn't been so appallingly stupid! He would have been glad to have someone besides Galina, Ruslan, and Mikail to talk to, but there wasn't much doubt that her head was as empty of thoughts as a blown egg.

When does pity call for self-sacrifice? he asked himself, as he trudged through the snow. *I feel sorry for her, but—the only way to keep her from my brothers' pranks is to put myself in their way, and I'm not sure I want to do that.*

Then again, this was supposed to be the poor creature's wedding-festival, the *one* time in her life when she should have a little happiness. Would it hurt him so much to try and give her that? It could be his wedding-gift to her, though she wouldn't recognize it and wouldn't appreciate it. The Holy Virgin Herself knew that, as soon as the wedding was over and Katya found out just how much Boris detested her, she would be made thoroughly miserable.

Let her have her happiness for a little. Even if that happiness is based on a lie. It could be worse for her. At least she's so fat that if Boris takes a stick to her, it probably won't hurt her as much as it would a thinner girl. He winced at that cruel thought. *Well, maybe I can save her from that, too. If it looks as if Boris is going to beat her, I'll get him to chase me until he's tired. Blessed Elijah knows I can outrun any of them now, I've had so much practice at it.* He looked up at the sky and the stars. *I hope you've noticed this, Holy God! I hope you're paying attention! Because I think I should have earned a chance to escape from here myself with all of this!*

With those virtuous resolutions firmly in his heart, he went straight to his bed. He couldn't get the girl out of the trouble she'd woven for herself tonight, but at least he could start "protecting" her in the morning.

And in the morning, he set straight out to do just that— only to discover that events had conspired against him. Or perhaps they had conspired *with* him, since his intention had been to make himself a target.

There seemed to be an unusual amount of noise as he made his way toward the great hall for his breakfast, and when he arrived there, he found out why. A wedding meant many feasts, including the great feast following the ceremony itself, and Ivan was no longer inclined to impoverish himself and deplete his stores of pork, beef, and fowl to provide those feasts. Last night after Ilya had left, Ivan had declared that there would be a great hunt, or rather, series of hunts, the next day, to provide the gathered throng with wild game for their tables. Virtually every man and even some of the women had greeted this announcement with a mingling of pleasure and relief—tempers were getting short as the tension around Ivan and Boris mounted. The folk in Katya's entourage found her behavior embarrassing, yet also felt guilt over not defending her; anyone who was out on the hunt wouldn't have to sit and watch her continue to make a fool of herself.

Every ridable horse in the stables was being saddled, all the dog-packs were ready and waiting out in front of the palace, and the hunters were catching a quick breakfast before going out ahorse or on foot to denude the countryside of game. Those servants who had no duties were going to course hare and rabbit. Lesser nobles were setting out afoot after game-birds. Those who were older, not so strong, and the women were taking the falcons to hunt flying game as well. One group of foolhardy, daring young men was going after bear. The rest were making up several mounted parties to chase deer and boar. The great hall was full of hearty, shouting men—and a sprinkling of women, just as hearty, if a bit more genteel. Even the space in front of the stove was crowded with a party of strangers, one of the groups Ivan had invited to the wedding. Ilya was about to retire to the dairy to ask advice of Mother Galina when hands seized both his elbows and he found himself sandwiched between Sasha and Mischa.

"So, Fool, care to join us on the hunt?" Mischa asked, baring his teeth in a feral smile. "I see you've got your coat and your knife—I think you must be."

Ilya let his jaw go slack. "Hunt? For what do we hunt?" He grinned vapidly. "I know a place where there is a hand-some flock of fish grazing; we could bag us a fine catch of fresh salmon out in the meadow!"

He wasn't about to get off that easily this morning. The brothers were obviously in a savage humor and looking for something to torment. Perhaps Ivan had warned them off Ka-tya until the wedding was over.

"We're hunting boar, little brother," Mischa replied silkily, his eyes narrowing as he feigned a feral smile. "Don't you want to hunt boar? You certainly like to eat it."

He nodded violently, hoping to appear cooperative, and thinking that God must have been listening a bit *too* closely to his thoughts last night. "Sure, boar! I can hunt boar! Just you watch me! I'm the best boar-hunter in Rus! I kill boar bare-handed! I kill bear boar-handed! Just you watch!"

"Good." Together, Mischa and Sasha propelled him through the crowd and out into the thin light of early morning, where a group of saddled horses was waiting. Before Ilya had a chance to say or do anything, he found himself up in the saddle, with Sasha at one foot and Mischa at the other. They were tying his legs to the stirrups, a move he found altogether disquieting.

"Ho, brothers!" he said, trying to sound jovial, "My boots are fine; they don't need polishing!"

"Relax, little brother," Mischa replied with a savage grin. "We're just making sure you'll get your chance to kill the boar. This way, the horse won't throw you off when he sees the boar and tries to run."

It was then that he saw that the horse they had put him on was one of the most skittish in the herd: young, just broken to saddle this year, and quite likely to be spooked by almost anything.

Except that it was also his friend from the apple-orchard, and *this* horse, at least, had his best interests at heart.

"Don't worry, boy," the horse said, rolling his eyes to look back at his rider. *"I think I know what they're up to. We'll play their little game, but we'll do it by our rules."*

That was all the horse had time to say before the boar-hunt was off, with the massive boar-hounds, all shoulders and jaws, ranging out in front of the horses, and the hunters carrying boar-spears and javelins at the ready. Ilya's horse was herded in front of Mischa's at the very rear of the group, and that told Ilya that all of this was his oldest brother's idea. He shouldn't be thrown—but when Mischa spooked his sorrel gelding, it was a good bet that he was meant to be stampeded through thickets of raking branches and possibly through some swampy areas as well. A skittish horse like this one could be counted on to try and scrape his rider off on tree-trunks, or knock him off with low-hanging branches. It was clear to him from Mischa's comment about his coat that his older brother intended the new coat to end up a ragged mess. That was

Mischa all over: If he could not have something, he would spoil it for the one who did have it.

"I'll do what I can to keep from bucking when he stings me, boy!" the horse called over his shoulder as the hounds belled ahead of them, signaling that they had found a scent-trail. *"I can't promise anything, though."*

The horses in front of them broke into a canter as the dog-pack broke into a run, giving tongue as they did so. Ilya caught sight of Mischa moving in on the gelding's flank with his riding-crop upraised. "Look out!" he warned the horse—and the crop came down on the gelding's rump with a savage slash.

The horse gave a very realistic shriek but managed not to buck. Instead, he put all of his energy into a great leap away from Mischa and tore off at an angle to the hunt at a full gallop.

"The Fool's horse is running away with him!" Mischa bellowed. "Send the dogs after them!"

This, of course, was the wrong way to stop a running horse, and Mischa very well knew it. But the rest of the party must have been in on the "joke," for somehow a group of mastiffs was pelting after the horse, baying on his heels. Ilya hung on for dear life, although it would have been a far worse case if the horse had really been running away with him. The gelding made every effort to keep his gallop smooth and to keep away from such obstacles as low-hanging branches, trees growing too closely together, and tangles of thorns. But the mastiffs baying and snapping at the horse's heels were enough to un-nerve any equine, and Ilya was amazed that his mount wasn't sent into hysterics. He looked back over his shoulder and saw that they had already outdistanced the "pursuing" hunters, who weren't making any kind of effort to keep up or come to the rescue. The dogs, however, didn't seem to notice.

"We'll see about this!" the horse snarled, and stopped, reared, and turned on his hind feet as soon as they were deep into the forest. It was a good thing that Ilya had been hanging on to the saddle with both hands, or he'd have had a leg wrenched out of its socket; the horse could move as quickly as a ferret, and he was in no mood to put up with the pack of mastiffs. He charged, and laying about him with hooves and

teeth, he scattered the dogs before him. He whirled again and faced the surprised and disorganized pack.

"What do you think you're doing, you idiots?" the horse snarled. *"This is your friend, the Boy-on-the-stove!"*

The pack-leader suddenly stopped in his tracks, sniffed loudly, and dropped his head and his ears. The rest followed his example. *"Beg pardon, boy,"* he whimpered subserviently. *"Hunt-master said to chase, we chased, you know—beg pardon—"*

The horse shook his head and neck violently so that its ears flapped and its mane whipped Ilya's hands. *"Well, now you know, so quit trying to bite my heels. The Monsters want him to get hurt, so we're going to make them think he's in trouble. Now, if you can manage to contain yourselves, I want you to follow me and bay as if you were chasing me."*

The dog's head came up, and his tail wagged slowly. *"We can do that, you bet! We can do that!"*

"All right, then—follow, and stop when I stop," the horse said, its good temper restored by their subservience. Its ears were up, and its tail flagged. It turned again and cantered off in a different direction, the hounds loping happily after, baying as if they were in full view of a boar.

The horse changed its course at random, apparently only doing so when he heard the hounds of the rest of the hunt belling in the distance. Ilya began to enjoy the ride, for the gelding had an easy canter, fast enough to be exciting, comfortable enough that Ilya was in no discomfort from the position he was forced by his bindings to assume. Although he had lost his hat, the upturned collar of his coat kept his ears warm, and although there no longer seemed to be any sun, it was still a good day for a ride.

Once the gelding was fairly certain there would be no pursuit, he slowed to a brisk walk, with the baying dogs trotting alongside, their tongues hanging out of their mouths.

Ilya hoped that the horse had some notion of how to find its way back, for he had never seen this part of the forest before. It didn't look to him as if anyone had ever hunted it this season: Snow lay untouched and pristine everywhere except on the game-trails, and there it was broken only by the tracks of wild animals. The mastiffs stared wistfully off after these tracks, but remained dutifully at the horse's side. The rest of the forest was heavily overgrown, and the light that filtered through interlacing branches of conifers and leafless hardwoods seemed unusually dim.

Finally the horse stopped in a small clearing where many game-trails crossed, and addressed the dogs. *"You can go back now,"* the horse said. *"Or go chase whatever you please."*

The mastiffs needed no second invitation. With the leader loping through the snow, they headed off down one of the other game-trails, noses to the ground, tails waving.

"Now, boy, you can untie your feet and we can be more comfortable," the horse said. He cocked his head and swiveled his ears to the side. *"I hear the hunt, but they aren't close enough to worry about. Maybe a couple of leagues away."*

"You can hear things that far away?" Ilya said, astonished, as he bent down, and with fingers still stiff from holding onto the saddle, worked the knots on his right leg loose and untied his right foot from the stirrup. The horse snorted.

"I can hear things farther away than that!" he said scornfully. *"Now, this is my idea. We'll wander about here until dusk, browse where we can find food, then go in the direction I last heard the hunt. Sooner or later, I'll scent the horse-scat, we'll hit their trail or our own, and we can follow it back home."*

Well, that sounded just like the idea that a horse would come up with, but since he couldn't think of anything better, he might as well go along with it. "So long as we don't go in circles," Ilya replied with a shrug, freeing his other foot. He shoved the pieces of rope into his pocket so that he could tie his legs back onto the stirrups later. Mischa shouldn't get the idea that he had enough wits to free himself. "I've heard of people who are lost going in circles for hours. I don't think either of us wants to meet a wolf-pack after dark."

He didn't bother to mention that only the horse would be browsing, and that he hadn't had anything to eat since last night. He wouldn't starve to death in a single day, and although being out in the cold on an empty stomach wasn't the best idea, he at least had the new fur coat to keep him warm.

The gelding just snorted. *"You seem to think I'm a dull-sensed human! I can tell my own scent from other horses',"* it replied scornfully. *"And I can tell fresh scent from old. If we start going in circles, I promise you, I'll know it."*

The horse plodded leisurely along the game trails, following a plan best known only to itself. Occasionally in the distance Ilya heard hounds belling, although it was so faint and far that he couldn't tell if it was the group Mischa was with, the smaller pack that had been sent to chase him, or some other hunting party. The horse found things to snatch at and eat from time to time, but Ilya's stomach was not pleased with the mouthfuls of snow he ate to stave off hunger-pangs. The birds here had left no berries on the bushes, and whatever fallen nuts there might be were buried under the snow, past finding. Ilya discouraged himself thinking with longing of the fine breakfast of hot bread and butter, of sausage and boiled eggs that he had missed. He resolved to start hiding boiled eggs and other things that wouldn't spoil in his room, and keeping a packet of such things in his pockets, just in case this happened again.

The horse stopped at a patch of old grasses poking up out of the snow, and Ilya caught sight of the tail of a squirrel whisking around the trunk of a tree. It occurred to him that if he could get a squirrel to hold still and talk to him, he might persuade it to part with some of its cache of nuts. "Can I talk to wild things, do you suppose?" Ilya asked the horse, after a long silence broken only by the sound of equine teeth grinding away at tough grass.

"If they understand the human words, I expect so," the horse replied. *"That would be the problem, you see. We who live with you have learned to understand your words, and now you can understand ours, but we aren't speaking the same language. So you could understand a wild thing, thanks to the Firebird's magic, but you may not be able to make it understand you."*

Well, that explained why he didn't have to bark for the dogs to know what he was saying, but it was a bit disappointing to know that he would probably not be able to talk a bear out of eating him, or that squirrel into sharing some of its hoard.

He thought about that for some time, wondering just why it was that the Firebird had given him this gift in the first place. Limited understanding of just one or two animals, seeing spirits—that could have come from the fact that she had been near him, that the magic had rubbed off on him a little. But she had brought him that cherry—and after that, he could understand all the animals he came in contact with, no matter whether they were talking to him or not. Why had she done that? And how had she known which window was his? He hadn't seen her again except in dreams—had she given him this gift out of gratitude for his silence? That seemed the most likely.

It could be a perilous gift, though, if it turned out that he was going to see more spirits, as well as being able to understand the animals. At the moment, he was feeling so desperate for a girl that he might well fall prey to the temptations of a pretty *rusalka*.

But that was supposed to be the way it was with the gifts of magic creatures: They had both advantages and disadvantages, and sometimes there were perils involved. On the whole, though, he was inclined to agree with Ruslan's assertion that to see the Firebird was the worst of bad luck. It had been *after* he saw her that Pietor had bolted and his brothers had beaten him and left him for dead. It had been *after* he saw her that he'd been forced into this role of the Fool.

If she was really grateful, she should have found a way to get me safely out from underneath my father's roof, he thought sourly. *Surely, if she could put the orchard-guards to sleep, she could do the same to everyone in the palace and give me enough time to steal a pair of horses and get farther away than Pietor did.*

If he'd had any warning, this very prank of Mischa's could have been his doorway to freedom—he could have put a lot of provisions in the lining of this new coat. The horse was certainly prepared to cooperate. Unfortunately, riding out in the winter with nothing on his person but the clothes he was wearing and a belt-knife was suicidal. He was prepared to take the horse's word for it that he could hear danger coming in time to avoid it—by day. But night would be a different matter, for neither of them could see in the dark, and the horse couldn't climb a tree to avoid the wolves.

The forest still didn't look at all familiar, and although Ilya could not claim to be the hunter that some of his brothers were, he *had* walked and ridden over a great deal of Ivan's land, and he thought by now he should have seen something familiar. Where had Mischa taken them? How far from the palace were they, anyway?

Tall, drooping pine trees had replaced most of the deciduous, and that made the forest seem even gloomier, for the trees blocked most of the light, and grew so closely together that it wasn't possible to see far off the trail. Ilya's stomach growled, and he was getting very cold, in spite of his handsome coat. His nose and ears were particularly cold, and he kept taking off his mittens to cup his hands over his ears to warm them and keep them from getting frostbitten. How much longer before they could turn back and try to find their way home?

An angry snort was the only warning he had that the gelding's hearing wasn't quite as sharp as it claimed. He looked up, and so did the horse, to see one of the sights every hunter dreads.

A huge wild boar, easily the size of a young bear, stood blocking the path. Blood dripped slowly into the snow from a wound in its shoulder—clearly one of the hunters had cast and missed. Now it was mad with pain and anger, and considered everything that moved to be its enemy, the same enemy that had hurt it. It filled the game-trail, and in the peculiar clarity of the moment, Ilya stared in fascination at it, its image filling his mind. Its tiny red eyes glared as the pig turned its head from side to side, clashing its tusks against the bushes. Every black hair on its body stood up, bristling, especially the hair of the ridge that began between its ears and traveled along its backbone. The blood from its wounded shoulder trickled slowly down its leg to pool in the snow beside its left trotter, as it pawed furrows in the snow with its right. Its breath puffed out in white clouds as it snorted, and he could smell its musky, feral odor as it grunted angrily at them. The yellowish, dirty tusks dripped foam; there was an old scar running along its snout where something had once clawed its face open.

The horse froze, caught between the urge to flee and the urge to stand still and hope the boar hadn't seen them properly. That moment of hesitation was all that the boar needed.

With a squeal of rage, the boar charged, slashing savagely

at them with its huge tusks, blood and foaming spittle flying in every direction.

That was all Ilya saw. In the next moment, he was flying through the air, with a tree-trunk coming at him. The moment after that, he knew nothing.

ILYA opened his eyes, his head aching horribly, wondering where he was and who had cracked his skull for him this time. Somewhat to his surprise, he saw only an interlacing of bare tree branches against a gray, overcast sky. Slowly, painfully, bits of memory came back to him. The hunt. Mischa and Sasha tying his legs to the horse. The horse pretending to spook, and running off. The boar.

I must have been thrown when the boar charged. Or maybe the horse bucked me off on purpose to get me out of the way. He didn't remember just what he'd hit to give him such a terrible headache, but it was probably something large and hard. One by one he moved his limbs and discovered that nothing was broken, or even seriously injured. Once again, it seemed, being beaten to a pulp on a regular basis had toughened him to a certain extent.

However, if he continued to lie here, he was going to be in danger from the cold. The coat had saved him so far, and that was another stroke of luck; in his old woolen coat he might have frozen to death before he woke up.

He listened, closing his eyes to concentrate, for any sounds indicating that the boar was still around. There was nothing, other than the occasional, melancholy *quark* of a raven in one of the trees nearby. Slowly, carefully, he sat up; his mouth filled with saliva as his stomach heaved in protest. He closed his eyes for a moment, hoping for the sensation to pass.

He was in the middle of a tangle of juniper bushes and couldn't see anything past the thick mass of branches around him. Another stroke of luck—that was why he hadn't broken anything but his skull. He must have cracked his head on the tree just above him, fallen straight into the springy juniper boughs.

The nausea faded, though not the headache. If he couldn't do anything else for it, he'd have to clap a handful of snow to his head to ease the pain a little. He listened again—and this time, he heard a groan of agony.

The horse! He wanted to rush to his friend's aid, but he knew if he tried, he'd probably pass out again. As quickly as his damaged head would allow, he fought his way clear of the bushes, shoving and pushing the spiky branches clear, eventually burrowing through them—and as soon as he broke free of them, tumbling headfirst into the churned-up snow of the game-trail, he knew that his luck had run completely out.

But not as completely as had the poor gelding's.

The horse had collapsed in the middle of the game-trail; blood sprayed over the snow all around it, and its hind-feet kicked feebly and without purpose, for his front legs were not so much broken as shattered. Splinters of bone poked whitely through the ruined flesh, and blood oozed into the snow from the savagely torn wounds.

Ilya gave a strangled cry, struggled to his feet, and ran, stumbling over hidden obstacles, toward the horse; but when he fell on his knees beside him, he knew that there was nothing he could do for the gelding. Such damage was irreparable, and the horse was dying even as he gazed helplessly into his eyes.

Those eyes were fogged with suffering, but there was still some sense and understanding in them. Perhaps that was the worst part of all, and the most horrible, that the horse should know it was doomed.

"Boy," the horse whispered. *"Boy, I'm sorry. I failed you. You trusted me to protect you, and I failed you."*

How could he think of *him* at a moment like this? "Don't be ridiculous!" he cried, tears choking his words and streaming down his cheeks to drop into the snow. "How could this be your fault? How could you guess a wounded boar would get this far away from the hunt?"

"I should have kept the dogs with us," the horse persisted. *"But I was so sure I could keep us both safe. I was so proud that I was strong, fast, and smarter than a dog. This is where my pride got us."*

"It's not your fault," Ilya sobbed, stroking the soft, warm neck in a futile attempt at comfort. "It's not your fault. I should have just let Mischa do what he wanted. I should have told you to run back toward the hunt."

"Be merciful, boy," the horse went on, as if it had not heard him. *"It will either be you or the wolves, and I'd rather it was you. Take your knife, and be merciful—and when I am dead, mount me backward as you did the donkey and cut some hair from my tail to make a bracelet with. Your luck will come back."*

The horse knew what was coming, as surely as the dark and the moon—and so did Ilya. The wolves would scent his blood and come to the easy kill; they would tear the horse apart, still alive. The least he could do would be to end his pain.

He'd hunted enough deer to know how to make the end quick and painless, even though he had only a knife at his disposal. Still crying, he moved around until he had the horse's head cradled in his lap. He cupped his left hand around its eye so it couldn't see what he was doing, and whispered in its ear, telling it how brave and faithful a friend it had been, assuring it that none of what had happened was its fault. With his right hand, he took his knife and made a quick, deep slash along the great, throbbing artery that ran up the horse's neck.

It was over in a moment, as a gush of blood poured out over the snow in a crimson flood, and the life ebbed from the horse's eyes. All the muscles relaxed, the eyes slowly closed, and the noble heart slowed, then finally stopped, along with the pain. A great shudder ran over the horse's body, a last spasm, then it lay perfectly still.

"I'm sorry," Ilya whispered, stroking the soft nose for the last time, weeping as he had never wept for himself. "If it hadn't been for me, you'd be in a warm stable right now. I'm so sorry. . . ."

He clambered over the gelding's barrel, mounting it backward so that he could cut that handful of hairs from its tail—because it had asked him to, and not because he thought it was going to change his luck. He stuffed them into his pocket with the rope and stood up, trying to think through his grief and the pain in his head.

I have to take everything I can carry. But I don't care how hungry I am—I won't eat him. I'd rather die first.

But he was bleakly aware that dying was an all-too-real possibility.

He loosed the horse's cheek-straps, pulled the bridle over

his head, and took the bridle and reins, setting them aside for the moment. The saddle was next; he unfastened the girth and cut as much of the girth-leather free as he could. He got the saddle-blanket off, then cut one of the stirrup-straps and the stirrup off. The saddle itself was of no use to him, but if he managed to live out the night, the rest might help him survive a little longer.

Unless he could somehow get back to the trail of the hunt, though, it might not be very long. Nevertheless, there was one thing that was certain. The scent of blood would soon bring a wolf-pack, possibly even before night fell, and if he stayed, he would be the tidbit before the main course. He had to get away from there, as far away as possible, before they came.

He didn't dare trace back along the trail that he and the horse had taken here; that was the way that the boar had gone. He could only go on, listen for the dogs, and hope they would lead him to people.

"I'm sorry," he whispered again to the horse. "I wish I hadn't been here. I wish you'd had a cleverer friend than me." And once again, tears filled his eyes and he turned away, blinded.

He took just long enough to roll his meager booty in the saddle-blanket, tie it with the reins, and sling it over his shoulder. He left out only the stirrup-leather with the dangling stirrup; he held that in his hand as an improvised weapon. It wasn't much, but it was better than nothing. If he'd had something more than a knife, he might have been able to cut himself a staff or a cudgel, but unless he found something already fallen, he'd have to do without.

He plodded along through the snow, which was surprisingly thin and getting thinner. That was a blessing, at least; he was able to get a good distance away in a relatively short time. Before too long it had gone from calf-deep to ankle-deep, then from ankle-deep to little more than the depth of the first joint of the thumb. He was able to get away faster than he would have thought possible, which put him out of immediate wolf-danger. He had no idea of the real passage of time; as he stumbled along, he had the sensation that time wasn't passing at all. But his head hurt so much that he knew better than to trust his senses completely; the only thing he knew that he had to do was keep moving. If he stopped and sat down, he would probably pass out, and if he did that, he *would* die.

But as the dim light began to fade, and night fell, it soon became obvious that he was not going to find the track of the hunt any time soon. There was no sign of human life anywhere: no scent of woodsmoke, no tracks, no sounds of hounds or voices. The woods themselves were weirdly silent, enough to make the skin on the back of his neck crawl, and he thought that he felt eyes peering at him from out of the shadows.

The light faded but never died completely, and that was enough to make him bite his tongue and wonder about going on. It *should* have been as dark as the crypt here, yet the forest was full of a faint, bluish light; it had no source, and yet it was possible to see everything in it. There were no shadows, not even beneath the thickest pine trees, but no obvious bright spots, either.

But in the end, he knew he had no choice: If he stayed, he would be tacitly giving up, and if he gave up, he would die. He went on, taking each step carefully, not only to save his still-aching head and to avoid tripping over something, but also to be able to listen for sounds out there in the semidarkness beyond the trees along the game-trail. He wasn't certain that he would hear anything coming before it was upon him, but it was better to try than not.

Finally, after what seemed like an eternity, he *did* hear a sound, but it wasn't the one he expected. It was the sound of running water.

The trail he was following seemed to lead toward the sound, and he followed it. If he could find a stream, there would surely be cress growing in it, and although the blow to his head had made him nauseous, he knew he would have to find something edible soon or he would be sick to his stomach. Where there was water, there was usually someone living along it, and if he followed the stream, sooner or later he would come to a dwelling. And even if all he found was a hunter's hut without anyone living in it, he would have shelter, and a door he could bar against the wild beasts.

He found the stream by stumbling into it; he was so busy watching the forest around him that he wasn't paying any attention to where his feet were going. He heard a splash, felt the cold around his ankle, and quickly pulled his foot back before the water could seep into his boot. He looked down at the bit of water, no wider than his forearm was long, and quickly realized that he was not going to find edible plants growing in it except by accident; the faint blue light of the forest did not extend into the stream, which was a winding path of blackness against the snow-covered forest floor.

But it would give him something to follow.

He had no idea which direction he or the stream was going in at this point, so he simply turned in the direction it was flowing and followed along beside it without crossing it. From time to time, he bent down and dashed a handful of the cold, sweet water over his aching head, or knelt down and drank directly from the stream. By this time, he was so tired that he was walking in a kind of weary daze; he knew that the state he was in was dangerous, but there didn't seem to be any choice in the matter. He certainly couldn't take a rest on the ground, and climbing a tree in this semidarkness was out of the question. He could only force his aching, exhausted limbs on, and hope that dawn wasn't far off.

In a way he was glad he hadn't taken the time to try to cut a staff; he knew if he'd had one, he would have been tempted to stop for a moment and lean on it, and that would have been fatal. He would have fallen asleep standing up if he had.

Father will send out searchers looking for his horse, I'm sure of that. Maybe I should have stayed with it. But the wolves were coming . . . maybe they'll all think the wolves got me when they got the horse. Poor horse. It was all my fault. If I hadn't seen the Firebird . . . if I hadn't talked to him . . . if I had just turned around and gone back to my room when I saw all the hubbub in the great hall . . .

From there, his thoughts wound to the usual conclusions: *. . . if I'd never been born . . . if I'd just given up and died in the crypt . . .*

Suddenly, he realized that he wasn't following the bank of the stream anymore, it was in front of him, and it seemed to have gotten much broader. Much, *much* broader.

He stopped and rubbed his eyes with his free hand, and slowly the truth dawned on him.

He stood on the shore of a lake whose waters sparkled under a sky that had inexplicably cleared, allowing the full moon to shine down upon it. But more inexplicable than the appearance of the moon and stars was the strange transition he had wandered through while his thoughts had been preoccupied.

There was no snow on the ground, not the slightest sign of snow, and although the air was chill, it was not *cold,* and his fur coat was growing a bit too warm for comfort. There were leaves on the trees, which rustled with a dry sound, and the tang in the air suggested that as he had walked, the land had gone backward in time from winter to fall.

He rubbed his eyes again, but nothing changed.

I can't have gone so far south that I've walked into warmer lands—could I?

A strange lassitude came over him, compounded equally of exhaustion both physical and emotional, of depression, and of a sense of being too overwhelmed to care about anything anymore. He plodded, exhausted, along the winding, contorted shore of the lake, barely able to put one foot in front of the other, and wondering with a tired fatalism what new disaster was going to present itself to him.

His answer came before he'd gone more than a fraction of the distance around the shoreline. As he rounded a concealing curve, he all but fell over a young woman sitting on a projecting stone and gazing out dreamily over the waters.

He was so dumbfounded at seeing another human being that for a moment or two all he could do was gape at her.

The moonlight fell fully on her upturned face as she twisted to look up at him. She was beautiful—heartbreakingly, stunningly beautiful, a perfect snow-maiden created by the hand of a master-artist. She was dressed in nothing but white—silken shirt, embroidered tunic, and flowing skirt; even the hair braided and wrapped around her head like a crown was a blonde so light it looked silver in the moonlight. Her skin was as pale as the snow he had left behind, and only her huge, dark eyes gave any contrast to the whiteness of her skin, her clothing, her hair. She turned those eyes on him and he thought he would melt beneath their power.

"Who are you?" she cried in alarm, as she started back a little, one hand to her throat. "Where have you come from?"

He couldn't blame her for being alarmed, and he hastened to soothe her.

"I am Ilya Ivanovitch; I lost the hunt I was with, then I cracked my head, I lost my horse, and then I lost my way entirely." He spoke as quietly as he could, and endeavored to look both harmless and helpless. "I'm awfully tired, my head hurts like anything, I haven't eaten all day, and I haven't the least notion of where I am. I don't suppose you could help me, could you?"

She stared unwinkingly at him, then suddenly smiled. "Poor man!" she replied in her sweet, breathy voice. "Poor, lost fellow—we don't see many strangers here, just a peddler or two, now and again. You quite startled me, coming up on me like that! But what a tale of misfortune! Poor Ilya Ivanovitch! Of course I shall help you!"

He wanted to kiss her, and not just because he felt such relief, but because her full, smiling lips looked so very kissable. And in the back of his mind, a suspicious little voice said, *You managed to calm her down* awfully *quickly, don't you think? She's a maiden, alone, by the side of the lake, and a stranger has just stumbled up out of nowhere. . . .*

Well, perhaps—but she smiled so charmingly, and looked up into his eyes so trustfully. He told the nagging little voice not to be foolish, that this lovely maiden was simply friendly. Not all families were like his, mistrustful, competitive, more ready to see an enemy than a friend—and hadn't she said they seldom saw strangers? She was simply sheltered and gentle, with no reason to think badly of anyone, even someone she had never seen before.

"I am sorriest to hear that you have hurt yourself," she continued, rising as slowly and gracefully as an exotic being in a dream, and reaching out to take his hand. Her sleeve drifted down from her outstretched arm like a cascade of mist. "I shall give you all the help in my power, but what would you have of me first?"

"You could start by telling me where I am—and who you are," Ilya said, finding himself getting lost in those huge, dark eyes, until the pain in his head and his growling stomach pulled him back with a start.

Yes, and she can't be a peasant, now, can she? said the

nagging voice. *Look at that dress—it doesn't look like any peasant smock, and it must have cost more than three of Katya's dresses combined. Look at that silver, that embroidery! Those are real pearls, there in the embroidery!* Ilya gladly obeyed the voice, using his examination of her clothing to sway a little closer to her. He'd never seen materials like that; they flowed about her, the skirt falling in cascades to the grass, with the soft sheen of moonlight reflected in the still water of the lake. He breathed in the scent of her—the scent of clean water, of water-lilies—

Really? You don't know that many boyars' daughters who are that clean. . . .

"My name is Vasilisa," she said, gazing deeply into his eyes, unaware of the little voice commenting suspiciously on her appearance. She did not seem to mind that he had not yet relinquished her hand; it lay in his, cool and perfect, a tiny sculpture with nails of pearl. "My father is the boyar—we dwell over there, on the other shore, across the lake. I often walk along the shore here at night, when the water is still and the mist rises. I often think that it looks as if our home is built among the clouds."

She waved her free hand in the direction of the other side of the lake. Ilya looked up and, for a puzzled moment, saw nothing there but thick mist obscuring the trees.

But in the next instant, the mist parted as if on command, and he saw an impressive palace rising above the water on the opposite shore of the lake, a palace with walls as white as the finest marble, as white as the mist on the lake itself. If someone had built a lofty hall out of the finest white birch, ornamented with the most fantastic carvings, it might have looked like this. It had dozens of windows, huge, ornamented porches, and was at least three stories tall.

How could the horse have carried me that far away from home? Surely Ivan or Gregori would know about this palace—this maiden.

She took a step nearer to him, still holding his hand, and he found he could not look away from her eyes. "There are few people here," she breathed. "And no young men of any rank, least of all sons of a tsar. I am lonely, Ilya, and I often come here to think about my loneliness, and wish for a young man to come and take it away. Have you been sent in answer to my wish, Ilya Ivanovitch?''

Now her eyes held very little of innocence and a great deal of promise. She pressed closer to him, looking up into his eyes, the warmth of her body a subtle caress all along his, leaving him no doubt of what she was offering. He wanted to say, *Yes!* but something held him back.

Perhaps it was because she had gone so suddenly from shy innocent to experienced seductress in the time it took a horse to canter from the palace stables to the orchard. Perhaps it was simply that any of his brothers would have had her down on the grass without thinking twice about it. Perhaps it was the fact that he had never heard of a boyar with a white-birch palace out here in the forest. Perhaps it was all of these things—for whatever reason, Ilya felt a sudden disinclination to take what she offered, and an equally sudden and strong wish to have his hand back. He stepped back a pace and managed to free it, just as his foot struck something that had been half-hidden in the grass at the girl's feet.

"Never mind that, it's just a bit of flotsam," she said, in an oddly cold and commanding voice. The voice had the opposite effect on him. He looked down at the obstacle and poked it out of the grass with his toe, peering at it with a slight frown on his face.

"It's just a fish-trap," she said in that same cold voice. "It doesn't matter, and it's empty. Leave it alone."

Why was she so determined that he not examine an old fish-trap? He looked closer, for he thought he saw something moving in the trap—a tiny, hopping form, a flutter of wings, a single, bright black eye. *It's a bird!* he realized. *A nightingale! But why would anyone put a nightingale in a fish-trap?*

Somehow, though, he didn't feel like asking Vasilisa directly. The bird looked up at him pathetically, its shining, frightened eye peering between two of the slats of the trap. "Help me!" it cried. "Help me! She means to drown me!"

Vasilisa made as if she was about to reach down for the trap. Ilya didn't even stop to think; he snatched the trap up before Vasilisa's hand touched it. It was made of brittle willow-withes; he wrenched at the slats with both hands, and in a moment he had broken it open with a splintering *crack.* It fell to pieces and the bird flew off like a shooting star, into the deep woods.

Vasilisa gave a horrific scream and flung herself at him, and Ilya found himself fighting with a vicious harpy of a woman. Gone were both the shy, demure maiden and the sweetly tempting seductress. In their place was a demon, a terror, a woman-shaped monster who spit at him and tried to bite him, who tore at his face with clawlike nails, and kicked and kneed him like one of his brothers in a wrestling-match. Only the fact that she was hampered by her skirts saved him from some painful damage. She clawed and struck at him while he protected his head with his arms, then tried to seize his wrists and drag him toward the lake with preternatural strength. Once she got a good grip on both wrists, she started hauling him to the water, and nothing he could do would get her to let go—he dug his heels in, and realized to his horror that she was *still* pulling him toward the water, while his heels made twin furrows in the earth. His wrists burned with a terrible cold that was worse, in its way, than fire, and try as he might, he could not break her grip.

It was at that moment that he knew what she must be: a *rusalka,* a water-spirit in the form of a beautiful girl, whose only purpose in life was to find ways to drown foolish young men. And that was exactly what she was going to do to him; she was near her watery home, and her strength far surpassed his. She had both of his wrists in a grip of steel, and she pulled him toward his death with a grim determination that nothing would shake.

He flung himself sideways, hoping to break her hold on his wrists, and by sheer good luck got his left hand free. He groped inside his coat for his knife and pulled it out, with some of the gelding's tail-hair wrapped around it, and some of his blood still staining the blade. He brandished it at her, not certain if a simple knife could hurt a creature like a *rusalka.* She cackled scornfully and reached for the dagger, unafraid.

At that moment, the unthinkable happened. Out of nowhere, out of the fog and the night air, a horse appeared—a horse of mist, as transparent as glass, but as real as the thing clutching his wrist. With mane and tail of streaming smoke, the horse screamed a challenge, and the *rusalka* answered it with a scream of her own. It reared up beside Ilya, pawing savagely at the *rusalka,* striking at her with sharp hooves made of ice and snaking its head about to snap at her with formidable teeth. Ilya would have known that head anywhere; it was the sorrel gelding! But *how*?

The *rusalka* might not fear a knife of steel, but she was afraid of a spirit-horse; she screamed again and loosed her hold on his wrists enough for him to wrench free of her. He whirled and ran as hard as he could back into the forest, away from both the stream and the lake it fed. He stumbled through the brush, clawing his way past branches without regard for his hands or his face. He fell and recovered too many times to count, juniper-branches whipping into his face, not caring whether he was on a trail or not, so long as he got away.

He heard pursuit, but it didn't last very long; as he had hoped and prayed, the *rusalka* couldn't venture far from her watery home. Still, he ran on; there was no telling what allies among the spirits this *rusalka* might have. Finally, when his sides ached and his breath burned in his lungs, he slowed and came to a halt in the middle of a tiny clearing.

Moonlight poured down on him and reflected off the snow filling the tiny glade. The chill of winter was back, the snow easily calf-deep again. Had he ever really been in that false-autumn, or had that been as much an illusion as the white palace? There was a flat rock in the middle of the clearing, projecting up out of the snow. He sat down on it and tried to catch his breath. What had gone on back there? Where had the gelding come from—the horse that he *knew* was dead? It must have been a spirit, but did horses have ghosts?

His sides hurt, and he thought he might have wrenched his ankle; it certainly hurt as if he had. His wrists burned where the *rusalka* had held them; when he pulled back the cuffs of his coat-sleeves, there were marks like burns encircling his wrists. He still had his knife, though, and with silent thanks to the spirit of the gelding, he cleaned it in the snow and resheathed it.

One thing was certain: He couldn't go on any farther tonight. He was exhausted, hurt, and too disoriented to find directions in the dark. He looked all around and, peering into the darkness, decided that one of the large trees surrounding the clearing looked possible to climb, even if he couldn't see.

The huge old pine tree had branches all the way down to the ground, and it was no worse than climbing a ladder. He continued to climb until he was well out of reach of all but the most determined of bears, and then took the reins, the saddle-girth, and his own belt and tied himself to the tree. It wasn't bad; there was a branch chest-high to a sitting man, and only a little farther from the one he was sitting on; he made a kind of pillow out of the saddle-blanket, wrapped his arms around it, and leaned over onto the next branch. Once he was in position, exhaustion did what nothing else could have done. Before he knew it, he was asleep, and he stayed asleep until he awoke the next day.

CHAPTER SIX

ILYA WOKE with ravens quorking nearby at dawn; sore everywhere, cold, starving, and so stiff he could hardly move. Once again, an overcast sky threw the forest into a gray gloom, and the clouds were so thick he couldn't even tell where the sun was. "This is not going to be one of my better days," he said aloud, startling the ravens into ungainly flight.

With some difficulty, he untied himself from the tree, rolled his meager belongings in the saddle-blanket, and tied the resulting bundle to his back, all without rising from the branch he was sitting on. Every movement hurt—and it almost did not seem worthwhile to climb down. He would still be lost, without food, with no idea how to get home. Even as high up in this tree as he already was, he couldn't see anything but forest. The only sound was the melancholy calls of the ravens in the next tree.

They're probably waiting for me to die.

He just couldn't seem to make the effort to move. He leaned back against the tree and felt something soft in his pocket. Pulling off his mitten and fishing around in the hopes he might have shoved a bit of bread in there, he encountered the hank of horsehair he'd taken from the gelding's tail. For lack of anything better to do, while he waited for the sun to burn off the overcast so he could get some direction, he braided the hair into a bracelet and slipped it on. Maybe it *would* change his luck; certainly the spirit-horse had saved him last night. Finally, after more time of just sitting, his thirst drove him down to the ground. Once there, he ate snow, which eased his thirst but did nothing at all for his hunger.

He thrashed around in the underbrush for a while until he came to a game-trail, and lacking any other direction, he struck out to his left. There were still no sounds of life, and if it had not been for the rings of tender flesh on his wrists, he would have dismissed the encounter with the *rusalka* as a dream. He stopped once to cut himself a staff, which gave him some help in the rougher spots in the trail, and late in the morning he came across another little stream and actually found some cress growing in it, which he devoured down to the last shred. His stomach was not convinced that this constituted real food, and continued to rumble complaints long after he had left the stream and gone on. A little later, he found a bush that still had a few rosehips on it, somehow overlooked by the birds. He ate those as well, though they were so acidic they puckered his mouth. Beside the rosebush was a fallen tree with several forms of shelf-fungus growing on it, one of which he knew was edible. He hunted out and ate every last scrap of this as well, though it was as dry as an old book, and he had to eat more snow to get the papery taste out of his mouth.

The longer he walked, the less he felt like going any farther. The forest seemed to go on forever, with no end in sight, no sign of game, nothing to give him hope. As a crowning touch to his plight, snow began to fall again, thick, and with a light wind to blow it around.

I should have let the rusalka *take me,* he thought with heavy despair, as he plodded onward, concentrating on getting one foot in front of the next. *What's the point of going on? The only way I'm going to find my way back home is by a miracle. Even then—if by a miracle I did get home again, Father would probably find a way to punish even the Fool for losing one of his precious horses.* The farther along he went, the more desperate his thoughts became, and he considered sitting right down in the snow and letting the cold take care of his problems for him.

But if he did that, wouldn't it be suicide? The half of him that was Christian was horrified at the idea of even thinking about suicide; if he killed himself, he would go straight to hell, and he'd already had a taste of what hell was like recently. But how could it be suicide if it wasn't he himself who did the deed, but the chill that did it for him?

Maybe I ought to go back and give myself to the rusalka *after all.* But wouldn't that be just as much suicide as sitting down and letting yourself freeze to death?

Would it? Or would it be more along the lines of aiding in a murder—his own?

But it was looking as if he was going to have only a choice in how to die—at the lovely hands of Vasilisa, by cold, by wolves and other wild beasts, or by starvation.

Of the four, at least death at the hands of the *rusalka* would be quick. He turned around, but he hadn't gone more than a few paces when he realized that going back to find Vasilisa was as futile an idea as trying to find his way home. The thick snow was already erasing his footprints from this path, and he'd passed several clearings that looked just like the one he'd spent the night above. He hadn't kept count of them; he'd never be able to tell which was the right one, and then he'd never be able to trace his panicked flight across the forest. The lake was as lost to him as his father's palace.

He turned around again, and just as he was about to give up and lie down in the snow, he spotted something brown lying atop the snow right underneath a hole in the trunk of an enormous tree. Just in case it might be something useful, he shoved his way through the snow, and discovered that it was a matted mass of dead, dried leaves, with a chestnut lying atop them.

He snatched up the nut, which was sweet and still sound, and peered into the hole in the trunk of the tree, then felt around inside it with the two fingers he could get in, thinking that it was too much to hope for, that squirrels had used a hole so close to the ground for a cache. But they had—not a large cache, but there were nuts in there! With a bit of work enlarging the hole with his knife, he was able to get his hand inside, and came up with a pocketful of sound nuts among the ones that insects or rot had gotten to. This looked as if it was an old cache, last year's rather than this year's; perhaps that was why it hadn't been touched.

He sat right down in the snow and cracked nuts, picking out even the tiniest fragments of meat, until he had devoured every morsel of his find. Chestnuts were better roasted than raw, but beggars couldn't be choosers, and he had no way to make a fire. Having a little more in his stomach revived him a little, and gave him the strength and hope to go on. He still did not dare to go off the game-trail in search of food; he was afraid that if he did, he could wander in the forest without finding another trail until he died. Game-trails at least led to and from water and clearings; he might find another stream with cress, or even a sluggish fish he could catch by hand.

But by late afternoon, when nothing more to eat had presented itself, the light had begun to fade, and he still had not seen a single sign of life, that hope and strength ran out again. He was so exhausted that he couldn't even look up to take note of his surroundings. Once more, it was all he could do to place one foot in front of the other, his eyes fixed on the sunken track defining the snow-covered trail in front of him, and he wondered if he ought to simply lie down in the snow tonight and take his chances.

He went on in this manner for quite some time, following the twists and turns in the trail, while the undergrowth grew denser until it hemmed in both sides of the game-trail. He began to grow dizzy with hunger and weariness, and it seemed to him, in a dull fashion, that his actual range of vision had narrowed and gone gray. Then it occurred to him that there was nothing wrong with his eyes—the bushes on either side of the trail were blocking out the light in a most peculiar fashion. He stopped, braced himself on his staff, and looked up, and saw that the dense evergreens growing beside him were very thick and very tall, more like a pair of parallel walls than bushes. The trail turned a little farther on, and he turned with it, now wondering how deer or other animals had made a trail through such thick shrubbery, and why. There must be something very important to them on the other side of it for them to have gone to such effort.

The trail divided; he took the fork to the right. It turned a time or two more, then ran into a dead-end. Now thoroughly interested, and no longer thinking of lying down in the snow to die, he retraced his steps and took the other way. In a few more turnings and dividings, the path through these bushes seemed very familiar—and it was beyond odd that the turns were at perfect right angles, as if they had been laid out that way.

Finally, it occurred to him *why* it seemed so familiar. Following this path was just like being in the maze that protected his family crypt from robbers getting in and ghosts getting out. Out of curiosity, he continued to make the turns he would take if he were, indeed, in a larger version of the family maze. When he ran into no more dead-ends, he stopped for a moment to consider how this could possibly be, for after encountering the *rusalka,* he was no longer able to take things as they appeared.

How did a copy of our maze come here, to be made of bushes? he wondered, with a healthy feeling of apprehension. *Is it just that our maze is a common pattern, and my great-grandfathers replicated it for our crypt? Or perhaps one of them came here, saw this maze, and copied it?* The second idea didn't seem too likely when he bent to examine the bases of the bushes forming the maze walls. If the bushes had been hundreds of years old, their trunks would have been as thick as his thigh; instead, they were only as thick as his wrist. They had been here for some time, but not more than twenty-five or thirty years at best. It might be that the family maze was a copy of a more famous one, for certainly Ivan would never have admitted that anything *his* family had was a copy of anything else, not even of the Great Tsar's.

But why had anyone planted a maze out here in the middle of the forest? Unless, of course, the gardener was some sort of forest spirit.

Ilya got a kind of chill, for there was a spirit who *would* know just what their maze looked like and might be inclined to copy it—their old house-spirit, the one Ruslan swore had gone away because Ivan didn't believe in or appreciate it.

Did our domovoi *plant this maze? What if he's still here?* He shivered, for the *domovoi,* though not as powerful or easily offended as the *bannik,* could still be deadly when provoked.

If I meet an old man in the center of this place—an old man who might be the domovoi—*I'll tell him what happened to me before I tell him who I am. If he knows that I am as despised by my family as he is, maybe he'll take pity on me.*

At any rate, it was worth going on and getting to the heart of this maze. It would protect him from wind and wild animals, and he would be able to spend the night in relative safety. And it might *not* be a copy of the maze he knew, after all. He had only made a few turnings, and they might simply lead to a more elaborate dead-end.

As the light faded, he plodded on, feeling relief at least from the biting wind, though not from the snow or from hunger. He didn't need to see to know his way through the maze; even the stupidest of his brothers had learned how to thread it in the dark, as it had been an ongoing "joke" for the eldest to take the youngest in blindfolded and leave them there without a light. They had stopped taking Ilya in when he was able to take the alternate route out and beat them back to the palace— the fun was in waiting to see if the terrified younger brother could get out in time for supper.

But this could not have simply *grown* here; not only were the twistings and turnings planned, but the bushes showed signs of having been trimmed recently, to prevent them from blocking the path, and it looked very much as if someone was attempting to train them to interlace their branches overhead, so that eventually the path would become a tunnel. Would a spirit go to all that trouble, or could it command the bushes to do what it wanted, instead of trimming and training?

There were no trees here, at least, and he had an unbroken view of the sky. As he walked, he watched it darken, still without the clouds clearing away, until it was as black in here as it was in the crypt-maze, though nowhere near as musty-smelling.

When he finally felt his way around the last turn and came out into the square clear space in the heart of the maze, where the crypt would have been, part of his answer was there in the form of a snug, beautifully built little house. This was no peasant hut or hunter's shack; this was more the sort of building that a boyar or tsar would have constructed as a hunting lodge. Though log-built, of sturdy trunks with the bark peeled off, there was nothing ramshackle or slipshod about it. Light shown warmly from its windows, which had panes of something opaque that kept cold air out yet let some light in. He couldn't tell what the substance in the windows was from here, but their golden light beckoned far too temptingly. The place was *so* well-constructed, in fact, that he was even more suspicious. How could anything be *that* well-built out here in the middle of nowhere, unless there was a supernatural hand at work?

Could this, in fact, be the hut of Baba Yaga? If *rusalkas* and *banniks* were real, why not the dreadful old witch herself? He didn't *see* any sign of chicken legs underneath it, and it was supposed to stand up on them at the mere sign of a stranger, but what if the witch already knew he was coming and had craftily ordered her hut to stay on the ground like a normal house?

Still, he knew the stories, and forewarned was forearmed. He knew better than to agree to do anything but the most simple of tasks, and Baba Yaga had a weakness for handsome young men and a tendency to underestimate them. If he knocked on the door, and an old woman answered it, he could act like a handsome simpleton. If *he* chose the work, she could not trick him into anything impossible in exchange for food and shelter. He could offer to split wood for her fire—yes, that was a good plan.

If it was any other kind of spirit—he tried to think further, but the breeze suddenly changed to carry the smoke from the chimney toward him, and he nearly fainted at the wonderful odors in it. It carried the scents of roasting meat and fresh bread, and his stomach growled so loudly it sounded like a bear stood here rather than a man.

It really *did* sound like a bear, and worse than that, it hurt. He gasped with the pain, dogs started barking inside the hut, and the door flew open. Three huge white wolfhounds bounded out of the open door and headed straight for him, followed by an old man in the long tunic and baggy breeches of a peasant, a spear in one hand, a knife in the other.

Ilya froze in terror, expecting to be torn to pieces in a moment, but the dogs had no interest in *him*. They gave him a perfunctory sniff, circled the house once, then came back and sat beside him, the leader giving a short bark. *"All's safe,"* the dog said in that single bark.

"No wolves, boars, or bears, eh? Well, if you're a man, come into the light, and if you're a beast, go your way," the old man called. "I don't hunt deer and fox on my own ground, unless I'm starving, which I'm not."

Ilya stepped forward, slowly, the wolfhounds following at

his heels, plumed tails wagging gently. The old man peered at him, but with the light at his back, Ilya couldn't tell what he looked like, only that he was old enough to have gray or white hair.

"Well, boy, *you* certainly look the worse for wear. Come in; I've plenty to share, and no visitors till spring." His voice seemed kindly enough; but was it the *domovoi?* There was no way to tell for sure. Presumably the *domovoi* wouldn't need dogs to protect him, but—

The scent of rich meat-juices was too much for him, and Ilya stumbled forward. The old man stepped aside, then took his elbow as he passed and guided him in. The dogs followed, surged past them once they were all in the hut, and went straight to the hearth, where they curled up.

"By Rod and Perun! You look *more* than the worse for wear!" the old man exclaimed, once he got Ilya inside and shut the door. "Here now, don't say a thing, just sit right there and let me get some food into you."

Ilya was perfectly happy to do just that, sitting down on the rough-made stool the old man pointed to, while his host swiftly carved up three slices of meat from the joint on a hand-built table, laid them on a thick slice of bread to serve as a plate, and handed it to Ilya. While Ilya hungrily cut bits of meat and bread soaked through with juice and stuffed them in his mouth as fast as he could, the old man cut a second slice of bread and topped it with a smear of honey, then poured a cup of home-brewed honey-wine and handed the cup to him.

The old man himself looked just as ordinary as any of the peasants and servants at the palace: tall, tough, and muscular. His weathered, wrinkled face sported a large gray moustache though no beard, and his shaggy, gray-white hair looked as if the only time it was trimmed was when he took his own knife to it. His blue eyes had a kindly and concerned gleam to them, and his clothing showed signs of long wear and hard use. Both the shirt and the breeches were the same off-white of ordinary rough woolen peasant-garb, with no embroidery or trimmings and only a single button carved of a slice of horn closing the shirt at the shoulder. His belt, made of oiled leather, held a formidable hunter's knife, and his boots, of the same material, showed even more wear than the shirt.

The hut itself had been built with great care and a love for craftsmanship; again, more like a boyar's hunting-lodge than a peasant-hut. It had an actual wooden floor, a stone hearth and a real stone chimney. The material in the windows looked to be plates of mica, carefully fitted into wooden frames and caulked with pine-tar and moss. The logs of the hut had been chinked with more moss and mud, so tightly that not even a hint of chill crept in. All of the furniture was hand-built, mostly of carefully bent and formed branches with the bark peeled off. The only things that could not have been made by the old man himself were the pottery, ironmongery, woven goods, and weapons. Ilya noted three pottery mugs, the pitcher, and several crocks. There were weapons and knives hung on the wall, and they appeared to be in good repair and functional. There were also some fine examples of ironwork: the kettle, pot, tongs, hook, and poker at the fireplace. The bedding on the bed included coverlets and blankets as well as some beautifully tanned furs. Bunches of onions and herbs hung from the rafters, there was a hand-fashioned splint-basket of tiny apples in one corner, another of nuts next to it, and other assorted supplies that were not immediately identifiable.

This place and this man had never had a woman around long enough to make any changes; both the man's clothing and his dwelling were of the sort only a bachelor would have. No woman could have resisted decorating the wool of his tunic with at least a little embroidery, and no woman would have left the house so utilitarian and unadorned. There were no curtains at all, for instance, and no fancywork on the bed-linens. Everything was entirely functional, with nothing to make it "fancy." A woman would have woven some rugs rather than use somewhat motheaten bear-and-wolf-skins; a woman would have painted the shutters and the splint-baskets with flowers and fanciful beasts.

Ilya was so hungry he ate most of the meat without tasting it; when he did slow down enough to gulp some of the potent honey-wine and eat the last few bites carefully, he identified it as venison, nicely seasoned and juicy. This man might be a bachelor, but he had learned how to cook with his limited foodstuffs, and do it well.

He finished the last few bites, drank about half the honey-wine, and his host handed him the honey-smeared chunk of bread he'd been holding. "Now," the old man said, when he finished the honeyed bread and the last of the wine. "You need sleep more than you need anything else, I'm thinking. Bide you there a bit, and let me pull out the trundle."

Before Ilya could say anything, the old man went over to the large bed and pulled a second out from beneath it. It wasn't much of a bed, more like a box filled with soft grasses and herbs, but the old man threw a coarse sheet over the filling and dropped a pillow, a blanket, and a bearskin down on it from his own bed.

"I use it for puppies when my bitch whelps," he explained, as he tucked the sheet in all around, "but on the rare times when I get a peddler through here, I can give him a safe night's sleep—it makes them more likely to pass here again, when stopping with me takes them so far out of their way. Most often when I need something, I have to go fetch it myself, and that's a long trip."

"I slept in a tree last night," Ilya said hoarsely, standing up and putting out a hand as he swayed. "And I meant to sleep on the ground tonight. *Any* bed, even a piece of your floor, is like a gift from heaven right now. Thank you. Thank you! May all the kind spirits bless you!" He shed his coat and fell into the bed as the old man stood aside. He stayed conscious just long enough to kick off his boots and roll himself up in the blanket and the bearskin. After that, he remembered nothing.

He woke with dim, golden light coming in the windows, and the old man had already tidied up the place without waking him. The man's bed was neatly made, the coverlet tucked in tightly; the floor had been swept, the dishes washed and put up, and the dogs were nowhere in sight, so they were presumably outside. The old man was quietly carving up the now cold roast into slices, chopping some and dropping it into a pot; turnip-tops on the table and the scent of onions told Ilya what some of the rest of the ingredients were. When he saw that Ilya was awake, the old man showed him a basin of water waiting for a wash, which Ilya was glad to take advantage of.

Ilya doused his face and neck with the cold water, making free of some soft soap in a box beside the basin. Seeing no other recourse, he took the basin to the door and tossed the dirty water outside; as he did so, the dogs came bounding up from out of the maze and slipped past him into the house, tails wagging. For a few moments, the small room seemed full of dogs until they settled themselves in their usual places, each with a generous bone to chew. Ilya wiped out the basin with his towel and set it back where he had found it. When Ilya was done, the old man offered him the stool beside the fire, and presented him with a breakfast of cold venison and bread, which he ate slowly and with more appreciation than he had the food last night. While Ilya ate, the old man shoved the trundle-bed beneath the larger one, and went out several times, bringing in firewood that he put in a rack beside the fireplace. Ilya offered to help, but his offer was cordially refused, and after Ilya tried to rise and couldn't, he gave in.

The old man waited until Ilya was clearly finished eating, then poured himself a cup of his own brewing, taking a second stool by the fire. "Now," he said, "I've been the one doing most of the talking. Tell me how you ended up here, back behind the north wind."

Ilya told his story slowly, leaving out nothing except most of the supernatural events, from the theft of his father's cherries onward. He went back that far under the premise that if this *was* the *domovoi,* he wanted the spirit to feel as much sympathy for him as possible. But in case the old man was a simple mortal, he said nothing of seeing the Firebird, nor of his own presence in the orchard—only that Pietor had failed as had Mischa and Gregori, and what Pietor had done that ultimately led to Ilya's own beating. He very cleverly managed to give neither his father's name nor the name of the village associated with the palace, just as he'd planned last night. Ilya also left out the fact that the gelding had spoken to him, but left in the *rusalka;* left out the spirit-horse that had come to his rescue, and left out the fact that he had recognized the maze. The old man listened carefully, nodding now and again but never interrupting, except to refill his mug with honey-wine. Ilya was careful not to drink too deeply or too often; he couldn't imagine how the old man drank his own potent brew without becoming tipsy. When Ilya came to the end of his story, the old man rubbed his nose with the back of his hand, and harrumphed a bit.

"There's no one in the world that you could be except the grandson of my old master, Vasily Gregorovitch," the old fellow said decisively, slapping his knee for emphasis. "That's who I copied my maze from, to keep out the bears and the wolves—they get tired of trying to follow scent about halfway in, except in really bad winters, give up, and go back out again. Only one of Ivan Vasilovitch's sons would know how to find his way in so easily, and damn if you don't have the look of your grandfather about you. I'm Yasha, boy; I was your grandfather's friend as well as his wolf-hunter; when your grandfather Vasily decided I ought to be turned out to pasture, I came here, built this place with a bit of help from him. I like silence, and I didn't like what Ivan was turning out to be—he was bad to his wife and worse to his men. So, what's your name, Ivanovitch? It's a damn shame young Ivan turned out to be more of a fool than you pretended to be, or he'd have chucked the other boys out and kept you. And who's your mother?"

"I'm Ilya," he replied, limp with relief. He'd actually *heard* of Yasha once or twice from Ruslan and some of the older servants, especially the hound-master, who swore that only Yasha could properly breed and raise the borzoi. Even if this was the old *domovoi,* Yasha was kindly inclined toward him. And if it wasn't—Yasha was *still* kindly inclined toward him. "I'm the middle son, from Ivan's second wife, Ekaterina."

"Middle son?" Yasha's eyebrows arched. "Two wives? I got the impression from you that there were more than three boys—how big a litter did he raise?"

"Eight, altogether, and he's on his third wife," Ilya replied, rubbing his arms a little to ease some of the aches still in them.

Yasha snorted in contempt. "Eight! All still at home!"

"More or less," Ilya sighed. "I told you that Pietor ran off with two of his best horses and a load of loot. I think that Ivan had planned to ship Boris off to his new father-in-law along with that poor dumpling of a bride, but he might use my 'death' as an excuse to call the wedding off and bundle her back to Papa." He laughed ruefully. "Dying this opportunely would be the only thing I'd ever done that would make

Father happy, I'm afraid. He'll be able to pick whether to use it as an excuse to hurry the wedding up or cancel it.''

Yasha shook his head. "Gods. And you the only one with sense in the lot. And my poor old friend Ruslan, how does he fare? I told him he ought to come with me, the way young Ivan was turning out, but he wouldn't leave your grandfather. Loyal to a fault, and now he's probably too old to come hunting for me." Yasha sucked at his lower lip thoughtfully. "I suppose I ought to think about going to fetch him myself; by now, he probably thinks *I'm* dead.''

"Well, he's safe enough, and he's got at least two friends," Ilya replied with truth, and went on to describe Ruslan's situation, Father Mikail, and Mother Galina. He tried to make it clear how much Father Mikail and Ruslan respected each other, and how Mother Galina would make use of her own indispensable position to see that they got decent treatment, if nothing else. Old Yasha nodded every now and then, but had the solitary man's habit of never interrupting until a speaker was finished with what he had to say.

"I told Vasily that the boy was going sour," Yasha said bitterly. "But Ivan was the only boy to survive, and he was precious; his opinions were taken as if he'd earned the right to voice them—whatever he said was taken seriously. By the time I left, the boy was a little buzzard, waiting for Vasily to die, impatient to have everything it took ten generations to build as if it was all owed to him.''

"Mischa's like that," Ilya ventured. "Maybe all young men are.''

"All young men are impatient to have a life, and that's understandable," Yasha replied. "But Ivan—he wanted everything, but never cared for all the work and effort it took to create what he wanted. When no one's opinion counted to him but his own, he didn't even have the respect to cherish and protect what his father felt was important, and what went into making up what *he* was." Yasha groped for words. Ilya remained silent while the old hunter searched for the way to say what he wanted to.

"It's this—I know all old men complain that young men pay no attention to tradition, but there's usually a reason for a tradition. Sometimes it's a reason that doesn't hold anymore, but there was *always* a reason for it. That's why it's important to listen to old men—they know the 'whys' as well as the customs. And a man without custom and tradition is a man without roots; he'll blow away in the first hard storm, and no one will ever miss him.''

''I think I see what you mean,'' Ilya replied, creasing his brows. ''If you don't have a tradition behind something, there's nothing to keep you from changing it every time you don't happen to like what's going on at the moment. And if you keep changing your mind and the way you do things, you'll never really figure out what is going to work.''

Yasha nodded eagerly. ''The reason traditions start is because they *work,* and someone probably paid a dear price to find that out. When you throw all that away, you're throwing away their lives and all they stood for and sacrificed along with it! When you throw it away, you're saying that your ancestors had nothing to do with what you are now, that your prosperity and your life all came into being because you were somehow so meritorious just by being alive that the world made it all spring up out of nothing just for you. And that was Ivan all over; throwing everything away so that he could make his own rules—and what has it gotten him? A houseful of contention, enemies in his own family, a wife who despises him, and the only son worth more than the earth to bury him in is the one that is the least regarded.'' Yasha snorted. ''So much for believing that every new idea has to be a good one just because it's new!''

He asked more questions about the incidents that had led to Ilya's becoming the Fool. Ilya obliged him, although he made no mention of the more outré supernatural elements of his story. He didn't talk about his grandfather Vasily and all his great-greats appearing in the crypt. And he continued to leave the appearance of the Firebird out of his story, and his own subsequent ability to hear and understand animals. At that point, the wolfhound bitch left her place at the fire and walked deliberately over to the two of them, gazing searchingly into Ilya's face. She was one of the most magnificent animals he had ever seen, an incredible specimen of her kind, with a pristine white coat, delicate muzzle, and huge, intelligent eyes. It was easy to see that the wolfhound currently leading Ivan's pack was out of her line.

"You ought to tell him," the bitch said directly to him, gazing at him with liquid brown eyes. *"He has the right to know, does my master, what has come into his house. I know that you would not harm him, but he has the right to know."*

"He ought to tell me what?" the old man asked her sharply. "What is it I have the right to know about my guest?"

Ilya's mouth dropped open, and he stared at each of them in turn, his eyes going from the dog to the man and back again in a manner that was probably quite comical.

The wolfhound turned her attention to her master, bending her slim, aristocratic muzzle to him. *"He ought to tell you he's Firebird-touched,"* she said. *"We can scent the magic on him, and we know that he hasn't told you everything that happened to him yet. He can talk to us, just like you can, and he is wearing a thing on his wrist that is also magic-scented, but it is a different scent from the Firebird."*

"You—the dogs—I—ah—I didn't know—" Ilya stammered. "I beg your pardon, but I thought—"

For the first time, Yasha interrupted him with a wave of his hand. "Never mind. I understand why you didn't say anything." He chuckled. "You probably thought I was like most people; that I wouldn't believe you if you started talking about Firebirds and being able to understand animals. It must have taken a great deal of courage to mention the *rusalka.*"

"Well, I have the marks on my wrists to prove she almost had me," Ilya replied with a wince. "And most people believe in the water-spirits. But I never heard of anyone who could speak with animals before, and I certainly never heard of the Firebird outside of a tale, and I don't think anyone else I know has, either."

Yasha chuckled. "I can certainly guess how you've been feeling. The gift of tongues is a strange gift to receive, especially if you aren't prepared for it. I got it years ago, from the *leshii;* I did one of them a great favor, and they gave it to me to help me be a better hunter. You thought you were mad when you started to hear the beasts, right?"

"I wondered," Ilya admitted. The old man laughed, throwing his head back and shaking his head.

"You poor fellow!" he chuckled, wiping his eyes. "At least the *leshii* told me what he was going to do. But yours is from the Firebird! I suppose you must have seen her. Is that who was stealing the cherries?"

Ilya nodded. "I was in the trees, watching, while Pietor took his turn at guard. I kept myself awake with pins. I didn't tell anyone about her. I couldn't; I didn't think Father would believe me, in the first place, and if he did, I was afraid he would try and catch her. He can't see or hear of anything valuable without trying to get it—you should have seen what he went through in order to get our prize stud! I guess that's why she made me the gift."

"But ever since you saw her, you've had terrible bad luck." Yasha nodded wisely, as the wolfhound bitch lay down at his feet. "Not too surprising. So, let me think back along your story. Since you could speak with beasts, most of them would have been trying to help you. So your horse didn't really run off, he ran away with you a-purpose, knowing what your brothers intended—that's why you aren't more knocked about than you are. When he got savaged by the boar, you had to kill him. And the gift of tongues—that's how you knew to rescue the nightingale from the *rusalka,* right?"

"Exactly." Ilya frowned for a moment. "I still can't imagine why she had a bird in a fish-trap."

"Terrible bad magic," the old hunter said, with a shake of his head and a sad and serious look on his face. "The water-spirits hate the spirits of the air, and they kill air-creatures to make the worst of their magics. That *rusalka*'s a mean bitch; I know her, and she's as much witch as spirit, and spiteful enough for twenty. Sometimes you can get the *rusalka* to like you and help you, but never her; she's the daughter of the boyar of the lake and never lets the other spirits forget it. Proud, petty, and vicious, and a good thing you had help, or you'd never have gotten away from her." He cast a sharp glance at Ilya. "You *did* have help, didn't you?"

Ilya nodded, and told the old man about the spirit of his sorrel gelding and the bracelet of horsehair he now wore. "Maybe it's foolish, but the horse did tell me to make and wear it. . . ." He trailed off.

"Let me see." Mutely, Ilya held out his hand, and the old

man examined the horsehair bracelet minutely. "Huh. Not one of the Night Wind's foals, or the boar wouldn't have touched him, but I'll bet he was telling the truth and he's Night Wind get, all the same. There's enough of her sons about to have sired or grand-sired your gelding. Your luck started to change about when you put it on, didn't it?"

Ilya thought for a moment, and realized with surprise that he was correct. "Come to think of it, you're right. After I made the bracelet and put it on, I found a few things to eat, and nothing harassed me on the trail. I never even heard or saw anything but ravens all day."

"That's it." Yasha smiled and nodded, and so did the wolf-hound, in a somber imitation of her master that would have been funny if both of them hadn't been so serious. "He's countering the Firebird's bad luck. He's not got enough of the Night Wind blood to give you *good* luck, but he can counter the bad. I'd wear that until the bad luck wears off, or she takes it off, but she'd have to see you to do that, and you'd probably have to do her a good turn again. She's already paid you for the last one."

Ilya pursed his lips in thought. "But why did I get bad luck in the first place just by looking at the Firebird?"

Yasha laughed, spreading his hands wide. "Who knows? She's a spirit-creature; they have their own rules! If I were to guess, though, it's probably something she does to make sure that those who see her can never catch her—if suddenly their luck goes bad, even if she doesn't know they're there, then she's a bit safer. If she can foul their luck, their nets will tangle, their snares will foul, their arrows will go astray, bow-strings snap, bows break. Of course, if anything came to catch her that had stronger magic to counter hers, then she would be in trouble."

Ilya sighed, then jumped as a knot in the fire popped. "I can't thank you enough for your hospitality," he said slowly. "And I can only think of repaying you by offering to help you, if I can."

"As a matter of fact, you can, if you don't mind a bit of hard work," the old man told him. "But first, you sleep a bit more, and eat a bit more, and we'll see to the chores tomorrow." He smiled, as Ilya belatedly wondered what he'd gotten himself in for. "Don't worry, I'm not the *domovoi* from your house; the Old Man was still in residence when I left, and being honored as was proper. If I were to guess, I'd say he took up residence in the hunting-lodge the master of the hounds built for your grandfather; it never had a proper *domovoi*, and it's the closest dwelling. The dog-master knows how to properly honor the spirits, and that may be the only reason why the *domovoi* hasn't given Ivan what's coming to him—that, and Ruslan is protecting the brat as he promised Vasily he would. I know he says he isn't, but I'll bet that he is. Maybe when Ruslan dies or goes away, the *domovoi* will make up for lost time, and no one I know would weep."

"Have *you* a *domovoi*?" Ilya whispered, looking over his shoulder.

"Of course," Yasha said matter-of-factly. "Don't worry about him; I know better than most how to honor spirits. You likely won't see him while you're here, he's shy—but he looks just like me. The *bannik*, on the other hand, I know is there, but I've never seen him."

At the mention of the *bannik*, Ilya realized how filthy he was. Some of his sudden longing for a bath must have shown in his face, for Yasha looked at him intently for a moment, then stood up.

"Speaking of our bathhouse friend, I am overdue for a steaming. I don't fire up the house as often as I should, being alone, but with two here, it's worth it. Care for a bath, Ilya Ivánovitch? You'll have to help me chop extra wood."

"It will be worth it!" Ilya exclaimed, getting stiffly to his feet.

The next hour or so was spent in readying the bathhouse and getting the fires going. Then they both chopped wood madly, replacing wood for the house-fire that they had used up in the bathhouse. When they were done—and Ilya made a point of chopping more than his share, more than old Yasha asked him to—they were both ready for that steam.

Yasha liked his steambaths the old-fashioned way—a bath, then a steaming, followed by a dash into the snow, a brisk beating with fir-branches, then another steaming. Ilya was quite content merely to douse himself with cold water from a bucket, but if the old wolf-hunter had toughened himself with this particular ritual, there was little wonder that he had survived so long by himself.

"Third steaming's for the *bannik*," Yasha said, leaving fir-branches, soap, firewood, and water ready. "And we could stand a change of clothing. I hate getting into dirty clothes when I'm clean, and yours aren't going to be fit again until they're washed and mended."

Ilya didn't ask where the old man was going to get clothing to fit him; he was too drowsily content after the hot steam, which had done wonders for all of his aches and pains, and even for his head. He wondered if Yasha had healing herbs in the honey-wine; there had been a taste there he hadn't recognized. It was a pleasant taste, to be sure, but quite unfamiliar.

They trudged back through the snow to the house; once there, the old man went up into the loft above the main room and came down with an armload of wildly disparate clothing. The only thing all the pieces had in common with one another was that they were clean, obviously had been worn at least once, and were a bit faded.

"That *rusalka* and her father are good for one thing," he said slyly. "When they're done with a victim, they haven't any use for his possessions, and they cast them up on the beach. I go gleaning there about once a week in the summer; most times I find nothing, but I've been here for years, and I haven't had to buy a stitch of clothing for myself in all that time."

Ilya wondered for a moment if he should feel squeamish about wearing the clothing of a dead man—but Yasha obviously didn't feel that way, and he was more familiar with ghosts and spirits than Ilya was. Finally, he bent to help Yasha in picking over the clothing.

"This ought to fit you, and this," Yasha said, picking out a streaked and faded red tunic of fine wool with an embroidered collar, and a shirt of light linen, a little discolored, to wear beneath. "And this," holding up a pair of black leather breeches. "I couldn't get into those, but I save what I can't fit, for patches and all." He tossed the clothing to Ilya, who caught it, and stripped off his own peasant-garb of wool. Then Yasha swiftly changed into a sober brown tunic and matching breeches with a modest amount of trim at the collar. Ilya sacrificed squeamishness in favor of clean clothing, and climbed into Yasha's offerings.

They fit perfectly. With the addition of thick stockings and his own boots and belt, Ilya's outfitting was complete, and he had to admit he felt much better. The clothing was scrupulously clean, and there was no sign of how the *rusalka* and her father had eliminated the previous owners.

Supper was venison stew, and afterward it was Yasha's turn to talk, telling simple stories of wolf-hunts and dog-breeding, made a bit different by the casual way he would refer to what his dogs had told him—and the way his borzoi-bitch would chime in with additions or corrections as needed. Finally, weariness, relaxation after the bath, and the honey-wine all caught up to Ilya. He pulled out the trundle-bed himself and fell into it, pulling the blanket and furs over his head. His last sight was of Yasha and the hounds discussing things over the fire.

In the morning he felt very much his old self, and woke at the same time as Yasha. He discovered that he need not have worried that Yasha was going to set him to impossible tasks; the chores that Yasha had in mind were all simple ones. He wanted help with chopping wood, for his old shoulders were not as pain-free as young ones. He also wanted help with a few tasks that needed two sets of hands: some mending of the roof of the house, the bathhouse, and his storage sheds. That was enough for one day, and the next two or three were similar. Ilya helped him with nearly everything, from tanning the stacks of hides he'd accumulated, to smoking the deer and boar he brought down the third day after Ilya arrived, to chopping a small forest of deadfall wood. Days of hard work always ended in the bathhouse, and at night Ilya slept and dreamed. He didn't remember what he dreamed, except that it had to do with the Firebird, and he felt an increasing certainty that she had meant more with her gift than merely to give him the means to understand the speech of animals. In the end, though, there wasn't much left to do; Yasha could go the whole winter without having to leave the clearing in the center of the maze if he wanted to.

"Well, you've seen to it that I needn't do a bit of hard work this winter, and that's a fact,'' Yasha said the night Ilya finished the last of the wood-chopping. The wolf-hunter laughed, as he often did. ''I'll have to be diligent in my hunting, or I'll run to fat! But now what will *you* do? Go back to Ivan? I can show you the way, if you'd like—maybe you could persuade that old fool Ruslan to come back here with you. By Perun, maybe you could talk the Christ-man into coming too, and see if we convert him or he converts us first! We could be four bachelors together until spring, then see if a pile of furs will buy you a pretty bride to take care of all of us!''

''I could go home and frighten Mischa—make him think I'm a ghost!'' Ilya replied. ''Then, maybe I could let things go back to the way they were, but only after I threw a good scare into him by coming in his window at night!''

Yasha laughed hugely at that, then sobered. ''The trouble is, you'd have a damned hard time convincing anyone you were a fool after wandering around in the woods for so long. I can go fetch Ruslan myself in the summer, and I will, since things aren't going so well for him. So don't think you have to go back because of him. You decide for you; what will you do? Go back, or go on, or stay here? You're welcome here, and no doubt of it.''

Ilya twisted the horsehair bracelet on his wrist and considered his options, slightly dazed by the fact that now he *had* options. ''I think, and no slight meant to you, Yasha, that I would like to go on. I think the Firebird meant something when she gave me her gift; I don't know what, but I want to find out.''

Yasha and the wolfhound bitch exchanged a look, and it was the dog who spoke first. ''*I told you no one who is Firebird-touched is ever satisfied with a common life again. I told you he was going to have to follow the scent of magic.*''

''Eh, well, you were right, dog,'' Yasha admitted and sighed. ''Good enough, and I can't blame you. But winter can be deadly in these woods; if you haven't found anything by the time the going gets bad, come back here and bide with me the rest of the winter, all right? We'll go after Ruslan in the spring, and maybe steal some of Ivan's horses, and then you can be off again in high style!'' He grinned ferally. ''There isn't a dog on that estate that will so much as bark at me, and the day I can't get past one of Ivan's stupid hired guards is the day I will lie down and die. Between me and my silver beauty here, when the horses get turned out for spring grazing, we could nip you a pair as smart as any gypsy, and no one the wiser. Then you could be off; maybe go to the Great Tsar, and sell your services to him as a horse-talker if you tire of chasing Firebirds.''

The idea had merit, Ilya had to agree. Certainly, if things were parceled out honestly, his inheritance would amount to far more than a couple of horses—and a horse-talker could command fees as high as any magician.

''I'll do that,'' he promised. ''But first—just say I have a trail I have to follow, at least to see if it comes to a dead-end or not. If it does, I'll be back.''

''Fair enough,'' Yasha agreed. ''Now, let's see what the *rusalka*'s leavings are, and how well we can outfit you.''

In the end, the *rusalka* outfitted him very well indeed. He had a pack, changes of clothing, a cloak to go over his coat in case he needed to sleep in the snow some night, a coil of rope, two knives, a sword, a bow and arrows, a spear, a fire-striker and tinder-box, everything a traveler might need to trek through the forest in winter. The only thing he lacked was a horse or a donkey, but in the winter, it would be hard to find animal fodder, so perhaps it was just as well he was taking only what he could carry. He knew that Yasha would have parted with the youngest of his three dogs if he'd asked, but he wasn't going to ask. He'd already indirectly been the cause of one animal's death; he wasn't going to take the chance of putting one of Yasha's precious wolfhounds in danger.

Yasha gave him a rough map of the area around his maze, to the best of his knowledge, but to the west the map was mostly a blank. ''I don't go there much,'' Yasha admitted, as they sat over the sketch just before Ilya shouldered his pack to leave. ''I'm a creature of habit, and there was never any-thing to the west that I needed to see.'' He rubbed his nose. ''Maybe there's something in the west that wanted me to feel that way, eh?''

''It could be,'' Ilya agreed. ''If there's any direction it feels like *I* ought to be going in, though, it's to the west. So maybe that ought to be my sign.'' He hoisted his pack to his shoulders and shifted until it balanced correctly. If he got into a fight, he could drop it immediately and have knife and sword in his hands in moments, for both were belted on over his coat.

"Good enough!" the wolf-hunter said. "Just remember my promise, and your own."

"I will, and you have all my thanks, Yasha," Ilya replied, taking a moment to study the old man's face. He was looking for something subtle—loneliness, the vague fear of being on his own through the long winter—and if he saw it, he was going to change his mind, put the pack down, and wait to see what spring brought. He'd already taken the wolfhound bitch aside and asked her if she thought Yasha would be all right when he left. Her opinion was that he would. But Ilya wanted to know for certain. After so long a time of being alone, Yasha could not hide his thoughts; he wore them as clearly as if he had them written on his shirt-front.

Ilya saw nothing in the old man's eyes that he had not already seen every day that they had spent together, and he felt the release of great relief. Yasha *was* used to being alone—and he wasn't precisely "alone" as long as he had the gift of animal tongues. He would be fine, and so would Ruslan. Yasha would not leave his old friend in Ivan's house a moment longer than he had to, now that he knew how things stood. Ilya had some thought that Yasha might well go after Ruslan as soon as his guest left, if the weather looked to hold for a while. Ilya was free to go wherever his need led him.

With a wave of his hand and an odd feeling of contentment, he plunged into the maze.

When he emerged again, according to Yasha, he was going to have to follow the outside walls of the maze until he was going due west. There was a game-trail along the outside, for birds and small animals sheltered in the dense bushes, and deer browsing there where grasses rooted at the base of the hedge. Then, the game-trail went westward, more or less, for at least a league; beyond that, Yasha didn't know, for he had never gone that far.

But with a pack full of supplies and food, and with weapons in his hands and at his belt, Ilya felt more confidence than he had in months. He followed the game-trail as Yasha had described it, with the wall of dense bushes to his right, and did indeed find a new trail striking off to the west that joined the one around the outside of the maze. The snow was not terribly deep, and there was no wind; the sun shone brightly down on the forest, and if there was ever a perfect day to strike out on a journey, this was it.

I know of the rusalka *and her father to the south of here— who knows what there might be in the rest of the forest?* he thought, with more of a thrill than a feeling of trepidation. *There might be anything! There might be the palace of a magician, the tower of a lovely, lonely sorceress, or an enchanted grove where maidens have been turned into statues, waiting for the kiss of a warrior to change them back into girls!* The world seemed fraught with possibilities, and Ilya found that he was paying attention to everything.

His first day passed without anything of real note happening, and the second and third were like the first. He used his bow to take down a couple of rabbits to make his supplies last a little longer—either there was a great deal more game in the forest here, or he had been so dazed and disoriented when he had wandered after the accident that he had missed all signs of the animals around him.

Or else, his luck had been so bad that all the animals had avoided him, and now he was enjoying perfectly normal luck, in which he hit some rabbits, fired at others and missed, and lost one arrow when it hit a rock and shattered. That was the way an ordinary day of hunting in ordinary forest should pass. Normal luck pleased him completely; it was pleasant to be able to hope that the universe would not *always* muster its forces against him.

But having had completely bad luck for so long made him very cautious. When he made camp, he would always stop at the first good place that presented itself, instead of trusting that something better might show up later. He never had to camp in the open, thanks to that policy. The first night he was on his own, he found a rough tripod of downed trees with a cavity beneath them just big enough to curl up in. The second night, he discovered a group of rocks at the edge of a ravine with a similar shelter. The third night, he made a rough lean-to beneath the branches of one of those enormous pines, a sheltered space beneath their drooping boughs. Although he sometimes wished the next morning that he *had* walked a little farther, there were always enough downed trees, groups of rocks, or sheltering glades to provide some protection if the weather turned bad. Yasha assured him that a fire was sufficient to keep off wolves and lynx, and suggested that he always have something solid on three sides of him, and he was usually able to situate a lean-to so that he had that protection and could sleep without worrying about predators. Between the fur-lined wool cloak and his coat, he slept as warmly and safely as if he were in the trundle-bed.

All the while, his sense that something was about to happen strengthened and made him aware of everything around him, from the winter-birds in the trees above to the tiniest movement in the woods beyond.

So when he came to a place where one large tree had crashed to the ground some time in the last summer, taking several smaller ones down with it, he didn't miss the hint of movement just as he rounded a turn in the game-trail, nor the scrap of reddish-brown fur lying oddly atop the fallen trunk. He ventured off the trail, cautiously, wading through fresh, unbroken snow up to his thighs in places. As he neared the tree with the fur on it, he saw that there was a split in the trunk, and that disturbed snow seemed to indicate that the trunk had moved a little, very recently. As he got even closer, he saw that the tree had caught itself a victim.

The scrap of fur was the tip of a tail, stuck in the split trunk, and the tail belonged to a live fox vixen, who peered up at him from behind the trunk, her teeth bared in a terrified snarl as he approached. It wasn't too hard to see that she was a vixen, not a dog-fox; not with the way her tail was being held. She alternated her actions among trying to frighten him off, trying to escape, and trying to hide.

"You poor little thing!" he exclaimed, seeing her terror. "Your luck must have turned as bad as my own was!" Something must have been holding the split trunk apart—perhaps a bit of wood wedged in the crack—that had given way as the vixen was hunting for mice in and around it, catching her tail in a viselike grip. She *could* get away by gnawing her tail off, but obviously that would be painful, and she hadn't gotten to that extreme yet.

Now, he was not a hunter, like Yasha, with a market for fur, and fox was not edible. He had no reason to want to kill the little vixen, and he never killed anything without a good reason if he could help it.

He didn't want to leave her here; she might have to gnaw herself free, which would be very dangerous as well as painful, creating a place for wound-rot to set in. If she didn't free herself soon enough, she could become prey for another animal: a lynx, a bear, or a wolf, perhaps. But he also had no intentions of getting bitten for his pains, and he couldn't count on the fox understanding his human words, as his friend the gelding had pointed out.

So he shrugged out of his pack, took the rolled-up cloak off the top of it, and while the vixen watched him with eyes that were nearly insane with terror, he threw it over her. The moment its folds fell around her, she began fighting it, snapping and whining with pain, but he picked her and the cloak up together and rolled her tightly in it, immobilizing her.

"Now, pretty little lady, you must stay still," he said, in as soothing a tone as he could manage. "I'm going to free your tail and let you go, but the job will go faster if you don't struggle."

Whether she heard and understood him or not, she suddenly stopped fighting, and remained a tense but unmoving bundle inside the entangling folds of the cloak.

After that, it was only a little work to take his hand-ax, cut a crude wedge from a bit of branch, jam it into the split trunk at the narrowest part, and hammer it home with the butt of the ax. The split widened again, and as the fox involuntarily flicked her tail, it came free of the wood.

Ilya picked her up again, took her over to a clear spot, and gently freed her of the cloak, stepping quickly away so she wasn't tempted to snap at him. She lay in the snow for a moment, as if dazed, then got to her feet and shook herself hard.

Then she craned her neck around and stared at her tail as if she didn't quite believe that it was free and undamaged, except for a bit of bruising.

Ilya smiled and chuckled. "There, you see," he said, very quietly. "I told you I didn't mean to hurt you. Now go run off, and find a handsome dog-fox. But watch out for this tree—the wedge I put in it may not hold any better than the last thing wedging it open did.''

She turned and looked at him, looked him straight in the eyes as wild things very seldom do. *''Thank you, man-child, I won't forget this. You might want to know,''* she said, slowly and clearly, *''that if you go on the way you have been, you'll come to the maze around the Katschei's palace.''*

Then, with a bound, she was gone, vanishing with that astounding ability that foxes and cats seem to share.

A maze? Around a palace? That piqued his curiosity as nothing else could have. Who besides Yasha had built a maze in the middle of the wilderness? And who besides a water-spirit would have a palace here?

Well, I'm not a bad hand at mazes; perhaps I can solve this one, and find out what a ''Katschei'' is.

First, he would make sure no other animal got caught in the same trap. Using the wedge he had already driven into the trunk, he split the fallen tree completely and left the two halves standing slightly apart.

He rolled up his cloak, replaced it and the hand-ax in his pack, shouldered the pack, and went back to the game-trail. *Katschei;* it had a strange, exotic sound to it. Maybe this was the ''scent of magic'' that he had been chasing.

There was another possibility, and it drew him irresistibly. Maybe there he would see the Firebird again.

ILYA had reached the maze the fox had told him about, and now he stared up at the strangest structure he had ever seen in his life.

It was a wall—a stone wall—reaching twice as high as he was tall. It was made of perfectly fitted square blocks of some polished gray stone, put together, so far as he could see, without the use of mortar or cement. The wall went for furlongs, perhaps a league, in either direction, and he had walked quite some distance to find the opening.

The only stone walls that *he* had ever seen had been made of fieldstone mortared together with cement. He had heard of marble, of course, and knew that it was supposed to be of surpassing whiteness, so he didn't think this wall could be made of that substance, but what *was* it? And why waste so much obviously fine material on the walls of an outdoor maze? The amount of labor implied in the construction of this wall made his head reel. How long and how many men had it taken to quarry and smooth all these blocks? How long to transport them? And how long to fit them together?

When the fox had said that there was a maze ahead of him, he had naturally thought of a simple little maze, perhaps of wooden fence-sections, or hedges, or, just possibly, rough fieldstone walls. He had never imagined anything like this! Either the Katschei was as fabulously wealthy as the Great Tsar and as mad as a cuckoo, or he was a sorcerer of unbelievable power. In either case, Ilya found himself eaten alive with curiosity. He had to find out what lay on the other side of the maze!

Still, if he stood here staring at it, he'd never get anywhere. He hitched his pack a little higher on his shoulders, made sure that his sword was loose in the sheath, and entered into the Katschei's maze. Surely it could not be that complicated; the sheer cost of building these enormous stone walls would make it impossible to construct a large maze. A few turns and he would be at the Katschei's palace, and find out just what a Katschei was. He was quite confident that he could solve this little problem in time for his midday meal.

It was a little before noon when he entered it; by nightfall, he was exhausted and hungry, and ready to admit defeat. He'd already made one attempt to find his way back out, and now he was completely lost. The maze went on forever, or so it seemed; monolithic gray stone walls on either side of him, twice the height of a man and with about as much space between them, and nothing whatsoever to relieve the gray of the stone, the white of the snow. He *should* have been able to retrace his steps by retracing his own path in the snow, but somehow he had come to an intersection where all four of the paths were trampled, and that was where he had gotten lost. He was just glad that this was winter and there was snow to melt for drink—for otherwise he'd be very thirsty by now.

He still could not imagine how anyone had ever built this place—unless it had been by magic. When he'd read of the legend of the Minotaur in Father Mikail's books, he'd never been able to figure out how those Greek boys and girls had managed to get lost in the Minotaur's maze——he'd pictured a maze like the one protecting the family crypt. His father's maze was frightening for a child, of course, and it took remaining calm to master it, but you couldn't wander about for more than half a day without finding your way out, if only by accident. Now he understood how people could wander for days in a maze and never know where they were. He was not certain that he could have found a ball of string long enough to mark where he had gone so far.

He came to another dead-end, and stopped, just as the sky reddened in the west. He'd tried to use the location of the sun as a guide, but not even that had kept him from getting lost. Now the sun was about to set, and he was faced with a decision: stop here, camp in this dead-end where he would at least be safe in three directions, or try to keep going with the stars as his guide?

As the light faded and he considered his options and the top of the wall, he suddenly grinned. It would be a great deal easier to negotiate this maze from above; the builder had probably never thought that someone trapped in his construction would climb to the top and make his way where he could see where he was going.

But if I'm going to do that, he thought, *I'd better try and get up there now, while I can still see.*

He set down his pack and took out his rope, tying one end to the pack and the other to his belt. He took off his sword and added it to the pack, knowing that to try and climb while wearing it was a recipe for comedy, but wouldn't help him much. Then he took a running start down the long leg of the dead-end and launched himself at the wall.

He hit it perfectly, but could not catch the top, and slid ignominiously down it.

He could hardly believe it, the first time it happened, thinking that he surely must have hit a slick patch. He removed his mittens, backed up, and tried again, with similar results. It was almost as if the top of the wall suddenly moved out of his reach just as his fingers touched it!

He tried several more times, including using the corners, and all without any success whatsoever. It was like trying to climb a wall of glass. When he tried to find finger-and toe-holds to scramble up the wall lizard-fashion, he failed again. There wasn't enough room between the blocks of stone to insert a piece of paper, much less his fingers, and there were no rough places or imperfections. When he tried to make an improvised grapple out of some of his equipment, there was nothing on the top of the wall for the grapple to catch onto. The moon rose long before he finally gave up and sat down in the snow, defeated by the monolithic stone giants guarding the Katschei's palace.

Now what am I going to do? Wander for days? If he'd had any notion that this was going to happen, he'd have marked the walls or the snow next to them with arrows, so he would at least have *known* how to get back out. *But maybe that would have failed, too. Maybe something or someone would have come along and erased the arrows. . . .*

He was too baffled to feel despair yet—he wasn't anywhere near out of supplies, and there was plenty of snow to drink, but what if this maze had guards patrolling it? The Katschei clearly didn't want visitors.

What if it has something worse than guards patrolling it? he thought with sudden dread. Ruslan's tales were full of hideous possibilities, from man-devouring tigers to demonic monsters. *What have I gotten myself into?* Now despair settled over his heart in a black pall. *What good is ordinary luck going to do me in a situation like this one? I could be drinking with Yasha right now, planning how we're going to get Ruslan and Father Mikail out without my father knowing. I could at least be outside this endless maze! I'm never going to find my way out of here—it would take a miracle to get me out of here now.*

But just as he thought that, he heard a sudden trill of song above his head, a bit of melody more often heard in high summer than the start of winter.

Birdsong? Here? Now?

It was a nightingale, but what was it doing here?

Startled, he looked up, but of course saw nothing; it was dark, and there was no way for him to see a dull-gray bird against the night sky. The nightingale, however, saw him very clearly.

"Boy! Boy!" she called. *"Look at me, boy! Hear me! I live in Katschei's garden! Follow, and I lead!"*

Was it the nightingale he had rescued from the *rusalka*? He couldn't imagine any other bird remaining in the north in winter. But how was he going to follow the bird when he couldn't see her?

He shouldered his pack quickly, and went to the end of the dead-end passage. When he came to the first turning, he found out how he was to follow her.

"Right! Right, boy! Right, and then follow, follow!" the bird sang gaily, as if she flitted through warm summer skies. *"Follow, and I lead!"* Evidently she was flying ahead to the next turning, and landing and waiting there for him. *Now* he had the aerial view he wanted, even if it was by means of a bird's eyes!

At every turning, the nightingale flitted overhead and sang his direction; he moved as quickly as he could, given the heavy burden of the pack, praying that she would not lose interest in leading him. And as he followed the nightingale through the maze, he began to sweat, until his fur coat seemed unbearably hot. At first he thought it was because he was moving at a quick trot and was overheating beneath the heavy fur coat. But then he saw that the snow was gone—

A few turnings more, and the feeling of the ground beneath his boot changed. He stopped for just a moment, pulled off his mittens, and knelt cautiously to feel it. With a sense of shock, he ran his hand over the supple blades of fresh, green grass. This was not just grass that was growing nicely, it was grass that had not yet felt the touch of frost.

Shock might have held him there for some time had the nightingale not circled overhead, warning him that this was not a good idea. *"Hurry, boy! The Katschei's guards look for wanderers! Follow, follow, or they find you!"*

That was enough to send him lurching to his feet and on to the next turning. No wonder the nightingale didn't feel the need to migrate to the south—she had summer here, in the middle of this maze! Perhaps that was why she understood the human tongue; she must have heard it here. And no wonder the Katschei had no trouble raising the walls of the maze itself—to anyone capable of keeping summer alive through the midst of winter, raising a few paltry walls to make a maze would be child's play.

Ilya stopped only once more, to pull off his coat and add it to the bundle atop his pack—he hadn't wanted to stop at all, but he was sweating so beneath the burden of fur that he simply couldn't stand it anymore. Once he had the coat off, it was as if he was running beneath a midsummer moon, the air was that balmy and warm. It even carried the scent of flowers, roses and other blossoms, quite as if it was not only summer, but spring as well, a mingling of three seasons.

The maze was changing as he got nearer to the center. The walls were taller, as if the Katschei wanted to block out every glimpse of the world on the other side of it. As if the maze itself was not discouragement enough! It was a good thing that he had the bird as his guide, for there was no pattern to the turnings that he had yet been able to discern. Perhaps there was a pattern here, but if so, it was too complicated for him to figure out on the run.

"Two turnings, boy!" sang the bird overhead. "Now one! Left, left—yes! Now you are here!"

Ilya rounded the last corner of the last wall and simply stood and stared. The Katschei's palace rose above the orchard immediately in front of him.

So this is the Katschei's palace, he thought dimly, then shrank back, afraid. What in the name of God am I doing here?

CHAPTER SEVEN

UNTIL THIS moment, Ilya had never in his life seen anything like the walls of the maze, and he was completely unable to conceive of the amount of work it must have taken to build them.

Now he had finally seen what the maze was protecting, and the Katschei's palace made the walls of the maze look insignificant.

He wasn't actually *at* the palace yet; it was clear from the trees before him, and the substantial amount of land between him and the structure, that there was a complex of orchards and gardens to traverse before he reached the building. The land covered by the maze and grounds alone must be as much as Ivan claimed for his palace, the family farms and fields, and all of the hunting preserve besides. But this palace loomed over the tops of the trees, lit up like a Christmas cake, an incredible confection of turrets and domes, of towers and twisting staircases, decorated in every color he had ever seen in his life.

Whoever the Katschei was, he seemed to be very fond of rainbow hues. Every dome was tiled in a different color: scarlet and blue and emerald green, some in multiple colors and patterns, every tower roofed in silver or gold. Each window had beautifully painted shutters, and although it was quite obvious that the palace was made of stone, it was made of a dozen different kinds of stone, cut and laid together, forming intricate geometric patterns up and down the walls. Doorways and arches were rimmed in carved alabaster so finely detailed that from here it looked like lace—Ivan had a collection of alabaster eggs, so Ilya knew what alabaster looked like, and this was either that fine material or something very like it—and the twisting pillars of serpentine, jade, onyx, and carnelian upholding porticoes and porches were twined with bands of gold. He couldn't even begin to count how many stories tall the structure was; he had to crane his neck to look up at it. He couldn't begin to estimate the number of rooms—two hundred? Three? A thousand? His father's palace wouldn't even qualify as an outbuilding to this place. A toolshed, maybe, or a gardener's shed, but anyone who lived in a place this grand wouldn't put even his gardener in a house like Ivan's palace.

Ilya had to rub his eyes, pinch himself, and look again to convince himself that he wasn't dreaming. Nothing had changed the second time he looked. And what was lighting the building? The walls were as bright as if the sun were shining on them! How was the Katschei doing that? He'd seen buildings with every window alight at a festival, but never for more than an hour or so, and he'd never seen anyone illuminate the *outside* of a building before. The expense in an hour's worth of lamp-oil or candles alone would ruin the richest man he knew!

Just as that thought occurred to him, the illumination went out, leaving the building lit only by the moon. A few of the windows still glowed with light from within, but many of those were winking out. He glanced up at the moon and realized that it was well after midnight; quite late, even by the standards of someone who owned a palace like this one. He had somehow arrived just in time for the occupants of the palace to go to bed.

And he didn't blame them for making the light go away—it would be impossible to sleep with all that light glaring in through the windows.

But now that the palace no longer commanded his attention, he noticed that there was a furtive light in the orchard itself, very near to hand. It moved and flickered, but never went far from one spot. It might be a good idea to go have a look at that light before he did anything else. The nightingale had already warned him about guards—well, maybe that was where the guards were. And in any case, it was pretty obvious that the Katschei was not particularly fond of unexpected or uninvited visitors, else why the maze? It would be the better part of prudence to go slowly.

But he was going to have a hard time being stealthy with a pack the size of his torso!

The moonlight was exceptionally strong tonight, and it wasn't difficult to see. He took time to examine the area where the maze ended and found a place where an animal—or a human—had tried to burrow under the wall, leaving a respectable hole just about the size of his pack. He stuffed his cloak and coat inside the pack, tied off the top, and wedged the pack down into the hole.

It just fit, with a little room at the top and the sides. He scraped in some of the dirt that had been left until the hole was full, scattered the rest to hide the hole in the grass, then went a little ways into the orchard and carefully cut a square of turf with his knife. He brought that back and squared off the hole, then fitted the turf over the top, stamping it down in place. When he was confident that the pack was as well hidden as he could manage, he looked about to see if the light was still there.

It was, and it was still in the same place, so he began to slip from tree to tree, moving toward it.

The outermost trees were of no kind that he recognized, and although they had neither flower nor fruit, their bark was fragrant in a way that made him think of—incense! Could these be incense-trees? Was this where the incense the traders said they brought from China actually came from? Were there trees like this in China, where the traders got their incense? Or was the scent merely coincidence?

There was no one to ask, and no way to find out, so his curiosity would have to go unassuaged. But beyond the first trees there were others that were quite familiar, though not in form.

The strangest yet most beautiful apple trees he had ever seen in his life were arranged with mathematical precision down rows in all directions. They were strange because he had never seen an apple tree with flowers, tiny applets, green fruit and ripe all on the same tree at the same time. The fragrance of the blossoms was utterly intoxicating, and as for the fruit, although he could not see the color, the aroma was mouth-watering. The mingling of the two scents was like nothing on earth.

If Father could see these, he'd forswear cherries forever, he thought, as the scent of lushly ripe apples wafted down toward him, tempting him to take one. *He wouldn't be able to stand not having a tree like this, or better still, an orchard full.*

Ilya *was* tempted by the fruit, but not stupid. Everywhere he looked, there was evidence of powerful magic at work, and the mark of someone very like his father in the level of his greed. There was the maze—and the guards that the nightingale had warned him about. Just because he had not *seen* anything like a trap here, that did not mean there were no traps here. The way in which the orchard was laid out made it easy to keep track of what was on the trees, and there was no windfallen fruit *anywhere* on the ground. He had the feeling that the Katschei was as bad as Ivan when it came to his possessions; that he made an inventory of every blossom, demanding to know why it did not develop into a fruit, and that he knew the placement and ripeness of every fruit on the tree. Where were the windfalls, if not on the ground? Probably thriftily (greedily) gathered up and sent off to be made into cider. There would probably be a price on these apples that Ilya would not be willing to pay.

I wonder what he does about insects? Ilya thought to himself, as another breath of fragrance wafted down toward him. *Or is that what the nightingale and her cousins are here for?*

As he neared the furtive, flickering light, it began to take on an air of familiarity, and as he got within sight of the source, he knew why it seemed so familiar.

Someone had not heeded the signs of vigilant greed here, and had paid the price. As he had thought, the fact that there were no visible traps did not mean that there were no invisible ones. Someone had been tempted to take the apples, trusting in her own magic to keep her safe, and had learned that the Katschei's magic was stronger than hers.

It was the Firebird, and she was trapped beneath a net that covered the entire tree. Where had it come from? How had it dropped down on her? The only answer could be magic. In comparison with the Katschei's ability to keep high summer in his orchard, such a magical trap must have been quite a trivial exercise in power.

The Firebird should have known that, but evidently, the apples had proved to be too great a temptation to resist in spite of that knowledge. Or perhaps she had trusted to her own magic to protect her. Now she was trapped. In an agony of terror, she tore at the net, trying without success to free herself. She changed as he watched, from a bird, to a mingling of bird and maiden, to a maiden as human as any Ilya had ever seen, though far lovelier than his own little milkmaids. In all these forms she ripped at the seemingly fragile netting keeping her captive, and in all these forms she failed to free herself. In her maiden and half-maiden form, she wept with fear, soundlessly, great crystal tears rolling down her cheeks as she circled the tree, endlessly trying to find some weak part in the net that she had not found before.

Part of him felt a rather nasty satisfaction that she had finally met her match and been caught in her thieving ways. After all, she would not have been caught like this if she had not been trying to steal fruit in the first place. And it could be said that all of *his* troubles dated from her thefts in his father's orchard. Despite the gift of animal tongues she had granted him, she had *not* taken the bad luck off, and that bad luck had nearly killed him twice. It *had* killed the sorrel gelding, who had done nothing to deserve his terrible fate.

But the rest of him ached with pity for her. She was clearly petrified with terror. Whatever the Katschei had in mind for her, it probably wasn't very pleasant, and if he was as powerful a sorcerer as he seemed to be, he could shrug off her bad luck as a goose shrugged off water. He'd caught her, hadn't he? That was proof enough that her bad-luck magic was powerless against his.

A creature like her shouldn't be kept in a cage and displayed! That was why he hadn't told his father about her, because Ivan would have wanted to catch and cage her. She beat at the net with slender, delicate hands, pulled at it until her hands were cut and bleeding, and still with no result. He'd seen animals caught in traps that looked like this, so frightened that they were the next thing to mindless.

It could be argued that she had taught Ivan a lesson in the

cost of greed—though whether he had learned anything from that lesson remained to be seen. With all the trees in this orchard, she couldn't possibly have taken enough fruit to make any real difference, anyway.

He could not possibly leave her like this, no matter if he did get a second dose of bad luck on top of the first. For that matter, by getting this close, he probably already had it, so he might as well help her and be done with it.

He walked straight up to the net, openly, and she fled in bird-form to the top of the tree, her eyes blank and staring with terror. "Be at ease, lady-bird," he said, as he drew his knife to cut the meshes of the net. "It's only me, Ilya Ivanovitch. Remember me, don't you? I saw you when I was up a tree in my father's cherry-orchard. You came to take his special fruit this fall, and he set guards, and you put them to sleep. Do you know how I kept from falling asleep myself? I stuck myself with pins. I'll wager you never thought anyone would do that, now, did you?"

He continued to talk to her without looking directly at her, in the voice he used to calm frightened horses, as he sawed at the fabric of the net. But it wouldn't cut, it wouldn't even fray, and it quickly dulled the edges of his blade. He regarded the ruined knife with a frown before reluctantly sheathing it, and studied the bottom of the net instead. It appeared to have a weighted edge, but a weighted edge shouldn't be so heavy that the Firebird herself couldn't lift it.

Well, "shouldn't" is relative, when you are talking about magic.

While he examined the net, she fluttered down out of the branches of the tree, changed again, and approached him warily in a form of a flaxen-haired maiden, pale and proud, with a cloak made of scintillating feathers. As he bent down to try and lift the edge of the net so she could slip out beneath it, she put out her hand in an involuntary gesture.

"Don't—" she said, her voice exactly as he remembered it from her singing, melodious and sweet—and just now, tense with fear. "Oh, don't, don't stay, don't try to help me! Flee, Ilya Ivanovitch, I beg you! The Katschei has many guards, and surely they will be coming soon. I was a fool to come here, and you will be a fool if you stay."

He heaved and grunted with effort, and discovered that although the net appeared to be perfectly ordinary, he could not lift the edge at all, any more than he could cut it with his knife. "I won't leave any creature in a net, lady-bird, not even fruit-thieves. You got me in a lot of trouble, you know. I could have done without seeing you that night. By the time your ill-wishing was done with me, I was in worse condition than you are now."

She wrung her hands—a gesture he had heard of in tales, but had never actually seen anyone do. She did it rather gracefully, actually. "Oh, *go*, Ilya Ivanovitch!" she cried, and another of those great crystal tears formed at the corner of her eye and trickled slowly down her face. "*Go*. You cannot cut the net, and you cannot lift it. The Katschei will kill you if he finds you, or worse! You cannot know how powerful he is, or how evil!" She gave a little sob, the first sound of weeping he had heard her make yet. "Perhaps this is only what I have deserved, for putting my ill-wishing on someone who never meant me harm. Now I have taken my ill-wishing from you, if that was what you wanted out of me. Now go, while you still can! I would not have your death on my soul!"

He left off trying to lift the net, and took a moment to look into her eyes. They were still the most beautiful, most expressive, and bluest eyes he had ever seen. "I won't leave you here, lady-bird. If he is evil, then that is all the more reason why I should help you escape. How could you have known I wasn't like every other man, who would see you only to desire you, and desire you only to cage you?"

The Katschei will be very angry when he finds the trap sprung and the prey escaped, he thought wryly. *Still, I think it might be a good thing for him to learn that he cannot always catch what he sets out to snare.* Certainly everything Ilya had seen so far bespoke arrogance as well as greed. He did not at all mind helping to teach this Katschei a little lesson. Perhaps he would learn, as Ivan had probably not.

She raised both hands, the fingers crisscrossed with welts and cuts, and clutched them on the meshes of the net, desperately. "Listen to me, and do not be a brave and well-meaning fool! The Katschei is a powerful sorcerer, and when he catches you, I promise that you will *wish* that he had killed you. You would not be the first young man he has caught in his webs of sorcery."

"Oh?" Ilya replied absently, as he looked carefully all around the tree. "And how is that?"

"He lives but to cause others grief and torment," she replied, still clutching the net. "He keeps twelve of the most beautiful tsarinas in all of Rus imprisoned here in his gardens. Each one of them is more lovely than the last. Whenever he hears of a beautiful woman of noble birth, he uses his magic to spy upon her, and if she is as lovely as those already in his collection, he kidnaps her, and puts her with the rest. The most powerful sorcerers in the land have tried to defeat him, and have failed, for they say that he sold his soul to the devil— yes! the very devil!—for power and magic, and the only person who could defeat him in magic would be another like him." Her eyes were wide and pleading, but he was not trapped in them the way he had been in the *rusalka*'s eyes. "I only know that he sold a part of himself to *some* dark power, for there is no one more evil, or more powerful, in all of Rus. Perhaps it is only that he has forsaken all things good and gentle to devote himself to harm and pain that has made him powerful. But he *has no weakness,* Ilya Ivanovitch. You cannot defeat an opponent with no weakness!"

"And how do you know all that?" Ilya asked, still studying the net.

"Because I have studied him," she replied, her head high. "I have asked the birds and the beasts here about him, and I have watched the comings and goings of his servants. I have sought information about him from every possible source, for *I* am a creature he might well wish to possess. I have seen much of what he can do with my own eyes. No sorcerer has ever been able to defeat him."

"So? If a sorcerer cannot defeat him, perhaps an ordinary man can," Ilya replied, stepping back a few paces and once again examining the net. There must be a way to release this thing, a way that did not require magic. Surely a powerful sorcerer, a greedy man like Ivan, would be just as suspicious as Ivan. He would not want any of his servants to have any magical power that could counteract anything of his own. So the release must be purely mechanical.

"A man?" the Firebird laughed hysterically. "A warrior, you mean? Do you think that none have tried? He makes no secret of the fact that he holds these beautiful women here—in fact, he makes certain that the tale is well known! He keeps them here as bait for his own sadistic traps! Men, warriors, boyars, all have come, some singly, some with armies, and all have met defeat at the hands of his magic. And when he catches the poor fools who think to rescue these maidens, he changes them into statues—but *living* statues, statues that can see and remember all that happened to them and all that continues to happen to them—statues that can see others coming to make the same mistakes they did, and can do nothing about it! This is but one of his amusements, and it is the mildest of the lot! Now *go*, and leave me to pay the penalty of temptation!"

"Oh, I think not," Ilya said casually. He had found the release, or so he thought; it was cleverly concealed, but precisely the same sort of release that dropped the ordinary bird-nets Ivan had draped over his trees. It was a rope sewn into the side of the net along one of the seams, but it moved in its pocket, and Ilya was fairly certain that it held the net together at the top. He pulled the rope—and to his immense satisfaction, the top of the net parted, and the net dropped to the ground in a neat circle around the tree.

The Firebird stood there stunned for a moment, and that gave Ilya the chance he had hoped for. He dashed in and caught her by the wrists before she could flee. She seemed to know everything about this Katschei, and he wanted to hear what she knew. At the least, he had to cross the Katschei's land—and at the most, well, there might be some profit here.

Immediately as his hands closed around her wrists, she changed into the form of the fiery bird, beating him with her powerful wings, trying to scratch him with her talons, and stabbing furiously at his eyes with her beak. He ducked his head and held on, though she buffeted his head with such force that he saw stars, and her beak scored a line across his skull that burned.

She changed again, into the half-bird, half-maiden, and fought him in that form as well, kicking at him and clawing and scratching, twisting and turning to get him to break his hold. He held her at arm's length and would not let go. The strangest thing about this furious battle was that she was absolutely silent—probably because any noise would bring the Katschei's guards. He took his cue from her and clamped his own lips shut, even when she stamped furiously on his instep and managed to kick him once in the privates. He saw more than stars then, but he kept his hold on her.

She changed back into the bird, then into the half-and-half, then into the bird again, trying anything and everything to get him to let go. He held fast through all of it, and finally, exhausted, she became a maiden again. She half-collapsed onto the ground, but fearing a ruse, he kept tight hold on her wrists, though he was afraid he was hurting her cruelly.

"Listen, cherry-thief," he said, before she could speak. "You made a ruin of my life, and because of what you did, my brothers nearly killed me twice. You owe me more than the gift of animal-speech; because of you I lost everything that I had—it wasn't much, but by the Holy Ghost, at least it was mine! I want your promise that you won't try to escape, and I want something more out of you than the removal of your curse and the ability to speak to the beasts!"

She drooped with weariness against his grasp. "Speak," she replied, her voice faint with exhaustion. "You have my promise that I will not escape until you give me leave. And as for what you want, if it is in my power, I shall grant it to you. I have no gold nor silver, although I know where such may be found, so do not look to me to ransom myself with treasures I do not have."

He let her go, then, and she sagged back against the trunk of the tree, putting her hands against the trunk to keep from falling. He was glad to see that he had not marked her wrists; he would have felt very badly if he had bruised her. "I want to know about this Katschei," he told her sternly. "You seem to know a great deal about him."

"I do; nearly all," she replied. "But not enough to keep me from daring his magic apple trees." As she spoke, she looked hungrily up at the apples hanging so temptingly near. "My kind—we require what is rare and sweet, and if it is magic too, it nourishes us the better. The nearest such fruit is in Egypt at this time of year, and I did not want to fly so far."

Ilya dared to seize one of the nearest apples, thinking that, since the trap had already been sprung, they were probably safe from a second such.

He was right; nothing happened, and he handed her the apple with a gallant gesture. She took it with a surprised smile; seized it and devoured it in the blink of an eye. "Tell me about this sorcerer, and all that you know about his powers and his palace. Tell me how to defeat the Katschei then, if you know," he demanded. "Tell me how to kill him, if he can be killed."

It can hardly be an evil deed to rid the world of such an evil creature, he thought to himself. *And even if I didn't do it myself, I could barter the information to the next boyar who comes to rescue the maidens, surely.*

"Oh, he can be killed," the Firebird admitted, seizing another apple herself and making it vanish after the first. He had never seen anyone eat so quickly, nor so daintily. "Not that anyone is likely to succeed. But—" she glanced around, suddenly wary. "We should not talk here. Follow, and we will go somewhere safer."

He had no fear that she would suddenly turn into a bird and vanish again; he trusted her to keep her word. As an afterthought, he picked a half-dozen apples and stowed them inside his shirt, then followed her back in the direction of the maze. Sure enough, that was where she led him, into a dead-end that was presumably safer than the rest of the maze. She no longer glowed so brightly, although she *did* shine in the dark, with a light that was a little like the light in the *rusalka*'s part of the forest. They made themselves comfortable, settling on the soft grass that carpeted the floor of the maze, and he gave her all but one of the apples, reserving that last one for himself. After one bite, he was glad he had; if one had somehow managed to blend the sweetest apple with the finest honey, and flavor it all with a hint of clove and cardamon, it *might* have approached the taste of that delicious apple. He ate it all, every bit of it, licking the seeds and the stem clean of juice. In the time it took for him to eat that single apple, she had finished all five of hers.

There was a faint light about her, although it was as if she was illuminated from some invisible source of sunlight or flame rather than lit from within, like a lantern. It wasn't the moon touching her, either, for this was a warm light, not the cool and silvery light of the moon.

"Now," he said, keeping his voice down, in case the guards might be within earshot. "Tell me about the Katschei."

"He cannot be killed like ordinary men," the Firebird told him. "In fact, one of his games is to allow the young warriors to close on him and stab him through the heart. He only laughs, then lets his demons seize them, for he *has* no heart, not in his body. There is no way to slay him with steel, not even by cutting off his head."

"No heart?" Ilya repeated skeptically. "How can he have no heart?"

"That was part of his bargain with the powers of evil, they say," the Firebird told him. "The evil ones took his heart of flesh and replaced it with a stone. Instead of a heart of flesh, he has a heart of black, enchanted glass, and the Katschei keeps *that* safe, let me tell you! It is true enough he has no heart, though whether that is of his own doing or the devil's, I do not know. It is true that the heart of black glass is what keeps him alive, and it is true that he has a stone in his chest instead of a heart, for I have seen men blunt and break swords upon it. To kill him, you must break that heart at his feet— but he keeps the heart in a diamond, which will only shatter if it is struck correctly."

"Oh, that hardly seems so difficult," Ilya said slowly. "It is not hard to shatter something if you know how."

The Firebird leveled a withering look at him. "The hard part is *getting* the diamond. The diamond is in a duck, the duck is in a rabbit, and the rabbit is in a locked chest to which only the Katschei holds the key. And as if that were not enough, the chest is in the top of the tallest oak tree in the garden, and the oak tree is guarded by the Katschei's dragon. The dragon is chained to the tree, and don't think that you can simply climb the tree by slaying the dragon at a distance. If you can see and hear the dragon, the dragon can see, hear, and scent you, and he will begin roaring the moment he does. Then the Katschei and his guards will come." She sighed. "Even if you could somehow get past the dragon, you must get the chest down out of the tree, and the only way to do that is to chop the tree down. Open the chest and the rabbit will run; catch the rabbit and open it, and the duck will fly out. Catch the duck, and you still have to break the diamond and get to the Katschei to break the heart at his feet.''

Ilya chuckled. ''Well, it does sound more like a task for a great hero, and not for someone like me. I confess that I had hoped that it would be easier to defeat this sorcerer; while I should like to do so, I think it might be simpler to fly to the moon and take up residence there.''

Still, I should like to have a look at these twelve maidens. I cannot believe that the twelve most beautiful women in all of Rus are held captive in a sorcerer's garden. For one thing, some of them must have begun to age by now, unless he has put a spell upon them that keeps age at bay.

The Firebird sighed with relief, and the pinched look about her eyes and mouth eased. ''I am glad to hear you say that, Ilya Ivanovitch,'' she replied softly, with real warmth in her voice. ''You have a good heart, and a true and noble nature. That is why I gave you the gift of tongues, for I could not take off the ill-wishing without seeing you, and I was afraid to come near you again.'' She was silent for a moment. ''I am sorry that you came to lose so much.''

''Not all that much,'' he said, truthfully, and found himself reciting his own history to a stranger for the second time. She was a sympathetic listener, and watched him with those remarkable eyes as if she found his words utterly fascinating. When he had finished, she sat silent for a moment, then stood. He followed her example.

''Well,'' he said, with growing reluctance, but knowing that it was the right thing to do, ''you have fulfilled your pledge, and I free you from it.''

''And I must go, for I cannot remain here and be caught by the dawn,'' she said quietly. ''If you will take my advice, Ilya, you will not go farther. The pattern to enter and leave this place is a simple one. You always turn to the right, but only by passing other possible turnings. You take the first turn to the right, then pass one and take the second, then pass two and take the third, pass five and take the sixth, pass eleven and take the twelfth—the pattern is the sum of the ones before it—and it repeats after you make five turnings. There *are* other ways out and in; that is merely the quickest.''

''Ah! I see!'' he exclaimed, and laughed. ''And it is a good thing that it is I and not one of my dolt brothers who stands here now, for they could not add one and two together and get the same number twice in a row.''

She did an unexpected thing, then, and seized his hand as the *rusalka* had, looking up earnestly into his eyes with her own of blazing blue. ''Please, Ilya, leave this place. Go no farther. I would not see you fall victim to one of those beautiful and heartless women—for the tsarinas have no more heart than their captor. They are alike in that, and I think perhaps that the Katschei chose them for that reason. Be wise, and go back to your friend the wolf-hunter, or on into the west. Sell your services to the Great Tsar as a horse-talker; he has many fine horses and most are mishandled. But do not stay here to serve the Katschei's humor. If you *must* stay, even for a little, beware of traps. The Katschei's guards are demons, and they are not very bright. You can trick them easily enough, and avoid them easier still, if you are not trying to rescue a tsarina. But go; go and save yourself, and grow to be a fine and noble man in the service of the Great Tsar.''

She released his hand as abruptly as she had seized it, and took a step back. She stooped down as gracefully as a swan and pulled a feather loose from the hem of her cloak, a lovely thing of blue and gold and red that shone like a star in her hand, shedding soft sparks of warm light.

She held the feather for a moment, cupped in her hand. ''You asked nothing special for saving me, beyond that I take away my misplaced curse, so here is my reward to you. If you ever need me, as often as you need me, wave this three times in the air, and I will come to you, unless death prevents me.''

She held out the feather, and he took it, dumbfounded at the magnitude of the reward she had gifted him with. Before he could say anything, even to thank her, she had turned back into the Firebird again, and launched herself into the air. She did not soar into the sky, she shot up into the sky, less like a bird and more like a comet with a fiery tail. In a moment she was gone, and he would have thought it all a dream but for the taste of honey and cardamon on his lips, and the feather in his hand.

He stood there for a moment, simply gazing at the feather, which was a marvel in and of itself. It changed colors constantly, the blue shifting into red, the red into gold, making ever-moving patterns across its surface. Little sparks seemed to form at the edges and drop off, but when he held his hand beneath the feather to catch them, he felt nothing. At length he tucked the feather into the breast of his tunic, extinguishing its light, and gave a moment of thought about his next move.

The logical thing would be to cross the Katschei's gardens—perhaps see if he could filch a few supplies out of the palace kitchen—and go on into the west as the Firebird had suggested. That would be easier than plunging into the maze again, for he was afraid that in the dark he would miss a turning, and if he missed one, he would be quite lost again. It might be smarter to try getting out the other side. But that assumed that the maze did not surround the entire palace, and he had a second thought that it probably did. Otherwise, what would have been the point of having it at all, if someone could get in simply by going around it?

I still wish to see these maidens, he thought, a bit rebelliously. *For all that the Firebird is a magic creature, she is still a female. I think she may be jealous of the beauty of the tsarinas, and that is why she warned me off them.* It would not have been the first time a woman told a man that this or that maiden was cold-hearted and cruel out of jealousy of her beauty. *And besides, it would be a pity to come this far and not see them. It would be like going to Africa and not seeing the Monopods or the Lyons.*

He decided to leave his pack hidden where it was for the time being. It would be much easier to scout through the gardens without it, and until he knew exactly what lay on the other side of the palace, he needed as much mobility as he could muster. Only when he had an idea of what he would be encountering in the western end of the grounds would he come back after it.

He slipped back into the orchard, and although he would gladly have used his favorite trick of going into the branches of the trees to travel above the ground, he decided against it.

Climbing into the trees might trigger a trap, and it would be decidedly ignominious if he had to summon the Firebird to free him from the same kind of trap he had freed her from.

Instead, he used what cover there was, flattening himself against the trunks of the trees, listening and watching for distant movement before slipping into another bit of shadow and hiding behind another tree-trunk. Without the Firebird's light, the orchard was very dark indeed, and it wasn't at all difficult to find shadows big enough to swallow a cart and donkey, much less one young man. But as the Firebird had told him, when he finally did encounter some of the Katschei's guards, they proved to be even dimmer than his brothers.

There were five of them, all bunched together in a group, and they were all carrying torches and arguing at the tops of their lungs. They certainly weren't making any effort at all to hide themselves. Perhaps that was because they counted on the Katschei's traps to snare intruders, and had no reason for stealth. Or perhaps they were simply stupid.

They didn't look much like his conception of a demon, given all of Father Mikail's horrific stories. They *did* have long, barbed tails and vestigial, batlike wings, both of which poked through slits cut in their clothing for the purpose. And they had horns, rightly enough—two had the horns of a goat, two of a cow, and one had the horns of a young stag. And yes, they had fangs or tusks like a boar sticking out of their lipless mouths. And they themselves were either bright red or ebony black, with yellow, goat-slit eyes.

But they weren't eight feet tall; they were half that. The tallest of them rose no higher than Ilya's breast. From the tattered and unkempt look of their clothing, they hadn't changed it in months, perhaps years. It was rumpled and food-stained; tears had never been mended and worn spots never patched. He was glad that there was no wind; it looked as if the odor of their bodies would gag a goat. Their armor looked like something put together out of what was left after all the real warriors got their pick. They had mismatched breastplates, ill-fitting arm-guards, chain mail that was too short, too long, or had holes in it, and silly little skullcap helmets. As Ilya hid behind a tree, he heard them talking, and it even *sounded* like his brothers arguing over something particularly stupid.

"Now *I* say," one of the Goat-horns declared, "that there is nothing, absolutely nothing to match a big plate of fried grubs and beans." He smacked his lips noisily, and the Stag-horned one made a gagging noise. Ilya peeked around the tree, and saw the Goat-horned speaker glaring at Stag-horn.

"Oh, grubs and beans is fine, if all you want is something filling with no flavor," asserted one of the Cow-horns. "But you take a big bowl of borscht, and you add a mess of fish-guts—now *that* is a meal fit for a man!"

Now Goat-horn glared at Cow-horn, while Stag-horn made more noises of contempt.

"You're *both* crazy!" shouted Stag-horn. "And you neither one of you has any taste whatsoever! Fish-guts! Grubs! Baby-food! Serf-fodder! Garbage! You give me a nice, juicy man-part, and you wrap it in bacon, and you put it inside a bread-roll, now *that* is what *I* call eating!"

The other two glared at him; the ones who had not taken part in this discussion tramped on stolidly, without taking any notice of any of the three.

"Where are *you* gonna get a man-part?" jeered Cow-horn. "Since when is the Chief gonna give a little frog like you a man-part?"

Stag-horn looked superior. "I got one the last time the Chief caught that boyar with all the followers." The others looked skeptical, and he began to puff up and look angry. "I *did*! He gave it to me himself! A nice, long man-part, fresh off one of the ones with the pikes! That's how I know! And I got promised another!"

"And that was how long ago?" Goat-horn scoffed. "Hell, all of us got a piece of man-flesh that day! You only got the man-part because you weren't good enough to rate a buttock!"

Stag-horn danced with rage, and the other two jeered at him.

It was at that point that Ilya realized just what part a "man-part" was, and he felt his own man-part trying to retreat into the safety of his body in automatic reaction. The five guards continued on into the distance, still arguing about food, as he quickly reassessed his first impression of the demons. They might not be very bright, but—well—they were man-eaters. Literally. And it didn't take being very bright for a number of them to swarm someone and take him down.

For that matter, they might be like their master: impossible to kill, or even hurt. In that case, they didn't *have* to be bright, just persistent.

He was even more careful after that.

The apple trees ended and pears began, with the same peculiar combination of flowers and green and ripe fruit on them. After the pears came cherries, then apricots, then, to Ilya's utter astonishment, oranges. He had seen an orange only once in his life, when Ivan got one as a bridal-gift for his third wife to impress his new mother-in-law, and he had never, ever tasted one. It took a great deal to resist the temptation to pluck one of those. The scent of the blossoms was positively erotic, and the sweet-acid scent of the fruit intriguing because, even though he didn't know how the fruit tasted, the scent still made his mouth water.

Finally, the orchard gave way to gardens; it was easier to hide here, for there was a great deal of shrubbery. This was clearly a pleasure-garden, for it was full of flowering plants and bushes, and little nooks and bowers for privacy. Ilya wondered why the Katschei had such things, when it was fairly obvious that *he* didn't use them, his visitors couldn't use them, and his servants wouldn't use them. Maybe it was just because the Katschei liked gardens?

The pleasure-gardens ended in a brick wall, hardly more than a foot or so taller than Ilya's head, and easy to climb. He seized the top and pulled himself up, thinking to take a peek before making the effort of climbing it.

He looked down into a walled garden softly lit by hundreds of pale, colored lanterns. It was lit because the garden had occupants, and when he saw them, he could hardly believe his eyes.

The rest of the palace might be deep in slumber, but the Katschei's captives definitely were not.

Inside the wall was an exquisite pleasure-garden not much larger than the great hall of Ivan's palace, with a fountain in the middle spraying perfumed water and hundreds of soft cushions scattered about among the flowers—more flowers than he had ever seen in his life, in more colors than he had ever known existed. Pretty little birds in golden cages sang from every corner of the garden, and the garden was full of girls.

That was Ilya's first impression, at any rate. Everywhere he looked, it seemed, there was another ravishingly beautiful maiden. He really hadn't believed the Firebird when she claimed that the women that the Katschei held were the most beautiful in Rus; now he did.

Nearest him was a black-haired, dark-eyed creature with the slow, languorous movement and costume of a woman out of a Turkish harem, dancing with sinuous grace to the music played by another girl. This one, who was strumming the balalaika to produce an unfamiliar melody in a wailing minor key, was black-haired and dark-eyed as well, but her complexion was duskier than that of the dancer, and her costume resembled that of an Arab rather than a Turk. The first wore gauzes so diaphanous as to be transparent, made into trousers gathered at the ankle and knee, a skirt over the trousers, and a thin tunic over both. The second wore a bright skirt of more opaque stuff, without the trousers, and with a tiny jacket that barely covered her breasts. Beyond them, two ice-princesses with silver-gilt hair and pale blue eyes clad in the heavily embroidered jackets and breeches of the women of the farthest north, the Sami, were playing ball, and beside them were another pair of goddesses with rosy round cheeks and hair the color of wheat-straw dressed like the girls of his own country, chattering over embroidery.

The remaining six, all wearing differing gowns and skirts and tunics, were playing a game of tag, skirts hitched up to show ravishing ankles and even calves, cheeks flushed, eyes sparkling, high, round breasts heaving with exertion. Five of the six were just as stunning as the previous half-dozen, but the twelfth—

Ilya nearly fell off the wall when he saw her. She was perfection itself. Golden hair, indistinguishable from the true metal, falling in two braids as thick as his wrist all the way down to the ground; huge, melting eyes as blue as a perfect summer sky; a sweetly heart-shaped face; a pair of winglike brows arching coyly above the enormous eyes; and a delicate nose and a rosebud of a mouth beneath. Her neck was so long and graceful that a swan would have envied it; her shoulders were as white and flawless as a pair of snowbanks. The body beneath a dress that matched her eyes to perfection was as supple as the Turkish girl's, with a pair of breasts like perfect half-melons, a waist so small he could span it with his hands, and curving hips that begged him to try. The glimpses of ankle and calf he caught as she ran told him that the legs matched the rest of her. There was nothing about her that was not exactly as it should have been, from the sound of her voice, as sweet and piping as a flute, to the ivory of her skin. She wore a gown of silk embroidered with gold around the collar, down the front, and at the hems, but she could have worn a sack and looked as lovely. If someone had taken the shape of Ilya's imaginative girl-daydreams and melded them into a single maiden, it would have been this one.

Ilya was smitten, in love "at first glance," as the tales said—and he knew he would never rest if he didn't try to rescue her from the Katschei's terrible captivity.

He pulled himself up and over the wall, and dropped down into the midst of the girls before they even knew he was there.

He had expected shock, squeals of fear; expected them to run from him at first. But instead, they surrounded him immediately, exclaiming over him in the most flattering of tones. They touched the hilt of his sword gingerly, chattered about the breadth of his shoulders, his strong arms, his well-muscled back. But it was the Turkish maid who was the first to address him directly.

"You must be a great warrior!" cried the Turkish maiden, the first to reach his side. "Oh, good sir, have you come to rescue us? What great king sent you, and what is your name?" Her big brown eyes gazed up at him so meltingly that, if he had not already lost his heart to the girl in blue, he probably would have lost it to her.

"To answer the last question first, I am Ilya Ivanovitch," Ilya said modestly. "I am a mere boyar, and not a well-known warrior, but I *shall* do my best to free you all. I vow it! No king sent me—I came on my own when I heard of you, and the terrible fate that has been inflicted on you."

That was not *quite* a lie, and it wouldn't hurt anything if they didn't know all of his story yet.

The maiden of his dreams neared, and perfect tears filled

her wonderful eyes. "It is a horrible fate, you are right, Ilya Ivanovitch," she said, in a voice that trembled. "It is all the more horrible that we know of all the bright and noble warriors who have tried to rescue us, and failed. We see them every day, for our Master makes us take a daily walk among them— or rather, among the statues that he made of them. You should fly this place, Ilya Ivanovitch, lest you become one of their number."

Nevertheless, as she spoke, she held out a hand, as if she would somehow be able to keep him there with that gesture. He seized the hand and kissed it while she blushed captivatingly. She was *so* different from the *rusalka,* who had truly been the kind of cold-hearted creature the Firebird had described. The *rusalka* had never blushed, never hidden her eyes or looked away. She had been as steady in her gaze as an owl, and as false as this girl was true.

"How could I leave, now that I have seen you?" he asked her. "How could I possibly leave you to such a terrible fate? Even if I were such a loathsome coward as to abandon you, I would be tormented for the rest of my life by the memory of you, the knowledge of what I left you to endure, and the dreams of what I might have done."

He made no indication that his "you" did not include all of the maidens, but his eyes never left the face of the twelfth as he spoke, and he did not let go of her hand. She blushed an even deeper pink, which did no more than heighten the color in her cheeks and spread no farther. Her little hand grew warm in his, and it trembled there, like a shy bird.

"Let us at least make you comfortable for a little," said one of the ice-princesses, and before he knew it, she had unfastened the belt that held his sword and knives. As it dropped, the other Sami woman caught it. Before he could protest, it had been whisked off somewhere, and the twelfth maiden was leading him to a softly lit bower where plates of sliced fruit and a pitcher of cool wine were waiting. He thought about resisting, then recalled that the lights were mostly out in the palace. Surely by now the Katschei was asleep. Surely he could take a moment to rest before he found a place to hide.

"*We* can hide you, if you like," whispered the Arab girl, in an uncanny reflection of his thoughts. "We can see to it that the Master doesn't find you. You can find a way to slay him and free us, and we can keep you safe until you can. We would gladly help you all we could.''

The twelfth girl nodded solemnly. ''None of the others got so far as this, or we would have helped them,'' she said, with tones of deep sadness in her melodious voice. ''We tried, but we couldn't get to any of them before the Katschei's guards found them.''

What were they doing, tramping through the gardens calling challenges? he thought, recalling how easy it had been for him to evade the guards.

Then again, perhaps they had been doing exactly that. At least one or two of his brothers would have been that stupid—and the rest would probably have tried to snatch fruit from the trees and triggered the traps, or walked openly along on the paths once they got through the maze. It was entirely possible that so far, none of the would-be rescuers had even the wits to try and *sneak* in. Hadn't the demons said something about a boyar with pikemen? And hadn't the Firebird mentioned those who had brought armies? Anyone with followers would certainly have issued a formal challenge, stupid as the idea was. In fact, they probably stood outside the walls of the maze with their armies ranged behind them, while the Katschei giggled hysterically at their self-important posing.

''You know my name, but I don't know any of yours yet,'' he said, looking from one lovely face to the next. ''If we have time enough—''

A chorus of feminine voices assured him that he had time enough, and they began, not only introducing themselves, but telling him how the Katschei had come to carry them off.

The stories were monotonously the same. The Katschei, it seemed, had a penchant for stealing these girls magically, transporting them from their very bedrooms on the eve of their sixteenth birthdays. They would go to sleep in their own beds, and wake up in a strange bed, a strange room, in the part of the palace called the maidens' tower. One of the other girls would be ordered by the Katschei to go in and explain things to the newcomer, then the Katschei himself would appear to reinforce that explanation.

Something that did seem rather odd to Ilya was that none

of them ever mentioned that she tried to fight or attempted to escape. They all appeared to become resigned to their state immediately.

But perhaps they do try and escape, and learn it's not possible. Or perhaps the ones that did *try became—examples to the rest on the folly of trying to escape. Perhaps what the Katschei did to those who ran was horrific enough that they don't care to think about it.*

They were allowed the run of the maidens' tower and this garden beneath it. When the Katschei summoned them to his throne room, they were expected to play and dance for him. Otherwise, he left them alone, except for the daily walks among the statues; he would appear for these if he happened to have made an addition to the collection, and he would take care to point it out.

They didn't lack for amusements, apparently. Their servants—who were ugly rather than monstrous, although they were far from human—could and would get them anything they craved. Musical instruments, books, the supplies for handicrafts—whatever they needed to pass the time. Clothing appeared magically in their wardrobes. One of the girls from Rus mentioned that she had purposefully destroyed every gown in her chest every night for a month, only to have new ones appear to replace all the old ones when she woke in the morning. Finally, she simply gave up. Likewise, jewels appeared for them to wear, sometimes objects so rare and precious that the girls knew they must be more of the Katschei's prizes, stolen, just as they were.

One of the ice-princesses and two of the girls from various parts of Rus had been taken not only on the eve of their birthdays, but also on the eve of their weddings. The Turkish maiden had been taken out of the harem of the Great Sultan himself; she had been a gift from a wealthy tradesman, and the Sultan had not yet summoned her to his couch. The Arab had been stolen from her father's house, where she was the only child, and accorded much more freedom than most girls of her race and religion. One of the girls he had mistaken for a maid of Rus was actually Circassian, and had also been in a harem, but like the rest, had not yet been touched.

There had been other girls—but either their beauty had not

lasted, or they had marred it themselves when they found that they were captive. They vanished in the night, and none of the twelve wanted to talk about them.

So, the moment they are no longer the most beautiful women in Rus, the Katschei . . . replaces them. I doubt that they become statues. A truly horrid possibility occurred to him that he couldn't help but think about. He already knew that the monstrous guards ate human flesh—and the girls, once marred or faded, were no longer trophies to be kept as the statue-warriors were. So, the most likely fate for them . . .

Maybe it's better not to know.

But the only story he was really interested in was that of his golden princess, and hers was the last tale to be told. He waited while she composed herself, for she had remained silent while all the others poured out their tales, and he sensed that it was painful for her still.

"My name is Tatiana, and I was the first maiden that the Katschei collected," she said, her head bowed over her hands. "You may not believe it, but this was once the simple palace of a boyar, and I was his daughter, his only heir. Although many of his people urged him to wed again and produce a son, he loved my mother too deeply to put aside her memory, and so I was to be the inheritor of all his lands. He was very proud of two things: myself and his orchards. He used to give great baskets of fruit as gifts to any visitors we had, presented by me in my finest gowns, and was a little inclined to boast of both the trees and my beauty."

"That was dangerous," said the Turkish girl solemnly. "That is probably how the Katschei heard of you, and he cannot hear of anything rare or precious without desiring it."

Two tears fell onto Tatiana's clasped hands, but her voice did not waver, it only became lower, perhaps with grief. "That is probably true," she admitted. "But it is too late to do anything now. The Katschei came—and yes, it was on the eve of *my* sixteenth birthday—and killed my father, turned all our people into horrid monsters, and built his palace where ours had been. He conjured it up all in a night, but that was not enough for him, for the next day he built the maze about the palace and our orchards, and began his wretched games." She looked up, and her eyes flashed, even as another two tears formed in them. "Oh!" she exclaimed. "How I wish I had been born ugly, or that Father had been less kind, less hospitable! It was with me that these horrid games began!"

Brave girl! To take the responsibility for all this upon herself! How good she is, as well as brave!

Ilya took up her hands again, clasping them tenderly in both of his, and tried to reassure her. "Tatiana, my own father is as greedy in his way as the Katschei, so I know how greedy men think, and please believe me when I tell you that this vile sorcerer would have done just as he has if you had never been born. He was only looking for a maiden of great beauty and a remote location—and if he had not found the two together, he would have set up his palace *somewhere* and stolen all these other maids. You are not to blame, not in the least."

She looked deeply and earnestly into his eyes as he spoke, as if searching for the truth there, and sighed deeply when he finished. "I thought that, sometimes, but I could not be certain that it was the truth, or only my wish. But if *you* say it, then I must believe it."

They gazed into each other's eyes for so long that Ilya lost all track of the passage of time and completely forgot to speak. After a while, she began asking him quiet questions about himself, and he answered her just as quietly, but his attention was on her and not his answers. He thought that the other girls began to steal away, one at a time, leaving him alone with Tatiana, and he blessed them for their consideration. Not that he was going to attempt anything with her—or nothing more than a kiss or a tentative caress. This was no heart to trifle with; he would not treat her as he had his light-of-loves—

But his reverie was rudely interrupted. "*Well!*" said a deep, sardonically masculine voice. "How very touching! What a charming picture! Someone should paint it on the cover of a lacquer box!"

Ilya looked up, startled. He and Tatiana were no longer alone.

Their little bower was the center of a circle of demonic creatures, all armed to the teeth, and looking considerably brighter than the guards he had evaded in the garden. There were no two exactly alike; some sported horns of various kinds, some bald heads, some had more hair than most women. Many had tails—horse-tails, cat-tails, wolf-and fox-tails, rat-tails, tails with barbs or hooks on the ends, tails with a ridge of spines. Their faces were all grimacing masks with yellow, slitted eyes, and their skins were every color, but all somehow unpleasant. Some had bestial muzzles, some humanlike faces. They were armored with a uniform of bronze chain with a hammered breastplate of bronze; they carried various weapons, but they all held those weapons as if they knew how to use them. Standing before them was someone who could only be the Katschei.

Ilya had pictured a spidery sort of creature in his mind, a wizened little man who let others do his work for him. Nothing could have been further from the truth. The Katschei was tall, taller than Ilya, and as dark-haired as the Turkish maid, but with strange, icy green eyes. His complexion was pale, but not pallid; he was not as muscled as a warrior, but he was not emaciated or gone to fat, either. His manner was languid, his wardrobe flamboyant, but Ilya got the distinct impression that both were meant to deceive. He wore breeches of silk brocade patterned in scarlet and gold, a black silk tunic, and a floor-length vest that matched the breeches, with black leather boots and a matching belt. His lids were lowered lazily over his eyes, and as he gazed on Ilya and Tatiana, a slight but unpleasant smile touched his lips. This was not a spider, this was a snake, a huge and powerful serpent, and his reach was much farther than most people would anticipate.

Behind him were the other eleven maidens, huddled together in a frightened knot. And of course, Ilya's weapons had been spirited off elsewhere.

But Ilya had one weapon that no one could take from him: his wits, and he used them now. Snatching up the Arab girl's balalaika, he followed his first impulse and sprang to his feet, striking a chord, and not a well-played one, either.

He began to play and caper about, precisely like the Fool his brothers were so familiar with. He had played this act when his brothers came in and found him at some task he didn't want them to know about. He had been at that game for so long that it was second-nature.

As the Katschei and Tatiana stared at him in bewilderment, he ran through his entire bag of tricks. He never finished the song; he dropped it in midstanza, pausing in the middle of his dance as if he had forgotten where he was and what he was doing. Then he brightened, and walked straight up to the Katschei with never so much as a hint of the fear he felt inside. The Katschei's demon-guards tensed and moved their weapons threateningly, but the Katschei motioned them to remain calm, and watched Ilya with surprise and a little sardonic amusement.

He knows he's safe from anything I can do; he doesn't know what my game is, and I'll wager he hasn't been surprised in a long, long time. Let's see how long I can hold his interest.

"Hoy, brother!" he exclaimed, seizing the Katschei's hand and pumping it vigorously. "So you are to wed my dear sister here! Well, congratulations! That will make us brothers-in-law! Hoo! We'll be a family then! And I can't wait for the two of you to make me an uncle, hey?" He leaned close to the Katschei, and noticed as he did so that the man's breath was as cold as if it came off an ice-floe, and bitter. "I know she's rather plain, brother, but she's the best cook in Rus, and you couldn't ask for a better heart. Besides, don't they say ugly women are best between the sheets? That the best girl after dark is an ugly one—because when the lights are gone you can't see her face, but she'll be grateful for your attention? And isn't it true that ugly women give birth to handsome sons?"

Then he capered away again and seized one of the surprised demons as it tried to restrain him, whirling it into a dance. Tatiana watched him with a blank look on her face, and the Katschei began to lose his look of amusement and became annoyed as the dance went on with no signs of stopping.

Finally he became quite disgusted, and lost all patience. "What *is* this nonsense?" he demanded of his demons, angrily. "I am awakened in the middle of the night because there is an intruder in the garden, only to discover that it is a fool! Who raised the alert?"

The guards looked uneasy, and shuffled and looked up at the sky or down to the ground—anywhere but at one another. Then one turned tail and tried to run.

It was the last action the poor creature ever took.

The Katschei frowned and pointed his index finger at the

retreating monster. There was a flash and a *crack,* exactly like a bolt of lightning. It left Ilya blinded and deafened for a moment, and where the creature had been was only a smoking, blackened hole in the turf.

Ilya ignored all of it, or pretended to. He dropped the balalaika and wandered over to the plates of fruit and the wine, neither of which he had touched until now. He began cramming his mouth with fruit, using both hands to stuff it untidily into his face. Keeping his body loose, he waited to see what the Katschei would do, how he would react.

"Take him up and bring him here," the Katschei said, his voice tight with anger. Ilya made certain not to tense up and not to resist when he felt two sets of hands grabbing his shoulders and dragging him to their master. The monsters deposited him on the turf at the Katschei's feet, and Ilya remained there, first gulping the last of the fruit, then wiping his mouth on his sleeve, grinning up at the sorcerer, making his eyes as big and blank as possible.

"Who are you?" the Katschei barked.

Ilya wagged his head from side to side. "Some days, I'm a dog, and some days, I'm a fool, and some days, I'm a fool dog of an idiot bastard," he said conversationally. "But most days, I'm the good fellow on the stove, Ilya-You-Blockhead. Hey! That's me!"

"I can see that," the Katschei remarked sardonically. "Who sent you? How did you get here?"

"I went to hunt boar with my brothers, but I got lost," he replied as pathetically as a child, and stuck his finger in the corner of his mouth, letting his lower lip tremble. "I got lost for a long time." He made his lip quiver. "I didn't like it, and no one came to find me." Now he managed to conjure a lump for his throat, and tears to trickle down his cheeks, mostly by thinking about the poor sorrel gelding. "It was dark, and there were wolves!" he wailed. "I was alone! I was *scared!*"

He began to cry hysterically then, and it wasn't pretty, for he drooled and howled like any small child would have, until the Katschei turned away in utter disgust. He rolled over and buried his face in his arms as he lay on the grass, letting his sobs quiet so he could hear what the Katschei would do next.

"Only a fool would be able to wander in here by accident," the Katschei shouted. "And you *let* him! What do you think I'm running here? A home for the feeble-minded?"

Ilya peeked out from underneath his arm. The Katschei glared at his sadly bewildered creatures, who looked entirely baffled by his question. They might be brighter than the ones that Ilya had evaded, but not *that* much brighter.

"Never mind," he snarled at last. "Half of you go beat the other half, ten lashes. Then the ones that were beaten do the same for the rest. And take this—*idiot* with you. Give him a couple of kicks and a couple of lashes, and throw him in the kitchen to wash pots. If he lives without one of you losing your temper and eating him for insulting you, the way you did the last fool, I'll give him the old one's place. We might as well get some use out of him while we see if he's going to survive."

"Don't we get to eat him now, Chief?" asked one of the demons hopefully.

"No!" the Katschei snarled, making the questioner cower. "First of all, you don't *deserve* any man-flesh, and second of all, he might have something that would make you even stupider than you already are—if that's possible. Make him useful; at least he's smarter than the kitchen drudges we have now. I think we can count on him not to try to eat the pots rather than scrub them. Now all of you, get out of here!"

Two of the demons separated themselves from the rest, grabbed him by his shoulders, and hauled him up unceremoniously. In keeping with his disguise as a fool, Ilya completely "forgot" he'd been crying, and with drool and tears still wet on his face, tried to dance with the confused monsters. That led to a comic tangle that was resolved only when two more pried him off the original two, and the first two managed to get his arms wedged behind his back and frog-marched him off to the yard by the kitchen. Once there, they followed the Katschei's orders to the letter. One lashed him a couple of licks with a stick; he fell down and began howling at the top of his lungs, just in case the Katschei was listening. The other kicked him twice while he was down, and he howled a bit more. Strangely, they neither hit nor kicked him half as hard as he remembered his brothers doing. Then they picked him up, hauled him in the kitchen door, and dumped him in the center of the kitchen.

The kitchen was as big as Ivan's entire palace, and Ilya had an uncanny sense that he had been here before—a momentary flash of memory of the laboring servants in Ivan's kitchen, looking like laborers in hell. But here, the creatures working bare-bodied over the tables of bloody meat, the roaring fires, and the red-hot ovens *were* creatures out of hell. . . .

Stone floors, stone walls, stone fireplaces, stone ovens—only the tables were of wood. And the place looked like a slaughterhouse; Ilya hadn't seen that many carcasses since butchering-time. Recalling what the guards had said about eating humans, he couldn't help but take an apprehensive, sidelong glance at the tables, and gratefully saw nothing but a cow, three deer, and five hogs. He resolved, though, to eat nothing but vegetables while he was here, unless he could certify himself what was in his meal.

A bulky brown creature the size of a small shed, with a bearlike head and long, clever hands looked up at their entrance and grunted.

"Whazzat?" it asked.

"Pot-scrubber for you, from the master," replied one of the monster-guards.

The kitchen-creature gestured with its chin, and Ilya's captors hauled him over to one corner where there was a huge kettle of water hot enough to have a bit of steam rising over it, a mound of dirty pots, and soap. There he was let fall. He sat for a moment, rubbing his sore rump.

"You heard the master, Fool-boy," said one. "He said scrub pots, you scrub pots."

Ilya nodded and picked himself up off the wet stone floor, which sloped in this corner, so that water would drain down into a hole in the floor. He tested the temperature of the water with a finger, and found that while it was hot, it wasn't as hot as it looked. With a sigh of mingled relief and resignation—relief at his narrow escape, and resignation for his short-term fate—he set to work scrubbing pots. It did amuse him to think of Mischa set to this task. Mischa would have gotten himself killed and eaten in the first moments of the encounter with the

Katschei—the only way he'd have been in the kitchen would have been as part of the evening dinner!

He'd never appreciated how much work it was to scrub pots. First the pot had to be soaked, to loosen whatever was crusted and burned to it. Then it had to be scrubbed with a boar-bristle brush until his arms ached, to get all of the crust off. Water slopped everywhere during this process, and in mere moments he was soaked from head to toe with cold, greasy water. But that didn't matter, because it was so hot in the kitchen he'd have been soaked through with sweat anyway. Now he was glad that he'd hardened his muscles with all that exercise and wood-chopping. After what seemed like hours of scrubbing, he finished the mound of greasy, blackened pots and pans, and looked up to see six monsters staring at him expectantly.

They all had eyes like saucers, and huge, lipless mouths, and they eyed him as if they were considering how well he would do to flavor the soup.

He jumped back—and all six of them stepped forward and took control of his wash-kettle. Two of them emptied the kettle of cold, grease-laden water by manhandling it over and tipping the contents down the drainhole, while the other four refilled it with pot after pot of fresh, clean, hot water. Then all six went away, vanishing somewhere in the depths of the kitchen, and two more monsters brought another heap of dirty crockery as large as the earlier stack. Ilya gave thought to trying to escape, but the one he now thought of as Kitchen Monster turned around and gave him a significant glare.

Run, that glare said, a gaze that measured and weighed him, and calculated just how many meals he would serve. *Go ahead and run, and the stew will have a little more meat in it tonight.*

Ilya shuddered and bent to his work with a will. The longer he scrubbed, the narrower his world became. He had never worked so hard in his entire life—not at the height of harvest, when not even the tsar's sons were immune from working in the fields, not when the sheep had to be sheared, not when he'd spent the whole day chopping wood for Yasha. His vision began to gray, and hunger gnawed at him constantly. At some point, he grew so tired that all that existed for him was the next pot, the scrubbing-brush, and the kettle of hot, greasy water. He couldn't even think, he was so tired.

Some time near dawn, he was allowed to stop. The monsters who came to empty his kettle did not refill it, and when he looked up, weary beyond words, he saw that the kitchen was empty. Even the Kitchen Monster had gone away.

There was bread on the table—that seemed safe enough. He took a half loaf, and found some onions, some cheese, and decided not to take any chances on anything else. He drank water from a hand-pump, using one of the bowls he himself had cleaned for a cup.

His hunger assuaged, he found that he was fighting to keep his eyes open. It was time to find somewhere to sleep.

He crept away as quietly as a cat, out into the fresh air and dawn-light of early morning, and looked dully at his hands, which were wrinkled and white with so much immersion in water. *Got to find a place to sleep,* he thought, vaguely. *Got to figure out how to get out of this. . . .*

But he was alive, he wasn't a statue, and he wasn't in the stew. He'd already come out ahead of every other man who'd attempted to get into the Katschei's domain. If he had to, he could scrub pots for a few days, while he saw how the land lay, and how to manipulate things to his own advantage.

He stretched, and felt every strand, every fiber of muscle in his arms and shoulders ache. If he kept soaking his hands in hot water, he'd lose the calluses he'd gotten from all of his weapons-practice and wood-chopping.

Well, *maybe* he could scrub pots for a few days. It would be a lot better to find a way to stay here and be ignored. He still had the sorrel gelding's bracelet, and the Firebird had taken off her ill-wishing, so now, for the first time in his life, he should be able to enjoy *good* luck for a change.

Ahead of him were kitchen-gardens, which would probably be better places to look for food than the kitchen itself. He rather doubted that the Katschei had put traps on the turnips and onions. It would be a lot safer to go pull up raw vegetables than trust to anything in a stew.

He remembered the discussion of food in the orchard and shuddered.

As if to demonstrate that his luck had turned, as he looked back to the palace to hunt for a place to sleep, he saw that a small door was standing open not far from the kitchen door.

Something made him drag his weary feet over to it, and peer inside.

It was a storage chamber, a rubbish-room, and from the look of it, no one had brought anything in or taken anything out for a very long time. Mostly what lay here was broken furniture, all piled up as if waiting for repairs that no one would ever do, and it was all coated with a thick layer of dust. But what caught his eye immediately was a bedstead, with four legs all broken off to approximately the same length, the feather mattress still in it. The mattress was a bit worse for wear, with holes in the cover and evidence that moths had been at it, but it was far better than anything he'd hoped for. And in a pile beside the door were rugs, motheaten furs, torn blankets, pillows with the seams splitting and feathers coming out. He seized an assortment and tossed them on the bed.

He closed the door behind him, and in the total darkness stumbled toward the bed and fell into it, too tired even to sneeze in the dust-cloud he raised. There were probably spiders and moths, probably mildew. But dust or no dust, mildewed or not, it was soft, the room was warm, and once he had tucked a pillow under his head and pulled some of the coverings over himself, he was asleep in less time than it took to think about it.

When he woke, he lay in his purloined bed for a long time, staring into the darkness and feeling every muscle in his arms and back aching as if he had never exercised them before in his life. *Should I go back to the kitchen?* he wondered. *They don't know where I am. Will they miss me if I don't show up?*

It was entirely possible that they wouldn't, but he decided that it wouldn't be a good idea to test that too much. On the other hand, he was supposed to be a fool, so maybe he could make himself so *very* useless that he would even be demoted from kitchen-drudge.

He unwound himself from his bed-coverings, wrinkling his nose at his own odor. *Another two or three days of this, and I'll begin to smell like one of these demons!*—and that thought triggered another, one that he couldn't quite get to come clear, so he let it simmer in the back of his mind, and felt his way to the door of his impromptu bed-chamber, listening carefully before opening it a crack. He didn't want anyone to know where he was sleeping; he didn't want to be hauled off to wherever it was that drudges were supposed to sleep, since he doubted it would be anywhere near as comfortable as the broken bed. It certainly wouldn't be as private.

The advantage of being in a palace this big was that if he could find a way to fit in, no one would pay any attention to him so long as it looked as if he knew what he was doing and where he was going. As long as he looked as if he had a job, it was quite likely that no one would interfere with him. So, his first task was to get himself dismissed from the kitchen-staff so that he was free to move about.

He peeked through the crack in the door, and waited until there was a lull in the activity in the kitchen-court before slipping out and quickly shutting the door behind him. He slumped his shoulders and shuffled his feet, shambling his way slowly toward the kitchen door, attracting several curious— and several hungry—looks. Well, so much for fitting in.

The problem was, he didn't look like one of the local inhabitants. Unless he could disguise himself, he was going to attract attention, unwanted and possibly dangerous attention. As long as he looked like the demonic equivalent of a nice, fat chicken, he was going to attract the demonic equivalent of underfed, overworked, and none-too-honest serfs. He could probably defend himself against one or two, but against a pack of them he'd need weapons.

He had barely stepped inside the kitchen door when the Kitchen Monster spotted him. "Airrgar!" it growled around the mouthful of strangely shaped teeth it was afflicted with. "Gerroork!"

Which he interpreted as "There you are, get to work!"

His interpretation was evidently correct, since the slovenly little creature doing duty at the wash-kettle scuttled away, and one of the other kitchen-staff gave Ilya a cuff across the back of the head that sent him stumbling in the direction of his appointed station.

He waded into the pile of greasy pots, waiting for the first bowl to come his way. And as soon as he got something breakable in his hands—he broke it.

He broke the next piece, and the next, finding ways to drop them that were quite noisy and increasingly spectacular. And every time he dropped something, he screwed up his face a little more, and started to whimper and tremble as if he was frightened. Which, of course, only made his hands less steady. He was using *all* of the lessons in "How to be an idiot" that he had learned to protect himself at home.

Finally, at the crash of the fifth or sixth pot, the Kitchen Monster turned toward him, fury in every line of it. *"Jijit! Oron! Ahellooooin?"* it bellowed at him.

He took that opportunity to jump back, as if startled, slip, and fall purposefully into the pile of stacked-up crockery waiting his attentions. His practices as his brothers cuffed at him made his aim so true that he fell without hurting himself in the slightest—but oh, the wreck he made of the dishes!

The resulting penultimate crash brought the entire kitchen to a standstill. And in the resulting silence, Ilya burst into noisy wails and a torrent of tears.

The Kitchen Monster screamed and stalked toward him, hands on hips. Ilya cowered and wailed, and babbled apologies, covering his head with his hands, and rocking back and forth. In this position he couldn't see anything but the Kitchen Monster's feet. After a few moments of tears and babbling, one of them began to tap. He took that as a good sign, and flung himself at the foot that wasn't tapping, burbling all over it, clinging to the ankle—which wasn't particularly easy, since the ankle was as big around as a tree-trunk.

"Ell," he heard the thing mutter. Then, "Ehisool Oua ear!" it said aloud, then presumably it pointed to two of the other monsters. "Oo. Oo. Eh ih ou, *ow!*"

Or, You. You. Get it out, *now!* That much, at least, he recognized.

Two large and bulky monsters pried him off the Kitchen Monster's ankle, hauled him to his feet, and got him out of the kitchen by cuffing him in that direction. Every time he stopped, or when they wanted him to change direction, they cuffed him—and once again, the lessons in evading his brothers' blows made it possible for him to avoid being badly bruised, although it *looked* as though they were knocking him to pieces. Once outside, they delivered another few blows until he sprawled on the ground, picked him up, and carried him a short distance, then threw him through the air.

He landed on something relatively soft, behind a screening of bushes, while the two monsters stomped off, grumbling to themselves. He remained there quietly for a moment, then sat up and looked around when it appeared that no one was going to do anything more to him.

He had landed on the palace trash-pile—as opposed to the kitchen-midden, which would have been much less pleasant. Here is where things went that were past being stored in rubbish-rooms. And it was in looking around at the contents of this trash-pile that the idea which had been only half-formed when he first woke up finally sprung into full life.

These creatures were anything but intelligent; he'd had ample evidence of that. All he had to do was to disguise himself as one of them—make himself look sufficiently unhuman—and he would be able to explore this place as much as he cared to. He would no longer look like a potential dinner, and since he hadn't yet seen an end to the variety of forms these creatures came in, just about anything he put together would probably pass muster.

He spent the morning scavenging through the trash-pile, and took his gleanings into "his" rubbish-room. Once there, he combined them with more things he found there. He found a bit of broken knife-blade, and by wrapping leather about it, he had something that would cut and pierce as long as he was patient. He cut himself many things out of old leather, and went to work building his disguise. Out of the motheaten furs he made a sort of head-gear, embellished with a pair of cow-horns. He made huge flapping ears out of old leather, and stuck those on the outside. With more leather, he created a false nose the size and general shape of a large, wilted carrot, which he could tie on around his head with a pair of strings under the head-gear. He decided to forgo fangs after one attempt to counterfeit them because they were so uncomfortable to wear. To counterfeit a misshapen body, he stuffed his shirt with rags to create a hunched back, and he cobbled up armor very like that of the orchard-guards with leather, bits of real armor, and pieces of metal from the trash. When he was finished, he put his disguise on, and went out to test it. He knew that he wouldn't have fooled a human for a moment, but as he shambled out of the kitchen-court and down one of the lanes, he attracted no attention whatsoever. The Katschei's monsters were possibly the dimmest creatures on the face of the earth. Evidently it was difficult for the forces of darkness to find good servants.

All I have to do now is stay out of sight of the more intelligent monsters and the Katschei himself, and I can go anywhere I want!

Now he was free—and able to roam the Katschei's property at will.

If there was any chance under the sun of rescuing Tatiana and the rest, surely now he would find it!

CHAPTER EIGHT

ILYA STOOD in a corner and held a pole at a semblance of attention—a curtain-pole, in fact, scavenged from the trash-heap—and tried to look like one of the other bottom-rank guards at the back of the Katschei's throne-room. Those who were at the lowest rank were given crude pikes and left to stand at "attention" all day whenever the Katschei was *not* in his throne-room. When the Master *was* on his throne, he had far more intelligent creatures guarding him.

Ilya had found the place he now held largely by accident, falling in with a group of guards going on duty, and ending up here. That was how he had discovered a way of getting meals without getting into trouble for stealing—falling in with a group of guards going on duty somewhere, falling out when they were dismissed, and following along with them to their meal. Since he'd stood duty with them, there was never any problem about getting dinner with them. They were always hungry when they came off duty—in fact, the guards seemed absolutely obsessed with food, talking about it incessantly when they talked about anything at all. The incident with the first bunch of guards in the orchard was absolutely typical of the bottom-rank monsters; there weren't too many things that they thought about or talked about. Food was one, sleeping accommodations—*sleeping,* not assignations with lady-monsters—was another, avoiding punishment was a third, and the punishments others had incurred was the fourth and last. All conversations revolved around those four topics. All Ilya could assume was that there were no lady-monsters, for the topic of women never came up at all. It was a strange life hese creatures led, and a curiously confined one.

No one ever questioned where he came from when he added himself to a group; they assumed he'd been assigned there. No one ever asked him where he went when he wasn't working; none of them ever had the initiative to go find a place *other* than their assigned barracks and bed to sleep. When he showed up at a particular meal, they made room for him without thinking about it. He even had an excuse for why he didn't eat much meat—instead, he mostly ate vegetables and cheese and bread, with the occasional bits of fowl that he could identify positively as being safe. His excuse was that he had stomach troubles or a toothache. Many of the monsters had stomach troubles; there were some poor souls who couldn't handle anything more than mush. It not only seemed that the forces of darkness couldn't get good servants, they couldn't even get healthy ones!

The others would pat him on the back in commiseration, then happily gobble up his share of whatever he had rejected. Among humans, that would have made him mildly popular, but these creatures didn't even have enough imagination for that. He'd have felt sorry for them, but he couldn't muster up a sense of pity. They *were* man-eating monsters, after all; if they knew what he was and why he was here, he would have been on the table rather than at it. They had done horrible things to other human beings, and he could never forget that, no matter how confined and pathetic their lives were.

They were at the bottom of the hierarchy here, like the hapless serfs his father used and abused. Perhaps that was why he thought he ought to feel sorry for them. The analogy only went so far, however, and it only took having one of them describe the last bit of man-flesh he'd had in reverent tones to make him lose any empathy he'd had for them.

Now, those at the top of the hierarchy here needed no one's pity, and this room was proof enough of that.

The Katschei's throne-room was as stunning and impressive as the exterior of the palace suggested, and Ilya was busy taking it all in while he was supposed to be on guard.

If the kitchen was big enough to swallow up Ivan's palace, the throne-room was big enough to swallow the palace and the grounds. The ceiling loomed so far above them that the many beautiful paintings up there lost a great many of their details. The ceiling was actually painted, and not in icons, either—not that it would have made any sense for a master of demons to have the face of the Virgin or Christ gazing down on him! Light came from a dozen constructions of crystal and brass, each the size of a table and supplied with hundreds of tiny lights. Ilya had no idea how these things stayed lit; they couldn't be candles, for the lights never flickered and never wavered. They couldn't be oil-lamps, for there was no source of oil. These shimmering creations sparkled and tinkled softly whenever a breeze moved the crystals against each other.

The walls were paneled in floor-to-ceiling mirrors, the clearest, most flawless mirrors Ilya had ever seen. When he thought about how much Ivan had paid for the single, flawed mirror his third wife had bought, he couldn't even begin to calculate how much these were worth. There was scarcely a ripple or an imperfection in the glass, and the reflections that they cast were indistinguishable from the original. Ilya couldn't imagine how the stupid guards managed to keep from walking into them. Possibly the only thing that saved them was that *they* were not allowed into the throne-room itself, only the gallery that ran across the back of it.

In between the mirrors were drapes made of silk. How anyone could use silk for draperies was beyond Ilya, and he knew that if his stepmother could get a single glimpse of this place, the Katschei's drapes would never be safe as long as she lived. She'd probably break one of the mirrors as well, and risk the bad luck that came of such an action, in the hopes that there would be fragments large enough to be carried away.

The floor was a mosaic of semiprecious stones of all kinds: jasper and sardonyx, carnelian and serpentine, soapstone and rose-quartz. Alabaster pillars carved in spirals supported the ceiling.

The throne itself could not be what it looked like—yet Ilya was becoming convinced that it *was*. It appeared to be jade, a huge, single piece of grass-green jade, carved into a throne with the backs and sides made of sinuous, intertwining dragons. It stood on a dais approached by three steps. The first step was made of a slab of rose-quartz, the second of amethyst, and the third of crystal veined with gold. The platform that the throne stood upon was built of sandlewood; Ilya could smell it from where he stood.

Behind the throne was a huge tapestry, but it was not woven of wool or linen, not even silk; it was made of millions of glass beads woven into a fabric. It depicted a snake devouring a bird, and if the subject had been more pleasant, the tapestry would have been gorgeous. As it was, the thing was stunning, in the way the light played on it and through it. The snake was a huge cobra, bright green, with the double-loop design on its hood in scarlet. The bird it was eating was yellow and red, and the background was a brilliant blue. The snake was outlined in gold, the bird in black, and each scale of the snake had been picked out carefully in different colors of green, each feather on the bird in varied yellows and reds.

There was no sign of the Katschei today; he didn't often come to his throne-room unless he had business with someone he wished to impress, and when he did that, he always summoned his captive maidens. Ilya had heard about this from the young women themselves. These sessions always began with a demand for them to dance and play for him, and ended with a scene in which he humbled their spirits and they pledged to obey him in all things. He could have dominated their spirits by magic, but he seemed to enjoy doing this without the use of magic. Ilya sometimes wondered why he bothered having a throne-room at all, he used it so seldom.

Thus far, Ilya had seen the throne-room, the outside of the Katschei's private rooms, the armory, the barracks, and the hall where the monsters all ate their meals. He was rather surprised to learn that there was a room where the monsters also were supposed to bathe—not that all of them did, or even most of them, but they were supposed to. He didn't use that room himself; he confined himself to cold baths in one of the garden-pools. He wouldn't risk the chance that one of them might come in and see him without his disguise.

He had also seen many of the gardens; and again it was strange, for the Katschei had all manner of gardens, and he allegedly set great store by them, but he seldom used them himself. There was the kitchen-garden, of course, and two herb-gardens, one for the kitchen and one for the Katschei's purposes alone. Ilya had considered going there one night and wreaking as much havoc as he could, but he doubted that such an action would have much effect on the Katschei's activities. There were many kinds of pleasure-garden; the maidens' garden, of course, was one of those. There was also a garden laid out like a tiny piece of wilderness, complete with artificial ruins; there was one laid out in geometric patterns. There was a water-garden, which featured linked water-lily-filled pools of fish, and fountains, waterfalls, and babbling streams, all completely artificially created and maintained. There was a rock-garden, and a garden of trees shaped into animals and cones, birds and cubes, and linked balls. He still had not seen all the gardens—he hadn't yet found the garden of statues, nor the one that held the oak tree and the dragon guarding it.

And the Katschei never left the palace to walk in any of his gardens, unless he did so when there was no one present to see him.

Ilya could not fathom this man. He took pleasure in nothing, so far as Ilya could tell. So why did he have all these things? Was it purely for the power of *owning* them? But where was the point in that, if you didn't enjoy them?

If *he* were the master here, he would spend every waking moment enjoying all the pleasures to be had here. He would be eating fine food, sitting in his marvelous throne-room, walking in his gardens with one of his lovely maidens at his side—

And that was another thing. The Katschei had twelve of the most luscious women in all of Rus living right under his roof, and yet he did nothing with them! Oh, no—that was not quite true. He had them dance for him, and he humiliated them, and presumably these actions reinforced his sense of power over them. But he probably could have had all of them fawning over him, if he had been kind to them rather than cruel. What maiden could ever resist the combination of good (if sinister) looks, a little politeness and kindness, luxurious living, and unlimited wealth?

Well, maybe Tatiana. But the rest had been going into arranged marriages, anyway—this could have been little different from going to a man their fathers had effectively bartered them to. So why didn't the Katschei exert himself to charm and win them, and then enjoy the fruits of that exertion?

Is it because he has no heart? Is that the price of his invulnerability and his immortality? To lose all pleasure in life, to be forced to an existence of cold chastity because there is no longer any desire? If so, the price was far more than Ilya would ever have been willing to pay.

But perhaps his father would have found it an acceptable bargain, had it been offered to him.

Ilya had learned one thing about the Katschei that the Firebird had not told him: The Katschei was said, by his servants and guards, at least, to be immortal.

And in an elaboration on what the Firebird *had* told him, Ilya had heard, as he eavesdropped unobserved on some of the more intellectually gifted of the servants, that the Katschei did not bleed if cut or stabbed and that he would live "as long as he cared to." So there was no point in getting him into a fight, cutting him up, and trying to get him to bleed to death; it wouldn't happen. He also didn't seem to be affected much by pain. The demons, however, *did* bleed, feel pain, and die. The Katschei had killed several out of pure pique since Ilya had been here, and had punished many more. So perhaps they weren't demons after all, and were merely monsters.

All of which merely pointed to the fact that it would be foolish and probably futile to try and attack the Katschei physically. The monsters stood between him and attack, and any attack that got as far as the Katschei himself would do absolutely nothing.

Ilya stifled a yawn and looked up at the ceiling, trying to identify the subjects of the paintings there. At a guess, they were scenes from ancient myths, such as the old Greeks and Romans had believed in. Father Mikail had a book about them once, but he hadn't let Ilya look at it too often, for he considered the subjects distasteful for any real Christian, since they often concerned gods and goddesses. He had reluctantly (and after much persuasion) allowed Ilya to peruse it, as he wanted Ilya to exercise his Greek and there were few books *in* Greek available to them. Ilya had then made an injudicious, if innocent, comment about how odd it was that the classical Hippocrates and St. Hippocrates were virtually identical except for the little detail of who they worshiped and swore by—and the book had been sent back to its donor.

Ilya rather enjoyed the paintings, and would have liked to see them closer—especially the paintings of the women, who were not what his stepmother would describe as "modestly dressed." He wondered how they were supposed to stay warm, dressed that way. Perhaps the climate in Greece, like that of the Turks, was warmer than Rus's.

There was no way to judge the passage of time in this room, but it seemed as if he had been standing there forever when the next group of monsters came to relieve them. The group Ilya was with moved out smartly as far as the doors to the throne-room—huge carved and gilded things so large it took two creatures to open one of them. But once they got past the door, their smart formation fell to pieces, and they turned into a mob, most heading toward their dinner. But Ilya had managed to hide a fair amount of food in "his" room, in part by filching it from the garden, in part by hiding it in his clothing at dinner, and he had heard that tonight's meal was to be a stew featuring insects. So he lagged behind the others until they outdistanced him, and when they were far enough ahead of him that they wouldn't notice his departure, he separated himself from the pack and headed for the kitchen-court.

Now that he was not with the others, he walked briskly, as if he was on an errand. As long as he did that, it was less likely that anyone would stop him, for these monsters walked briskly only when they *were* on an errand. If they were wandering about on their own, they shambled and shuffled, taking as much time to get from one place to the next as possible, and generally looking guilty about it.

It wasn't quite sunset. The kitchen-court was full of activity when he got there, so he simply walked straight over to the corner nearest his door—but not directly in front of it—and grounded his makeshift pike, standing at rigid attention. No one stopped to ask him what he had been sent to guard; no one stopped to ask him anything at all. It made no sense by human standards—who would have sent a guard to stand at attention in a kitchen-court?—but it didn't have to.

The moment that the court was quiet, he slipped into his hideaway. As soon as the door was closed tightly behind him, he groped for the shelf he had built just inside the door, and found the candle-end he had put there; a little farther along was a fire-starter. This was a small cast-iron pot with a vented lid with a coal in it; he was able to get a fresh one every morning from the kitchen when they swept out the ovens. He'd gotten the fire-starter pot by stealing it from a table in one of the halls; perhaps elsewhere it was used for incense, but it worked just fine as a fire-starter. He uncovered the coal, which glowed at him like a baleful red eye, and blew on it, applying the wick of the candle to it at the same time.

The wick caught, and he set his light in the puddle of wax by the door and pulled off his headgear and nose, which were the least comfortable pieces of his disguise.

He had tried to use the Firebird's feather as a light, but it hardly glowed at all in here, and eventually he just kept it in his shirt, where it would at least be safe. It was a distinct relief to be in his room at last; although the most dangerous moments for him were when he was not with a group of lesser monsters engaged in some task, he was always nervous when he was out. At any point, one of the lieutenants could spot him, and then his masquerade would be over. *If* he was lucky, he could still play the Fool and the Katschei might find his costume amusing. If he was not lucky, the lieutenant would simply assume he was another intruder, and he would be in the soup.

Literally.

He rummaged about in the storage-chest he'd repaired and came up with bread, cheese, a turnip, and onions. That was enough for dinner, and he could replenish the bread and cheese by staying up tonight until the Kitchen Monster and its staff had gone to bed and raiding the kitchen for leftovers. Or he could hide more in his clothing the next time he went with the others to eat.

Eating with the monsters always made him nervous, though, and he didn't like to do it too often, only when he hadn't been able to restock his supplies as well as he liked. He wished he dared raid the orchards as well as the kitchen-garden; he hadn't had anything sweet for so long that his teeth ached when he thought of an apple or a pear.

The fruit was strictly reserved for the Master, though what he did with all of it was a mystery. No single man could eat the bushels of fruit that the orchards produced every day. Each piece of fruit was counted and had to be accounted for, however, and the Kitchen Monster's special task was to take the fruit and produce elaborate dishes and preserves for the Master's table.

Maybe the fruit serves as tribute to whatever gave him his power in the first place. Or maybe it goes as bait to catching creatures like the Firebird.

Ilya ate his dinner slowly and thoughtfully, while he decided what his direction tonight would be. He had spied on Tatiana and the others at least every other night, although they had no idea that he was watching. He wondered what she had thought when he had suddenly turned into the Fool before her very eyes. Had she thought he was mad? Or had she realized that it was part of a plot?

He wished he could tell her that he was not only still alive, but was still working to free her and the others, but he knew he didn't dare. The Katschei probably had them all under his control so thoroughly that they would be forced to tell him anything they knew. They were certainly under compulsion to delay any rescuers who got as far as the maidens' garden and maidens' tower, and to take the weapons if they could. That much was common knowledge among the monsters; Ilya had not yet found out just where the weapons were kept. He also hadn't gone back for his pack yet—perhaps that ought to be his task for tonight. There were a great many things he could use right now in that pack, including a change of clothing.

So once it was dark, that was what he did; stealing regretfully past the lighted walls of the maidens' garden, and moving on into the orchards, with his pike clutched at the correct angle as if he were one of the regular guards.

He told himself not to count on the pack still being there; he hadn't done a particularly skillful job of concealing it, and by now the monsters might very well have uncovered it, particularly if the patch of sod he'd transplanted to cover it had refused to grow. But as he came to the first walls of the maze and began to walk along them, he saw to his relief that the patch of sod, while still visible as a patch, did not appear to be disturbed. Although it was fully dark at this point, the castle itself provided enough reflected light for him to see clearly.

With a quick look around to be sure that no one was near,

he dug up the sod and found his pack still waiting beneath. It was a little damp, but only on the outside. After some quick consideration of how he ought to proceed, he decided to carry it openly, just as if it was something he'd been sent for.

He was actually within sight of his shelter when the possibility he had most been dreading came to pass.

"You there!" snapped a harsh voice, as he turned into the kitchen-court. "What are you doing? Where are you going with that?"

He stopped dead in his tracks, and turned slowly. Behind him was one of the Katschei's lieutenants, an odd, purple-skinned creature, tall and curiously attenuated, as if someone had taken a normal man and stretched his limbs and body. The creature wore a one-piece black garment that clung to its limbs and covered it from neck to ankle. Its head, a round, fur-covered ball, with tiny, shiny, round black eyes—eyes like a pair of black beads—and a stubby snout of a nose was crowned with huge, flaring, pointed ears, exactly like a bat's.

"What is that?" the creature asked sharply.

Ilya cringed, but did not move any nearer. The creature peered at him, squinting, as if it was shortsighted. His only hope was that it *was*, and that it would not penetrate his disguise. "Rags, sir-m'lord," he mumbled, his voice trembling. "Cleaning rags."

The creature wrinkled its nose fastidiously, and its ears quivered as Ilya shifted his weight from one foot to the other. "Rags? And where are you going with them?"

"Yon storeroom, sir-m'lord," Ilya replied. Fortunately, he didn't have to hide his trembling, for he wasn't certain he could have. The creature had only to see him clearly and demand that he open the pack, and it would all be over.

It frowned and peered at him more closely, taking a few steps nearer, as Ilya's heart nearly stopped. "I don't remember seeing your type before. . . ." the creature began.

Ilya shuffled a few steps backward and decided to take a chance. "Please, sir-m'lord," he pled desperately. "I got to go. I got to put these up. I got to get back. They tol' me t' get back quick, sir-m'lord. I'm late already—I won't get no supper if I don' get back quick. . . ."

Perhaps it was that last which convinced the creature to let him go. Certainly, if he'd been a hero in disguise, he wouldn't have been worried about food! The demon waved a hand at him. "All right, off with you," it said with contempt. "And try to think a little less of your stomach and more of your duties."

"Yessir!" He made his attempt at a bow as comical and awkward as possible. "Thankee, sir! Right away, sir!" He kept bobbing up and down until the creature lost interest completely, turned on its heel, and stalked around a corner. Only then did Ilya retreat to his hiding place.

Once he was safely back in hiding, he sank onto the bed and shook for a while. *That was far too close. This isn't going to be as easy as I thought.*

Finally, after his heart stopped pounding, he plundered his pack, concealing his belongings all over the room, just in case someone happened to come in while he was on duty somewhere and decided to poke around. His cloak and coat went into the pile of old bedding, his clothing he stuffed into a pillow that had long since lost every feather it had once been stuffed with. All his other belongings went into piles of rubbish, so that it was not immediately obvious that these things were *not* rubbish.

Everything, however, but his spare knives. Those he put on his belt, immediately, and felt much, much better. It was hard to believe that he had spent these several days in the company of monsters, for the most part completely unarmed, and had never once needed a weapon. His luck had been extraordinary. At least now if several of them cornered him, he'd have more than a stick to defend himself with.

There should still be time to explore another garden and gather up some supplies from the kitchen-garden, now that he had things he needed. He wished he had a sword—but he'd have a hard time explaining his possession of one, so maybe he was better off this way.

I'd better get the supplies first, though, he thought ruefully. There wouldn't be anyone in the kitchen-garden at this hour— all the kitchen staff were working at full gallop, putting together the nightly feast for the Master. The Katschei hadn't had visitors since Ilya arrived, but his lieutenants, those creatures he entrusted with commanding his lesser minions, were entertained nightly.

The lieutenants, from all Ilya had been able to judge, did not share the dining habits or tastes of the underlings. This bewildered the lesser monsters, whose table-manners were nonexistent, and who saw no need for such amenities as forks and napkins, and who used their knives more often to threaten one another over a choice "dainty" than to carve their food into bite-size portions. Nor did the lieutenants share the lesser creatures' preference for "edibles" that Ilya preferred not to contemplate. They ate what humans did, for the most part, though their food was a notch or so above that served at Tsar Ivan's table. The Katschei, of course, ate dishes of the kind Ilya used to daydream about, when he pictured himself as a sultan or in a favored position at the court of the Great Tsar, the Father of All Rus.

Ilya took a pillow that he had emptied of feathers to use as a bag and slipped into the kitchen-garden. He was always careful to take his thefts from the ends of rows which had already been picked that day, so it wouldn't be obvious that someone was helping himself. There were several sorts of vegetables that he hadn't been able to touch yet, and every night he pillaged the garden, he looked longingly at them. It wasn't hard to get weary of turnips and parsnips.

He'd been hoping for three days that the Kitchen Monster would *finally* get into the radishes so that he could take some, and today it had happened. It was with great pleasure that he helped himself to a dozen. There were always turnips, and he took two, but today someone had begun harvesting a row of beets, and he got one of those as well. And they'd begun to pick the peas! He'd been lusting after those sweet peas for longer than he'd been watching the radishes. Carrots were still off-limits, and beans, rhubarb, and most of the greens, but he helped himself to those longed-for peas. His supplies would be more varied now than they had been since he came here. He slipped back into his hiding-place with his bag bulging with produce, reflecting that now he was no better than the Firebird, pillaging where he did not belong.

A heavy mist had begun to arise while he was in the garden, and by the time he got done storing all his plundered vegetables, it had become quite thick. This might have been the result of the difference between the summery weather in the Katschei's gardens and the winter weather outside the maze. But rather than deterring him, the presence of the mist encouraged him to go exploring; any patrols would not be able to see him. He was beginning to know and understand these monsters very well; in thick mist, they would huddle together in one spot on the grounds that if they went out in it, they might get lost. And indeed, they probably would. Their sense of direction wasn't bad; they simply didn't have one.

His goal tonight was the garden beyond the one with the sculpted trees. He checked the coal in his little iron pot, and found that it was still alive, blew out the candle, and ventured out into the mist.

The curious thing about the mist was the way it gathered up the light from the castle and dispersed it, making it *look* as if there was more light without making it possible to actually see anything more. It turned the gardens into a milky sea, as if he were wandering about underwater. The mist thinned a bit as he reached the shaped trees, but the moment he got on the other side of the hedge dividing that garden from the next, it thickened again, quite without warning. He literally took a single breath and the mist closed in all around him.

At that point he knew he had made a mistake in coming out into unknown territory. The mist shut him inside a tiny space that moved with him, and he couldn't see more than the length of his arm.

He turned around and tried to make his way back to the tree-garden, but even though he couldn't have been more than a few dozen paces from the hedge, he couldn't find it. He took three dozen steps—and there was nothing. Three dozen more, and he still hadn't found it, and by now he should have run right into it. There was no shadow in the mist to show him where the hedge was, nothing at all but himself and the mist.

For a moment he panicked, his heart racing with fear; then he forced himself to calm down. It wouldn't do any good to start running around, hoping he'd bump into the hedge; what he needed to do was to start a search in an ever-widening circle. Most people circled when they were lost, anyway.

And it didn't matter. It wasn't as if he was lost in the forest.

The only thing that would be out in the gardens tonight were the monster-guards, and he already knew that they would stick close to a few spots where there was light and perhaps a fire. Even if he didn't find the hedge, by morning the sun would burn the mist away, he would make his way back to the kitchen, and he could go spend the day sleeping. He didn't *have* to stand duty like the other monsters, and he already had enough food to keep him for the day. He didn't have a superior now to miss him, and if he didn't show up, no one would be curious about where he was.

He began moving cautiously in a sunwise circle, or trying to, at least. The great danger was that he would encounter something out here that was smart enough to recognize that he *wasn't* one of the Katschei's monsters. If that happened, he could only hope that he could kill it before it raised an alarm.

At just that moment, he bumped into something cold, hard, and human-shaped.

With a stifled yell, he jumped back, his heart pounding, his throat closed, ready to flee or fight. Without his making a conscious decision to draw a weapon, the knife was already in his hand.

Nothing happened. There was a dark shape in the mist where he thought the thing he had bumped into was. It didn't move, and neither did he. He strained his ears, but heard nothing but his own harsh breathing.

He didn't even hear the unknown breathing, shifting its weight.

What is this?

He took a cautious step forward, then another, and finally came face-to-face with the other. He put out his hand and touched that face.

And encountered a cool, smooth surface; not entirely like stone, but definitely not alive either. It was a human face, though, and as his fingers traced the features, they seemed to be constricted in a grimace.

That's odd. All the other statues have either been completely grotesque or beautiful works of art.

He felt farther down and encountered what might have been the folds of clothing, had they not been cool and hard. That was when he knew he had finally found one of the two gardens he'd been looking for. Either he had found the garden holding the men who'd been turned into statues, or the Katschei had an incredibly lifelike sculpture. Judging by the fact that every single detail of a warrior's garb was present in this statue, including a couple of places where leather armor had frayed and roughened due to wear, he rather doubted it was just a sculpture. He didn't think an artist would know of or want to reproduce that sort of detail.

As he explored the form, he recalled belatedly that Tatiana had told him these "statues" continued to experience everything that went on around them. What must this fellow think, being groped in the middle of the night by a complete stranger?

"My apologies, friend," he murmured to it. "I wasn't taking liberties, I was just trying to figure out what you were. I beg your pardon for any embarrassment I've caused you. You ought to know that I'm hoping to be able to cure your condition by eliminating the cause, if you catch my meaning."

He didn't dare get more specific, just in case the Katschei had the means of interrogating these petrified fellows.

"Just try to believe," he added, "and wish me luck, if you'd be so kind." He bowed a little, and backed slowly away.

In the time it had taken him to examine the statue, the mist had lifted considerably, and now he was able to make out more shapes in the garden. There were quite a few of them, and it made him wonder soberly just how long the Katschei had been at his games. There was no way for the maidens to judge the passage of time in a place where every season was like every other season, unless they kept track of the lengthening and shortening of the days—and he rather doubted that they paid a great deal of attention to such things. In their place, he wouldn't.

He made his way carefully over to three of the other statues, and found that of the four he examined, three were typically warriors of his land, and one was clearly a Turk. So, it appeared that the Katschei had cast his nets widely, and had caught a diverse lot over the years.

Could they speak with one another, locked as they were in shells of magic? Or were they forced to stand mute, even among themselves, while others came and went in their garden prison? He thought that such a fate would be likely to drive one mad—which was probably the Katschei's intention in the first place. Every time he thought he'd taken the measure of the Katschei's cruelty, he encountered something worse.

He left the fourth statue to itself, and decided not to examine any of the others; there was nothing to be gained, and a great deal to lose, if he caused these imprisoned warriors any distress.

He looked up at the sky, trying to judge by the moon if it was time for the kitchens to clear out. He guessed that it probably was, and the sooner he headed in that direction, the better: The exterior lighting of the palace would be going out soon.

The mist settled again as he reached the water-garden, and the palace lights went out about the same time he got to the first of the pleasure-gardens. He reached the kitchen as the last of the weary pot-scrubbers scuttled off to whatever hole it slept in; he recognized it, a thing with the muzzle of a dog, the horns of a goat, and the tail of a donkey. He waited, but heard nothing stirring in the kitchen itself. He nudged the door open and slipped inside.

There was bread on the table, hot and smelling like nothing this side of heaven, waiting for the morning. Tempting, tempting, but he knew better than to take any. It would be missed.

Take nothing that will be missed. . . .

One such theft he might get away with, even two—the drudges would be accused, would deny they had done anything, and be punished anyway, since they would deny it whether they were guilty or innocent. But after a third incident, traps would be set, and he would be caught.

Freeing Tatiana was a larger goal than filling his belly with hot bread. In this place of great greed, it was easy to become infected with even smaller greeds, but if he allowed them to tempt him, he doomed himself and his cause. He had never quite understood the words of the Paternoster so clearly before; to be afflicted with many small temptations daily, any one of which could be his downfall, was to understand just how powerful a "small" temptation could be.

So he crept around the hot and deserted kitchen, making his way by the furtive light of the fireplaces, where great carcasses roasted for the morrow, turned by mechanical devices rather than dogs or small boys, as was the case in Ivan's palace. As the flames blazed and died, depending on whether an errant bit of fat escaped the dripping-pan and hit the hot coals, he took a half-loaf of bread here, a forgotten sliver of cheese there, and hovered for a moment, wondering if he dared trust the end of a ham that had been discarded with a few shreds of meat still on it. He wished he could see the entire leg-bone; was it pig or something else?

His hunger for meat was great, but he decided to risk something else. By the time the carcasses on the spits were done, the thinner meat on the ends of the legs would be charred and useless. And now that he had his knife, he could carefully pare away the hot meat and crackling skin while it was still good, and by the time the Kitchen Monster arrived in the morning, there would be no way to tell that anything had ever been taken. Two oxen, a deer, and a pig were turning above the flames, and Ilya carved careful bits off all four, his mouth watering at the savory aroma.

He had just gotten himself and his booty into his hideaway, and was settling down to a feast, when a ground-shaking crash just outside his door made him leap for the candle and snuff it out. It sounded as if someone had used a battering-ram on the kitchen door. He waited, trembling in the darkness, for something to come pounding on his door to break it down; he had taken off his disguise in order to sleep, and he couldn't possibly get it on in the dark, since he didn't know where half the pieces were at the moment. With his nerves keyed up, he listened for some clue as to what was going to happen, but heard nothing but his own pounding heart.

Finally, unable to bear the tension anymore, he slipped to the door and cracked it open.

In the middle of the kitchen-court was a wagon. There were no horses nor oxen hitched to the singletree, and the wheels were broken off at the axle, as if it had been dropped there. It was laden with all manner of bales and boxes, and there was no one whosoever in sight.

He blinked, trying to figure out what, precisely, had just happened out here. *What—why—* Now it was not the tension but his own curiosity that impelled Ilya out into the courtyard. He kept a watchful eye and ear on the rest of the court, ready to shoot back into hiding like a frightened mouse if he caught even a hint of anyone coming, and moved step by silent step to the wagon.

It was heavily laden with boxes, barrels, bags—he peeked inside one of the bags, and saw with dumbfounded surprise that it held a huge wheel of cheese. He looked in another and found hams. He poked at a third, and decided it must hold dried beans.

And now he recognized this wagon for what it was—a load of staples, going from the country into a large town, one too large to supply all its own needs from the fields and farms around it. His father sent their surpluses into one of the greater towns several times each year, especially in winter. So *this* was how the Katschei got his supplies! There were always wagons that went missing, and it was usually supposed that robbers took them. Perhaps sometimes that was the case, but it seemed, sometimes, the robber worked by magic, while the horses were unhitched and the drivers sleeping. A great many otherwise-puzzling lacks were explained—as far as Ilya had learned, there were no dairy cattle here and although there was butter and cheese in the Katschei's kitchens, there was never any milk or cream, sour or sweet, nor any sign of a dairy.

So the Katschei is a thief, and I have been eating at the table of a thief. Somehow, oddly enough, that eased his own conscience about his thefts in the kitchen and garden. It seemed only just that the great thief should have his own possessions nibbled on by the little thief.

He poked about in the wagon a little and found several more whole hams. This time, knowing that what had not been counted could not be missed, he made free with the smallest one, a pannikin of butter, a pot of honey, and with one of the smaller wheels of cheese. Now he need not scuttle about in the kitchen like a rat when the craving for something besides vegetables came on him.

He carried them away with a sense of triumph, and stowed them all in old barrels, which he hid in turn under broken furniture. And with the sense of having done a good night's work, he finished his belated dinner and went to sleep.

*   *   *

LYA had been waiting and watching for the better part of the morning now. "So, Ali, do you think it will be a fine day today?" the odd little demon who tended the gardens asked the statue of the Arab. The monster cocked his head as if he was listening for a moment, and nodded. "Yes, I think so too. I'll be certain to keep the pigeons from using you as a sunning-perch this afternoon, I promise. I'll leave a puppet to chase them off."

The statues in the garden looked even stranger by day than they did by night, because they had been painted to look like living men. The painter was the monster in charge of the gardens, a rabbity little fellow with no fangs, only huge buckteeth and a harelip, a long, limp tail, and long, floppy ears like a hound's. In color he was a faded blue all over, and seemed to be covered with a short, soft fur. He wore nothing but a pair of breeches cut off at the knee. Ilya had never seen him eat anything but vegetables, he never even killed so much as a pigeon, and the other demons despised him. He was lonely, poor fellow, and this was one monster that Ilya *could* find a reason to pity. He had painted the statues to appear more life-like so that he could talk to them, for no one else would talk to him.

Ilya had been watching him for two days now, making up his mind if he was going to befriend the little fellow. If he was ever going to find the dragon, for instance, this monster would be the one to consult. This morning, after spending part of last night watching his Tatiana sitting by herself and em-broidering while the other maidens played at blind-man's bluff, he made up his mind that it was time to actually do something, even if he wasn't quite sure what, yet.

He strode through the gate in the hedges with a confident air—which, of course, caused the rabbit-monster to ignore him. In this little one's mind, anyone with a confident air could not possibly have anything to do with *him.*

"Ho, friend," Ilya addressed him, startling him so that his floppy ears stood straight up for a moment. "I've been as-signed to help you, they tell me. So, where do I start?"

"You?" he squeaked. "You've been assigned to help me? But—but—you're a warrior—"

"I've stomach troubles, friend," Ilya said, drooping a bit,

as if it pained him to confess the weakness. "I'm no good for fighting anymore, and they won't keep a fellow around who isn't any use, if you take my meaning."

The demon shuddered, as if he knew better than Ilya what happened to monsters that were no longer useful.

"To tell you the truth," Ilya continued, lowering his voice so that the rabbit-demon put his own head close to Ilya's and cocked up the ear on that side, "I never really could get to like fighting, killing, and maybe that's why I got sick. Didn't have the *stomach* for it, eh?" He chuckled, and after a puzzled moment, the rabbit-demon got the joke and chuckled too.

"Well, if you've really been assigned to help me, the best place to start would be with this garden," the little fellow said, but doubtfully, as if he really didn't believe anyone was going to help him and that this was all a joke on the part of the other monsters.

"Fine," Ilya replied heartily. "I've often wondered just how it is that one stout fellow can tend all of the gardens and keep them in the kind of shape that pleases the Master. He's damned hard to please. I'm Ilya, by the way."

Now the small monster brightened. "Do you really think so? That I do a good job, I mean? I'm Sergei."

So these creatures have names just like the rest of us! How odd! I would have thought it would be Razzlefratz, or Gezornenplotz, or something. None of the other monsters had ever given him a name, and he hadn't volunteered his own until now, thinking that "Ilya" would not be sufficiently demonic.

"Of course you do, and you know how you can tell? Nobody complains, not ever." Ilya grinned at him and slapped him on the back, doing his best not to make little Sergei stagger. "Now, how *do* you manage this?"

"Oh, I couldn't, if it wasn't for the puppets," Sergei said modestly, his face turning a slightly darker blue. "Look, I'll show you now, since you'll be doing this too."

He went to one of the box-benches and took out a strange little beast about the size of a rabbit. It had a hard carapace, like a beetle, pincers that looked like clippers, four pointed legs, and two tails. One was a pointed paddle, and the other a wicked-looking stiletto-tail.

"These are the puppets," Sergei explained as Ilya hunched

down next to him. "There are sets of them in each of the gardens, and they won't go beyond the hedges. The Master made them, and every day you take them out and tell them what to do for the day. Today, for instance, in this garden the grass needs to be trimmed."

Sergei held the puppet up to his face, and although Ilya couldn't see any ears, he got the eerie feeling that the creature was listening to the demon. "Now, puppet, today I want you to cut any blade of grass that is longer than my thumbnail," he said, slowly and carefully. "Don't touch anything that isn't grass." He plucked a blade of grass. "This is grass," he said, holding it up before the puppet. "This is my thumbnail," he continued, doing the same thing with that digit.

He put the puppet down in the grass, and it immediately set to work, trimming a path as wide as its pincers could reach, exactly the height of Sergei's thumbnail. Sergei looked up expectantly. "Now you try."

"I have an idea," Ilya said. "What do you do about all the grass clippings?"

"We'll have to rake them up when the puppets are done," Sergei replied, his ears drooping. "The puppets aren't big enough to rake. It's a lot of work—"

Ilya grinned and reached into the box-bench, pulling out a puppet himself. He held it up to his face. "Today I want you to find all the pieces of grass that have been cut and chop them up into twenty smaller pieces with your clippers," he said. He held up a bit of cut grass. "This is what the pieces of grass you are to chop up look like. They aren't standing up like the others. Don't touch any of the grass that is standing up, only the loose pieces of grass."

He put the puppet down in the path the other one had cut, and sure enough, it followed along, slower than the first, chopping the grass clippings fine until they sifted down among the roots to form a nice mulch.

He looked up expectantly at Sergei, who stared at the puppet, dumbfounded, then looked at him. "How did you think of that?" he demanded, his pinched little face alight. "How *did* you think of that?"

Ilya shrugged, concealing his alarm. He had forgotten just how unimaginative these monsters were; had he just made himself conspicuous? "I don't want to rake any more than you do," he replied. "Stands to reason, if you chop something up small enough, you don't have to worry about it. Bet we can do that with everything these things trim off, eh?"

"Ilya, this is wonderful!" Sergei said, with unfeigned pleasure—the first real pleasure, other than in food, Ilya had seen one of these demons show. "This is absolutely wonderful! It will take them longer to do a job, because we'll have to use half clippers and half choppers, but *we* won't have to do it!"

"That was the idea," Ilya told him, with a broad wink. "Now, let's get the rest of these little fellows going, and then we can spend our hardworking time enjoying the sun and this garden." He looked around ostentatiously. "I've never been here; you'll have to show it all to me."

"Delighted!" little Sergei crowed. "Now, the puppets are all in the box-benches along this path; you go that way, and I'll go this. Just set them down anywhere; they'll wander about until the whole lawn is done."

Ilya followed Sergei's orders and was finished in a reasonably short period of time. The little bright green creatures scuttled about like so many giant beetles, making paths that meandered about the lawn, and avoiding the shrubbery, the flowerbeds, and the garden path. He watched them for a moment, then got to his feet and went the other way, looking for Sergei.

He found the little monster setting out the last of his puppets. "There!" Sergei said, getting to his feet. "Now we simply watch them and see that they don't get stuck in corners or something of the sort. Telling them how to get out of a corner is more than they can handle, so we have to keep track of them."

"What happens when they're finished working?" he asked. "When there's no more grass or clippings?"

"They each come back to the bench they came out of, and we put them back in." Sergei cast a quick glance around the garden, checking on the progress of the puppets, and nodded, satisfied. "You said you've never been here?"

"Never," Ilya told him. He stretched, as if enjoying the sunlight. "Never been out of the orchard. So, what is this place? It's certainly handsome."

"One of the Master's favorite gardens," Sergei said earnestly, waving his arms about to indicate the breadth of the place. "This is where he puts all of the warriors he turns into statues."

Ilya contrived to look impressed. "Really? I didn't know that. Do you know who they are—I mean, were? That would be really interesting."

"I know about all of them!" Sergei said proudly, raising himself as tall as he could. "When the Master brings the maidens here, I listen when he tells them, and I remember everything. I have a very good memory."

Which is more than can be said of most of these monsters!

"Why don't you give me a tour, then?" Ilya replied. "I've never even seen *one* of these statue-warriors, much less all of them at once."

Sergei was only too happy to oblige, pointing with pride to Ali ibn Hussein, the Arab prince who had arrived with a contingent of fierce desert warriors; Viktor Terenko, a powerful boyar who had done the same. There were hunters who were known to have killed powerful bears and tigers, heroes who had fought in famous battles; there were boyars and a *tsarevitch* and even a sorcerer or two. All told, there were several dozen of these statues, but not all of them were what Sergei called "the special ones." These stood in their own little grouping, and there were twelve in all, but the twelfth was off in a corner, and Sergei pointedly ignored him. Ilya was extremely curious, however, and walked over to the statue, which was positioned so that its back was to them. That arrogant back seemed oddly familiar, somehow, though he couldn't quite place it.

Ilya walked around to the front of the statue, and found to his shock that he was staring into the face of his brother Pietor, who had a surprised—not to say stupefied—expression.

"Who's this?" he heard himself asking.

"Oh, some nobody." Sergei dismissed Pietor with a shrug. "I painted him up so he'd match the others, but I don't really talk to him. He was wandering around in the maze for a while; he didn't even know about the maidens before he got here. But he found his way into the maidens' garden and challenged the Master to single combat, winner takes all, and the Master was bored enough that day to oblige him. And of course, since the Master had fought him, and he *was* a *tsarevitch*, or so he said, the Master felt obligated to put him with the others." Sergei snickered. "Lucky for him, otherwise he'd have ended up in the stew, like his horses did."

I wonder how Pietor likes being called a "nobody"? He must be ready to burst with anger inside that stone shell of his. I'm surprised there isn't steam rising off him. I wonder if he recognizes me? Probably not. He can't be so stupid that he thinks I'm a monster, but I doubt he can see past this leather nose.

"He certainly sounds stupid," Ilya remarked and walked away. "I've heard that these fellows can hear and see everything that goes on around them. Is that true?"

"The Master says it is, and he should know." Sergei paused beside the handsome boyar and patted his knee fondly. "I like to talk to them, anyway. And after I painted them up to look more lifelike, the Master thought it was funny, and it really gave the maidens a turn the first time they saw what I'd done. You should have heard them squeal!"

Ilya examined the boyar again, and had to admit that Sergei had a talent for this sort of thing. The statues did look lifelike; Sergei had an eye for detail, and there was nothing slipshod or garish about what he'd done except for the colors of the clothing, which were rather loud. The faces, hair, and hands were astonishingly lifelike.

Ilya faked a laugh. "The maidens squeal a lot, and they do it for the stupidest reasons," he replied. "Can't imagine why these fellows would want to have anything to do with such a lot of flighty flitters."

"Nor me." Sergei shook his head. "So, what else would you like to see? We have to walk around the garden now and again to make sure the puppets are all right, but otherwise all we have to do is stay here till they're finished."

Ilya thought about asking more questions about the statues—for instance, could the Katschei's magic be broken?—but decided not to show too much curiosity. "Do you have anything you like to do?" he replied. "Some game or other, maybe?"

Sergei looked wistful. "I don't suppose . . . I don't suppose you play naughts and crosses, do you?"

Sergei seemed surprisingly intelligent for one of these monsters, but it was logical that the demonic equivalent for a challenging game like chess was the children's game of naughts and crosses. Ilya feigned enthusiasm; what was the harm? Sergei might be the closest thing he had to a friend here. "Naughts and crosses! That's my favorite!"

Little Sergei positively glowed, every short hair on end, he was so pleased. His ears perked up, and even his limp tail acquired some life. "How about a few rounds, then, while we wait?"

Ilya had spent more tedious mornings, especially while he was playing the Fool, so it wasn't too bad. In fact, it was rather like entertaining a young child in such a way that he didn't realize he was being entertained. It got to be something of a challenge to make sure that Sergei won games, rather than having them *all* come out as draws. Ilya did his level best to make sure that when the last puppet chopped up the last bit of grass, Sergei was slightly ahead of both Ilya and the games that had ended in draws.

That made Sergei very happy, as did the wedge of cheese he won from Ilya as a side-wager. "I never get cheese," he said sadly when Ilya had proposed the bet. "I don't much like meat, but I like cheese. I suppose I could bet you some turnips, though."

"Turnips are fine," Ilya said, smacking his lips and rubbing his stomach. "Good for a fellow with tummy troubles, eh?"

When the tallies were counted up, and Sergei found he'd won, he took the cheese with a mixture of glee and guilt. "I get cheese as often as you get turnips," Ilya assured him, which, after last night's theft, was certainly true. Sergei didn't even tuck the cheese away in a pocket after that; he devoured it on the spot, then they went to collect the puppets. The lawn was immaculate, with not a sign of scattered grass-clippings.

"Now," Sergei said cheerfully, as they put away the last of the puppets in the garden. "We have to go set the puppets running in the vegetable gardens. That will take a bit more time—we have to set three on each row. One to weed, one to cultivate, and one to kill insects. That's what the stinger on the end is for, and they can really only get the large, slow ones, like caterpillars. We have to have the birds get the smaller ones.''

''They can't be set to do three things, then?'' Ilya asked with interest.

Sergei shook his head. ''Only one thing at a time, and only one thing in each day.''

Interesting.

''I'll have to leave you there; there's one garden I have to go do myself,'' Sergei continued. ''I'm the only one *it* recognizes, and *it'll* kick up an awful row if *it* sees anyone else.''

''It?'' Ilya raised an eyebrow. ''Just what are you talking about?''

''Well, I'm not supposed to talk about this, but you *are* my assistant and all. . . .'' Sergei paused, and motioned to him to lean down so the little fellow could whisper in his ear. ''It's a *dragon*. The Master has a dragon chained to a tree in the next garden. It's guarding something, I suppose, or else it's a pet. Or maybe he does something else with it.''

''A dragon?'' Ilya asked with interest. ''Really? I've never seen a dragon. That'd be worth a look at! I don't suppose there's any way you could get me a look, is there?

''Well . . .'' Sergei said, looking a little worried. ''I don't suppose there'd be any harm in you looking in at the gate. The dragon's pretty shortsighted; it can't seem to see that far. It doesn't usually see me until I'm halfway down the path.''

''Then I'd like to have a look. Please?'' Ilya urged. It was the ''please'' that did it; Sergei was so unused to being addressed politely that he surrendered completely.

He led Ilya to a thick wooden gate in a garden wall; Ilya looked up as Sergei was unlocking the gate, and saw one tree that towered above the rest over the top of the wall. Was there a chest in the topmost boughs? There was certainly *something* dark and vaguely rectangular in the shadows behind the leaves. Ilya didn't want to think about how tall that tree really was. Half as tall as the palace, maybe. It would not be easy to get up there, assuming you could get past the dragon.

Sergei got the door unlocked and opened it, motioning to Ilya to come up beside him. ''You can look, but don't say anything,'' he said quietly. ''*It* knows my voice, but *it* doesn't know yours, and if *it* starts a row, the Master will come out.

He doesn't like having to come out for no reason, and he'll have both of us beaten.''

Having seen the Katschei's anger when Ilya played the Fool for him, there was no doubt in Ilya's mind that Sergei was being accurate and honest. And it was quite possible that the Katschei would know if Ilya put a single foot inside the forbidden garden. He nodded, and peered over Sergei's shoulder.

There at the end of the lane was the trunk of an enormous tree. It was too far away to say if the tree was an oak or not, but there was no reason to think that the Firebird had been wrong, and anyway, it didn't really matter what kind of tree it was. The trunk was so huge that Ilya guessed all twelve maidens could encircle the trunk with their arms outstretched and barely have their hands touching.

There was something else encircling the trunk, and it wasn't maidens. It lay in coils, like a giant serpent, but no serpent was ever as colorful as this one: red on the belly, shaded into purple along the sides, which shaded in turn into blue on the back and the ridge of spines—metallic gold glinted at the edge of scales and the tips of the spines. There was a suggestion of wings lying in shadow along the back, like the dark blue shadows of storm-clouds. Ilya couldn't see a head, but he didn't need to. He'd never seen a dragon, no one he knew had, but if ever there was something he would immediately *call* a dragon, this was it.

And it was huge, not like the bear-sized creatures he'd seen in drawings in Father Mikail's books. Not that *they* weren't formidable, with their armored bodies and huge fangs and claws—but this creature wasn't just formidable, it was impossible. When the Firebird had told him about the oak tree and the dragon, this was not the picture he'd had in mind.

He retreated, and Sergei locked the gate after them both. ''I'll come back here after I show you what to do in the vegetable garden,'' the little fellow said. ''I'm really glad you're helping me, Ilya. I'll be done long before dark, and I used to have to work until moonrise to get everything done, even with all the puppets helping.''

''How can you work around that creature?'' Ilya replied without thinking. ''I'd be too afraid to move! I can't believe there's a chain in the world that could hold it if it wanted something!''

Sergei laughed quite cheerfully and completely without fear. "It doesn't pay any attention to me, that's how. The Master took me to it, and now it knows me, and I'm nothing more to it than one of the puppets. It would make short work of anything that came in here, though."

Ilya shivered. "I can believe that. Well, let's see to the vegetables, eh?"

His mind was still trying to grasp the size of his foe, and the size of the tree he was going to have to climb. Assuming he could get past the dragon, or kill it, how would he ever climb that tree? There weren't any limbs anywhere near the ground, at least not that he saw in those few moments.

But climbing the tree would obviously be the least of his problems. That dragon was the size of a barn. Something like that would eat a lot, and he had no doubt that the Katschei kept it sharp, a little underfed, so it would be particularly keen to attack anything it didn't recognize.

Could he poison it? What would poison a dragon, anyway?

He and Sergei arrived at the vegetable garden with Sergei chattering away while he answered absently. Evidently Sergei didn't notice that he was preoccupied, possibly because the little fellow had been so used to talking to himself that he didn't notice the long silences.

Here in the vegetable garden, the puppets were in small boxes at the end of each row of vegetables, and they were just like the ones in the first garden. Sergei sent the weeders out first, showing them the plants that were supposed to be in their row, and telling them to cut off everything that didn't look like that particular plant. Then he sent out the cultivators, which were to use the pointed paddle on their first tail to dig gently around the base of each vegetable. Then came the insect-killers, whose job was to kill the caterpillars, snails, and large beetles.

These had to be watched more carefully than the grass-cutters; their tasks were more complicated and they tended to get into trouble more often. Since the weeders were cutting off everything that didn't look like a particular plant, only one type of vegetable could be worked at a time, and the puppets that had been used once for weeding could not be used on a different kind of vegetable. That meant that as soon as they were done with a row, the weeders had to be collected at once and put away.

Once Sergei was certain Ilya would be able to take care of the vegetable garden, he went off to tend the dragon-garden, leaving Ilya alone. Monsters from the kitchen-staff came and went, giving him no more than a single, incurious glance. Even those who had seen him as the pot-scrubber didn't recognize him.

Tending the puppets was tedious, but far less tedious than doing any of the weeding or cultivating by hand would have been. Ilya let his mind work on the problem of the dragon while he added a little variety to his work by picking off bugs that were out of reach of the insect-killing puppets and dropping them in the puppets' paths. When Sergei returned to help, he saw what Ilya was doing and did the same.

They finished the kitchen-garden in the late afternoon, helping themselves to whatever vegetables they chose by way of a moving lunch. Sergei insisted that this was fine, that it was a privilege of his job, and Ilya was not going to disagree with him when it allowed them both to "graze" at will. Certainly none of the other monsters stopped them or interfered with them. Ilya finally got some of those carrots he'd been coveting, and ate his fill of fresh peas.

"I must go tend the maidens' garden now," Sergei said. "And I know you will understand that it is something I must again do alone. The Master does not allow anyone in there except himself and his chosen servants. He doesn't want to frighten the maidens so much that they get sick and ugly."

"Of course," Ilya replied, although he was disappointed. How could he not have been? A chance to see Tatiana—but of course, she would recognize him, and by virtue of the spells of the Katschei, be forced to betray him, so perhaps it was just as well. He could always watch her over the wall tonight, now that he no longer had to hunt for the dragon. "Is there another lawn I could clip, perhaps?"

"The water-garden; it won't take long, and that will be one we will not have to do tomorrow," Sergei replied immediately, and with gratitude. Ilya knew why. It wasn't likely that a real monster would have volunteered for extra work. "Then when you are finished, you might as well go straight to dinner. Don't wait for me; this will take me some time, and I seldom eat with the others, anyway."

Ilya nodded sympathetically; he had noticed that the few monsters who did not share the rather bizarre culinary tastes of the others tried to avoid eating with them as much as possible. This was not because they found the others' food distasteful to look at, but because the others tormented them about it. "I'll just get my bowl of mush and get off to bed, then," he responded cheerfully. "I'll see you in the morning!"

"Don't bother to come too early," Sergei called after him. "We can't work until after the dew burns off; the puppets can't take the damp."

Ilya nodded and waved, secretly relieved that he wasn't expected to get to work at dawn, and went off to the watergarden. Once again, the puppets were in a box-bench, and as there was precious little lawn in this garden, they were soon done. He got into his hideaway with no trouble, and settled down to a feast of bread and ham, cheese and honey. He eyed the wheel of cheese, decided that there was no way that he could finish it himself before it dried out, and decided to share it with Sergei from now on. Unlike the rest of the monsters, Sergei seemed capable of things like gratitude.

Didn't Tatiana say that the Katschei had turned all the people in this palace into monsters? he thought to himself. *I wonder if Sergei is one of those? He's certainly the most likely.*

But if that was the case, he obviously didn't remember being human, although perhaps that was in the Katschei's interest. The monsters wouldn't continue to serve him if they remembered what they had been. Perhaps that explained why they were so stupid as well; this was the Katschei's way of making sure that his victims wouldn't regain their memories. Or it was a side-effect of removing those memories.

Well, that was all speculation, though it had been rather delightful to find Pietor staring at him in the guise of a statue. Given all of the misery Pietor had caused him, it had been a moment of sweet revenge.

But he wouldn't want even his brother to remain frozen in the form of a statue indefinitely. If Pietor had been here for as long as Ilya thought—assuming he'd been caught by the Katschei a few days or weeks after he'd fled Ivan's palace and holdings—that was long enough. And how humiliating, to be thought a "nobody" by a little blue monster who *no one* respected or regarded!

What a sweet, sweet revenge it would be if I could kill the Katschei, marry Tatiana, and become the tsar of all this land, and free Pietor. He'd have to be grateful to me, and if he stayed here, he'd have to obey me. That would be marvelous.

It would be marvelous *if* he could do it, and right now, that didn't look very likely.

Well, how was he to dispose of the dragon? Getting into the garden would be easy: He could either climb the wall, or the next time that Sergei went inside, he could jam the lock. *I could ask Sergei about the dragon and find out if it has any weaknesses at all.* He had the depressing feeling, though, that there weren't any. Even if it was monumentally stupid, it didn't have to have anything other than relatively good eyesight and a keen sense of smell and hearing to be able to protect that tree.

I could poison it, if I could keep it from eating me *and go for what I'd poisoned.* That was worth looking into, *if* he could discover what would poison it, if the poison didn't make it sick so that it threw up its dinner before its dinner killed it, and if he could get enough poison into it to kill it in the first place. Anything that big would require a *lot* of poison.

I could feed it something that would kill it, other than poison. Dogs often died from eating the brittle bones of cooked fowl; maybe the same thing would happen to the dragon. It couldn't be cooked fowl, though; it would have to be something like tiny bits of metal or broken glass. He'd have to find a way to hide it in pieces of food small enough that the dragon would bolt them whole.

I could attack it. Yes, if *he* was monumentally stupid. That was not a good idea in the least. Unless, of course, he could discover a weakness in it.

I could lure it to the end of its chain, then attack it. That had promise, provided that its bellowing didn't bring the Katschei.

But of course, Sergei had already said that it would start

raising a row as soon as anything got halfway down the lane, and that the Katschei always responded when it made noise. *Naturally he does, and in person—if I were he, I would too. That's his heart up that tree, the one vulnerability he has.*

He decided not to go look at Tatiana tonight. That would be adding too much torment atop everything else. No, the best thing to do would be to sleep on the problem. Maybe he'd have answers in the morning.

HIS answer came, not that night, but several nights later, when his sleep was broken by the sound of another wagon crashing to the ground outside his door. He made sure that no one was going to come unload it immediately before slipping out to investigate.

And that was where he found his answer, for the wagon was full of dressed fowl, frozen as hard as little boulders and stacked up like a pile of snowballs in their burlap bags. One of those would be a tempting morsel for a dragon—too tempting to resist, maybe?

He filched one and ducked back into his room. Just in time, too, for although the last wagon had been left till morning before anyone unloaded it, a moment after he had closed his door, he heard the sounds of feet slapping the pavement and irritated muttering. Someone had roused workers to come take the contents to a safe place before they thawed.

His heart beat faster for a moment, when he cracked his door and peeked out, as he realized just how easily he could have been caught. He closed his door again and sat back down on his bed, wondering if stealing the bird had been worth the risk.

There was no way he could stuff enough poison in that one chicken to kill a dragon. The only poisons he could get his hands on all grew in the gardens, and would require barrel-loads to kill something the size of that beast.

But there had been his other thought: metal shavings and broken glass. His big problem with using those had been in trying to find a way to stuff them into something without them falling out again. That wouldn't happen with a bird; he could fill the body-cavity and sew it shut, just as if he were going to cook it.

As to how to get the dragon to take it—well, the best thing he could think of was to get into the garden, get as close as he could without arousing the creature, then toss the chicken at it and hope it got close enough for the dragon to reach it.

He went back to sleep and spent the day as usual with Sergei, who was looking much more cheerful and content now that he had help and someone to talk to. Ilya kept thinking about the chicken thawing back in his room, hoping that it wasn't thawing so quickly that it would start to smell and possibly attract attention, and trying to plan how he would sling the stuffed bird at the dragon.

When he and Sergei got done for the day, he gave the little fellow a huge wedge of cheese to go with his evening meal. Sergei was so grateful he hardly knew how to respond.

Ilya had planned this carefully, however.

"You'd better go and hide this somewhere, or take it where you won't be seen to eat it," he cautioned. "You know how the other fellows are: If they see it, they'll try and take it away from you."

"Oh dear, you're right!" Sergei responded with alarm. "I'd better go—I know just the place! Oh, thank you again, friend Ilya!"

He hurried off quickly. Ilya smiled to himself. He'd given Sergei such an enormous wedge, nearly a quarter of the wheel, that the little monster would never be able to gobble it down in a hurry. That got Sergei out of the way for the afternoon and evening.

He got in and out of his hiding place with the now-thawed chicken, though at such a busy time of the afternoon it wasn't easy. The chicken was beginning to get ripe, but not so much that it had made an odor in his room, just enough so that it would not be amusing to handle. Still, that might make it attractive to the dragon. He headed straight for the trash-heap; if there was anywhere in the palace that he'd find what he needed, it would be there.

He couldn't find any metal bits, but he did locate broken crockery (perhaps the very pieces he himself had broken in the kitchen) and some broken glass. He hoped that those would do, and he added anything he found that looked hazardous, just on general principle. He soon discovered that stuffing a chicken with broken bits of glass, which are quite likely to cut the handler, was not an easy task. He was concentrating so hard on it that he didn't notice that he wasn't alone until a shadow fell on him.

And by then, of course, it was too late.

ILYA lay facedown at a pair of all-too-familiar boots, and blubbered.

"And he was a-stuffin' this rotten chicken with trash, Master," the monster that caught him reported. "So I thought I'd better haul him to you."

It had been Ilya's misfortune to be caught by one of the Katschei's more intelligent lieutenants, one with unimpaired vision, who was able to see through his disguise. Without a word, the monster had grabbed him by the collar and hauled him in front of the Katschei himself.

Ilya heard a great sigh of exasperation, and one of the boots moved to toe him in the side.

"I suppose it's too much to ask you what you thought you were doing?" the Katschei asked in pained tones.

"Ev-ev-everybody else was stuffing chickens!" Ilya wailed. "I wanted to stuff a chicken too! All I w-wanted w-was to s-stuff a chicken, and they w-wouldn't g-g-give me one!"

"Cook says he threw the idiot out because he broke everything he touched," the lieutenant continued. "Then he disappeared."

"Disappeared." The Katschei groaned. "To most of those cretins, if he draped a cloth over himself he'd disappear. Why is it so *hard* to get intelligence out of them?"

The lieutenant prudently didn't answer, and the Katschei didn't wait to hear one, anyway. Once again, the boot-toe prodded Ilya in the side. "Just what were you doing with that ridiculous hat and that nose?"

Ilya wailed even louder, drool running out of the corner of his mouth and mucus from his nose. "I-I-I wa-wa-wanted to l-l-look l-l-like everyb-b-body else!" he howled. "I wa-wa-wanted to b-b-be l-like everyb-b-body else! I w-wanted t-to s-stuff a chicken!"

"I hate to say this, Master, but he's telling the truth," the lieutenant said.

Of course he was; just in case either the Katschei or his underling was as good at ferreting out lies as Mother Galina had been, he was strictly telling the truth. Everybody in the kitchen *was* stuffing chickens today, and he *had* wanted to stuff a chicken—his way. And of course he wanted to look like all the monsters!

"He's too dangerous to keep, too worthless to make into a statue—and as I said before, I'd be afraid to feed him to the troops, or they might become more stupid than they are now," the Katschei said in disgust.

"If you kill him, they'll find him and eat him anyway, no matter what you do with the body," the lieutenant warned.

The Katschei groaned. "What a waste of magical power! Well, never mind. It can't be helped; it would take more to burn him to ash, and I don't dare leave the burning to the staff—they'll just decide to cook and eat him instead. I want him out of here before he really does some damage."

Oh, Holy Virgin—help me now! he prayed desperately, as he lay curled up in a ball with his eyes tightly shut.

"Begone," said the Katschei.

There was a moment of vertigo—then Ilya gasped and his eyes flew open as cold struck him like a physical blow.

He was outside the maze, lying in the snow, while more snow fell out of a dark gray sky like a thick curtain of white.

CHAPTER NINE

ILYA HAD on nothing more than his shirt and breeches and the boots he'd been wearing; no coat, no cloak, no hat. He didn't even have the rags he'd stuffed in his shirt to make a hump; he'd stopped wearing the hump when he started working in the gardens. It was already horribly cold; an old proverb said that Father Winter killed more foreign invaders than all the armies of Rus combined. The sun was going down and it was going to get colder in a moment. He was going to freeze to death before he ever got to the part of the maze where winter turned to warmer weather.

Assuming he could remember how to get that far in the first place. He couldn't count on a friendly nightingale coming to help him twice, and right now he could hardly remember his own name, he was so cold. . . .

Already he was shivering uncontrollably, his teeth chattering so hard he was afraid they might start chipping. And he wasn't anywhere near the entrance to the maze, either. He was going to have to *find* the entrance first, before he could even try to get to the warmer part.

Shock gave way to panic, and his mind went numb. He couldn't think of anything except that he was going to die.

He was going to *die*. He was going to die out here in the snow, and the Katschei didn't even think he was important enough to turn into a statue. He wasn't going to die because the Katschei recognized him as an enemy, he was going to die because the Katschei thought he was an idiot, and too dangerous to be around his imbeciles because he might get them into trouble.

Get up. Get out of the snow, Ilya. Your father couldn't break you, your brothers couldn't break you, and you made more headway against the Katschei than anyone else so far. Don't give up now!

He got to his feet, pulled his collar up around his ears, and wrapped his arms tightly around his chest. If he was going to die, he wasn't going to do so lying down in the snow in despair. But the wind picked up, growing stronger as the sun went down. He shoved his way through snow that had drifted up to his waist, hoping the exertion would get him warm enough to survive.

You have to keep moving in a situation like this. You can't stop moving; if you do, you'll drop, and if you drop, you'll die.

If only there was some sort of shelter! But he couldn't see anything for the snow, and he was afraid to get away from the wall of the maze or he'd lose it. As he stumbled through the drifts, though, he *did* start to feel a sensation of warmth, right at about the level of his heart.

Maybe I'm warming myself up a little. Maybe if I can run, I can keep myself warm. Encouraged, he tried harder, hoping to find the entrance of the maze before the last of the light faded, hoping to spread that tentative warmth farther. The warmth under his crossed arms increased, but it didn't seem to spread much past his chest. In fact, it was all concentrated in a single spot, exactly as if he had a warmer with a live coal in it tucked into his shirt right there.

Was it all an illusion? He wanted to stop and check inside his shirt to see if there was something he'd forgotten.

The Firebird's feather? Maybe—and if ever there was a time to use it, that time was now! But with the wind howling round him, if he pulled it out, it would be snatched right out of his hands! *No, I can't stop now, I have to find the entrance of the maze. Whatever is going on, it just might keep me alive long enough to save myself.* The bit of warmth was just enough to keep him going, just enough to keep him from giving up, and enough to help keep him from getting so cold that no amount of willpower could prevent him from sinking down into the snow.

The maze wall made an abrupt right-angle turn and continued on. He followed it, but now he was fighting his way into the wind. He could hardly feel his feet; he kept his hands tucked into his armpits or he knew he would risk losing fingers to frostbite. The wind drove snow into his face; his exposed skin burned, and he would have given just about anything for a rag to wrap around his head to protect his ears. His high collar didn't seem to be doing any good.

The light failed then, and suddenly there was nothing around him but blowing snow. He stopped where he was, unable to see where he was going, unable even to see the wall. Any step he took might be a step in the wrong direction. He was completely lost, and the wind wasn't helping give him any direction, for it seemed to be blowing around him, coming from all directions at once.

This is it. I haven't a chance.

"Hey, boy!" The barked voice came out of the dark, and something small, furry, and warm brushed up against his leg. *"You want to get into the maze, I bet! Follow me, I can get you there!"*

He looked down, and he could barely see the dark shape of a fox against the white of the snow. A slim muzzle lifted in his direction as the fox looked up at him. *"I'll stay with you, just follow where I lead you."*

The fox moved off, and he stumbled after her. She took great care not to get more than a step ahead of him, so that he could always see her vague shape against the snow. He would never know how long it took to find the entrance to the maze, because everything blurred into a fight against the wind and the cold, but eventually she whisked off to his right, and he followed, to find that he had blundered into a place hemmed in by walls on both sides, windless and calm. He was in the maze! The snow fell straight down here, and without the wind it almost seemed warm.

The first thing he did was take his hands out of his armpit and clap them over his ears. They burned as fiercely as if he'd dipped them in a fire, but he gritted his teeth and endured the pain until his ears and his hands were the same general temperature—cold, but not frozen.

"Hey, boy, did you know your chest is glowing?" the fox asked with some interest.

He looked down at his chest, and there *was* a faint patch of glowing light visible through the fabric of his shirt, about where the spot of warmth was. He reached into his shirt and brought out the Firebird's feather. He'd kept it with him at all times, waking or sleeping; keeping it had become such a habit he'd actually forgotten about it until now. Then again, it had stopped glowing once he was inside the Katschei's palace and gardens, and he'd wondered if the Katschei's magic had over-powered the Firebird's.

Once it was in the open, it redoubled its light, until it was as bright as a good lantern. Holding it over his head, Ilya found that he could see for some distance. He had not dared to have real hope before; it had only been determination that kept him on his feet. Now, for the first time since he found himself outside the maze, he began to hope that he would survive.

"Now it's your turn, boy," the vixen told him. *"I don't know my way around in here."*

"Don't worry, I do," he replied, and holding the feather up, he led the way into the maze.

Even though it wasn't in his shirt anymore, it did cast a faint warmth over him, wherever the light from it fell. It wasn't enough to make him comfortable or even close, but it did keep him from freezing; exactly like wearing a very light cloak.

He followed the pattern the Firebird had taught him for navigating the maze, repeating it over and over: take the first right, then skip one and take the second, skip two and take the third, skip five and take the sixth, skip eleven and take the twelfth, then start over again. The falling snow thinned, then stopped altogether. Gradually, the snow-cover grew lighter: from knee-deep to calf-deep, from calf-deep to ankle-deep, then finally to a thin covering that barely showed the impressions of his soles. He started trotting the moment the snow got down to ankle-deep, and this time the exertion *did* warm him. The feather streamed back from his hand like a torch-flame. The snow-cover seemed to stay as a thin layer for a long time, but eventually it vanished, leaving him with only grass beneath his feet.

He paused then, for just a moment. The fox looked up at

him expectantly, but a little puzzled, as if she was curious about why he had stopped.

The truth was that he was wondering if he ought to wave the feather now. The Firebird was afraid of the Katschei, and had told him more than once that she was no match for that powerful sorcerer, and he wasn't at all certain that he had the right to ask her to help, or that she would agree to help him. But there was no doubt in his mind that he needed her; at this point, unless she would help him, he couldn't think of any way he could defeat the dragon and kill the Katschei.

For that matter, he didn't know if he could do it *with* her help, but at the moment he couldn't think of any way he could succeed on his own.

He also wasn't certain if he should go farther in and wait or stay here and wait. He decided to compromise: He would wave the feather but keep going. Being a flying creature, she should have no trouble spotting her own feather as a glowing spot in the dark maze, even through a snowstorm, and there was no point in wasting time waiting for her that he could be using to get closer to his goal.

Once, twice, three times he waved the feather over his head. The light from it flared for a moment, then resumed its steady glow. Satisfied that something had happened, he continued on into the maze.

At some point he stopped shivering, and farther on he actually began to feel warm again. When that happened, he suddenly wanted to sit down; he was absolutely exhausted. It came on him all at once, and he stumbled and nearly fell; he knew if he *had* fallen, he would not have been able to get to his feet again.

"Fox!" he called out. "I have to rest. I'm about to collapse."

"*I could use a chance to breathe, myself,*" the fox replied, swishing her bushy tail. "*Just pick the spot, you're the leader in here.*"

He waited until he was about to begin the turn sequence again so that he would remember where he'd left off, then stumbled into one of the dead-ends. He went all the way to the end, the fox still trotting beside him, and eased himself down onto the turf at the end of the passage. He stuck the end of the feather into the turf so that it stood upright, like a candle.

"*I don't suppose you have anything to eat, do you, boy?*" the fox asked without hope.

But as a matter of fact, he did. He'd taken to keeping a meal of bread and cheese with him at all times, wrapped in a clean rag, since he never knew how long he might be kept away from his hiding-place. He still had that packet on him, for the Katschei's lieutenant had not even given him a cursory search, had not even taken his knife. Why bother, when the Katschei couldn't be killed, anyway?

He pulled the slightly squashed packet out of the breast of his tunic and shared the generous chunk of cheese with the fox. The cheese was fine; the bread was a flattened pancake, but it still tasted good. The food made *him* feel better, and the fox looked distinctly more cheerful when she'd eaten. She didn't bolt her portion as he thought she might; she nibbled at it daintily, enjoying every crumb.

They had both just finished their portions when the Firebird appeared, flying just above the top of the maze, her blazing feathers dimmed so that she showed as hardly more than a ghost of herself. Evidently, she didn't want to draw too much attention to herself this close to the Katschei's palace. She dipped down into the maze itself when she saw them, skimming the ground exactly like a swallow chasing insects, until she reached them. Then she swooped up a little, and dropped down beside them with scarcely enough breeze from her wings to stir Ilya's hair.

She glowed brighter for a moment; stretched and grew to human-height even as he got to his own feet. A moment later, with a motion of her wings as if she were tossing back the sides of an enveloping cloak, she transformed herself into her maiden-form.

She stood before him in a gown of golden feathers, with a cloak shaped like a pair of folded wings lying softly on her shoulders. She was not, to his eyes, as heartbreakingly beautiful as his Tatiana, but she was lovely, more beautiful than anyone *but* Tatiana. Her hair, the color of golden embers, flowed loosely along her shoulders, and was confined by a band of gold with a single stone exactly like one of her blue eyes set at the front. Her sharp little face with cheekbones like sculptured arches looked up at him wisely. Her thin lips smiled, but not as if she was amused at his predicament; rather, her smile was a little sad, as if she found him in a place where she had hoped he would not come.

"Ilya Ivanovitch, you called me, and I have come as I promised. You have been in the Katschei's home, I see," she said without preamble. "And having got that far, I suspect you have fallen in love with one of his maidens."

How did she know that? he thought with astonishment, but he certainly could not deny it. "I *have* lost my heart to the captive maiden called Tatiana," he replied with a sigh. "I went into the Katschei's domain because I was curious, but now I cannot live if I must be without her. Firebird, I *must* rescue her!"

The Firebird bent her head with a sigh of her own. "I warned you," she replied softly. "And I wish that you would remember all of that warning. In the Katschei's domain, nothing is what it seems, neither as simple nor as complicated, as innocent nor as safe. The only constant that you may be certain of is his deception."

He shook his head. "Lady, you cannot argue with your heart," he responded. "It goes where it will, and not where you would have it go. I saw her, and I loved her in that moment; I have watched her without her knowing for some time, and I do not love her any less for what I have seen of her. If anything, I love her the more."

Her head remained bent a moment longer, and he could not see her face. "How well I know that one cannot love where one wills," she murmured, with another small sigh. "And how well I know that the heart cannot be commanded by good sense." Then she raised her ageless and wise eyes to his again. "So, tell me what you have done thus far, and I will try to counsel you."

She sank down on the grass with the grace of a falling feather, and he sat beside her. The fox curled up between them both, her intelligent gaze going from one to another as they spoke. The feather served to light their conversation; it seemed to him that she had deliberately dimmed her magical light tonight. He told her all that he had done so far, ending with his capture and expulsion.

She tapped her lips with a finger as she thought, her fingernail reflecting the light of the feather with a pearly iridescence. "Well," she said at last, "the notion of poisoning the dragon was a good one, but I fear that it does not eat. That is why it needs no tending. I believe it is a creature like the gardening-beetles, but much more complex. It slays the creatures it captures quite handily, but they go to feed the Katschei's minions, not the dragon itself." She shook her head sadly, her hair flowing with the movement. "I have eyes and ears everywhere in the Katschei's realm, for all the birds tell me what transpires. The birds watched him build the creature, and have watched it carefully ever since then."

He felt utterly crestfallen, for that was the one question he could have asked Sergei and didn't. Shaking his head, he could only curse his own stupidity.

"I am sorry that I did not tell you that," she added, looking a little crestfallen herself, "but I was trying to dissuade you from going into the Katschei's realm, and I was hoping that I had. It never occurred to me that if you saw the thing, you might try to kill it. You are one man alone, and such a thing would daunt an army. Even less did I think you would venture near enough to try to poison the beast."

"Oh, even if the dragon *did* eat and I had tried, it probably wouldn't have worked," Ilya admitted. "I probably couldn't have gotten the chicken close enough to him without getting too close myself, and getting caught."

"And even if you had," the fox observed, licking her paws, *"I had a cousin once who was poisoned—he cried and whined for a long time before he died. The Katschei would know at once that something was wrong, for the dragon would surely have cried and roared in pain as the glass cut its stomach. Surely such a thing would give it a terrible bellyache."*

"That is a very good point, fox," Ilya admitted, and rested his chin on his hand, discouraged and depressed. "Now I don't know what I could possibly do to get rid of it, and get rid of it I must, if I am to get at the heart."

"I don't suppose I can persuade you to give up the attempt, can I?" the Firebird asked, without much hope.

He shook his head. "As long as I live, I shall try to free her," he replied. "I will live in the rubbish-room beside the kitchen forever, if need be. My disguise is still good among the lesser monsters, and the monster called Sergei will help me simply by standing as my superior. I can work in the gardens and steal whatever other food I need; I simply will have to be careful that I am never seen by the Katschei or any of his lieutenants. If I grow old there, I will still keep trying."

The Firebird sighed and shrugged. "Then I must help you, however mistaken I think you are," she told him, looking quite depressed. "Both because I have promised, and because you are deserving of help."

"This could be fun," the fox observed, eyes sparkling, tail swishing happily. *"I will help, too. What is life without risk? Besides, it is summer there and winter here; you can probably get me more cheese, and I know there must be many mice to catch there, and few things to catch them."*

Ilya closed his eyes for a moment with relief. "Thank you. Thank you both."

"Just remember me with cheese," the vixen grinned up at him, tongue lolling. *"Now, this beast—could we lure it away, and shut it up in some other place? One of my cubs lured a troublesome dog away once, and we managed to lure it right up to a bear's den. The bear ate it, then we went and ate the hens the dog was guarding."*

"It's chained to the tree," Ilya said regretfully. Then another idea occurred to him, and he turned to the Firebird. "Could *you* sing it to sleep, as you did my brothers in the orchard?"

"No," she told him firmly, but with regret, for that would have been the easiest answer for all of them. "The dragon is like the garden beetles. It can hear quite well, but it cannot *respond* to anything it has not been commanded to." She smiled sadly. "I tried that, once. I hate the Katschei, and I am afraid of him, and I thought perhaps I could succeed with trickery where the warriors had failed with force. I cannot put it to sleep any more than the garden beetles would come to your call or pay attention to a conversation in the garden above their heads."

Ilya ground his teeth in frustration, for it seemed that the dragon was almost as immune to attack as the Katschei. "Tell me everything you know about it, please," he asked the Firebird. "Maybe I can think of something while you talk."

She nodded, her thick hair swaying like a curtain of embers spun into strands. "The dragon is a creation of the Katschei," she began. "It is heavily armored, and I do not know if its armor has any weaknesses, for I have never heard of anyone harming it. It has keen senses, and anything that it hears or scents that is out of the ordinary will alert it, even in the depths of sleep. If it is aroused, it will watch and wait to see what roused it. If it is a human or animal that it does not recognize, it will roar, as a guarding dog will bark. If whatever it is comes within reach of the chain, the dragon will try to kill it, although it will not eat what it has killed. You cannot tempt it to lunge against the chain, for it knows precisely how long the chain is and will always stop a little short. But because it knows precisely how long its reach is, the moment you come into that reach, it will strike like lightning."

Ilya nodded. "Does the Katschei always come in person when the dragon begins to make noise?"

"Always," the Firebird affirmed. "No matter what time of day or night it is. If the dragon is engaged in killing something, he never breaks the fight off, but stays until the end. He likes to watch," she added with a frown.

"Typical," Ilya muttered, and thought for a moment. "Does the dragon ever make false alarms?"

The Firebird looked uncertain. "I suppose it must, but I would not think that such a thing would happen very often. Still, it must sometimes see a wild animal such as a deer that has somehow threaded the maze and come that far, or a very large bird such as an eagle-owl. Those are large enough to make it sound a false alarm."

Ilya grinned, for Ivan had once had a guard-dog that barked at *everything*. If it saw the grass moving in a way it thought suspicious, if it heard something it did not recognize, it barked a full alarm. Ivan eventually grew tired of the noise and got rid of the dog, for he could not go a full night without having his sleep disturbed.

"The Katschei is not infallible," he said with confidence. "And what is more, he is quite well aware that he is not infallible. He said as much in complaining about his own monsters. So he must know that the dragon can sound a false alarm. Now, he might not mind one false alarm, and two or three times of being awakened would only annoy him a bit—but what if the dragon was to sound the alarm *all night long*? What would he do then?"

Now the Firebird looked interested, and the fox nodded approvingly. *"Now you are thinking like a fox, boy!"* she said, her ears perked sharply up. *"If he was a farmer, he would shut the dog in the shed."*

"I do not know what he will do," the Firebird said slowly, "but he is most likely to think that something has gone wrong with his creation. And he is *not* likely to think that he needs to fix it at that very moment. I do not know what he will do, but I think that we should try and find out."

Ilya rose, picking up the feather and putting it back in the breast of his tunic.

"Lead on, boy," the vixen said, getting to her feet and swishing her tail. *"The best time to find out is tonight."*

ILYA had made several advance preparations in the garden that day. For one thing, he had stuffed the mechanism that locked the garden gate with clay, and Sergei had never noticed the difference. He opened the gate stealthily, and the fox slipped in with him, then he knocked the clay out of the mechanism so that it would lock behind them, leaving no trace that anyone had gotten inside. As he closed the gate, the Firebird landed on a branch just above his head, once again in the form of a bird, but with her fiery feathers muted to almost nothing. They stood together at the end of a long lane that led directly to the great oak tree. It looked to Ilya as if there were lanterns or torches all around the clearing that held the tree and the dragon, for it was as bright as day down there.

The Firebird bent her head down to him. "You and the fox take it in turn to tease the dragon," she said, though the words came strangely accented out of her beak instead of lips. "I will keep watch for the Katschei and call warning in time for you to get to hiding. Find hiding-places first, before you go to tease the beast. Ilya, you be the first, and fox, you the second."

"Sounds like fun," the fox observed cheerfully. *"Let's get to it!"*

She trotted down the lane with Ilya coming cautiously behind. In the light from the circle of lanterns, he could see only three great coils, like three fat necklets of amethyst, ruby, and sapphire, twined around the base of the tree. But as Sergei had warned him, the moment they got about halfway down the lane, those coils began to stir.

In another moment, the dragon's head came into view, as it peered into the shadows of the lane suspiciously.

Ilya expected smoke to wreathe up from its nostrils, but evidently this dragon was not the fire-breathing sort. Instead, a long, scarlet forked tongue lashed out from the front of its mouth, twitching nervously before being withdrawn.

Around its neck was a brass collar as thick as Ilya's waist, and a bronze chain as thick as his thigh hung down from a ring on the collar. Its head was shaped like a lizard's, with a ridge of spines running from the middle of the forehead on down along the neck. Its eyes were a deep, bright yellow, and Ilya could not yet see its teeth, for it had not opened its mouth, but he suspected that they would be as long as his hand, at least.

The fox scampered off to the right, off the lane; Ilya took a moment to go to the left. The dragon was not yet alarmed, but it was aroused, and he knew that it was listening carefully to every move he and the fox made.

This was not such a bad thing, since it distracted the dragon from the Firebird, who was flying up into the branches of the great oak tree to hide herself.

It took Ilya some time to find a hiding-place for himself, but eventually he found one, in an ornamental pond. The end nearest the lane had been allowed to grow over with reeds and other water-plants; he paused long enough to cut himself a hollow reed to breathe through, and then stepped back onto the lane.

Now the dragon was restless, up on its feet, and prowling back and forth on the chain, peering into the shadows beneath the trees. One of the strangest things about it was its ability to move with very little noise. It had worn all the grass beneath the oak tree away with its prowling, and had polished every exposed rock to a shiny gloss. It was obvious, now that it was moving about, that its wings were purely ornamental; they were much too small to have ever carried it in flight. Its claws weren't ornamental, though; wicked scimitars of gold, they were as long as Ilya's arm, and as highly polished as the rocks.

It was quite obvious how far the dragon's chain stretched, but Ilya had no intention of getting even that close. All he had to do was get near enough that the dragon would start to make noise—

Which it did, as soon as that thought had crossed his mind. It finally caught sight of him, recognized that he was *not* someone it knew, and let out a furious bellow.

And that was where Ilya stopped, although he did not stand still. Instead, he danced in place, waving his arms at the dragon, taunting it, and capering about like a grouse at mating-time. The dragon responded by leaping at him, stopping just short of the end of its chain, and standing there, cutting deep furrows in the ground with its claws and bellowing. Ilya had never heard such a noise before: Part growl, part howl, and part roar, it was louder than anything but the loudest thunder, and far more irritating. No one could ever hope to sleep through that! It spurred him on to wilder capers, just to see if he could get a higher level of noise out of the creature.

A sharp, piercing whistle carried over the dragon's screams, and Ilya sprinted for his chosen hiding place. He took a deep breath as he dove into the pond, but the shock of the cold water nearly made him lose it. He kept his eyes open as he swam, staying underwater until he reached the water-plants. He pulled the cut reed out of his shirt and poked it above the surface of the water cautiously, holding himself in place with both hands anchored in the roots of the plants sunk into the mud. It had occurred to him that the Katschei might have the equivalent of hounds, and here in the water his scent would be lost. The vixen, of course, could probably trick any hound ever born.

He had just gotten as comfortable as he was likely to get underwater, when a burst of light illuminated the end of the pond. A trail of moving lights passing by the water told him that the Katschei had come to see what had alerted his dragon. Shortly thereafter, the bellowing stopped.

Ilya concentrated on his breathing. It was difficult to get enough air through a tiny little reed, and that gave him something to think about without worrying his head over what the Katschei was doing. After a while, the lights passed by again, and silence and darkness fell over the garden.

Cautiously, Ilya poked his head above the water, still well-concealed by the reeds, taking in a deep breath of air, slowly and silently, just in case there was still something waiting out there. Once again, the garden was empty, but he heard the dragon snorting impatiently beyond the trees, the clanking of the chain as it moved, and the grating of its claws on the ground.

Now that he was used to it, the water wasn't all that cold. He stayed in the pond for the moment, figuring that he would be colder if he got out and stood in the breeze in soaking-wet clothing. He took the opportunity to explore the pond further, and found several more hiding places in it: beneath the low arch of an ornamental bridge, under an overhang of rock, and best of all, just behind a waterfall. He decided to use the bridge next time, when he heard the dragon bellowing again. He moved to his chosen spot beneath the bridge, and found to his pleasure that he could actually see a small section of the dragon's "yard."

The fox was much more daring than he would have been, actually diving in and out of reach of the frustrated serpent. She yipped at it insolently, and as she got out of reach, she gave a barking laugh. Sooner than last time, the same sharp whistle rang out, and the fox whisked out of sight, so quickly Ilya didn't even see her move—one moment she was there, and the next, there was just a patch of leaves quivering at the edge of the clearing. Ilya ducked under the bridge, a venue that just left his nose, his eyes, and the top of his head above water. He felt safe there, even if someone happened to lean over to look beneath the bridge, for he was down at the end of the arch, with some supporting rocks hiding him on either side. With any luck, here in the darkness his head would look just like another rock.

This time he did see a little of the Katschei's procession; the magician led a small parade of torch-bearers and lesser flunkies; none of his lieutenants were with him. Most of the monsters were smaller than the Katschei, and the sorcerer himself was resplendent in breeches, ankle-length vest, and tunic of black silk trimmed in gold. He got only a glimpse of them, however; soon they were out of sight, and he strained his ears to hear anything at all.

The dragon stopped bellowing, and in the silence, the Katschei's irritated voice rang out like the sharp crack of nearby thunder.

"Search the grounds!" he snapped. "And this time, do it right! Whatever is irritating my pet *must* be here, and I expect you to find it!"

The Katschei's minions scattered about, searching dutifully through the garden grounds, but Ilya noticed that they did not look as closely as humans might have. They didn't bother to *hunt* for clever hiding places, although the problem might simply have been that they didn't have enough imagination to guess where clever hiding-places might be. They looked under bushes and peered squinting up into the trees, but they seldom searched areas too small for a human to hide in.

For whatever reason, although several of them thudded over Ilya's bridge, they never once looked under it, and he was entirely safe the whole time. During all of this, their master waited with a scowl on his face and his arms crossed over his chest. With a mutter of annoyance, the Katschei received their negative reports as they came to him by ones and twos, and when they were all gathered again, he stalked away with them, anger in the very set of his back.

Now it was Ilya's turn again, and he was quite ready to play his part. He got out of the pond at the grassy verge, where the water dripping from him wouldn't be so obvious, and worked his way through the plantings to the dragon's clearing.

Now the beast was extremely suspicious and fully aroused; it took one look at him and began screaming in frustrated rage. Once again, he teased and taunted it, and it tore up huge clods of earth and even moved the huge boulders in its anger, for it knew it would not be able to touch him and didn't even try. This was a good thing, for if it had gone to the end of its chain and torn up the ground there, that would have pointed to the place where he had stood while he teased it. He danced in place as much to keep warm as to arouse the beast; with the breeze on his wet clothing, he was *cold,* and he couldn't wait to get back into the relatively warm water.

The expected whistle came, and he raced back to the pond, launching himself at the water in a flat racing dive that carried him most of the way across the pond under the water. He felt for the rocks where the bridge was with his hands in front of him, found them, and came up beneath the bridge. He had a few moments to settle himself beneath the end of the arch, and then the Katschei arrived for the third time. He cursed the incompetence of his minions; the sorcerer's voice carried clearly across the water. The poor monsters bumbling along in his wake were trembling and visibly unhappy, expecting punishment or even death at any moment.

Once again, the Katschei ordered a search of the grounds, and once again the monsters came up empty-handed. The Katschei glared about him as if he wanted to make the garden itself give up its secrets. Then he glared at the monsters as if he dared any of them to give him an excuse for violence.

But these were evidently veterans of his anger, and they had more sense to do anything other than stand with their eyes on their feet and tremble. The Katschei cursed, and stalked out again, followed by the terrified monsters.

Ilya waited, but for the moment, nothing happened, and the dragon settled down again, grumbling to itself. The time stretched, the dragon shifted restlessly, and there was no sign of the vixen. He wondered if the fox had lost interest in the game, and debated getting out to tease the dragon himself, but at that moment the little vixen came trotting up to the water's edge, her nose in the air, sniffing carefully for his scent.

"Boy!" she called softly. *"I have your scent. Are you near the pond?"*

"Here," he whispered, swimming out from under the bridge. He stayed in the pond, looking up at her. She trotted briskly over to the bridge and stood at the end of it, looking down curiously at him.

"It seemed to me that for the best effect, we ought to let the dragon settle down and its master get to sleep, or else to get interested in something and forget about the dragon," she said, and chuckled heartlessly. *"Let him just get comfortable,*

or begin to amuse himself, and then we'll rouse him out again. He won't like that!''

"You are a *very* clever, cunning little vixen," he replied with admiration. "You couldn't have come up with a better idea to irritate him out of all countenance!"

She frisked with pleasure at his praise, bouncing a little and whisking her tail from side to side. *"I come from a long line of cunning foxes,"* she said modestly. *"I do wonder why the Master didn't leave one of the little fellows to watch and guard, just to see why the dragon is bellowing."*

"He can't," Ilya replied gleefully. "The dragon would only scream at whatever he left to watch for him. The only way he could find out what is going on would be to stay here himself, and I doubt that would ever occur to him."

"Too important to do his own work, hmm?" the fox replied with fine contempt. She settled down at the edge of the pond and regarded him thoughtfully. *"Well, why don't you tell me about what's here while we wait for Master Oh-So-High to get himself into a comfortable position? All I saw was a tiny bit of the gardens that we passed through. I'd like to know what's here before I decide if I'm going to take up residence."*

Ilya described the various gardens that they had briefly passed through, and the way that they were tended. He told her about the kitchen and the kitchen-midden, the trash-heap—and admitted the lack of chicken-yards, stables, and other places where there would be livestock and rodents. The fox licked her lips as she contemplated what he told her.

"I can think of places for mice, and places for moles," she said with satisfaction. *"And lots of places to hide, which is just as important, unless I were to den up during the day with you. I wouldn't mind that, and I could keep mice out of your food."*

"That assumes that we can't get this to work," Ilya reminded her. "If we do, we'll have to work quickly, for we may not get a second chance. Once the dragon is taken care of, however the Katschei does it, the next thing will be to get the chest down out of the tree and get it open."

"I won't be much help in climbing. What's in the chest?" the fox asked, curiously.

Ilya described the chest and its contents. The fox tilted her head and squinted up her eyes, as if she wasn't certain she had heard him correctly. *"That is altogether too strange to even think about,"* she said, and shook her head until her ears flapped. *"The very idea of ducks inside rabbits makes the inside of my head itch! How were you going to kill them?"*

"I hid a knife and my bow and arrows in one of the garden-benches of the garden with the statue-warriors in it when I put away the garden-beetles earlier today," Ilya replied. "When I thought I was going to be able to poison the dragon, I had figured on prying the chest open. If the rabbit gets away from me when I open the chest, I ought to be able to shoot it, then kill the duck."

"Maybe," the vixen said with skepticism. *"Remember what the Firebird said. Nothing is as simple here as it seems."*

"Right now, let's just concentrate on the dragon," Ilya told her. "We'll worry about the chest *if* we can get it out of the way."

"Good plan." The vixen licked her lips, and looked over her shoulder. *"And by now, I suspect that the Master has settled in to enjoy whatever he's doing. So now I'll go make sure he doesn't."*

She trotted off, and Ilya swam back to his hiding-place beneath the bridge. A moment later, the dragon bellowed with rage again, this time from the far side of the oak tree. The vixen had teased him over to a new place, which was a good idea. Now there would be no way of telling exactly where they were hiding.

The Katschei took a bit longer to return, and he was in a fine rage himself. This time, he brought with him two of his lieutenants, who were a great deal more human-seeming than the usual monsters. Once the dragon quieted, he ordered a general search, then turned to these two.

"You take the far side of the garden, and you take the near," he said, his voice tight with anger. "Direct these fools; they think that if they search everything obvious, they've done their jobs. I'll have to stay here and see to it that the dragon stays quiet; it would take three days to make it understand that all of you are to be permitted here. So make this quick—I want my dinner, and I'm getting very weary of this."

The lieutenants made no reply, or at least not one that was

audible to Ilya. He tucked himself back under the bridge as far as he could get, holding very still and breathing deeply, so that if he had to duck underwater and hold his breath, he could at a moment's notice.

Sure enough, this time when the monsters searched around the pond, the lieutenant directed them in a close examination of the verge, and had them poke their spears into the reedy section. If he had been under there, he'd have been stuck, and it would all have been over right then. When they came to the bridge, he was ready, and ducked underwater as one leaned down with a lantern in his hand to examine the area beneath the bridge. *He* could see the lantern and the vague blob of a head, but he was quite certain that the monster couldn't see a thing because of the reflection of the lantern in the water. The head and lantern both withdrew, then reappeared briefly on the other side of the bridge with the same lack of results. He waited until he heard the water-muffled thuds of its feet going off the bridge before he rose cautiously out of the water.

His view from beneath the bridge was limited, but he had no intention of trying to improve it. He was probably safe where he was, and he didn't need to know what the searchers or the Katschei was doing. The lanterns of the searchers moved through the garden in the middle distance, and he took a deep but silent breath, just in case someone had remained behind to watch and listen for a clever intruder hiding under the water.

He was glad it had been the fox's turn to torment the dragon; if it had been his, he would have left splashes and water at the verge of the pond. They wouldn't have been visible, but there would have been an obvious place with wet grass where the rest of the grass was dry. If the lieutenants had noticed that, it would have given the searchers a real reason to concentrate on the pond.

Finally, all activity in the garden ceased, and eventually the vixen trotted up to the pond again.

"*They've gone,*" she said, her voice full of satisfaction. "*I had a good time; I managed to slip in behind them, and I followed along as they searched. This is as much fun as tricking a pack of hounds. The master is* really *angry, by the way. He's cursing a great deal, and muttering.*"

Ilya had to chuckle at the tone of her voice. "I don't doubt it," he replied. "The Katschei wouldn't like being called away from something he wants to do, and he wouldn't like being made a fool of. We're doing both to him, and what is worse, he must be thinking at this point that there's something wrong with his dragon. He'll hate that even more. He knows he can make mistakes but admitting it is a different matter."

He climbed carefully out of the pond, and spent some time dripping at the edge until he was damp rather than wet so that he wouldn't leave any telltale splashes when he got out. It didn't matter that this was going to take some time; all that mattered was that he didn't leave any signs. He shivered in the breeze, but better cold than take any risk when he was so close to his goal.

It worried him suddenly that now, after days and weeks of accomplishing little besides discovering where things were and how the Katschei organized his domain, *if* he was going to succeed in destroying the sorcerer, everything would have to be done in the next few hours. It was as if a horse he was riding had gone from a slow and sleepy walk to a full-out gallop with no warning whatsoever.

Yet he had no choice in that, and never had. If he'd only thought about it, it would have been obvious that once he eliminated the dragon, he would have to get the heart *immediately*. The Katschei would hide the heart somewhere else or replace the dragon with another guardian within a short period of time. And once Ilya got the heart, he would have to use it *immediately*. The Katschei would certainly notice if his heart was missing! He might even have some magical way of telling that it had been removed.

All that had always been the case; he had just been so busy, first in trying to survive and find the dragon, then in trying to think of ways to get past the dragon, that he had not bothered to think the entire situation through. He didn't like moving on with no plan; it made him feel entirely unsettled and uncertain. And the fact that if he got past the dragon, all the rest of his task would have to be accomplished before dawn, was positively frightening.

"You're having second thoughts?" the vixen asked, shrewdly.

He shook his head. "Not second thoughts—just worrying that we may not have enough time to do what we have to. Get rid of the dragon, then get the chest, then get the heart and get to the Katschei, all before dawn. If we can't get it done by then, we'll be in grave danger, and we may lose the heart—and dawn is only a few hours away."

The little fox sat down and scratched her ear meditatively. *"Well, we can only make our plans as far as getting that heart. After that, who knows? One thing at à time, and we still don't know that the Master is going to lock his dog in the shed for barking too much. If he doesn't, we'll have to think of another plan."*

He chuckled at her simile. "True. And you had better go hide. As soon as I am dry enough, it will be my turn to make the dog bark."

The vixen gave a wordless yip of agreement and trotted off. He waited a little while longer, until he was certain that he would not be leaving any wet splotches on the grass, then gathered himself and made a tremendous standing leap out onto the lawn, so that if he did, anyway, the splotch wouldn't be *right* beside the pond. He had left some water at the very edge, but only about as much as a fish jumping there would leave.

Then he went off to perform his dance for the dragon, capering and taunting it until its shrieks of rage reached new heights of volume and shrillness. He knew, as the Firebird warned him and he dove into cover, that if the dragon ever got hold of him, it wouldn't leave enough for the monsters to eat. The dragon was as frustrated as its master, and taking it all very personally. It not only screamed with rage, it danced with rage, its jaws snapping on air, its claws rending the breeze, as if it wanted him to know what it *could* do if it caught him.

Once again the Katschei and his minions came and went, and it was clear that the sorcerer was growing more furious by the moment. This time the fox evidently decided that it would be much more fun if she alerted the dragon before the Katschei even got out of the garden gate; the little cavalcade hadn't been gone more than a few moments before the dragon began bellowing again.

That, evidently, was the final straw. With a shriek of rage that very nearly rivaled the dragon's, the Katschei came storming back in the gate and up the lane at the head of his frightened troops.

He was so very angry, in fact, that Ilya couldn't understand what he was saying. Either he was cursing in a strange language, or he was so angry he'd become incoherent. Or—he was invoking magic. The sorcerer left a small trail of destruction in his wake, as his path along the lane was marked by great flashes of light and thunderclaps. As the Katschei stormed past Ilya, he shook his fist at a small garden statue, and a bolt of lightning came out of nowhere and shattered it, leaving only fragments and scorched earth. He walked right into the dragon's clearing without pausing to stop it from screaming as he had before.

Ilya wondered if he was going to treat the dragon as he had the statue, and braced himself for the thunderbolt. But there was no clap of thunder, no flash of light. The screaming stopped, but differently from the other times. Before, it had tapered off, finally resolving into upset grumblings and snorts. This time, the dragon's shriek was cut off in the middle, as if it had been throttled.

Then, in the silence that followed, Ilya heard a sound he had not expected to hear: the clank of the great bronze chain dropping to the ground.

The Katschei stalked out again, followed by his torch-bearing monsters, muttering under his breath. "I have had enough for *one* night!" he snarled to his lieutenants. "That will hold the idiot creature until I can get some sleep...." And there was more in the same vein until the Katschei got out of earshot.

There was utter and complete silence in the dragon clearing; there wasn't even the sound of a talon scraping the earth as the noise of footsteps vanished into the distance. The garden gate slammed shut with a tremendous crash. Then there was nothing, no sound whatsoever. The few birds that had been in the garden had all left when they first teased the dragon, and now everything else in the garden was too afraid to make a sound.

Some time passed while Ilya held his breath, wondering

what to do next. What had the Katschei done? Had he "shut
the dog in the shed"—or had he turned it loose to destroy
whatever irritated it the next time? That was one possibility
they had not discussed, and even the Firebird would not dare
warn them if that was what had happened, for the dragon was
perfectly able to climb the tree and go after her.

It was *his* turn to go tease it, and just at the moment, he
was not inclined to get out of the pond, lest he find a dragon,
loosed from its chain, prowling the garden paths. Like many
hunters, it could have turned silent and stealthy when it had
finally been turned loose to hunt on its own rather than guarding the tree. He waited, straining his ears, every nerve and
muscle tense with dread, wondering what had happened. He
listened until he got a headache, until his jaws ached from
clenching them, until his back felt made of ever-tightening
wires.

Finally, just when he thought that his nerves were going to
snap from the strain, he heard a soft call from above.

"Ilya, little vixen, come out," the Firebird sang quietly, so
quietly that her words could not have gone much past the
clearing, though her song probably reached all the way to the
gate. "Come and see how the Katschei has treated his pet!"

Ilya clambered out of the pond with no thought for leaving
telltale splotches and hurried into the clearing, dripping as he
came. For one half-crazed moment, he thought that the Firebird had somehow turned traitor and that he was going to be
killed—for the dragon was indeed unchained, the bronze chain
detached from its collar and cast aside. It glared into the garden, but it was not glaring at Ilya, and after a moment he
realized that it wasn't glaring at anything.

The dragon was standing stock-still and frozen; its eyes,
though glittering, were curiously lifeless. It had become a huge
bejeweled and shining ornament, no more alive than the bridge
or the rocks. Light from the lanterns all around the clearing
reflected from its ruby, amethyst, and sapphire scales, from its
topaz eyes, its golden claws. Ilya stared at it, sure that this
was all a trap, and that in a moment it was going to leap on
him. But it did nothing of the sort, not even when the vixen
trotted up and sniffed at its foot.

For a moment he could not imagine what might have happened.

Then he knew. The Katschei had turned his own pet into a statue to keep it quiet!

"Hah," the vixen said with satisfaction. *"So the master muzzled the dog instead of putting it in the shed! Or maybe he hit it in the head to put it to sleep!"*

"It certainly looks that way," Ilya replied, strolling up to the quiescent creature, as the Firebird circled down out of the highest branches of the tree, hovered for a moment just above them, then dropped down beside them. "And we have at least until morning to decide *how* I am going to get at that chest."

In the brilliant lantern-light he examined the tree itself. There were no limbs anywhere near the ground, and the trunk of the tree nearest the ground was smooth and without many hand-and foot-holds. Climbing that part of it would be a risky business, if not impossible, seeing as he had no equipment with him whatsoever to allow him to do so. Now what was he going to do? He looked up into the tree; the top was barely visible as a darker shadow against the sky. How high up was it? He hadn't been able to estimate from outside, and now he couldn't from up close.

How to get into those lower limbs? Once he got that far, there were places he could climb, handholds, rougher bark. The higher he went, the easier it would be.

He studied the situation for a moment, then realized something: Although there were no limbs anywhere near the ground, the dragon's chain made a perfectly good ladder. It was wound once around the tree, but higher than the dragon's head, perhaps so that the dragon wouldn't tear at it and get himself loose. From the chain, he could easily reach the lowest limb. So the only question was, how heavy was that chest? Could he get it down by himself?

"What is the chest like?" he asked, rubbing his hands together to warm them, and wondering if his wet boots were going to rub his feet raw before he finished climbing. *Maybe I'd better take them off and climb in bare feet. Yes, I think that would be better; I think my boot-soles would be too slippery. . . .*

"The chest is made of wood, bound with bronze. You could

easily carry the chest down on your back, if you can get into the tree," the Firebird murmured softly. "It is not very heavy. But there is a problem—"

"We don't have the key," Ilya replied immediately. That had bothered him, but not much. So long as the chest was made of ordinary wood, they *could* get into it.

"Yes. And the creatures in the chest are not natural," she added. "They are very, very swift. You might be able to shoot one, but you would never get a second arrow off in time."

The vixen looked up the tree. "*I might get the rabbit, if you could break open the chest,*" she offered. "*But you have to turn it loose down here. I can't get up there.*"

"The chest is perfectly ordinary wood, and it could be broken open without harming the creatures inside. But what to break it open with?" the Firebird countered. "We haven't an ax—"

"I have an idea," Ilya replied. "This is all hard ground here. If I dropped the chest, it should smash. If it smashes, the rabbit will leap free. If it doesn't smash, we'll think of something else."

"*And with luck, I can get the rabbit,*" the vixen said, licking her lips with anticipation.

"All right, then—let me get my bow and arrows," Ilya said, with a confidence he did not feel. "Then we'll see how good my climbing skills still are."

IT was a very odd and disconcerting thing, to be climbing up a huge bronze chain beside a dragon. The creature was quite beautiful up close, every separate scale edged in a fine line of gold, and as hard and shiny as a porcelain plate. The chain was an easy thing to climb, as easy as a ladder; it had plenty of hand-and foot-holds, and Ilya swarmed up it with relatively little effort. Removing his boots had been a good idea; his feet were still tough and callused from the summer, and gave him better control than wearing his boots.

From the top of the chain above the dragon's head he was able to reach one of the lowest branches, and from there he could find enough purchase in the bark to make his way slowly up the trunk.

Then it just became work: making sure he was firmly anchored by at least one hand and foot while he reached for a new hold, clinging to the bark with his fingertips, studying the next few feet of trunk for a new set of holds. All the while he was doing this, he hung on while his arms and legs ached, and his back complained loudly that this was a bad idea. When he reached a branch he was able to rest for a little, standing or sitting on it until some of the burning sensation left his limbs before he went on.

He looked down after a while, and wished that he hadn't. The dragon was as small as a toy, and the vixen the size of a bug, and he *still* wasn't at the top yet! The vixen gazed up at him, the dragon glittered, and the lamps defined a neat half-circle of light. He looked out and found that he was above the tops of the trees around him. He was on the wrong side of the tree to see the palace, but he sensed its presence. What was the Katschei doing? Did he sense something wrong? Or was he so angry and annoyed that he was not paying any attention to anything but his own anger?

The Firebird kept him company and helped him by finding easier routes along the trunk. She stayed in bird-form, flitting from branch to branch while he toiled his way upward. He wondered why *she* couldn't have retrieved the chest at first, but then it occurred to him that as a maiden she wouldn't have the strength to climb this high, and as a bird she couldn't carry the chest. If she somehow opened it while it was still in the top of the tree, the rabbit would escape among the branches or would plunge to the ground. Being a magical creature, it would probably survive the drop just fine, and escape. Or, as big as these limbs were, it could run off into the foliage and they'd never find it.

No, he had to do this the hard way; there was no escaping that fact.

He climbed and rested, climbed and rested until it seemed that he had been climbing all night. He looked out again, and was able to see most of the gardens below him, and the walls of the maze in the distance, shining under the moon. Strange; there were thick storm-clouds all around, except over the Katschei's land. There, the sky was clear, in a distinctly defined circle. So the Katschei could control the clouds, too!

The trunk got smaller until it was no thicker than an ordinary tree's. The Firebird was above him now, perched beside the chest, which was cradled in a "nest" where several branches grew out of the same fork, tied in place with perfectly ordinary rope. The chest wasn't all that large, after all, and there was enough rope wrapped around it that he should be able to use it to tie the chest onto his back. He looked down again and regretted it; the ground was moving.

No, it wasn't the ground, it was the tree, swaying in the wind. And from this height, the vixen was just a red dot on the brown earth. . . .

If he fell, there wouldn't be any need to bury him. He'd create his own pit where he impacted with the dirt.

No one he'd ever heard of had ever been *this* high. This was crazy. What was he doing up here? Why had he let the Firebird talk him into this? He was going to fall! He was!

Suddenly a great and terrible fear washed over him; he couldn't move, he could only cling to the trunk of the tree and whimper, with his eyes squeezed tightly shut. Every second, he expected to fall. If the wind picked up, it would pluck him right off the trunk. Or it would shake him loose, like a ripe apple. Or the top of the tree would break off and fall, taking him with it—

This was no fear caused by magic, it was a perfectly natural and sane fear of falling to his death at any moment.

"Ilya," the Firebird said, clearly and calmly, just above him. "Ilya, look at me."

"I can't," he said weakly, squeezing his eyes shut, as his stomach squeezed itself into a fist-sized ball. And he couldn't; he couldn't have gotten his eyes open if Tatiana had been sitting there beside him.

"Ilya, *look at me.*" There was magic behind those words, a coercive magic he had never heard the Firebird use. He could not withstand the command in her voice, and cracked open the eye nearest her.

She had transformed to maiden again, and sat casually on one of the boughs, not even holding on with both hands. "Come up, Ilya," she said. "It is not so far. Look! The branches are fully wide enough that you will be secure! See how stout they are?" And to prove her point, she bounced a little on the one she was sitting on.

He wanted to cry, to scream, to whimper and cling to the bark. He couldn't move, couldn't free so much as a finger. But he couldn't let her see that he was paralyzed by his fear, either. After all, *she* was afraid of the Katschei, and yet she was here helping him. Couldn't he face his fear of falling?

Slowly, with infinite caution, he loosed the grip of his right hand and moved it to a higher handhold. The Firebird smiled at him encouragingly. It took all the courage he had, and he was sweating as if he had run a mile on the hottest day of the year, but he managed to inch his right foot off the branch it was braced against and onto a higher one.

Little by little, he inched his way up the trunk those last few feet of the way. He had his cheek pressed into the bark so firmly it rasped his skin when he moved; he had to free each finger separately, while his arms and legs trembled and fear became a terrible, chilling nausea. Up he crept, like a lizard, handhold by handhold, each one paid for in sweat and terror, until he sat next to the chest on the side opposite from her. He didn't remember the last few feet, or how he'd gotten to that position.

She had already untied the rope that held the chest in place and was dragging it over into her lap. "Get into the fork, where the chest was, and I will help you tie it on your back," she said with authority, and he was not going to argue with her. The meeting of all those branches formed a secure little cup, and although it was not as good as being on the ground would have been, it was better than clinging to a limb.

He crouched there, with his eyes closed, trying to pretend that he was on the ground as she tied the chest onto his back, making a kind of harness of the rope that passed over both shoulders and around his waist. "I am knotting it over the chest, but when you get to the lower parts of the tree you can cut the rope," she said by way of explanation, as he felt her shifting and tugging at the rope. "There. It is *quite* secure."

Now came the worst part—the climb down.

Climbing up had been difficult, the last part nightmarish, but the climb down with the chest changing his balance and threatening to pull him over at any moment was hellish. The Firebird stayed with him the entire time, helping to steady him where she could, but in her bird-form she wasn't much help, and in her maiden-form she simply didn't have the reach to climb.

A thousand times he was certain that he was going to slip and fall, but each time, shaking and sweating, he managed to save himself. Sweat dripped into his eyes and soaked through his tunic, and the stiff breeze that had sprung up chilled him under the clammy tunic. At that moment, if anyone had asked him if he wanted to abandon the task, he probably would have said yes. He kept his eyes strictly on the tree around him until he reached the point when he thought that the trunk was just about the same size that it was at the level of the ground. He got himself securely onto one of the enormous limbs and made certain of his footing. Then he looked down.

The relief he felt when he saw that he was no farther above the ground than he would have been in the top of an ordinary large oak was so tremendous that tears sprang into his eyes and he had to stop a moment to wipe them away. This might be as good a place as any to drop the chest from.

He was standing on the top of a huge limb, as broad as a highway, which stretched out just above the dragon. He walked along it and sat down when he was right over a section of polished boulders deeply embedded in the barren ground. Those would certainly crack the chest open, if anything would.

He took out his knife and cut the ropes holding the chest to his back, and lowered it onto the limb beside him. Then he got out his arrows and his bow, a small but powerful weapon that Yasha had given him, made of laminated sinew, horn, and wood.

"Are you ready?" he called down to the fox.

She grinned up at him. "*Quite,*" she replied, getting to within easy leaping-distance of the cluster of boulders and readying herself to spring, hind-legs gathered in a crouch that would send her after the hare like a second arrow.

He took a deep breath. They would have only one chance at this. If they failed now, the Katschei would recapture the creature holding his heart and find another place to put it where it would be safer. He could not even *begin* to imagine what that would be.

And if they failed now, there was a very good chance that the Katschei would catch him, and he wasn't going to be able to feign the Fool successfully under these conditions. He *would* die if that happened, or worse. But probably he would die; the Katschei could not take the chance that someone would free him from the statue-spell.

He readied an arrow on his bow. It all came down to this, this single moment. *Now. Before I lose my nerve.*

He kicked the chest—and then the world slowed about him.

The chest fell—it seemed to float, it fell so slowly. But everything was like that, including himself. Only his mind raced on—or was it that the world was going at its normal pace, and his mind was outracing it?

The chest tumbled as it fell, ungainly, and he held his breath, bringing the arrow up to bear on it even though he wouldn't be firing it at the chest. The best thing would be if it landed on a corner—

It hit the boulders, small end first. He watched huge cracks form along the sides, watched the top fly off, bouncing along the ground. The splintered planks went in every direction, and the brass straps binding it twisted and deformed.

He watched as a huge hare the size of a small dog leapt free of the debris and pelted off in huge jumps, as fast as a shooting star, heading for the undergrowth at an astonishing speed.

But as fast as the hare was, the vixen was faster. She was a streak of red, a dull-copper lightning-bolt. The little fox intercepted the track of the hare, leapt at the same time as the rabbit, and caught it in midleap. Her jaws closed on its throat; she did a fast somersault in midair as it tried to rake her underbelly with its powerful hind-feet. She landed, shook her head violently, breaking its neck, then transferred her grip to the belly, ripping it open with a single tug.

But instead of blood and entrails, a duck exploded from the belly-cavity, wings pounding, heading for the sky above the trees.

As if in a dream, Ilya raised his bow slowly, sighted slowly, loosed an arrow that drifted away from his bow. He reached for a second arrow—

But there was no need. His first arrow flew straight and true, and pierced the duck squarely through the chest. The bird dropped to the ground without a sound.

The vixen had already vanished, taking the hare with her as her well-earned reward. Ilya scrambled down the rest of the tree-trunk as fast as he could, hitting the ground at a dead run, until he reached the duck. His knife was already in his hand although he didn't recall unsheathing it, and he seized the duck and slit it open.

A diamond the size of two fists put together fell out of the belly of the duck; embedded in the diamond was something dark, with a strange and unsettling glow to it. He stared at it, reached for it—

The Firebird screamed as dozens of monsters fell upon Ilya and his prize, and seized them both.

``I should have known you were too foolish to be true,'' the Katschei said, and the bored resignation in his voice did not hide the undertones of cold rage.

Ilya could not actually *see* the sorcerer; his wrists had been bound behind his back, and he had been forced into a kneeling position with his head down, and staring at the inlaid floor of the Katschei's throne-room. Up above him on the dais, the Katschei lounged, surrounded by the twelve maidens. That much Ilya had seen before the Katschei's monsters threw him to the floor and one of them put his boot in the small of Ilya's back to keep him bent over.

"I should have guessed that it simply wasn't possible for anyone as monumentally stupid as you appeared to be to be able to penetrate my maze, much less survive for an instant among my minions," the Katschei continued into the otherwise silent throne room. "And *now* what am I going to do with you?"

Ilya did not reply; he merely licked blood off his split lip and remained silent. The less he said, the more he might learn—and at the moment, he would take *anything* that would give him a moment more of survival.

"Please." Ilya recognized the voice of the Arab maid, soft and exotically accented. She sounded frantic, which was flattering, at least. "For once, for the love of Allah, be merciful. . . ."

Ilya wished he could see what was going on up on the dais, but he didn't dare raise his head. If he did, he'd be kissing the floor again. "I do not care what Allah thinks of me, dear child," the Katschei replied, with a sardonic chuckle. "And it would be far too risky to be merciful to this one. He's too clever. And, I suspect, too persistent. No matter what I did to him, short of death, he would find a way out of it."

At this pronouncement, the other eleven joined the Arab maiden in pleading for his life, their voices mingling in a clamor of shrill intensity, Tatiana's voice ringing above the others. "Has he not proved a worthier foe than all the rest?" she said, in clear and ringing tones. "Surely you cannot merely execute such a foe! Should he not be exalted above the others? Given a special place among your trophies?"

"Oh, a special *fate*, surely," the Katschei responded, his voice utterly cold and expressionless. "One who had my own—fate—in his hands, oh, he surely deserves a special *fate*. And it is well for you, my beauties, that you could not be the source of his oh-so-accurate information." By now, that voice was so full of deadly promise that it sent ice down Ilya's spine. "And I would like, very much, to know who told him what he knows. I intend to find it out before he dies."

Silence fell again, and then he was gazing at a pair of shoes. Not boots before his eyes this time, but soft, black silk slippers. The Katschei grabbed him by the hair and wrenched his head up so that he was looking into the sorcerer's eyes.

The eyes of someone with no soul, he thought. *It is not his heart that the Katschei has bartered for power, it is his soul. His heart was merely the promissory note.* He could not look away from those terrible eyes, so full of emptiness, and yet so very avaricious.

"You are going to tell me where you learned about the chest," the Katschei said softly. "Eventually. But you are going to entertain me first, to make up for spoiling my entertainment earlier this evening."

Whichever monster had his foot in the middle of Ilya's back removed it. With his hand still gripping Ilya's hair, the Katschei hauled Ilya to his feet. It felt as if the sorcerer intended to tear Ilya's hair out by the roots. Tears of pain sprang into his eyes, but he kept his mouth tightly clamped shut, for he knew this was nothing compared with what the Katschei planned for him. The Katschei let go of his hair, grabbed an arm, and flung him into the arms of two of the sorcerer's lieutenants.

"Cut his bonds," the sorcerer said shortly. "Then make him run the gantlet a few times to soften him up. I want to think about an appropriate fate for him before I do anything."

One lieutenant, a strange creature with long, spindly, attenuated limbs and a small body and head, looking oddly like a four-limbed spider, cut his bonds while the other held him. The second one looked *exactly* like one of the hairy demons of Father Mikail's books, complete with horns, grotesque expression, goat-eyes, and cloven hooves. Ilya faced the Katschei's throne and dais as the spider-man sliced through the tough rope with some difficulty.

Ilya studied the situation, looking for any advantage; the maidens were arranged six on each side of the throne, with the Katschei's diamond-heart in a niche just to the left of the throne, where the sorcerer could keep an eye on it. Tatiana stood a little aloof from the rest of the maidens, her hands clasped tightly against her breast, biting her nether-lip. As she got a good look at him, though, for just a moment her expression changed. She looked stunned, as if she had been expecting someone else.

She must have been stunned because she was still confused by his fool act, and thought he had been mad. She was stunned now to think he had been so incredibly clever—

Clever. He glanced quickly around, knowing the throne-room as he did, and was dismayed to see *competent* guards at all the entrances and exits, even the ones that were not obvious. There were guards below the windows above the level of the floor that let in light to shine on the throne during the daytime. And there were archers in the gallery above. The Katschei was taking no chances.

He had no chance to think past that moment; the spider-creature cut through the last few strands of his bonds; the demon spun him around, and he saw what he was to face to "soften him up."

A double line of the Katschei's monsters faced him, all of them armed with clubs, whips, or other unedged weapons. It was obvious what was going to happen. He would be forced to run between them, back and forth, until the Katschei thought of something else to do with him. At some point, he would be asked who it had been that had told him the Katschei's secret—but that was a mere bagatelle; the Katschei wanted to know only if it had been someone in his own household. Ilya could tell him anything, even that the Firebird had done it. That might not satisfy him, since he was bound to want as many victims as possible right now. There might, possibly, have been fear in the Katschei's eyes. The sorcerer who thought himself immortal had been very close to death, and knew it.

A shove in the small of his back sent him stumbling between the two lines, and the rain of blows began.

He stumbled between two demons with whips, who cut his shirt with their quirts before he could get to his feet and stagger on. His skin stung and burned where the lashes had fallen, and the next blow, aimed at his head, hit his shoulder instead and numbed it to the elbow. The demons were shouting and cheering, taunting him and catcalling as he staggered on.

I have to keep my head. If I can keep my head, I can come out of this with less damage—if I can dodge out of reach of the ones with heavy clubs and take the blows from the ones with whips and sticks—

He did just that, dashing under a pair who flailed clumsily with clubs that were too heavy for them, and allowing another pair to cut him with riding-crops. Two more had training-whips, and got in several cuts on his back, which tore his shirt to ribbons and felt as if the flesh had been flayed from his bones.

Instead of running straight through, he lurched down the line in a zigzag, avoiding the deadly blows and letting the monsters with lighter weapons strike his back and arms, as he held both arms cupped over his head to protect it. The pain was incredible—but it was no worse than one of his brothers' beatings.

Not as bad, really, he thought, dazedly. *I can take this.* Each of those light slices hurt dreadfully initially, but he could still move, still think—

He staggered to the end of the gantlet and fell flat on his face; everywhere he'd been whipped burned like a trail of fire, his arms and hands felt fat, swollen, and numb, and he was a bit light-headed.

Don't move. Make them do the work. Delay everything, Ilya. There's a way out of this, if only you can see it. He waited for the demons to haul him to his feet and face him in the right direction again. Every moment that he wasn't running the gantlet bought him a little more time.

Unexpectedly, three of the maidens broke away from the group around the Katschei's throne. They ran out among the demons, surrounded him, and tried to shelter him with their bodies. "Leave him alone!" cried one of the Sami women angrily. "Kill him and be done with it, or let him go! Stop torturing him, you heartless beast!''

The demons hauled them off, gingerly; the Katschei glared at them. Then he stretched out his arm and crooked his finger at them, and all three jerked as if he'd pulled on chains attached to their throats. With a cruel smile, he gestured again, and step by step, they stumbled back up the dais to the places they'd abandoned.

But that didn't shut them up. The moment they reached their places, they began pleading or haranguing, according to their temperaments, and the others joined them, as if aware that if they *all* made a fuss, the Katschei would be unlikely to concentrate on any single one of them to punish. The Turkish girl beat on the stone of the dais with her little fists, as if she would like to pound the Katschei with them, and the other Sami launched into a long series of vituperative curses in her own language.

The demons ignored all this. Once again, with a shove, Ilya was propelled into the gantlet. The demons hadn't changed positions at all, and once again he was able to evade the worst blows and even gain a bit more time by ''falling,'' tumbling out of the way, and staggering to his feet again. Now, though, he was getting more than a little light-headed; not disoriented yet, but the blows that did reach his head were making him dizzy. The Katschei would probably have noticed that Ilya wasn't getting the kind of punishment the sorcerer had planned, except that the maidens were distracting him with their pleas and wails.

He landed on his face again at the other end of the gantlet

and as he waited limply for the demons to haul him to his feet for a third round, he carefully assessed his physical condition. There was a lot of pain; now his entire back felt raw, and he could scarcely feel his arms. There was blood streaming down his back and trickling along his ribs, and his shirt was in ribbons. But he looked worse than he was.

No, this was not bad. Not bad, but not good, and it was never going to get any better. If he was going to do something, it would have to be now, before it got any worse, before the Katschei managed to silence his captives. There would never be a better moment.

The demons who picked him up were not hanging on to him with any great vigor, and he saw his chance.

He gathered himself, and before they could propel him into the gantlet again, he got his feet set and went into swift and surprisingly certain motion.

He threw his weight to one side, pivoting on one foot, and managed to fling the right-hand demon into the left-hand one. That broke their grip; putting his head down, he charged them, catching the first one in the stomach with his head. The demon grunted and went down, the second grabbed at him but missed, and Ilya continued his charge, heading straight for the goal he'd set himself when he knew he was in the throne-room.

The maidens saw their chance—or reacted without thinking, it didn't matter which. They fled the dais and ran back and forth through the throne-room, screaming at the tops of their lungs—no more able to escape than he was, but fully capable of complicating an already chaotic situation. Some of the demons tried to grab at them, and more than one of the girls reacted to this insult by further hysterics.

As the maidens shrieked and ran among the confused demons, confusing them even further, Ilya reached his goal: a small table with a heavy statue on it. He seized the statue and, evading the grasping hands of one demon and the flailing club of another, he whirled, hurling the statue with all of his might.

It crashed through the stained-glass window to the right of the throne, shattering it. And as soon as it left his hands, Ilya reached into what was left of the breast of his tunic and pulled out the Firebird's feather, waving it above his head desperately three times.

As the demons closed in on him, he held the flaming feather above his head, praying that she would come, for she was his only chance.

CHAPTER TEN

JUST AS the first of the demons reached him, and grabbed his arms, the Firebird came, and it was obvious that *she* had been waiting for his summons. His heart rose with hope and elation—she had not deserted him!

She flew in at the shattered window, filling the throne-room with the light of her feathers, but her purpose was not to attack.

Instead, she was singing, singing her magical lullaby with all of her soul. She went straight to the center of the room and hovered there, all of her concentration on the song, hanging in the air like a fabulous, gem-studded carving or an enchanting glass ornament, oblivious even to the archers who had their arrows trained on her.

Don't shoot! Ilya pled silently with them, as they stared at her in fascination, half-mesmerized by her beauty and the coruscating plumage that shivered and shed sparks of many-colored light as she sang.

Every note was shaped perfectly, every phrase exquisite. But Ilya was not at all interested in hearing that song—the opposite, in fact. He stuffed his fingers in his ears, as demons began dropping to the floor, by ones and twos, all around him.

First to go were the lesser creatures, the poor twisted and deformed things that looked the least human. They dropped immediately, falling like so many weeds in a frost. The next were tougher, though, as they swayed in place, eyelids drooping, while they fought to stay awake. In the gallery above, the arrows of the archers in the gallery slowly drooped, the archers likewise swayed and fought to keep their eyes open—then they lost the battle, arrows and bows fell from nerveless fingers, and the archers themselves dropped where they stood, draping their misshapen bodies over the railings of the gallery.

"Stop her!" the Katschei bellowed, his voice muffled by the fingers Ilya had in his ears. "Don't listen to her!"

Futile order, for the song was getting past his fingers, and despite the throbbing, burning agony of his back, Ilya's own eyes were beginning to feel heavy. Ilya dared the full song for a moment, tore loose the rags of his shirt, and stuffed them into his ears, then seized a dagger and sliced a shallow cut across the back of his hand to keep himself awake.

The pain jarred him alert again. The maidens were already asleep, draped gracefully along the steps of the dais. The medium-level monsters were falling now, as the lieutenants fought to keep their weapons in their hands and their eyes open. But they could not keep their weapons trained on her, and there was a clatter all over the throne-room as more and more of them lost their spears, clubs, and bows as they fought just to stay on their feet.

Meanwhile, the Firebird continued to hover, wings fanning the crystals in the great hanging lights until they chimed together in harmony with her song, her eyes closed in concentration, her head tilted back as her song soared ecstatically.

Ilya moved; he worked his way toward the dais one step at a time, moving very slowly, and avoiding the strengthless hands that reached for him. If the Katschei forgot he was there, or thought he was a demon—

Seeing that his minions were falling, the Katschei stood up, fighting off sleep and swaying where he stood, and began to chant in that strange language he had used before. All of his concentration was on the Firebird, and it was clear to Ilya that he was trying to muster the power for a spell to stop her. But his words faltered, and he was having trouble concentrating.

Now the last of the demons were dropping, their weapons clattering to the floor, their bodies collapsing into ungainly heaps.

Ilya felt sleep creeping over him, and sliced his hand a second time, the sharp pain cutting across the spell as the knife cut his flesh. The Katschei wavered, almost fell, then regained his concentration.

Now the confrontation narrowed to a battle of wills between the two, the demon-tsar and the Firebird. She sang on, her voice retaining all the power and purity it had when she began, but slowly the Katschei's voice gained in strength.

Ilya froze for a moment—the Katschei's voice rang out in muffled triumph through the rags in his ears. He had overcome her spell—and now he was about to unleash his own. In a moment, she would be blasted from the air.

And Ilya made a last dash for the niche beside the throne, and lunged for the diamond with both hands.

Caught unaware, the Katschei realized his mistake too late. He tried to turn his attention from the Firebird, tried to aim the terrible spell he was about to cast at Ilya instead.

But Ilya seized the diamond, as the black thing at the heart of it throbbed and pulsed. He whirled toward the Katschei and raised it above his head.

"No!" the Katschei screamed. *"No!"*

And Ilya threw it with all of his strength, while his injured back screamed in protest, smashing the diamond at the sorcerer's feet.

A soundless explosion of light caught Ilya in the chest and threw him through the air to land a dozen feet from where he had been standing. The Firebird ended her song in an unmusical squeal, and when the light cleared away, she was gone.

The black thing that had lived at the heart of the diamond billowed up and out, a cloud of evil, oily smoke, filled with flashes of reddish light and the suggestion of eyes. The Katschei staggered backward, falling into the embrace of his throne, staring up into the cloud as it loomed over him, his mouth open and his face twisted into a rictus of pain.

The smoke rose higher, then bent over toward the Katschei like a wave about to break. The Katschei tried to fend it off with his upraised hands, screaming, a high, thin wail, as every piece of glass in the throne-room shattered.

The black cloud dropped and enveloped him completely, hiding him from view, cutting off his scream.

There was a second explosion of light, then a bolt of lightning crashed through the ceiling of the throne-room and struck the place where the Katschei had been, blinding and deafening Ilya where he lay. Howling down out of the breech in the ceiling came a whirlwind, laced through with more lightning. Ilya clung to the floor as the wind hurled furniture, drapery, screaming demons, and debris around the room in an orgy of destruction.

For a moment he thought that he was going to die; he was certain that the ceiling was going to come down and bury them all. He sheltered his head in his arms in an attempt to protect himself, as the floor trembled beneath him and the room shook with the angry roar of the whirlwind.

Then, suddenly, it was over.

He raised his head, and his jaw dropped.

He was lying on the floor of a very fine great hall, perhaps a bit larger than the one in Ivan's palace, and with better appointments, but essentially the same. The polished wooden floor was well-kept, the walls were decorated with highly polished carvings of birds and beasts, as were the beams overhead. Behind him was a tiled stove that gave off a gentle warmth. Before him was a modest dais, with three steps leading up to a platform that supported a fine, carved wooden table and matching chairs. Behind the table, the wall was graced with a luxurious hanging of embroidered felt with a pattern of flowers, trees, and deer, and a matching piece ran the length of the table. Good beeswax candles stood in three candlestands on the table, adding their clear light to the lanterns on the walls. More tables had been stacked with their benches against the walls. On the dais, twelve lovely maidens, seated at the table, were slowly awakening and sitting up.

Around Ilya, a crowd of men-at-arms and servants, serfs and the well-born, were also awakening from slumber and getting to their feet.

We did it! he thought wonderingly. *We did it! We slew the Katschei and broke all his spells! Tatiana is free, and tsarina again!*

Ilya stood up with the rest of them and blinked, for once feeling as stupid as he had pretended to be. But before he could say or do anything, those nearest him finally came out of their own daze to *notice* him.

"It's him! The hero!" shouted one, and "Savior!" shouted another. Soon they were all shouting and cheering, picking him up and carrying him to the dais, where he was shoved up next to Tatiana. Caught up in the excitement, he seized her in his arms and kissed her, while Tatiana's un-enchanted subjects cheered him as if they would never stop.

They did, eventually, run out of breath—but just at that moment, a handsome, hawk-faced man in the robes of an Arab prince, and a tall and beautiful fellow dressed in a costume only a *tsarevitch* could afford, entered the hall, took one look at him, and flung themselves at his feet.

"God be praised!" the *tsarevitch* cried, crossing himself, then kissing Ilya's hand while Ilya blushed and tried to make him stand up. "I heard your promise, and I prayed that you would be able to free us! May heaven bless you, Ilya Ivanovitch!"

The Arab rose from his kneeling position long enough to take the massive golden necklace from his own neck and place it around Ilya's. "Allah be praised!" he said in perfect Rus. "And praises to you, Ilya, son of Ivan! You are the bravest man I have ever seen!"

That only started the cheering all over again, as two of the maidens detached themselves from the group and rushed into the arms of the former statues. And no sooner had the cheering stopped again, when another three warriors entered the hall, and it all began anew.

Someone brought Ilya a new shirt, and the maidens stripped the old one off and dressed the wounds on his back with their own hands before he put it on. It might have belonged to Tatiana's father; it was silk, but rather too big in the stomach for him. He belted it around himself with his own sash and tucked the Firebird's feather back next to his heart. He noticed that it was no longer glowing; it was a lovely feather, but otherwise perfectly ordinary.

All the while, the former statues came in by ones and twos, falling to their knees at his feet, and swearing allegiance and eternal friendship with him—and then one of the maidens would fling herself joyously into the new fellow's arms, and the celebrating would start up as vigorously as before. It was a little embarrassing, but very exciting; Ilya hardly felt the pain of his back at all, but he did know that his face must be quite red from blushing.

"It wasn't all me," he kept saying, "There was the vixen, the Firebird, the nightingale . . ."

But no one would listen to him. Tatiana clung to his elbow as if they were already wed, and her father's chief allies and warriors declared that they would have no other for tsar.

Finally Tatiana herself waved her hand, imperiously, and the cheering died down. "Of course I shall wed Ilya Ivanovitch," she announced, a high blush on her own cheeks. "How could I fail to reward the great hero who saved us all with the greatest gift in my power to give?"

Then *she* kissed him, and the room erupted.

All except for one man, who had come in during the speech and now stood silently and sullenly at the foot of the dais, looking up at Ilya with a face so sour with envy that it would have set anyone's teeth on edge.

It was Pietor—and there were no welcoming maidens for *him*. All of them had claimed their chosen warriors. As Ilya and Tatiana finally ended their embrace and the cheering died, Pietor walked stiffly to the dais and bowed his head slightly.

"Well, brother," he said, his tone so ungracious that the Arab clapped his hand to his scimitar's hilt, and the *tsarevitch*'s eyes flashed with anger. "It seems you have had some amazing good luck."

Ilya raised an eyebrow, and held Tatiana a little closer. "Good enough to free you, apparently. Would you care to stay for my wedding?"

Pietor brushed chips of paint from his shoulders and shook them out of his hair. "I suppose I'll have to," he said rudely, and there was some angry muttering among the other newly freed warriors.

"You *could* go back to Tsar Ivan afterward," Ilya replied, tenderly and sweetly, savoring the bite of his outwardly mild words. "I'll be happy to give you three horses and all that you need to do so, and the proof that you were not at fault in the matter of the cherries, if you will bear him my filial greetings and give him word of my new prosperity."

Pietor turned red, then white, then red again, and Ilya's new friends chuckled.

But what else could he do but accept? His gear was gone, his horses had been eaten by demons, and he was stuck in

Ilya's court without a groat to his name. He didn't even have a coat of his own. It was a moment of revenge so sweet that Ilya nearly choked on it, and sweeter still was the knowledge that Pietor would be telling Ivan that his most despised son had become a hero, killed a powerful sorcerer, and won the hand and kingdom of a beautiful tsarina. Ivan would look at his aging, soured wife, his home full of contention and strife, his narrow little kingdom, his cow of a daughter-in-law, and probably have apoplexy.

It was wonderful, and Ilya savored every moment of it.

ILYA looked down from the tower room where the accounts were kept, watching his eleven new friends and their brides-to-be in a carefree snowball fight in the courtyard, and sighed. He wished that he had chosen any other maiden but Tatiana, and yet he would not have wanted to deprive any of *them* of their chosen brides. Not all of the former statues were so fortunate—the maidens *they* had come to save were among those the Katschei had disposed of when their beauty faded with age or they proved intransient. Some were remaining as Ilya's retainers, for they no longer had homes to return to, and others were going out to seek their fortunes, or taking service with the other eleven who still had homes and kingdoms to return to. It seemed that, for the favored eleven, their stories were all to have reasonably happy endings, but his—well, Tatiana was happy. And he was prosperous. That ought to have been enough.

It isn't enough, though, he thought sadly, as Abdul romped with the carefree abandon of the youngest of the statues, a Sami warrior who was only fourteen but as fierce a fighter as the oldest boyar among them.

In the tales, no one ever mentioned that the heroine was an idiot, spoiled, and selfish. Ilya would rather be up here in the tower with the keeper of the accounts than spend more time than he had to listening to her chatter endlessly about *her* life, *her* wants, *her* clothes, *her* friends.

She was as shallow as a rain-puddle, and couldn't speak coherently on any subject except herself. Ilya had gotten more sense out of the vixen than he did out of her, and at least the vixen had been honest in her self-interest.

And the Firebird was willing to sacrifice all she had to help us. . . . Tatiana wouldn't have even begged the Katschei for my life if the others hadn't been doing so first.

That was bad enough, but she was willful as well, and it was quite clear that her father had spoiled her beyond belief. She had only to see a thing to want it—much like the Katschei—and she would pout and cry that he did not love her if he did not get it for her. If she had her way, her little kingdom—quite prosperous on its own—would have been ruined in a fortnight. She had never done without anything she wanted, and unfortunately, her sojourn as the Katschei's captive had drastically raised her standards.

She was just as beautiful as ever, but that was *all* she was. Anything having to do with displaying herself, she did, and did well; she danced and sang, played games, and groomed herself to perfection. But her world began and ended with her; he had never seen anyone so self-absorbed. Even his father, selfish as the old man was, took some thought for the prosperity of his realm and the well-being of those in it. She seemed to be of the opinion that as long as *she* was happy, her kingdom was fine.

He had thought at first that this shallowness was a symptom of the relief they all felt at being free at last—that she would soon be the sensible and sensitive creature he knew in his heart she truly was. But—no. Lovely, spoiled, selfish little Tatiana was exactly as he now saw her, and he was forced to admit to himself that the wonderful woman he had created in his mind out of his few glimpses of her over the wall was just that: a creation of his own mind. He had built up an entire personality in his heart that had nothing to do with the real maiden; in fact, the times he had seen her, she had been on her best behavior because she wanted something, or had just been given something, or just was too tired to misbehave. Now he saw the real woman, but after he had already pledged to wed her.

And he was going to spend the rest of his life with her.

I'm going to spend the rest of my life with a woman who wants to pick our warriors by how muscle-bound and handsome they are, a woman who uses up all the milk in the dairy to take a bath when there are children here whose mothers can't nurse them, a woman who sends her little page out into the snow without a coat to pick holly so she can have a cheerful bouquet to look at since there are no flowers here anymore. I'm going to spend the rest of my life hearing, "If you really love me"; "It's my kingdom and I can do what I like"; "But when the Katschei kept me in his palace, I had this—"

He winced.

But she was lovely. There was no doubt about that. He would be the envy of anyone who didn't know what it was like to endure a torrent of tears because Tatiana could not have another rope of pearls, since her old rope of pearls did not *quite* match her pearl earrings.

He'd solved that particular problem by having her maid get the old rope and the earrings for him; he'd had one of the better craftsmen take a few pearls from the rope and create new earrings, and presented the new set to her *as* a new set. Now as long as she never went looking for the old ones . . .

His eleven new friends—how he envied them! Their brides were not *quite* as beautiful as Tatiana, but they weren't quite as shallow, either. The Sami women and Aisha the Arab girl in particular seemed sensible *and* beautiful. And the other couples didn't seem to have the difficulties he had.

He had hinted to a couple of the men that he was having a few little difficulties with Tatiana. Abdul had laughed.

"So she pouts! Beat her, my friend! Allah decrees that a man shall have an *obedient* wife, cheerful and eager to do his will, like my own Aisha. And if she does not, then she must be shown discipline!" He chuckled. "This must be your first wife, eh? Aisha will be my fourth. The first is for stability, for she will rule the house. The second and third are for children. The fourth—ah! The fourth is for pleasure, and my dear one knows that she will be my little treasure, but she also knows she must obey, not only me, but my senior wives. With his first wife, a young man is often confused, afraid that he will be cruel. But I tell you, it would be cruel to allow her to run wild like a mare in the desert, who is useful for nothing and will soon get herself into trouble. No, beat her, and she will come to love you for it."

Prince Igor had said much the same thing, eliminating the part about multiple wives. Even his Tatiana's advisors had hemmed and hawed, and suggested that she had been over-indulged and would benefit from a little loving restraint.

Ruslan said that the Firebird was a tsarina in her own right. I doubt that her staff would think she needs "loving restraint."

After that, he hadn't mentioned his troubles again to anyone. It was easy enough to hide them, for Tatiana never had her tantrums in public, only when they were alone together or had caused problems with her staff and servants, which he had to solve. Most of the time no one even knew she caused those problems because he solved them before they became public knowledge. In fact, one of the old advisors had congratulated him on how well he had gotten Tatiana to settle down, since she formerly caused near-riots among the staff on a weekly basis!

And the staff of servants had more than enough on their hands with the great weddings to take place in another four days. Poor things; no one had *ever* had to plan for the wedding of twelve extremely important couples all at once.

They were all, all twenty-four of them, to be wedded on the same day—in part because the young men wanted to take the maidens back to their homelands immediately, as it would have been a terrible thing for the girls' reputations to return to their homes—unwedded maids with young men—unchaperoned and unprotected. And in part because the warriors who had traveled farthest had brought entourages with them—men who had (when they had not wound up in the stew) been transformed into more of the Katschei's monsters. Now they were all back to human form, and they were eating their heads off, emptying Tatiana's stores at a terrific rate. It was dreadfully difficult to feed them all, even with parties going out daily for game.

It was also difficult that hunting was one of the daily activities; not sport-hunting, but serious game-hunting, conducted in a systematic way with an eye to rounding up enough game to feed all the hungry mouths in the palace. A small stream of gold was going out into the countryside, and wagon-loads of provender arrived daily. It would be a relief when all these people were gone, and the quickest way to get them gone was to get all the young men married to their maids so they could go home with honor and rejoicing.

It would have bankrupted the little kingdom, except that the cellars and attics were stuffed to bursting with the treasures the Katschei had stolen. When spring came, the factors could take those treasures, a few at a time, and sell them, and Tatiana's coffers would be quickly replenished. But for now, well, it would be sad to say good-bye to all his new friends, but there was no way that Ilya could play host to them for much longer.

You would think, with all that treasure, that Tatiana would be the happiest maiden alive. Although the clothing the Katschei had given his maidens was often magical in nature, and their more elaborate costumes had vanished when he did, the jewels were stolen and real enough. Tatiana had a chest of jewelry that was a real *chest,* not a miniature; it was as large as the dower-chests most women owned and stored their linens in. And the other maidens had pressed on her and on Ilya some of the jewels they did not care to take with them— pieces that had unpleasant memories. In addition, there were yet more precious things that the Katschei had not yet gotten around to decking his captives with, and Tatiana had access to all of that.

And yet—and yet—and yet—she was not content. She wanted the wardrobe that the Katschei had given her—silks from Chin and velvets from the west, gauzes from Hind and furs from the north. She wanted flowers and fruit in midwinter, strange foods from around the world, a bathhouse like the Turks had—not just a steamroom, but a huge pool of warm water to float in for hours. She wanted attendants to massage her with fragrant oils, to tend her complexion with creams and unguents, to buff her nails and rub her feet. She wanted a dozen girls to embroider for her, read to her, sing to her.

Was she going to get *any* of this? Not in the heart of Rus. Not without finding another powerful sorcerer.

Had she resigned herself to this fact?

Did pigs fly?

And the Firebird was content with a bit of magical fruit and the freedom of the sky. . . .

Ilya was just glad that the wedding would be soon; as soon, in fact, as a priest could be brought (the monsters had eaten the last one). There would be a mass wedding in the morning for the eleven captives and their chosen brides, and a separate wedding in the afternoon for Ilya the Hero and his lovely tsarina.

Perhaps when the wedding is over, she will settle down. Or perhaps children will settle her. Perhaps all of her discontent is only that she longs for children. Some of the older women here had assured him that her discontent could quickly be cured with children, who would soon absorb all her attention. They swore that once she became a mother, she would lose all her self-absorption and selfishness.

Or, she will find wet-nurses for them the moment they are born, and never see them again except when she wishes to pose with them around her. He hated to think that of her, of *any* woman, but it was a possibility.

In the meantime, he had tried his best to be gentle with her. But it was obvious that he was going to have to take on the management of the kingdom, for she didn't even know how to manage her own household, and she didn't care to learn.

But why can't I help but think that even that poor sow my brother married has a better heart? At least she doesn't try to hurt anyone.

As he watched, the snowball-fight in the courtyard dissolved, and the combatants declared a truce and went inside. There was a tap on his door.

"Come," he called, and the cook timidly poked her red face in the doorway.

"Sir, the lady Tatiana has just ordered me to have the gardener beaten," she said, tentatively.

Ilya sighed. "What for this time?" he asked without hope. *The Firebird never complained about anything.*

"She wanted strawberries yesterday, and he told her it was impossible, it was midwinter. She stamped her foot, said, 'The Katschei had strawberries in midwinter, and you'd better have them tomorrow.' So today, she sends—no strawberries, of course—and now she wants the gardener beaten."

"Don't beat the gardener," he said, groaning. *Poor Sergei! Even when he is no longer a monster, he is still being abused!* "Tell everyone I order the gardener to be left alone. For God's sake, tell the gardener to go visit his married children or his mother for a while until the tsarina gets over not having fresh fruit in midwinter. If he isn't here, she can't keep bothering him for impossibilities. Have you strawberry jam put by?"

The cook nodded.

"Then make her strawberry tarts with the jam, and she'll forget all about it. Make sure you put a lot of beaten cream on them, and she'll never know they're made with jam and not fresh berries."

The cook beamed, as if he was the cleverest man in the world, and bobbed a little bow at him. "Thank you, sir! I'll do just that! Thank you!"

She took herself out again, still uttering effusive thanks, and Ilya moaned.

Is it that these people can't think? Or is it that she has them so baffled that they've forgotten how to think?

Or maybe it was just that they'd gotten out of the habit of thinking, back when they were monsters. In some strange way, their lives were much easier when they weren't allowed to think. Hard to believe, but that cheerful, red-faced woman had been the hideous Kitchen Monster that had ruled the Katschei's kitchens with an iron fist.

On the other hand, I don't work in the kitchen anymore; I'm the Master. Maybe she still rules the kitchen with an iron fist, and I just never hear about it.

If only he had a little magic—not to bring strawberries in midwinter for Tatiana, but just to remind him that there were more things in life than trying to keep his bride-to-be from insulting and damaging her own staff. Something that would bring a little sparkle to his day, and remind him of what he had been and done.

Magic. It seemed that the Katschei had taken all the magic with him, that it had vanished completely away. He hadn't seen anything magical since the Katschei's spell was broken. He'd listened as hard as he could, but didn't get a hint of conversation when the dogs barked. None of the horses exchanged pleasantries with him. He guessed that magic was gone from his life, along with his ephemeral freedom.

In its place was duty, a duty that was becoming a burden more and more with every day that passed. And in the past few days, not an hour went by when he didn't wish he could just pack up and leave.

I can't abandon her. I have to stay here, for her sake, and for the sake of her people. If I left, I'd be breaking my pledge to her, I'd be leaving her people at her mercy, and I'd be leaving her to the mercy of the next Katschei to come along. And one would; maybe not so powerful, or so evil, but one would. She's too beautiful not to become a prize. And she's almost helpless without me; she can't take care of herself or defend herself. It's not her fault that she's spoiled, and the only way to unspoil her is to teach her. She can be a wonderful person, I know she can.

But he rather wished it had been Pietor who had rescued her, and not himself. Pietor would not make a bad tsar. He had a better temper than Ivan, he kept his cruel streak under control when it came to the servants and serfs, and he had a shrewd head on his shoulders when it came to finding others who were clever enough to take the burden of managing things. Pietor had made friends among the stable-people and the guards, and that alone proved that he didn't treat people as badly as Ivan. He wasn't bright, but he had managed to plan his own escape, so he wasn't as stupid as Ilya had thought.

Granted, he expected women to be like dogs, there when you called them, and otherwise at your feet.

Well, no one was perfect.

But it wasn't Pietor, and I made my promises and I have to stick to them.

Two of the former statues—two of the first that the Katschei had created—were neighboring boyars who were helping out with provisions for the horde that Ilya was playing host to. The Katschei had taken over and preserved their lands when he defeated them, thus ensuring that *they* had lands to return to. They had told him that they had both made bids to Tatiana's father to wed her, but it had been largely for the sake of her land. Being neighbors, they *knew* what she was like, and while in their cups, they had told him that not even her great beauty would have tempted them if she had not come with such a prize.

Now, though, they were more than happy with the girls they'd gotten.

"We probably would have gone to war with anyone who

had married Tatiana,'' Vladimir had said last night, over drinks. ''Just because, frankly, anyone who married her might come after *our* land just to help satisfy her. But *you* don't need to worry, brother. I wouldn't dispute a single grain of sand with you!''

Ilya yawned, and had to put down the pen to rub his eyes. He hadn't gotten much sleep last night. He hadn't been getting much sleep *any* night, actually.

I keep dreaming of the Firebird.

But not as a bird, not anymore. He dreamed of her as a maiden, mostly alone, mostly weeping. Last night he had dreamed that she was weeping in the famous apple-orchard, and when he awoke, he found himself standing under the trees in the moonlight, where he'd sleepwalked. Thank God he'd put on his boots in his sleep, or he'd have been getting married minus a set of frostbitten toes!

But his heart ached when he thought of her, weeping so hopelessly, as if she were still trapped in the Katschei's net. Why was she weeping? Surely *her* life was no different— except, perhaps, that there were no more magical fruits to eat here. But she was a bird, a magical bird; she could fly into the south, the warm and sultry south, and eat magical figs from the trees grown by the djinn, feast on pomegranates and oranges from trees tended by *efrits,* and on almonds and dates watched over by peris. She could go anywhere she wanted. He was the one who should be weeping, trapped here in a world without magic, with a woman who was a lovely, spoiled, selfish doll.

And a jealous doll. She wanted all of his time; wanted to know exactly where he was at any given moment. If he even looked at one of the other maidens, she questioned him crossly about what he thought of the girl. She didn't want him to have any friends, and tried her best to separate him from the ones he'd made. Only custom and his own persistence kept that from happening now, but once all the men he'd rescued were gone, she would have a freer hand.

He spent more and more of his time mending the things she had done without even thinking about them. This morning he had countermanded her order that the cows should not be milked before *she* was awake, so that she could have milk warm from the udder for her breakfast and to wash her face in. Never mind that this would throw the dairy into utter chaos, delay work for hours. And never mind that the cows would be in agony as the milk strained their swollen udders. *She* wanted milk that was warm and absolutely fresh.

He told them to keep a pail of milk near the fire so that it would stay warm until she woke, and she would never know the difference.

Thoughtlessness. Casual cruelty. Every day saw another instance—sometimes more than one, for today it had been both the milk and the strawberries.

How am I ever going to civilize this woman? he thought despairingly. *How am I to handle her?*

Whether he liked it or not, it looked as though his entire life was going to be spent in serving her—seeing to it that her whims didn't destroy anyone, seeing to it that she was happy so that at least there would be no more tantrums and tears. There would be very little time in all of that for himself.

At least when I was the Fool, my time was my own. He little thought that he would ever look back on *that* time with regret and nostalgia! *And when I was with the Firebird—I was completely happy. Perhaps a creature of magic such as she is could never care for a mere human, though.*

But for Tatiana's part—except for the moments when she wept that he did not love her because he could not provide her with something impossible—*she* seemed utterly content. She hung all over him in public, draped herself on him during their chaste meetings in private, kissed him on the slightest provocation. She seemed astonished at his cleverness and, to her credit, praised him openly and generously whenever there was an opportunity to do so. When he smoothed over a difficulty with the staff, she thanked him so prettily that for a few moments, he actually forgot that she had been the cause of the difficulty in the first place. And when he was with her and she wasn't chattering, he fell in love with her all over again.

Until she opened her mouth, that is.

But it was clear to him that she was entirely enamored of him, and had no idea that he did not reciprocate those feelings as wholeheartedly as she did. He couldn't bear to abandon her and break what little heart she had. But he couldn't help but contrast her desperate clinging with the Firebird's independence of spirit, and wish with all his heart that it was the Firebird he was to wed on the morrow, and not Tatiana.

But it's my word and my honor at stake here. What is happiness if your word can't be trusted and you have no honor?

That was a question that had no answers. In fact, the only answer to his current unhappy restlessness was this:

The only happy endings are in tales. The rest of us make do with what we have.

But for a man who had tasted a magic cherry, talked with a vixen-fox, and fought a battle of wits, wiles, and spells with a Firebird, that was a very unsatisfactory answer.

THERE were two gypsy bands in the courtyard playing conflicting mazurkas, a troupe of musicians in the great hall playing the cushion-dance, and a peasant-group in the great barn performing harvest-songs, all of them making as much noise as possible, and all of them at least partly drunk. Eleven couples were now man and wife, even the two Moslem couples, who bent their faith enough to allow that a marriage performed by a Christian was binding enough so long as a proper Moslem rite was performed when they got home. The priest, for his part, was flexible enough that with coaching by Abdul, he managed a semblance of a Moslem ceremony. So everyone was happy, and the wedding-feast was in full force.

The climax of the feast was to be Ilya and Tatiana's wedding, and Ilya gazed at his bridal finery with a sad and reluctant sigh. The splendid outfit laid out on the bed could have been a set of fetters and shackles, the way he felt about it. He had put off the fatal moment for as long as he dared, but now there was no choice. This was the end, the end of magic, of hope, of freedom, and the beginning of a responsibility and a duty that would never end until he died.

And with damned little reward, except for prosperity.

He was coming to realize that having prosperity without happiness was much akin to eating too much sugar: Initially one felt pleasure and satisfaction, but sooner or later one ended up sick.

"Off with you," he told his attendants, finally. "I can dress myself.'' *Thank God my friends are so busy celebrating their own weddings that they didn't feel the need to play attendant. I couldn't order them around.*

"But—" said one old man, the most senior of the servants. Ilya turned and glared at him, and he snapped his mouth shut.

"I can dress myself," Ilya said firmly. "I've *been* dressing myself for years." The six attendants bowed and let themselves out, leaving him alone with his wedding-costume.

He sighed, sat down on the edge of the bed, and began, slowly, to array himself for—what? He felt as if he were going to an execution; his own. Breeches, fine scarlet wool. Silk shirt of a pale gold. Coat, matching the breeches, decorated with gold braid and embroidery. All thriftily cut down (at his insistence) from feast-day clothing that had once been Tatiana's father's, in part to make up for the extravagance of her wedding-dress. Typically, she had not recognized it when she saw it on him, which was just as well, he supposed. A brand-new pair of boots. A magnificent sash, gift from Abdul. A curved knife, with a gold hilt in the shape of a bird's head, and a gold sheath, from Feisal.

He held up the knife, and the sapphire in the eye winked at him; where Feisal had found it, he had no idea, but it was not a bird of prey, as was common, but another, more splendid creature. *A bird of gold. A bird of fire—*

Tears sprang into his eyes, and he buried his face in his hands and wept for his loss. Now, too late, he knew that the woman he really loved was the Firebird. He was deeply, irrevocably in love with a creature he had not seen except in dreams since he had broken the diamond at the Katschei's feet.

Oh God. Oh, Holy Virgin. Oh Rod and Perun! What have I done to myself? What have I done to her?

He didn't know what had happened to her after that moment. All he knew was that the initial explosion of light had cut her song short, and when the light faded, she was gone.

Did I somehow drive her away with that? If I did, why didn't she come back?

Could it be that the terrible forces he had unleashed had harmed her? If that was the case, then he would never, ever forgive himself.

But he didn't know, and he didn't think he would ever

know. All he knew was that he had somehow abandoned his true love for a false one, and his life was in ruins because of that foolish choice.

He reached into the breast of his tunic and pulled out the lovely feather, which never left him, not even when he slept. If Tatiana knew, she probably would have demanded it for herself or told him to throw it away.

Never.

He gazed at it sadly, stroking the soft vanes with one finger, tracing the patterns and colors in it. There it was—the living symbol of everything he *really* wanted. Freedom, magic, and wonder, all the wonder in the world. This was a night full of stars so big and bright that it seemed all you had to do was to climb a tree and pick them like cherries. This was a *rusalka* singing to herself as she combed her hair beside her river. This was a laughing fox, a falling star, a talking nightingale, the faithful spirit of a horse who *might* have had a touch of the Night Wind blood in him. . . .

And he was about to give all this up, forever, to go into a captivity that meant the end of anything but care and responsibility. He was going to spend the rest of his nights beside a woman who wanted his soul, giving up the one who had given him freedom.

"*Ahem,*" said a brisk little voice at the door.

He turned, suddenly angry that his attendants had disobeyed his orders, and stared in fury at the open door.

The door was open, but the doorway itself was empty.

"*I said,* Ahem," the voice repeated.

He dropped his gaze, startled. Sitting squarely in the middle of the doorway was a vixen-fox, tidily licking a paw clean. His mouth dropped open and he gaped at the dainty creature, feeling very much as if he'd just been hit in the back of the head with a club.

"*Very nice feast, Ilya Ivanovitch,*" she said conversationally, ignoring his shock. "*The chicken is particularly good. And the cheese is superb.*"

"Ah, thank you," he stammered, his eyes wide. "I'm glad you came—I would have sent you an invitation, but I didn't know how to find you."

Where has she come from? Where has she been? Why is

she here now? And why can I hear her speaking now?

"*No matter; my family is inclined to invite themselves,*" she replied with a droll tilt of her head. "*Your selection of refreshments is quite superb.*"

"*Yes, indeed, although I favor the white cake and the currant-bread, personally,*" said another, sweeter voice to his left.

He turned to the window, and there on the sill stood the nightingale, preening her wings.

"I hope you both had your fill," he managed, wondering what this all meant, what had really brought them. Was it simply goodwill? Or were there—*could* there be other forces at work here?

"*Oh, we did. But there really is something you should see, Ilya Ivanovitch,*" the vixen said cheerfully. "*And we came to tell you about it.*"

"*Precisely.*" The nightingale nodded, her entire body bobbing.

"I'm a little busy right now," he replied inanely. "I'm about to be married, you see."

"*Well, this is about getting married,*" the nightingale replied. "*Now if I were you, I'd go pay a surprise visit to my bride right now, this very moment. It's very, very important, Ilya Ivanovitch.*"

"*And I would take witnesses with me,*" the vixen added. Was there a certain malicious enjoyment in her voice? If so, he didn't think it was at his expense. "*Plenty of big, strong witnesses who are also your friends.*"

"*We will see you later, I hope,*" the nightingale said and flew off. When he looked back to the doorway, the vixen was already gone.

But—surprise visit to his bride? Whatever for? What could Tatiana possibly be doing at this moment that it was important he see her? For one wild instant, he wondered if perhaps she was a shape-shifter—or that she wasn't Tatiana at all, but the Katschei in disguise. . . .

No, that was ridiculous, and if something like that had been true, she would have killed him and taken *his* place. She wouldn't be planning to marry him.

They never gave me bad advice before. . . . Severely puzzled, but willing to follow their directions, Ilya went out into the rest of the palace to see who and what he could gather up.

He managed to run into Lev and Vladimir as soon as he entered the antechamber to the great hall; the latter was a famous bear-hunter who had gone to challenge the Katschei to single combat, and the former was one of his neighbors, who had taken a small army to come to Tatiana's rescue. Both of them had become firm friends with him, Lev because Ilya understood animals, and Vladimir because Ilya understood the proper running of a household.

"Our brides have gone to make themselves beautiful all over again!" Lev called out, clapping him on the back. "So we're here to make sure you are still doing well. Not too nervous, I hope?"

"Actually," Ilya said, seeing the perfect opening for what would otherwise be a very strange request, "I've—forgive me, but I have a terrible feeling about Tatiana. A premonition." He laughed weakly. "Please, don't think I'm being foolish, but I keep remembering that the Katschei had a habit of kidnapping his maidens on their wedding day—"

"No, that's not foolish!" Vladimir said with alarm. "And we have no real proof that the monster is *dead*, after all! I do not want to wake up and find I'm a statue again, and not a happy bridegroom in my loving wife's arms! Do you think we should look in on Tatiana?"

"I do," Ilya replied, relieved. "And you don't mind if I come with you, do you? I would feel much better if she were being guarded."

"Well, your brother Pietor is doing that," Lev said ingenuously, "but it still wouldn't hurt to check." He frowned. "Premonitions are a serious business. There could be something seriously wrong here."

But Ilya was still thinking about the previous statement, for it was entirely out of character for his brother to leave any kind of a festival where there was even a chance of finding a toothsome wench to go along with a fine meal. *Pietor? Now why would Pietor volunteer to do anything that took him away from a feast?*

Now more puzzled than ever, but beginning to have a glimmer of suspicion, Ilya followed along in the wake of his two enormous friends.

Surely not. Surely neither of them are that *treacherous, or that stupid. . . .*

Tatiana's rooms were at the back of the palace, secluded and separated from the noise and bustle of the wedding feast. In fact, as they passed through the doors of the first and outermost chamber, her rooms seemed strangely quiet for those of a bride who was supposedly being readied for her own wedding. Where were all the attendants? Where were the servants? There should be a great deal of giggling and teasing going along with the primping and preparing.

Now Ilya was really alarmed, and so were Lev and Vladimir, who exchanged a look of dismay.

"It's awfully quiet in here," Lev said slowly, stating the obvious.

"Do you think?" Ilya began.

The other two exchanged another look, this time of alarm. "*The Katschei!*" they exclaimed at the same time, and heading for Tatiana's bedroom, burst open the door without knocking.

There was a feminine shriek, but not for help. This was the shriek of someone who had been caught doing something very wrong—mingled fear, despair, and dismay.

There was also a masculine roar of outrage mixed with fear and a touch of guilt, in a voice that Ilya knew very well indeed, for he had heard it roar other things, on a daily basis, for most of his life.

Coming in behind the other two, he caught only a glimpse of what they must have seen clear—Tatiana, sans her lovely wedding gown, sans any clothing at all, for that matter. In bed.

With Pietor, who was also showing a great deal of naked flesh.

Suddenly, a great many things fell into place with a mental click. Tatiana's surprise when she saw that the man who had vanquished the dragon was *not* who she had expected. Pietor's sullen reaction to Ilya's triumph. Little remarks made by both of them over the past few weeks. The way she had put him off from time to time. The way Pietor had vanished during times when Ilya wasn't certain where Tatiana was.

Pietor and Tatiana. Well, well, well.

Tatiana was breathing heavily, her eyes wide, her hair disheveled. Each breath came closer and closer to a shriek, until she finally managed to work herself up to a full-blown case of hysterics in a remarkably short period of time. She clutched the sheet to her breast and pointed dramatically at Pietor.

"He forced me!" she screamed, tears starting in her eyes. "He told my servants he was here to protect me, then he sent them all off, and he forced—"

Pietor backhanded her; she fell back into the pillows, a red mark standing clear on her cheek, and Lev and Vladimir started toward him, faces black as thunderstorms. Ilya restrained them with a hand on either arm. "Don't," he said in a low voice. "I think we ought to hear this."

"You treacherous bitch!" Pietor spat at her, completely ignoring the trio at the door in his anger. "You were the one who came sniffing and whining at my heels! You were the one who kept saying you wanted a real man for a husband, instead of a milk-and-water half-priest! *You* sent the attendants away, *you* asked me to come 'guard' you in case the Katschei came back, and *you* were the one who was the first out of her clothes and into bed! *You* were the one who couldn't get enough of my 'little man' for the past week! 'It doesn't matter,' you said. 'He'll never know I'm not a virgin,' you said. 'If I get with child, it will still look like him anyway,' you said!"

Ilya's friends were growing angrier and angrier with every word Pietor uttered, but strangely, Ilya grew calmer and calmer.

Her devotion—it was all an act! She isn't in love with me! If her own people hadn't insisted on it, she never would have agreed to marry me!

If he had never come down here, he would never have known about this. Tatiana would have concocted some story about why she was no longer a virgin—or else she would have faked it; she was perfectly capable of that. He'd heard stories. . . .

She probably would have had some excuse to keep Pietor under this roof. He'd have been cuckolded in his own home by his own brother—who might very well have decided to take matters into his own hands and get rid of Ilya. When a beautiful woman, a pile of treasure, and a kingdom were at stake, Pietor would hardly worry about a little thing like fratricide when he'd been perfectly capable of beating that brother to a pulp on a regular basis.

If he'd come here alone, there might have been a terrible "accident" on the verge of his own wedding. How tragic for the bride. How pleasant for her that she had Pietor to comfort her in her grief . . . how kind of him to marry his brother's bereaved betrothed to see that she was well cared for.

But he had witnesses—large, honest witnesses who were also friends of his. And what they did not know was that he now had the escape he had never dreamed possible. An escape with honor intact.

Well, his, anyway. After this moment, there wasn't enough left of Tatiana's honor to fill a thimble.

A terrible, wonderful, heart-filling joy overwhelmed him, and in the clarity of that moment, he somehow managed to feign a rage befitting the Katschei.

"*You!*" he thundered, pointing an accusatory finger at his trembling bride. "How dare you! I risk my life, my soul to save you, I honor and cherish you—*I* could have taken everything I wanted from you and left you with nothing, but no! I permitted you to retain the title and land that *I* rightfully won! I asked for your hand, in good faith and allowing that you might refuse me, and *you* pledged it, before God and your people! Oathbreaker! Harlot! Whore! You couldn't even wait until after we were married to cuckold me! You're more shameless than a bitch in heat! You have broken your vows, your word—you aren't even worthy to wash the feet of your scullery maid!"

"And *you,*" he continued, turning to his brother. "I rescued you, gave you more than you stole from our father, trusted you, and this is how you repay that trust! What did you intend to do, kill me so that you could take my place?"

The look of startled guilt on Pietor's face was clear enough for even Lev and Vladimir to see, and as one man, they clapped their hands on the hilts of their knives in warning, stepping instinctively to put themselves between Ilya and harm.

"Ha!" he cried. "Well, then, *take* her! No one else will! But don't be surprised if your neighbors celebrate your wedding by bringing armies to greet you! The two of you may go to hell together, for I will not be here to see it!''

He turned on his heel and stormed out, breaking into a run as soon as he got out of sight of his two friends, for the last thing he wanted them to have was a chance to dissuade him. *So they don't want Pietor as a neighbor—well, I don't blame them, but they can certainly take care of that little problem themselves. Not only do they have armies of their own, but they have a great deal of treasure to buy more warriors with.*

Once in his quarters, he worked quickly. One saddlebag he filled with golden jewelry that had been presented to him over the past few weeks; it made for a heavy pack, but gold would buy him a great deal more than he could carry off in the way of provisions. He packed the other bag with personal gear and clothing. *Sword—knives—bow and arrows—spear.* He turned to the armor-stand in the corner of his room and took everything but the armor itself. All the weapons were of the finest make, all left behind when the grand palace became a normal palace. He slung a grand sable cape, fur inside and out, over his shoulders and rolled the blankets on his bed into a rough but serviceable bedroll. Thus burdened, he made his way a bit clumsily down to the stables.

He dropped his loot in a heap just inside the stable door, startling a stableboy who was enjoying the company of a milk-maid and a bottle of honey-wine. The two tousled heads popped up out of the straw, and both began to stammer something; he cut them off with a gesture.

"You!" he barked, pointing to the girl, who was hastily pulling her skirts down and her blouse up. "You go to the kitchen and get me bread, cheese, meat, and onions, traveling food, enough for six or seven days; put it into a sack and bring it here. No, wait, bring extra bread and cheese as well. Now go!"

"Y-y-yes, sir!" the girl stammered, and scrambled up out of the straw to run off to do his bidding. She edged past him and broke into a run as soon as she was out in the open.

"You!" he continued, pointing at the stableboy. "You get me enough oats and sweet-feed for a week, and make it up as a travel-bag. Then get me a good brush, two blankets, and a hoof-pick. Get a pack-saddle and lead-reins. Bring them all here."

"Sir!" the boy jumped up to do as he was told.

Meanwhile, Ilya went straight to the two best horses in the stable. The first he saddled and bridled for his own use. The second, as soon as the boy brought the things he'd asked for, he harnessed up as his pack-animal. Neither would be particularly burdened, which meant that he would make very good time.

The girl returned with a surprisingly heavy bag. "I put a couple of bottles of honey-wine in there, sir," she said, bobbing shyly. "And a nice big piece of wedding-cake. Since you won't be getting any?"

He looked at her sharply; she gave him a demure but knowing smile. "The place is in an uproar, sir," she whispered. "They're looking for you, and threatening to hang your brother. That Arab, they've had to keep him from cutting the fool's head off twice now, and I don't know how much longer they can keep holding him back if that Pietor doesn't stop saying stupid things."

"I hope he doesn't," Ilya replied heartlessly. "I hope you didn't tell them where I was."

"Me, sir? No, sir," she replied promptly. "You aren't going to forgive her, are you?"

"Would you?" he countered.

She made a little face. "Not if I had any sense. You can't change a goat into a lamb with a wedding-ring." Then she reached up, grasped his head, and gave him a kiss, much to his own astonishment. He stared at her, and she giggled.

"I never kissed a hero, and I don't think I'll ever have another chance!" she said gaily, and ran off.

With a shake of his head, he finished loading the pack-saddle, added a few more things he and the boy thought might come in handy, like a coil of rope and leather-tools, and mounted up.

As the dairymaid had said, the palace was in an uproar, but people were running *toward* it and inside it, not away. No one stopped him as he rode out of the stables. No one even noticed him until he got to the front gate.

But then he heard someone calling his name, and pulled up a little. He looked back over his shoulder.

Tatiana, wearing a shift that looked to have been thrown on over her nakedness, her face tear-streaked, her hair a mess, her nose red as a hawthorn berry, ran after him, sobbing.

"Ilya!" she cried, her voice thick. "I beg you! Come back! I love you, I cannot live without you! I will do anything for you, *please*! Forgive! Forgive!"

She looked every inch the ruined bride, and for once, she looked *normally* hysterical. This might have been the first time in her life that she was not putting on a performance for the benefit of an audience.

So why ruin it for her now?

He turned abruptly away from her and set heels to his horse, leaving her to cast herself down in the snow, sobbing heart-brokenly.

"Forgive!" she cried. *"Ilya!"*

He made it through the gates—out onto the road—and out into freedom.

The moment he passed the gates, his horse broke into a canter, and he let it, laughing out loud for the first time since he had gotten himself into this mess.

I'm free. Free!

"Well, boy, I hope you brought me bread for this journey!" the nightingale sang out, as she winged in overhead, darting about his shoulders as if she were chasing insects there.

"And I hope you remembered my cheese!" the fox laughed, bursting out of a snow-covered bush and leaping along at his horse's heels.

"Bread for you, and cheese for you, and wedding-cake for all of us!" he shouted back.

"Wedding-cake! And what are you going to do about the bride?" the fox asked, as he slowed the horse to a walk to save it.

"Me? Nothing. If Feisal doesn't kill my brother, I expect the rest of them will force him to wed her. After all, he's not only despoiled her, he's robbed them of a hero!" He laughed again. "Pietor probably doesn't want her now, but that's too bad. And I bet that once the wedding's over, the dividing will begin; I wonder how many of the Katschei's treasures she'll get to keep now?"

"Not many, I bet," the vixen observed, looking up at him shrewdly. *"And I bet some of the lands get carved away too."*

"If not now, then later," Ilya agreed. "They pledged not

to fight with me, but they have every reason to fight with *him*."

"*So what about the bride?*" the nightingale asked. "*She seemed very unhappy.*"

"I'm sure she is," he replied, a bit more soberly. "Maybe that clout to her head woke her to the fact that just because a man is gentle and treats a woman like a precious object worthy of respect, that doesn't mean he's a milksop. And just because a man tells her what a fine piece of masculinity he is, that doesn't mean he's admirable. Pietor is going to beat her, like Ivan beats his wife, and probably on a fairly regular basis. He'll insult her to her face, humiliate her in front of his guests, and betray her with her maids and servants. If she cries, he'll ignore her; if she throws a tantrum, he'll have her locked in her room; and if she does something stupid with the household, he'll beat her. She'd better hope the servants will be too afraid of his anger to make life difficult, or there will be a lot of dirty floors and bad meals from now on."

"*You sound sorry for her,*" the nightingale observed. "*Are you having second thoughts?*"

"I am sorry for her, and no, I am not going back to her," he told the bird firmly. "She opened the door of my cage and she shouldn't be surprised that I've flown away."

"*I told you he was smarter than that,*" the bird told the vixen smugly.

They rode for most of the afternoon; as shadows started to lengthen, and he judged that he was a safe distance away, he took out the Firebird's feather. It wasn't glowing with the fierce, magical light it had shown before, but it was no longer dead and lifeless, either.

Carefully, reverently, he raised it over his head and waved it—once, twice, three times. With each wave, it glowed more strongly, until after the third time, it was burning as brightly as a torch.

He didn't have long to wait, either—like a shooting star she came streaking over the tops of the trees toward them, a long trail of sparks following her tail. He shoved the feather back into his shirt, jumped off the horse's back, and began running toward her.

She swooped down to the ground and transformed in midair

going from bird to maiden, from flying to running, in the blink of an eye. She rushed to meet him, and he her, until they fell into each other's arms and he swung her around and around until they were both breathless.

Then he put her down and cupped her face in both his hands.

"Listen!" he said, gazing into those wonderful eyes. "I love you. I think I loved you from the moment I saw you in the orchard. I never want to be parted from you, no matter what it takes, no matter what you ask of me. I would cross the world for you, go to live in foreign lands, fight all your enemies, and still find time to pick berries for you!"

To his joy, she flung herself into his arms again, sobbing with relief and joy of her own. "I could not bear to stay and see you taken by another!" she cried, holding him tightly. "I love you, Ilya Ivanovitch! I would rather never fly again than have to be without you!"

"Well, I would never ask that of you!" he replied, and kissed her until she stopped weeping and started laughing instead. "Now—what are we to do, and where are we to go?"

"My home—" She faltered for a moment, looking up at him. "It is far from here, a long and hazardous journey—but will you make it for my sake?"

"Did you need to ask?" he retorted, and kissed her again. "Will you fly or ride before me, my lady?"

"I will ride, for a little." She smiled, a dazzling, joyous smile, and wiped the last trace of tears from her cheeks. "And then when it is dark, I shall guide you to a safe place to rest."

"And you shall guide me to a safe place for *us* to rest," he responded as he mounted, and gave her his hand to mount up and ride before him. She put her foot on his and leapt lightly into the saddle, nestling into his arms as if she had always been there and would never leave.

"And we lived happily ever after!" The fox laughed gaily, as the nightingale caroled a wordless song of happiness; he touched the horse with his heels, and they rode together into magic, and legend.

TOR
BOOKS The Best in Fantasy

ELVENBANE • Andre Norton and Mercedes Lackey
"A richly detailed, complex fantasy collaboration."—Marion Zimmer Bradley

SUMMER KING, WINTER FOOL • Lisa Goldstein
"Possesses all of Goldstein's virtues to the highest degree."—*Chicago Sun-Times*

JACK OF KINROWAN • Charles de Lint
Jack the Giant Killer and *Drink Down the Moon* reprinted in one volume.

THE MAGIC ENGINEER • L.E. Modesitt, Jr.
The tale of Dorrin the blacksmith in the enormously popular continuing saga of Recluce.

SISTER LIGHT, SISTER DARK • Jane Yolen
"The Hans Christian Andersen of America."—*Newsweek*

THE GIRL WHO HEARD DRAGONS • Anne McCaffrey
"A treat for McCaffrey fans."—*Locus*

GEIS OF THE GARGOYLE • Piers Anthony
Join Gary Gar, a guileless young gargoyle disguised as a human, on a perilous pilgrimage in pursuit of a philter to rescue the magical land of Xanth from an ancient evil.